ALSO BY MICHELE JAFFE
Published by Ballantine Books

SECRET ADMIRER
LADY KILLER
BAD GIRL

LOVERBOY

LOVERBOY

MICHELE JAFFE

BALLANTINE BOOKS • NEW YORK

This book is for my dad, Peter Jaffe,
from whom I learned everything important I know.
With gratitude, respect, admiration, and love.
7×7=49 (see, I was paying attention)

Honest love, which is the kind belonging to noble men—that is, to men with a good and virtuous spirit whether they are rich or poor—does not come from desire, but from the mind, and has as its only aim the transformation of the lover and the beloved, so that ultimately the two merge and become one.

—Tullia D'Aragona
On the Infinity of Love, Venice 1547

ACKNOWLEDGMENTS

Oh, boy, did I have some help on this book. A veritable trainload of people lent knowledge or moral support at different times, but I would like to single out for thanks: SWAT Officer Matt Cabot of the Thornton Colorado Police Department for his invaluable information about police matters and SWAT operations; Lois Leveen, the queen of the knock-knock joke, for sharing her genius; Meggin Cabot and Holly Edmonds for their helpful suggestions on the manuscript in its pupa stage; Marc Shell for teaching me everything I know about plagiarism; Linda Marrow, Gina Centrello, and everyone at Ballantine Books, for the ceaseless toil they expend on my behalf; Susan Ginsburg, the best of all possible agents, who inspires awe, gratitude, and feelings of unworthiness in me every single day; and Dan Goldner because for some inexplicable reason he keeps putting up with me, making me the luckiest woman in the world.

Everything nice in the book is their doing. Everything naughty, my fault.

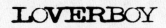

LOVERBOY

CHAPTER 1

"I hope you're better with zippers." The girl giggled into his shoulder as he fumbled with the lock.

"I am," he said, humorless. Sometimes he still had trouble with how to talk to girls. It wasn't hard to get them to come home with him, just to talk.

He focused on how the thick beige paint was scarred around the knob where generations of undergraduates had made drunken attempts to get their keys in. He was not drunk, but his fingers were trembling.

Finally he did it right and the door groaned open. He shoved against it, kissing her hard to push her inside. He was better when he wasn't talking, with his eyes closed. They didn't bother with the light but stripped off their clothes right there. He backed her toward the water bed and finally had the warm, reassuring feel of a female body under his.

"Ohhh, this is nice," she murmured, wrapping her legs around him and pulling his chest over hers.

Newton's third law: For every action there is an equal but opposite reaction.

She ground her hips up to meet his and he slid inside of her. She was warm and soft and nice-smelling, baby-powder deodorant and red wine. The numbers floated through his head as his hands moved over her skin.

A car sets out for its destination at 5:45 A.M. It travels five miles at 45 mph to a stop sign. It does not stop completely, but slows, before accelerating to 60 mph for four minutes.

He pictured the car's headlights speeding over the hunkered-down forms of the frozen trees along the straightaway, silhouetting them against the hard-packed snow, as his body moved against hers.

"Harder." She moaned, biting his shoulder. "Do it to me harder."

Newton's second law: Force is equivalent to the product of the mass of an object and the speed at which it is traveling.

He leveraged all his weight and pounded into her.

For six minutes the car's speed fluctuates irregularly between 35 and 75 mph.

He could imagine the driver rolling a Tic Tac around in his mouth to cover the bitter taste of reheated coffee and leaning forward with a squint as if the extra inches could improve his vision through the thick morning fog.

"Oh, angel, that is good," the girl said into his shoulder as his lips, his teeth scratched over her neck.

If the car continues to accelerate—

"Oh yes, just like that."

—and the road begins to slope downward—

"Oh God, am I close."

—the arrival time of the passengers at their final destination—

"Right there, oh yes yes—"

The ringing phone cut through her cries.

He gripped her to his chest to still her and reached out for the receiver.

"Hello?"

"I am so glad I reached you. Oh God, it's terrible, terrible. There has been an accident. The car missed a curve and—" On the other end of the line he heard someone take a deep breath. "Your father is dead."

He felt the girl tightening around him. He asked only, "When?"

The voice on the other end of the phone paused. "I beg your pardon?"

"I said, when did it happen?"

"I see. Ah, they are giving the time of death as six-oh-four."

"Six-oh-four," he repeated. "Thank you, Nelson."

"Was that important?" the girl asked, pouting slightly as he hung up.

"Nope. Sorry, babe. Now, where were we?"

"I don't think I want—"

He cut her off and, gripping her bottom to him with adrenaline-strong hands, picked up where he had stopped.

If the road begins to slope downward—

Her eyes lit up and she sighed, "Oh yes*ssss*."

—and the car's brakes give out—

"Right there!"

—the arrival time of the passengers at their final destination—

"Oh angel, yes, yes, *YES!*"

—would be 6:04 A.M.

"My God, you are a force of nature," she whispered to him later when he was inside her again.

Newton's first law: an object in motion will stay in motion unless acted on by an unbalanced force.

He smiled to himself and said, "I sure am."

He smiled to himself again, years later, as he sat at his desk and let his fingertips run along the edges of the fragile paper that recorded his triumph that day. There had been several obituaries, but this one from the local paper was the one he liked best. *Beloved father, survived by only son,* it read, the words like poetry to him. He had been the one to survive. He had won that round.

Let the games begin.

Just like he would win this one.

Gently he closed the album and rested his fingers on the words deeply embossed in the rich leather, letting the shapes of the letters, F-A-M-I-L-Y-R-E-M-E-M-B-R-A-N-C-E-S, seep through his fingertips. For five minutes he sat soaking up their feel and message like a divine incantation.

Then he put away his scissors and glue, slid his newest creation into an envelope, clicked off his desk light, and locked up. It was time to go.

Ready or not, here I come!

CHAPTER 2

Mayo Clinic Hospice, Rochester, Minnesota

The long corridor was silent, the bleached pine floor gleaming softly under the new coat of wax the cleaning crew laid down at 10:30. It wasn't really pine, Imogen Page knew, just a veneer over plastic, peeling up near one corner in front of the door marked *Exit.* Real wood would make too much noise, and noise was not allowed here. This was a place for quiet. Everything about it was quiet, the pastel walls, the nubbly cotton upholstery. Quiet plants, nothing fancy and tropical, hung in the rooms. Blinds let in only diffused light, telephones hummed rather than rang, doors closed slowly, gently on special hinges, never slamming. Everything was muted, quiet, expectant. Waiting for death.

The place was so wrong for Sam. Sam had never been quiet in his life. Sam who bubbled with life, with vitality, Sam who yelled rather than talked, guffawed rather than laughed. Sam could fill a room with himself. Big Sam, strong Sam, Sam who had protected her and cared about her. Her brother Sam.

He could not be dying.

Imogen turned from the window and looked at the man in the bed surrounded by plants and balloons and silly marker drawings. Hardly a man anymore, just the elements of a man, skin and bones.

Like some Renaissance painting of a death's head. God, he was small. He must have lost fifty pounds in the last three weeks.

He might live as much as two months, the doctor had said. *But there is really nothing we can do for him.*

But he was healthy and strong and alive last month, her mind shouted. Last month in Hawaii they had played in the waves outside the little house they were sharing, like the carefree teenagers they never had been, jumping up and down, chasing sand crabs, watching the palm trees wave at night. They had drinks in pineapples with happy faces attached to the outside by toothpicks, had tucked paper umbrellas behind their ears. One night they had walked so long on the beach—Sam telling stupid jokes, her laughing at them in a way she never laughed with anyone else—that they were too tired to make dinner and they had not even cared.

She had wanted to pound her fist on the doctor's desk as he sat there smoothly weighing his words. Dr. Stephen Gold. He was her age, maybe a little older, and looked rich and well fed. He had the forearms of a tennis player, slightly tanned, and Imogen found herself wondering if he'd taken his wife (wedding band on his left hand) or his mistress (no tan line from the wedding band) with him to his most recent medical conference in the tropics. He had not gotten that tan in Minnesota, and she could taste the remnants of his infidelity on the air around him. He was smug, the way someone can be who deals in the great mysteries, in Life and Death, capitalized. Life and death were her business too, but not like this. Not uppercase proper nouns. Not Sam. Not her brother.

What do you mean *nothing*? she had wanted to holler at the tanned philandering tennis-playing doctor. Don't you understand this is impossible? Don't you understand that while you may leave here with your mistress for a quick fuck, when I leave I have nothing, no one besides Sam? Don't you understand that he can't die? He is Sam, strong, the strong, athletic one. The Olympian. I am the one who should die, me, the smart one, the useless one; leave Sam.

Please, she had wanted to plead, this is a mistake. Please, she had wanted to scream, this cannot be happening.

"I see," she had said quietly.

"The best thing you can do," Dr. Stephen Gold continued, looking not at but over her, "would be to get him into a hospice. He needs more care than you can give at home, but he'll be more comfortable there than in an intensive-care ward. And there is nothing we can do for him here at the Mayo Clinic."

"I understand," she had said. And for the first time in her life, it was a lie.

Imogen Page was absurdly good at understanding things. It was her job to understand, to make sense of things no one else could explain, interpret inconsequential patterns—codes, riddles, chess patterns, stab wounds—into meaning. But suddenly, listening to the doctor, it had all broken down. From that moment on, she did not understand anything. Every day she understood less and less. Every day from that day she recognized less and less of Sam in the body lying on the bed in front of her.

Every day he went away a little more, and now there was almost nothing left.

Moving slowly to remain quiet, she left the hospice room. She did not know why she bothered to tiptoe, why she still bothered to leave when she had to cry. Sam had not opened his eyes in two days. He couldn't hear them, the nurses assured her as they talked about his condition with her in front of him. He was no longer sentient, the doctors said. But she did not, could not believe them. She turned her steps into the veneer corridor.

As soon as she got that plastic wood under her feet, she began to run. Gulping for air, she made it to the women's room and locked the door behind her. Imogen Page would not let anyone see her cry, turned away from the mirror so she wouldn't have to watch it herself. She backed up against the door, pressed her shoulders to it, and sobbed. Arms crossed over her chest like an ancient pharaoh's mummy, she leaned her head against the cold mint green tiles of the walls and screamed with rage, tiny screams that only she could hear in her head. Despair and anger flooded over her in waves and she felt buffeted by them, hurtled against the sides of her empty, lonely being. Just as suddenly as it came, the storm hovered, and disappeared. She found herself huddled in the corner of the tiled room, her hands gripping her thighs, her eyes squeezed shut.

She cleaned her face with the rough paper towels in the hospice bathroom and that pink powdered soap they used to have in the elementary school locker room the year they lived in Oregon, the year before—

When she had scrubbed away the signs of her tears, she returned to Sam's room.

He was just as she'd left him, but the room tasted different to her. Faintly peppery. She looked around and saw that his hand had moved. She reached out to replace it over his stomach, over the other one, in the proper handshake of death, and his eyes opened.

"Gigi." He did not say the word, just mouthed it, but she knew what it was, knew he was saying her name, his name for her. He pinned her with his gaze and lifted his arms slowly, slightly, into the air.

"Do you want me to prop you up?" she asked, rushing to his side, pushing the button that bent the bed forward.

She looked at him expectantly. He shook his head and, grasping one of his thin wrists with the other—those gold medal–winning wrists that had been so supple—raised both arms in the air in a circle.

"The bed is up as high as it will go, love," she whispered, moving close to him.

A tear of frustration leaked from his eye. His mouth, lips cracked and dry, was open partway. He smelled like plastic bedclothes and decay. He lifted his joined arms again.

A circle. Like a glass. Imogen grabbed the cup of ice shards that stood ready on the table beside the bed. He must be thirsty. "They like to suck on the ice when they can't eat anymore," the nurse had said. Imogen held a small piece of ice tenderly to his lips.

Sam jerked his head away, lifted his arms again.

She was trembling with inadequacy now. "I don't know what you want, Sammie," she said, pleading. "I don't know how to give you what you want. I don't understand."

He looked at her again, right at her, with his eyes clear in a way she hadn't seen in weeks. They were the eyes she knew again, pure blue eyes like hers, trying to tell her something. There was a plea there, a message. A question she couldn't read.

Her eyes stung and there was a lump in her throat. She would never swallow again, she thought.

She turned the light on over him, adjusted his pillows, tried again with the ice, almost manic now, trying anything, brushing tears out of her eyes before he could see them, but he just kept looking at her, a little sad. Finally he raised his arms in a circle again and mouthed a word.

Brother and sister stared at each other, for the first time unable to communicate. There was love in his gaze at her, so much love, and fear, but there was something else too, and she could not fathom what it was.

At last Sam leaned back into the pillows she had arranged, his arms fell down, and his eyes closed. Resting. She listened as he took a breath, shallow, peaceful, and another one. Another. There was a horrible rattling sound, a sound Imogen would dream of forever. It was the sound of death, the last sound, the last breath.

He was gone.

In desperation she wrapped her arms around him, cradling the wispy-haired head against her shoulder, holding on to him, holding the life inside him, hugging it in with her body, but it was too late. There was no more life. There were no more breaths left. Sam was gone.

Gone. It was then that Imogen understood. At that moment she understood, that too-late moment, understood what the linked arms had meant. She understood with a crashing clarity. And the understanding, when it came, was worse than death and worse than sadness.

Too late.

She sat and held Sam's hand in her own, rocking back and forth, crying silently, holding on until the fingers were stiff and cold. Then she placed them on his chest and summoned the nurse. That night she walked out of the hospice for the first time in two weeks. She did not notice the weather or the size-twelve footprints outside her brother's window or the fact that someone had plowed her car out for her. She did not feel sad or angry or any of the things she expected to feel. She tasted, for the first time in her life, nothing.

The obituary reported that Samuel Page died at 4:54 A.M. on Saturday, of a blood infection. The Olympic gold medalist in fencing, it went on to say, was survived by his sister, Imogen Page, the FBI agent who had solved the Connoisseur killings.

The obituary was wrong.

Imogen did not know that yet, would not know it for a long time. But the man reading it in the airport lounge did.

When he was done with it, he carefully folded the paper and slipped it under the arm of his hand-tailored overcoat. The camel cashmere fabric was great with his tan complexion, and several women turned to look at him as he strolled by. He could feel their gazes on his back. He wore aviator sunglasses so his eyes weren't visible, but at six foot four he was hard to ignore.

He played a game in his head, guessing what people were saying about him as he passed. "Isn't that . . . ?" he guessed the brunette in the tight red sweater sitting at the bar asked the bartender. The bartender would nod. "Sure is. Like to be in his shoes, I tell you."

"I'd like to be in his pants," the brunette would say. "Playing with his *you know what*."

The man in the camel coat worked to keep back a smile. People always said things like that about him. He knew how he looked: rich, powerful, successful, well groomed. A man without a care in the world. And he knew it was true. Or almost.

Because, as it happened, he was very care-ful. Full of care. Very careful indeed. A bright, boyish chuckle at the pun erupted in his throat, and evaporated as quickly as it had come. No time for that right now, he chastised himself. He was that other man now, the man who did not laugh. And there was still so much to do. So much to see to.

So many people to take care of.

CHAPTER **3**

Las Vegas, Nevada. Four days later.

Benton Walsingham Arbor knew something was wrong the minute he stepped out of the cockpit of his plane. Absent from the tarmac was the light blue 1966 Thunderbird convertible that should have been waiting for him to slide into the driver's seat; present instead was a brand-new black Arbor Motors X37 with J. D. Eastly behind the wheel. That told the whole story.

"What happened to Sadie?" Benton asked as he closed the distance at a run. "Which hospital is she in, how bad is it, has someone seen to Eros, and who is flying in from Mass General?"

J.D. glanced at Benton through the tobacco-colored sunglasses he always wore and said, "Good to see you too, Benton."

There was no love between the two men at the best of times, and this wasn't one of them. He and J.D. usually limited their communication to long, tense silences. Benton said, "Tell me what the hell is going on."

"Nothing has happened to your grandmother."

"Then why the hell are you driving?" Benton asked, ready to get out of the car. He hated not being in the driver's seat and J.D. knew it, even knew why. But the man wasn't budging.

He said, "Something else has happened," maneuvering around

the plane and out of the airport, turning onto Tropicana. "Something bad."

As a veteran cop, Det. Sgt. John Dillinger Eastly had delivered a lot of bad news in his time, but Benton could tell that this time he was struggling. J.D. said, "Rosalind is missing, Benton. Presumed kidnapped."

Benton forced himself to breathe. Think. Said, "Ransom demand?"

"Not yet. We don't know how long she's been gone, but the last time anyone spoke to her was yesterday morning. We just found out at eight-thirty this morning, when the spa called because she failed to show up for her massage appointment."

"Police?"

"Everyone's on the case. This should fall under my jurisdiction, since I'm overseeing the Violent Crimes Task Force while the boss is in Texas—"

"What is she doing there?" Benton asked, thinking maybe he could get her back for this.

"She's working on the twelve bodies of those women they found when they were tracking the space shuttle debris. Active serial killer case."

Or maybe not.

J.D. went on, "I called the FBI and told them we at Vegas Metro would prefer it if they let us handle Rosalind's disappearance ourselves, and I also notified the CIA. Given what she's been working on it seemed wise."

Rosalind Carnow was one of America's foremost nuclear physicists. She was also Benton's closest friend and, according to the tabloids, his paramour. That was pressing the truth, but it was true that they had known each other since college and had served as each other's dates for every important occasion for the past seventeen years, from debutante balls to banquets at the White House. In the past, Benton had asked her to marry him a dozen times at least, and each time she had said no. Each time, he respected her more for it.

Rosalind had come to Las Vegas a week before Benton to meet with some scientists from the University of Nevada, and have a few days of pampering before the craziness of the Las Vegas Invitational began. After the invitational came a party celebrating Benton's grandmother Sadie's recent wedding to Eros, the godlike Greek half her age with whom she had been living ("in sin, glorious, glorious sin," as she told everyone) for the past three years and whom she had quietly married the week before. Rosalind was supposed to be spending the next few days wrapped in mud and seaweed and covered in hot rocks and cool towels at the hotel spa, while Benton disappeared into the mountains for four days of solo rock climbing. After that, he was supposed to show what the new line of Arbor Motors cars could do on the track at the invitational, and Rosalind was supposed to watch, and make faces at him and chastise him for still racing when he was much too old. And they were supposed to go to dinner and gamble a little and laugh a lot and not dance because Rosalind hated to dance. It was supposed to be a really super ten days.

Everyone knew things always went the way they were supposed to. At least when Benton planned them.

"Damn it," Benton said, pounding a fist into the beryl-wood dashboard. "Damn, damn, damn. I should have thought of this. I should have been here. I should not have let her come by herself."

J.D. said, "Are you done?"

"What? Showing emotion? Does it bother you?"

The dark glasses flashed in his direction. "Actually, I meant trying to find some way to make this your fault."

"It is."

J.D. gripped the steering wheel harder, and to Benton it was a toss-up: was the man trying to keep from laughing at him or ripping into him. Except that J. D. Eastly didn't laugh. When he finally opened his mouth it was to say, "If someone wanted to take Rosalind, they would find a way to do it even if you were lying in bed next to her."

"You know what?" Benton said, barely waiting for him to finish. "I don't want to talk about it right now." Letting "with you" hang. "I want to think some things through."

J.D. shrugged and kept his eyes on the traffic in front of them.

Benton stared down at his clenched hands, opened them, and smoothed his palms over nonexistent wrinkles in his faded jeans. Despite the sun pouring through the sunroof of the sports car, it was cold inside his sweater. The rust-colored cashmere one, the one Ros had given him for Christmas that year. He'd worn it and his jeans because that was how she liked him best, and he loved to make her happy. "You almost look relaxed when you're dressed like that," she teased him, running her hand through his hair. "Of course, I know better."

She did. She knew him better than almost anyone, and what he felt for her went deeper than for anyone else. She depended on him, had been depending on him for more than twenty years. They argued constantly about everything from quantum mechanics to the merits of silk umbrellas, but only once in the nearly two decades of their friendship had they ever really fought.

"Jason," Benton said aloud without realizing it.

J.D. nodded. "I wanted to wait for you to get here before we called. I thought you should be the one to tell him."

Jason Carnow, Rosalind's sixteen-year-old son, was the product of her brief and tempestuous affair with Walter North, her adviser during her first year of college. In love with Rosalind himself, Benton had been furious when he learned of the affair, and the two of them had not spoken for a year. Not until the winter night Rosalind showed up at his dorm room without a coat but with a baby in her arms. Benton had paid off the waiting taxi, taken them in, and from that day on been the closest thing to a father Jason had ever really known.

At sixteen, it was clear to everyone that Jason Carnow had inherited not only his mother's classic good looks, but also her genius.

He had finished high school two years early, and instead of going on to college, he'd taken a job helping catalog lizard species in Costa Rica. The only thing he cared about more than lizards was his mother, and he was every bit as protective of her as Benton.

"There's no reliable way to reach him," Benton said finally. "He's camped somewhere deep inside the rain forest. I haven't even gotten an e-mail from him in three weeks. And it's probably better. At least until we know more facts. He would not take it well. He'd go out of his mind worrying about her."

J.D. said, "Yeah, better for you to be the only one doing that." And then, "If you're done *thinking*, let me tell you about our progress."

The way he drove it took them less than five minutes to get the rest of the way from the airport to the hotel, but that was plenty of time for his report.

"So you—the police—have nothing," Benton summed up as they pulled into the hotel driveway.

J.D. heard the correction as they got out of the car, Benton blaming him but pretending not to be, typical, not saying what he really meant. *Diplomatic* was how he was sure Benton would describe it. He decided to ignore it. "Nothing yet. But the CIA has already got agents on the ground, and it's getting Metro's—and my—full attention."

J.D. broke off as a swarm of reporters descended on them. The clicks of a dozen shutters going off were drowned out by the shouted questions of the press.

"Do you know who has her?"

"What have they asked for?"

"Is it true you were going to leave her for the Countess of Lille?"

"Is there any evidence that terrorists are behind the disappearance?"

Channel Four, all the networks, even *Newsweek*, J.D. noticed, scanning the crowd and ignoring their questions. Pretty good turn-out. He watched Benton handle it all smoothly, answer the questions, smile for the cameras, and wondered how he could do it without hating himself. Did he not care? Or was he just so used to being the center of the show?

The crowd surged like a tide and ebbed to one side at the insistence of the Bellagio security guards, and a woman in a well-tailored taupe suite with a clipboard appeared in front of them. She said to Benton, "I'm so sorry about that, Mr. Arbor. We tried to get rid of them before you got here but . . ." Her voice dropped and she looked warily at the reporters. "You are in your regular suite on the third floor, villa three-oh-three. The police finished half an hour ago and we sent housekeeping up, so everything should be in order. We are all very concerned about Dr. Carnow."

Benton took the key and gave her in exchange one of his famous smiles, but J.D. saw it vanish as soon as they were past the press. Don't waste that good stuff on peons, he was thinking as Benton said, "You sent over a forensics team. That means you think she was taken from the room."

"It was the last place anyone saw her." They walked by the elevators and toward the door of the service stairs that led up the two flights to the VIP villas. Stepping inside, they nearly collided with a bellboy who was struggling to keep hold of a hairless rat terrier wearing a Burberry sweater.

The bellboy stopped and stared at them, surprised to see guests in the stairwell, but his attention was immediately diverted when the dog turned around and bared its teeth at his neck. "Calm down, Lancelot," he said, quickly taking the last flight of stairs down to the kitchens and the dog dining room. "Please, Lancelot, it's just me, your friend, Cyril."

Benton nodded in the direction of the disappearing dog and said, "I see my cousin Julia is here."

"She and Cal arrived a few days ago. Second honeymoon. Or third. I lose count."

J.D. kept his tone neutral, and he knew Benton wouldn't press him. Julia was one of the reasons for the tense silences between the two of them. At least, that was what Benton thought.

"You said the suite was the last place anyone saw Rosalind," Benton reminded him as they stepped from the flecked linoleum of the service corridor onto the plush carpet of the third-floor hallway. "Who was the last person to see her?"

"Chambermaid. Her name is Selina Cortez. She came to make up the room Friday around ten-thirty in the morning and Rosalind asked her to stop back in later. Selina got the impression that there was someone with her."

Benton frowned. "Someone with her? The kidnapper?"

"If it was, then the kidnapper is someone Rosalind knew. Selina thought there was someone in the bedroom. A man."

"The chambermaid saw a man with Rosalind?"

"She didn't *see* him. She just had the impression that there was someone else there." The shadow of relief in Benton's expression gave J.D. an unwanted flash of sympathy for him. He knew for a fact that there had been a man sharing the bedroom with Rosalind. He'd keep that to himself, he decided, as well as whatever his forensics team turned up from the sheets and towels he had sent over, although he was positive it wouldn't be much. At least not much conclusive. J.D. knew what the tabloids did not, that Benton and Rosalind's relationship had for years been more of a friendship than a love affair, but he also knew how Benton reacted whenever he thought Rosalind was seeing someone else.

"I'll want to see that forensics report," Benton said. "I am sure you weren't thinking about withholding it from me."

"Of course not, Mr. Arbor."

Benton picked up his pace and J.D. let him go, sauntering behind and only catching up with him as he reached suite 303. Before either of them could ring the bell, the door was opened by a distinguished-looking man in a tuxedo and white tie who bowed to them both.

"Good afternoon, gentlemen," he pronounced with a deep British accent. "I am the butler."

J.D. looked at the man's hotel-issued plastic name tag. *Pete Greer. San Antonio, TX.* He wondered in which part of Texas he had picked up his accent.

Benton said, "Good afternoon, Pete. Could you——"

Whatever else Benton might have said was cut off by a voice from beyond the foyer, exclaiming, "Oh, Benton, thank God you are here."

Seven words that J.D. knew Benton had heard a thousand times and never tired of. He saw Benton turn the smile on again and followed him into the living room beyond the entry hall. Benton's grandmother was there, flanked by his cousin Julia and her husband, Cal, on one side, and Eros on the other. Behind them, on the terrace, two uniformed police officers were conversing with a guard from Bellagio security. Next to them was the taupe velvet chaise longue that Rosalind always claimed, her favorite scarf still draped over the side.

A romance novel in Spanish was lying open on it, part of her attempt to teach herself the language before she went to visit Jason in Costa Rica. An orchid plant and a glass with a smudge of purplish-black fingerprint powder stood on the round table alongside it. To J.D. it looked like a memorial to a life interrupted.

It must have looked that way to Benton too, because he seemed to snap into action. He jammed the piece of Juicy Fruit gum into his mouth, leaned toward J.D., and said, "I want the security tapes, all of them, from the hotel starting from the two days before Rosalind disappeared and going until right now. I want her phone records, both here at the hotel and her cell phone. And I want to be deputized by you so I can partake in the investigation."

J.D., speaking slowly on purpose to piss Benton off, said, "Partake? Don't you mean take over?"

"Very funny." Benton now faced the butler. "I would like a large pot of coffee, very strong, and a gallon of orange juice, no pulp."

"That has already been taken care of, sir," the butler said. "Detective Eastly sent over orders this morning."

Benton turned to J.D., looking, for the first time, genuine. And surprised. "You didn't—"

J.D. put up a hand. "Look, whatever there is between you and me, it has no place here. Only Rosalind matters." He thought it came out sounding like he meant it.

Apparently Benton did too. He held out a hand to shake and said, "Thanks." Then he crossed into the living room, bent to kiss his grandmother on both cheeks, and said, "Don't worry, Sadie. I'll take care of Rosalind. I've got the situation under control."

Under control—under control—under control, Benton repeated over and over again, bending forward and standing up mechanically like a marionette, as the man sitting in front of the television set rewound and replayed the end of that scene on the security tape later that night. The screen flickered spasmodically in the dark room, carving frightening shadows in his features. He was sitting much too close to it, he knew, but no one was going to yell at him about it. No one ever did.

Stop. Start. Stop. Start. Under control. Under control.

"Liar, liar, pants on fire," he taunted the television as Benton endlessly repeated his jerky bow. "*I'm* the one with the control. Remote control," he added, waving the black box in his hand. "Get it, Ros? Remote control?" He turned toward the woman in the La-Z-Boy recliner next to his. She was sitting straight up, and the way he'd spread the blanket, you couldn't even tell she was bound into the chair. Even where the clear fishing line was visible, it was hard to see in the dark room. All in all it was such a cozy scene, the two of them at home watching TV. He smiled at her. "Pretty funny, huh?"

Rosalind did not say anything, just kept staring at the screen with eyes still blank from shock and the sedative he'd given her.

They were always like this at the beginning, he knew, but he was still disappointed. He liked it when his friends laughed at his jokes. And Rosalind had such a nice laugh.

Oh well, there was always tomorrow. And the day after that. And the day after that. He'd take care of Rosalind. He had everything under control.

CHAPTER 4

Minneapolis, Minnesota

Imogen watched a red-parkaed child skate Spirograph figures over the surface of the frozen lake as Irwin Bright slowed to take the corner of Sam's street.

"Kathleen and I would be delighted to have you stay with us," he repeated for the fourth time, and for the fourth time Imogen shook her head.

"No. I want to stay at Sam's. Plus, I have to take care of Rex."

"Rex?"

"His goldfish. I promised."

Irwin nodded. Drove. Finally broke the silence, saying, "It was a lovely service. Sam would have liked it."

Irwin Bright was famous among his colleagues in the department of cognitive science at the University of Chicago for being honest to the point of brutality, which made his delivery, when he did try to lie, abominable.

Imogen could not keep herself from smiling at his effort, though. "Sam would have hated it, you mean. The church, the flowers. Aunt Caroline insisted."

"That part, yes. But the number of people who came. And those who spoke. That would have made Sam happy. And the gospel choir."

She had to agree with him there. The gospel choir that had arrived at the end, all in purple robes, and broken into song would have earned an ear-to-ear grin from Sam, and not only because of how much it upset Aunt Caroline.

"What are *those* people doing here?" she had leaned over to Imogen to hiss, but for once Imogen was not concerned with her disapproval. Marcy Tate, the leader of the choir and the assistant principal of Anwating Junior High, winked at Imogen as she led her group on in song after song until the entire church was singing.

Everyone but Aunt Caroline, who had seized her son Nathaniel's arm and dragged him from the nave.

"That was horrible, devil's work," she told Imogen in clipped syllables on the icy front steps of the church afterward. "I can't believe you allowed that."

"Those were Sam's friends," Imogen explained. "He sang with that choir."

Caroline slashed a hand through Imogen's words. "It was a disgrace. You've disgraced our family. Again. Nathaniel and I are leaving. We have a long drive ahead of us back to Madison. I lost an entire day of work for this, and now I don't even know why we came."

I do, Imogen thought as she watched her tall, silent cousin hold the door of this year's Camry open for her aunt. You came so you could have an excuse to see Father Donald tomorrow and get whatever weird thrill you get from saying, "I have sinned, I was angry at my niece because she was not devout enough," and let him praise you. She tasted burned leaves and lime, the way she always did when she was with her aunt, regrets, remorse, and disgust warring together. Most of the disgust was directed at herself for not being over this by now. The lime was the real taste, the burned leaves the remembered one of the air in the attic of the perfect house, like all the other perfect houses on the street, that she was locked in whenever her sinning mouth got her in trouble. It took a lot of time alone in the dark to get the sin out of a girl as wicked as Imogen was. Especially once Sam had smuggled all those *How Things Work* books and a flash-light and some of those icing-covered animal cookies up there for her.

Thinking about Sam brought the heart-clutching sense of lone-liness back, and Imogen forced herself to look at Irwin Bright. She owed it to Irwin not to burst into tears right there in his car. In fact, she owed him everything.

Only in college, while taking a seminar with him, did she learn that what she did was called synesthesia, that it was a rare condition that made her senses overlap. While most people smelled scents, saw sights, and heard sounds, sights, smells, and sounds were trans-lated by Imogen's brain into flavors. The school she and Sam had gone to in Oregon embraced the idea that any expression was a valid expression, so she'd never realized she was different. But after their parents' death, when they were moved to a suburb of Madi-son, Wisconsin, with perfectly groomed lawns and perfectly normal children, Imogen quickly learned that it was not acceptable to make statements like, "The Battle of Gettysburg was slightly minty at the beginning, then became very sugary." At least not if you didn't want people taunting you at lunch, asking, "What does this taste like, Page?" and giving you a kick. Or, in junior high school, pulling down their pants and demanding you to tell them what flavor they were.

She heard Sam's voice in her head now, saying, "Put that little Popsicle away, Albert, before you lose it."

Sam who taught her how to stand up for herself, Sam coming to her rescue, always there, Sam making her laugh and keeping her safe. Sam gone. *Oh God, Sam, how can you be gone?*

Imogen dug her nails into her palms to keep from crying.

It was Irwin who had explained how the mingling of her senses made her acutely aware of patterns, and also unusually—perhaps uncomfortably—empathic. Who explained that some people con-sidered what she did a gift.

She wondered if she could give it back to them.

When she had finished her graduate work, it was Irwin who

submitted her name to his friend at the FBI as a candidate for their new Cognitive Science Unit, and encouraged her to take the position they offered her. They were doing great things, he said, combining psychology, neurology, biology, philosophy, to try to understand the patterns that motivated people—from the politicians who governed America's enemies to serial killers. It was a perfect match, a perfect opportunity for his best student to shine as she deserved to rather than having her talents smothered in the petty day-to-day wrangling of academia. Imogen shrugged off his praise and figured that he could tell she wouldn't last three years trying to make it in the academy. But when she had resigned from the FBI a week before, she felt like she was betraying him more than anyone else, and it still made her sorry.

"Have you given any thought to what you are going to do next?" Irwin asked, trying to sound nonchalant.

"The Tom Thumb minimart on the corner is hiring," she said.

"I'm serious, Imogen."

"Me too. I'd get an employee discount on fish food." She was dodging, but "What next?" was a question she dreaded. Dreaded the feeling that if one of the Pages had to die, it should have been her, not Sam. No one would have wondered what Sam was going to do. Sam attacked every part of life as if it were his favorite pizza. Sam who, with his grades and Harvard diploma, could have been anything and decided to be a sixth-grade teacher in a public school because it was his sixth-grade teacher who had encouraged him to learn to fence. Sam loved everything he did, and everyone loved Sam. Imogen remembered the phone call she'd received the night before from a nervous eleven-year-old boy, asking if it would be all right if he brought Épée, the class hamster, to the funeral, because he had been Sam's special friend. Hell, even hamsters loved Sam.

"Our place in Hawaii is always at your disposal," Irwin went on. "Yours and, ah, Rex's. But there is also a visiting professorship open at the university for next semester. When I mentioned you might be available Dickinson went nuts. Begged me to do whatever I could to get you to take it. You would not want me to disappoint the chair of my department, would you?"

The idea of Irwin worrying about the opinion of anyone in the field was comic. Imogen said, "I'll think about it."

"I know I couldn't teach you much, but I thought I'd at least taught you not to lie."

"I will, Irwin," she said. "I really will think about it. I'll ask Rex what he thinks." They were at the end of Sam's block, nearly at his house. Neatly plowed driveways with trucks and the occasional Big Wheel cut off the street like spines on a fish's skeleton. The neighbors across the street from Sam still had their Christmas lights up, Imogen noticed, and someone had built a snowman in their yard.

Irwin pulled to a stop near the curb in front of Sam's house, and Imogen almost began to cry when she saw that the neighbors had shoveled the front walk for her. Not for her, she reminded herself. For Sam.

Irwin turned off the motor and reached over to unhook his seat belt, but Imogen stopped him.

"Thank you for the ride, Irwin. Give Kathleen my love."

"She'd never forgive me if I let you go in there alone."

"I want to be alone. You know that you and Kathleen are the closest thing to family I have besides Sam, and if I wanted to be with anyone right now it would be you two, but I think I really need some time by myself. Please? I'll call you tomorrow."

Irwin did not like it, she could tell, but he nodded. He sat in the car and watched her step carefully up the path toward the front door. She turned around and waved and stood, hands on her hips, staring at him until he started the motor and drove away.

Irwin was already halfway down the street when the man came quietly around the corner of the porch behind Imogen and reached to grab her.

CHAPTER 5

"Gigi," the man said, holding his arms out to her. "I am so sorry."

Imogen stopped at the sound of his voice and turned slowly toward him. "You know I don't like it when you call me that, Lex."

Lex's face tightened slightly and his arms dropped. The gesture reminded Imogen of Sam, and she had to squeeze her eyes against the tears.

"Imogen," Lex said, not noticing. "Let's go inside."

"No." She crossed her arms over her chest and glared up at him. "Why are you here, Lex?"

"Look, it's freezing. We can talk better inside."

"I don't want you inside. I don't want you outside. Go home. Go back to D.C. Sorry you wasted a trip."

Lex hesitated for a moment, his face growing grave. "He's back, Imogen."

Imogen put her hands over her ears. "I am not listening." Her mittens muffled the sound of her own voice inside her head. She started humming the theme song to *WKRP in Cincinnati*, Sam's favorite show, to block out what he was saying. When he still wouldn't stop she said, "I quit, remember? I can't hear a word you say. I don't know what you are talking about."

"He's done—"

"NO!" This time it was a yell. Her mittens came off her ears. "No more. I don't do this anymore."

Lex shook his head. "You went on leave because your brother was ill. What are you going to do now that he is gone? Run away back to Hawaii? You are only thirty-two years old. Are you going to spend the rest of your life sitting around and feeling sorry for yourself?"

"You bastard." The words drifted by Lex in frozen syllables as she passed him and went up the front steps of Sam's house. Her house now. No one's house.

Lex, uninvited, followed her in. "Look, Imogen, you're the only one who has ever been able to figure this out."

"I don't work for you anymore," she told him pointedly.

Her jaw clenched and she felt her cheeks get hot. The same way they had the night she came home early and found Lex bare-assed, being spanked by his secretary on their two-week-old couch. It was a hell of a way to learn that your fiancé was into S&M, Lex had agreed, but couldn't she try to see things from his point of view instead of standing there laughing?

No. She'd left, never giving him the chance to explain. Never even trying to forgive him.

What Lex would never understand was that it was because she was not forgiving herself. Would not understand it was because she knew she had been lying to herself, pretending that things with him were great, ignoring the red-wine taste of falsehood every time they kissed.

Imogen considered not forgiving herself one of her primary talents. Which was probably why, despite the subtle warning taste of licorice in her mouth, she did not really throw Lex out. By not throwing him out, she knew she was probably going to go back to work. And going back to work was something she could never forgive herself for.

As she slammed cabinets and drawers looking for the fish food, she was only dimly aware of the buzz of Lex speaking, only barely letting herself listen to what he was saying, that the man they were calling the Hide-and-Seek Killer had struck again.

"We got another one of his collages," Lex said, holding a glossy photo out to Imogen. She would not look. She intently measured out Rex's food and sprinkled it into his bowl.

"It's the sixth one. It's just like the others."

Imogen knew that meant it was a photo of a carefully staged, elaborately detailed crime scene, a crime scene that did not exist. Yet. That *yet* was the hook, the temptation the killer used to lure her and all of them in. Because buried within the collage would be clues and riddles that, when solved, would tell them the identity of the victim and the location of the body. The crime scenes themselves were not like the collages, they were much more bare, but one thing was constant: the center of the collage was always taken up with the chalk outline of a body. A body in a tortured posture. The body at the actual crime scene would be found that way too.

On the top of this photo, as on the top of the previous five, there would be a date. It had taken the FBI team assigned to the Hide-and-Seek Killer three victims to realize that the date was the date of death. It was usually sixteen days from the date the FBI received the picture, giving them two and a half weeks to find the crime scene and figure out the clues. Or, as in the past, two and a half weeks to fail.

Imogen had been brought onto the case a week after the Bureau received the fourth collage. She had made a name for herself and the fledgling Cognitive Science Unit of which she was a member two years earlier with the Connoisseur serial murder case. The case had been passed to the Cognitive Science Unit—or Cosy, as it was called, at that point still deridingly—when Behavioral Sciences failed to turn up any leads.

Cosy was different from other profiling units because its agents were authorized to act in the field, not simply consult with local law enforcement, and because they used a broader variety of techniques to identify suspects. It was becoming clear that the media attention lavished on serial killers was changing the way those killers behaved, helping them alter their behavior to fool or thwart the FBI. The Behavioral Sciences model of the white, male serial killer between the ages of twenty-four and thirty-five was increasingly out-of-date, as the Connoisseur case proved. It had been the big test for Cosy, and Imogen knew that many people had expected—even hoped—that she would fail. In retrospect, she almost wished she had.

She still had the light scar near one eyebrow that the last battle with Professor Martina Kidd, the Connoisseur, had left, and there were more scars inside. The case had cost her—time, sanity, happiness. Sleep. And confidence. She still sometimes woke up to the sound of Martina saying, "I see so much of myself in you, dear. So much to admire."

Imogen's boss, Elgin, landed a promotion, and Imogen herself became a bit of a celebrity, but it was only later, when she alone among all the operatives and computers of the FBI had been able to decipher the meaning of the Hide-and-Seek Killer's fourth collage, that she really attained star status. In fact, the FBI agents got to the crime scene only two hours after the girl had died, rather than three days, which had been their previous best record.

Lex unknotted his scarf, making himself at home. "You know Elgin as well as I do. He wouldn't have wasted a cent of his budget to send me out here if he did not think it was important."

Elgin was the head of Cosy, and Lex was his right-hand man. Or rather, his left-hand man. Literally, since Elgin had lost his left arm as a private in World War II. They had joked about that, once.

"You're the best Cosy's got—hell, the best the Bureau's got— and we need your help," Lex insisted against her stubborn silence. *He* had no trouble with social lies. His fingers moved to the buttons on his coat, and Imogen's eyes followed them, frowning so hard that he let his hand drop.

"You don't have me. I don't work for you. You know, I took up boxing when we broke up."

"Needed a way to get rid of all that pent-up sexual energy," Lex said, thinking he was joking.

Imogen clenched her hands. "Get out of here."

"Look, it doesn't matter what you think of me. I'm not even sure you know yourself. What matters is that he's taken another one. A woman."

"Stop it." Imogen's voice was low and she had her hand up, palm facing him. "Do not make this my responsibility."

"Why not? You know you are just being stubborn because Elgin did not listen to your recommendation after you deciphered the fifth collage. Because instead of sending a team to Boston like you told them to, he sent a team to Chicago on Winston's recommendation."

"Stubborn," Imogen repeated, shaking her head. She looked at Lex. "And?"

"And I lied to you about it. But once you'd sorted out the collage we wanted you out of it. We wanted you to concentrate on that document for the NSA. And we knew you would react too strongly if you got too close to the vic."

"Louisa Greenway."

"What?"

"Don't call her 'the vic.' Call her by her name. Louisa Greenway. Sixteen years old, gymnast, liked to baby-sit, favorite band 'NSync, favorite color purple. Remember, I even gave you her name?"

"Right. You are that good. You even gave us the name." Lex shook his head and gazed at her with his hangdog eyes. She knew that he knew the effect the look had on her.

She turned away.

"Look, Gigi, I'm sorry. The Bureau is sorry. We made a mistake. We should have listened to you. An organization like the FBI makes decisions all the time, and some of them—remarkably few—end up as mistakes. That's just the way it is, and if you would stop to think about it instead of acting like a spoiled toddler who didn't get her way you'd see it too."

Imogen swung back toward him, and her cheeks were blazing now. "*Didn't get my way? Is that what you think this is about?* That I am sore because you listened to someone else? How do you sleep at night, Lex? How do you sleep knowing that we could have saved Louisa Greenway if you had just listened to me? I would like to know, because I can't sleep at all. I keep seeing her body. Seeing her—" She turned her face away and closed her eyes.

"Gigi—"

She shook her head once, sharply, to silence Lex's voice. She could still picture the crime scene. What the Hide-and-Seek Killer did to his victims was unspeakable. It was as though he could not decide whether he loved or hated them. It was unclear whether death, once it came, was a curse or a blessing.

Imogen had untangled the riddle of the Hide-and-Seek Killer's last collage with time to spare. But another agent, whose father was something multistarred in the Pentagon, had come up with a different analysis, a different city. Too cheap to send out two teams, Elgin had gone with the better-connected agent's analysis, raiding a strip club in Chicago and leaving Louisa Greenway to die in Boston. When Imogen learned this, she knew she was finished at the FBI. She could not be a member of an organization that wrote off lost lives on a financial ledger as easily as it wrote off overpriced desk sets.

At least, that was what her letter of resignation said, and in those terms. It sounded good. It was an easy reason to give, but it wasn't the real reason and Imogen knew it, even if she didn't want to admit it.

Every time Elgin called her into his office to pop the cork on a bottle of cheap champagne as a celebration of her success, she'd been thrilled at the approbation. She basked in his avuncular approval, wallowed in Lex's protestations of love, grinned at their compliments, lapped up their promotions. Felt like she belonged somewhere.

Until she realized what it really meant to be good at her job. That thinking like a killer meant viewing all people through a lens that pinpointed their weaknesses, their secrets, their darkest fears. The horrible things they could be capable of. Trusting no one, being suspicious of everything. And worst of all: that despite the new feeling of having to be always on your guard, having to come into your apartment every night with a gun in your hand and check all the closets and behind the bathtub curtain and under the bed before you could relax (whatever that was); despite never using a tablecloth because someone could use it for concealment or to throw over your head or to strangle you with; despite coming to see every item in your kitchen as a potential weapon and every hardware store as a killer's paradise; despite having to sleep with a night-light again even though you were in your thirties; despite the way it warped you; despite all that, sometimes innocent people like Louisa Greenway would die.

That was when she realized she'd sold her soul for a case of Asti Spumanti.

Since then, the price had gone up. Up way beyond what the FBI could afford.

At first she had only taken a family leave to care for Sam. But she had sent in her resignation the day he died. Sent it and faxed it, to be sure it got through. It was the only thing she did that day.

"Elgin says you'll have his unconditional support," Lex was telling her when she came out of her thoughts.

Imogen said, "I want you to leave now."

Lex went on. "You'll be the head of the team. On-site. Whatever you say, goes. The collar will be yours too." He lowered his voice. "Gigi, he's escalating. You are the only person who can save the next one."

Elgin, through Lex, was offering Imogen all the plums she could pick. It was the offer of a lifetime, a career-making offer. Her case. Her team. Her criminal.

"I quit," she said again.

"I'll just leave the file in the kitchen," Lex replied. On his way out, he stopped and wrapped his arms around her and kissed the top of her head. She stood ramrod straight in his embrace, willing it to be over.

"How's Carol?" she asked when he finally moved to the door.

Lex turned around. "We broke up," he said, paused, gave her the hangdog look. "You know, if you wanted, I could stay tonight, or for a few days, and we could—"

Imogen shook her head violently. It was not only herself she was good at not forgiving.

For the next four hours she did everything she could to avoid going into the kitchen. She put on Sam's flannel pajamas with the flying toasters on them and ordered the spiciest takeout she could find and ate from the container with the plastic utensils that came in the bag. She drank a bottle of red wine she found in the dining room from the porcelain cup in Sam's bathroom that had held his toothbrush. She flipped through the *Grieving for Not-So-Dummies* book Irwin Bright had given her.

You're the only person who can save the next one.

At nine Imogen opened the file. At three A.M. she called Elgin's home number in Arlington, Virginia. When her flight touched down in Las Vegas it would be 8:15 A.M. local time.

CHAPTER 6

One thing he knew for sure, you could never be too careful. He sat on the floor with only the desk light on so he wouldn't wake Rosalind, and went over his gear again. To the left, the shoes, black, not new, not too old, the soles slightly worn in. Khaki pleated pants with one belt loop ripped, but in the back so you couldn't really tell. The belt too, rubbed bare in the back, occupational hazard, but looking okay in the front. Short-sleeved button-down shirt, off-white with thin brown stripes, pilling under the arms from years of wear. The jacket to wear over it all, a pencil and a pair of aviator glasses in the inside pocket. The glasses were a little too slick, a little jarring with the rest, which, he felt, gave it all realism.

He pictured himself wearing the clothes out. Sitting at a dark bar with a sports game playing on TVs behind it, eating peanuts one by one, drinking club soda through one of the little red bar straws and playing video trivia at twenty-five cents a pop. The girls who worked there would call him the Professor, because he always got the answers right, and say privately to one another that probably his wife left him for someone else, sad, he seemed like such a nice man.

Ha!

He laughed out loud at the thought, then slapped a hand across his mouth, remembering Rosalind sleeping behind him. She had not been any fun that night, and he'd had to cut short their activities and give her a double dose of pills because she was so squirmy.

He knee-walked across the room to watch her while she slept now. She looked nice like that, with her eyes closed and her mouth covered with tape. Sometimes she made a little snoring noise, which reminded him of his mom. It was funny, his mom used to say she slept in the guest room because she couldn't stand his father's snoring, but she snored too.

One difference between his mom and Ros was that Rosalind didn't wear any jewelry, while his mom loved it. She always was wearing something gold or shiny. Whenever he thought of her, he thought of her earrings.

He remembered one time, sitting on the back porch of the house, off the kitchen, holding his puppy in his lap. He didn't hear the door open but then the automatic hinges on it sent it banging back, *knock knock*, and he turned around and she was standing there.

It was before sunset and the light made her hair look gold, made her look like a model, the perfect image of the perfect mom. She smiled a perfect mom smile and sat down next to him, her arms open.

"Come here, angel," she said, gathering him onto her lap. He remembered letting his fingertips touch the gold hoops dangling in her ears. He liked it when she wore them but it made him nervous too, because mostly they were for when she was going out. He kept his gaze on her earrings or her lips, not her eyes. He didn't like eyes.

"Is it time to play now?" he asked, wanting her to deny that she was leaving. Almost every day at that time they played a game. Sometimes it was Mother May I. Sometimes it was Simon Says. And sometimes it was Hide-and-Seek. Hide-and-Seek was the boy's favorite. He was very good at it. One time she didn't find him for hours. She had been so scared she called the police, and when he came out she was shaking all over and her lips were red from her biting them and she smelled sweaty and she cried because she was so happy to see him. That was when it became his favorite. Because it showed how much she loved him.

He felt her pause. He stared at the earrings, hooking his finger through one of them. "You're going away, aren't you?"

"Honey, you're hurting me," she said, unwrapping his fingers and holding his hands in one of hers. With the other hand, she tipped his face up so he'd have to look at her eyes. He squinted. "I'm going away for a little while. I'll be back sooner than you think. You take good care and I'll come back for you. Then we can play."

"Promise, Mommy?"

"Of course. Would I leave my loverboy?"

He shook his head and she had kissed him and hugged him so tight the puppy squealed.

It had squealed a lot more, six weeks later, when he wrung its neck. He had to do it because the puppy looked so sad all the time now that his mom wasn't there. He was careful when he did it not to get any blood or pee on his clothes. He didn't want his father to say he had disgraced the family by going out with his pants all messed. Didn't want his father to yell that he was a disgusting little shit and threaten to slap him silly. It was his fault his mother didn't come back, he knew. She had found another boy to love. A good boy who didn't sometimes miss dinner because he was taking apart the radio and who would PAY ATTENTION and look you in the eye when you told him to. She went away because of him. Because he was not good enough. Because he had not taken good enough care.

That would never happen again, he swore.

Using tweezers, he lifted the piece of paper from between Rosalind's fingers where she had been clutching it when she went unconscious, and slid it into an envelope. Carefully.

From then on, everyone would stay until he was done playing.

CHAPTER 7

Las Vegas, Nevada

Imogen kept her sunglasses on as she threaded her way through the airport terminal, counting on them to narrow her field of sensation. She held her carry-on bag close to her to keep the jar she'd put Rex into that morning steady. She didn't know what airplanes did to goldfish, but he wasn't looking that good.

Her head was swimming with tastes, plasticky sweetness from the clinking of the slot machines paying out, spice from the sheer wash of colors and light, an undertone of lime, still, although now she wasn't sure if it was her own disappointment or that of others she was sensing. There were people everywhere but none of them were really at home, and for a woman who had spent her life feeling out of place, the strange magnetism of Vegas—where no one and everyone belonged at once—was potent.

"First trip?" the cabdriver asked as he squealed away from the terminal curb. Imogen, watching the skyline—pyramid, Eiffel Tower, New York City, Italian campanile—rise in front of her, nodded once, carefully adjusted Rex's jar against the backseat, and forced her eyes back down to the computer printout in her lap.

She checked one more time to be sure, although she had been sure since she first spotted the name on the third page. The sheaf of paper had been waiting for her at the Minneapolis airport, along with the ticket on the charter flight Elgin had shoehorned her onto. She'd been sandwiched between a sleeping man in a business suit on her left and Ralph—"You've probably heard of me? The Samoan Elvis?"—on the right, whose card was poking her thigh through her pants pocket in case she needed anything. "Anything at all, little lady," said with a wink-smile, more fatherly than flirtatious. "When Elvis is in the building, the sky's the limit."

Imogen had felt sorry for Ralph, for his retouched sideburns and chipped chrome glasses and the sour-cherry taste—loneliness—that the shiny patches on the creases of his light blue leisure suit evoked, but she had not had time to talk to him. Elgin's parting words to her on the phone that morning—"I'm trusting you. I hope I'm not making a mistake. Don't you dare screw this up, Page"—kept repeating in her head. Her case, her team, her sole responsibility if it failed. She was not going to let that happen.

She was suddenly aware that her cabdriver was talking to her again. "Mind if I ask, what's your game?"

"I beg your pardon?"

"What do you play? I like to guess what people play, sort of a hobby of mine. You'd be surprised how often I get it right. You, for instance. You're a roulette player, right?"

"No. I don't play."

The cabdriver's tongue clicked a rebuke. "This is Vegas. You heard of Shakespeare? It's like he said: 'All the world's a game and the men are but petty players.' "

Imogen decided not to correct him. Said, "Oh," and returned her eyes to the printout on her lap.

"Yep. And do you know what it means?"

She sighed and gave up working. Stared instead at the fraying collar of his rust-colored Members Only jacket. Did that brand still exist? "I can't imagine."

"Life is just one big game. If you're not playing, you're getting played. You ever heard the saying there are three things you can't get back once you've lost them—money, time, and a good woman?

That's it, man. Every decision's a gamble. Of course, you probably don't care much about a good woman."

"You'd be surprised." Imogen's attention moved to the dashboard. It was covered with toys—a hula girl, Elvis, three different dogs, a dinosaur, a Smurf, a miniature Barbie in an astronaut suit—all glued or suction-cupped on, half of them nodding or swaying in time to the motion of the car. Looking at them made her nauseous, and her eyes fixed on a card the driver had paper-clipped to the notepad next to the steering wheel. *Don't like my driving? Call 1-800-Jerkoff.* She found herself wondering if it was a real phone number as they screeched up to the hotel.

"Don't forget what I told you," the cabby admonished.

"I'll keep it all in mind. Thank you."

"You bet. And don't forget the receipt. You'll want it later."

Imogen gathered her change and her luggage from the trunk of the cab, too focused on keeping Rex upright to pay attention to the man in the beige short-sleeved button-down with the thin brown stripes, the khakis that were missing a belt loop, the shoes, just enough worn in, who was watching her. Too busy bracing for what was about to happen to see him smile despite himself as she pushed through the revolving glass doors of the hotel. Too far away to hear him whisper, "On your marks, get set, go!"

CHAPTER 8

Sitting in the chenille-upholstered chair that faced the Bellagio security chief's desk, Imogen had a lot of time to consider the fact that Lex didn't have the kind of pull he thought he did. When she had illegally called him from her cell phone in the airplane bathroom—Elgin encouraged his personnel to do this because the phone company had trouble keeping track of calls made that way and they often ended up being free—Lex had promised to have everything on the ground in place for her. But so far, while she'd been offered water, tea, coffee, cookies, a free gym pass, and a limited-edition engraved pen, she had not been offered access to Rosalind Carnow's suite, unlimited assistance, or any of the information she'd requested.

She took a sip of cappuccino out of the fancy porcelain cup, and reminded herself for the third time that strangling members of the Bellagio security staff with a phone cord would not fall under the FBI guidelines of interagency cooperation Lex liked to recite.

She had thought only thirteen-year-olds wore Drakkar Noir cologne, but the young security officer sitting across from her seemed to have bathed in it. His blond hair was cut very short, and he had a small piece of toilet paper under his chin that he'd forgotten to remove from when he nicked himself shaving too fast that morning. Imogen guessed that *Burt Weiss, Eureka, CA,* had been given the assignment of rushing in on short notice to deal with her because he was the lowest man on the Bellagio security totem pole. It was not his fault that he was standing between her and what she wanted, she knew, but it might soon be his problem. She gripped the handle of the fancy cup harder as Burt smiled apologetically at her over the telephone receiver and explained, "His wife is just getting him out of the shower." He returned his attention to the phone. "Hello, Mr. Strand? It's Burt, sir. Yes, I'm covering for Grouse. Sorry to call you so early but Miss"—he looked down at the business card in his hand—"Imogen Page is here to see you." He lowered his voice as if they were not sealed in an office, as if the information were an infectious virus. "From the FBI."

The man on the other end of the phone did not lower his voice as he made clear what he thought of the FBI. Imogen imagined he was a retired cop, and she was accustomed to how most cops felt about the feds, but she did not really care. Their dislike could not keep them from cooperating, and the barest minimum of cooperation was all she needed.

"Please explain to him that I need access to the room right away."

Burt put up his hand and, nodding, keeping his eyes on Imogen, said, "Yes, I understand. Yes, I'll do that. Yes, sir."

Imogen heard the line click before he'd finished saying goodbye, but Burt's face was relieved as he replaced the phone in the cradle. "Everything is all set. Detective Eastly should be here in less than ten minutes for your briefing."

Imogen frowned. "Detective Eastly?"

"J. D. Eastly, with the Las Vegas police?" Burt said. His tone practically shimmered with admiration. "He's on the major-incident squad and he's baby-sitting Violent Crimes while the big boss is out of town. Of course you've heard of him—John Dillinger Eastly, you know, the baseball player? All-star and everything. He quit to become a cop, but he does all those fund-raisers for Little League. On TV? Where he says, 'Stay focused, don't lose your cool, and keep your eye on the ball,' and then he hits a ball toward the camera and you see that written on it is 'only full-on losers do drugs.' Something like that anyway. Maybe more catchy, what the advertising people make up."

"I imagine it would be catchy."

"Anyway, he's the one who is coming to brief you."

"I don't need a briefing. And actually, I'd rather have a few minutes up there by myself."

"Detective Eastly is very good at this sort of thing, ma'am. You really ought to wait for him. You'll enjoy meeting him."

I bet, Imogen thought. There was no question in her mind that J. D. Eastly was going to protest against letting her have the case. In her experience, local cops either welcomed FBI assistance with open arms because they were overworked and delighted to have the help, or shunned them like a fungus as interlopers, but either way, they did not rush over to give them briefings.

Imogen peered at Rex in his jar—did fish sleep? Could she have killed him already? No, his fin was moving, thank God—then pulled the latest collage out of her bag and tapped it against the desk, looking at it idly as she tried to figure out what to do next. She was tempted to handcuff Burt to his chair and go up to Rosalind Carnow's suite on her own, but she had a feeling this was not the approach that would earn her the willing cooperation of the Bellagio security force or the Vegas police. Not that their willing cooperation was exactly necessary, but—

Imogen's hands stopped moving. She had spent hours studying the collage, particularly trying to figure out the meaning of the images in the upper center, but she had always looked at it right-side up. Now she was holding it upside down, and now suddenly the message came into focus. Unmistakable, gut-wrenching focus.

She pushed back her chair and started gathering her bags. "Burt, I'm afraid I can't wait any longer."

Burt, startled, looked up from the *Word Hide-'n'-Seek* book he had been working on. "I'm sure Detective Eastly is—"

"Take me up there now." When he did not move, Imogen leaned

across the desk toward him. "Burt, are you standing in the way of my doing my job?"

"No, ma'am. It's just that Detective Eastly said he did not want the feds"—*dicking around* was the phrase she'd heard his boss use on the phone, but apparently Burt didn't think that was exactly appropriate for a girl fed—"confused by the crime scene."

Imogen almost laughed. "I think I can handle it. I do not mean to be a pain but I really need to get in there. Now. I can call Washington and have them explain it to you if I have to, but I think we would both rather it didn't come to that." She didn't know where that bit of television-cop dialogue had come from, but she hoped the words sounded menacing enough that Burt would not think to ask whom she was going to call or what they could possibly do to him. Lex, for example, would have laughed in her face for an hour if she'd phoned to say she was having trouble getting past a hotel security guard.

She must have made it seem good, because Burt relented almost instantly. That was bad for him as far as getting in good with J. D. Eastly went, but lucky in another way, because without realizing it, Imogen had already slipped her handcuffs out of her bag and was getting ready to use them.

As soon as she was alone in Rosalind Carnow's bedroom, everything extraneous—Burt and what she had just seen in the collage and the events that led to her being in Vegas—disappeared from Imogen's mind. It was a beautiful room, off the main space of the suite, with a set of French doors that opened onto the terrace. Imogen turned her head around slowly, orienting herself among the soft camel-colored furnishings, then slipped on her sunglasses and began to work.

She started with the drawers. Two of them were empty, and two others contained silk underwear and nightgowns so beautiful that they could only have been packed for a weekend with a lover. Imogen lifted a brand-new claret-colored peignoir from the tissue paper wrapped around it. Her mother had worn nightgowns like that to bed every night, but hers were usually—

What was she doing thinking about her mother?

Imogen dropped the robe and shut the drawer quickly.

Concentrate. The regular ticking of a clock somewhere in the room gave everything a minty undertone as Imogen moved past a marble table toward the armoire. She pulled open the doors.

Her mouth was suddenly flooded with the taste of licorice.

Danger.

Nine years of sharing a recess schoolyard with Albert DeKlerk made her response automatic. Her fists were up as she spun, kicking first. Her boot made a good thud as it connected with her attacker's midsection, and she was aiming for his eyes when he grabbed her ankle and twisted.

Imogen fell sidewise, upturning the marble table, and her attacker was on top of her, pinning her hands with his wrists, her legs with his thighs. She could not move.

She said, "You are under arrest."

CHAPTER 9

Benton would have bet that nothing could make him laugh that morning, but he had not wagered on Imogen Page.

"I am under arrest?" he asked, looking down at the woman squirming beneath him. He flicked off her sunglasses.

"Yes." She squinted up at him. "Let me go."

"What if I don't?"

"Then you will be in even more trouble. I am a government agent, and if you don't release me right now I am going to have you taken in for assault and battery, in addition to resisting arrest."

"Oh," Benton said, shifting slightly.

That was all the woman needed. Her knee rammed upward into whatever she could find and he sprang away from her.

"Argh," Benton said, holding his knees to his chest. "Oh, man." He opened his eyes and saw that he was looking down the barrel of a gun. It was being held perfectly steady in the hands of the woman looming over him.

She said, "Stay down or I'll shoot your balls off," and he thought he might fall in love with her.

He rubbed his thigh with his palm and said, "I hope your aim with firearms is better than your aim with your knee. You missed your objective by three inches."

"You don't know what my objective was. It worked, didn't it?"

"Sure. Might want to practice that for the future, though. You favor your left. You're doing it with your gun, too." He started to stand.

She said, "Down."

"Five minutes and she's already got you backed into a corner. Must be some kind of record."

The woman stepped sideways, got her back to the wall so she could look at the man who'd just come in and still keep her gun on him. Nicely executed, Benton thought.

"Who are you?" she demanded.

"Detective J. D. Eastly, Las Vegas Metro Police," he said. "That's Benton Arbor. And you must be Imogen Page."

Imogen Page. Benton liked the name too. He said, "Nice to meet you, Ms. Page."

"Special Agent Page," J.D. told him. "She's from the FBI."

There went the love affair. "FBI? I thought you told me you had that angle covered."

"I thought I did," J.D. said. "I just found out this morning. Sorry." He didn't sound sorry. He sounded amused.

God, Benton hated that guy.

Benton Arbor. Imogen repeated the name to herself. Where had she heard that name before? Then she thought, *Oh no. Not* that *Benton Arbor.*

Of course. Her first lead investigation and she had to come head-to-head with Benton Arbor, the playboy automotive mogul whose wry face smirked out over supermarket checkout lines across America from the covers of at least one tabloid a week. Usually he was wearing a tuxedo or climbing out of a helicopter or doing some 007-ish thing in front of one of his Arbor Motors race cars rather than sprawling on the floor of a hotel room in sweatpants and an inside-out T-shirt with his hair smashed to one side, but there was no question that it was the same man. And it explained Rosalind Carnow's

collection of lingerie, since she and Benton were linked as a couple—
at least when he was not squiring topless European princesses around
tropical resorts.

This was not what she had bargained for. Dead people, killers,
okay. Rich socialites, no. Imogen found herself wondering where
she would end up if she made a break for it and scaled the wall at
the back of the terrace. Running jump, grab the top of the wall, she
could be over in three seconds, and then—

The babble of voices and the mingled scent of three aggressively
different perfumes cut into Imogen's thoughts. She looked up to see
that her crime scene had been invaded by a dozen people, half of them
in police and security uniforms, the other half civilians. Both bad.
Benton was on his feet, leaning over and speaking to a small group
dominated by two women. One of them was petite and nervous-
looking, wearing a fur coat and slippers and possessively clutching
the arm of a man in lemon silk pajamas. The other, whose age could
have been anywhere between forty and seventy, was tall and strikingly
beautiful and, Imogen realized with surprise, fondling the behind of
a muscular olive-skinned man half her age.

Imogen watched Benton talking to them, addressing them tenderly and a little condescendingly, and anger bubbled up inside her.
Even rumpled, as though he had just gotten out of bed, he looked so
thoroughly at ease in the surroundings. So in control. Their eyes
met over the heads of the crowd and he smiled at her slightly. A
smile that probably got his way with any woman he wanted. She
wanted him, all of them, out of there. Now.

"They worship him," a gravelly voice said behind Imogen, and
she turned to see a tall, slim brunette lounging in the double doors.
Her face resembled that of the woman with the younger man, but
thinner and colder. "I'm Julia Arbor, Benton's cousin. I play the un-
predictable, rebellious, and yet devastatingly charming character in
the family." Imogen tasted almost no irony.

A small hairless dog wearing a red angora sweater shivered between Julia's ankles, hissing at everyone in the room. Julia looked

neither at the people she was talking about nor at Imogen, but beyond both to where J.D. was leaning against the wall of the suite. Imogen noticed that he kept his smoky glasses on, looking like Mr. Cool Guy.

Julia said, "The woman with her hand on that Greek god's ass is Sadie, our grandmother. Sadie and Eros are newlyweds, that's why she can't keep her hands off him. Of course, the fact that his body looks like it was carved from marble doesn't hurt. The other woman, the shrew in the winter coat, is Benton's mother, Theresa, with her latest husband. I think this one is called Pierre."

Abruptly, Julia's gaze left J.D. and turned to Imogen. Imogen was surprised by its directness, and by the chill she felt as it swept over her from head to foot. Julia frowned, as if something dissatisfied her, and said, "Are you *really* from the FBI?"

"Yes. I'm Special Agent Imogen Page."

"That was rude of me," Julia said, not apologizing. "To look at you like that. I'm not at my best in the morning." She offered a hand and a smile. "I thought an FBI agent would be more drab, less, I don't know, sparkly eyes and kiss-me lips. Can we be friends? In addition to being Benton's cousin I am also Rosalind's best friend, and I want to help in any way I can."

Sparkly eyes and kiss-me lips. Imogen looked longingly at the back wall again. Then she said, "Actually, what I would really appreciate right now is if you could——"

A man impeccably dressed in a pressed shirt and perfectly creased trousers came up then and touched Julia's arm. His hair was wet and combed back, as if he had just gotten out of a shower. "Love, I've been looking all over for you. I just saw Wrightly come in and I thought you should be the one——"

Julia nodded and the man was about to go but she pulled him back. "Cal, I want you to meet Imogen Page. She is from the FBI. Isn't that incredible? Imogen, this is my husband, Cal Harwood. He's the engineering genius behind Arbor Motors. And not bad in bed either."

Cal was in the process of stammering as another man joined them. He was unshaven and rumpled and the only person in the room besides Imogen not to look morning-fresh and perfectly at home. Unlike everyone else, he seemed absolutely agitated, and Imogen liked him for it.

"Julia, what the hell is going on?" he demanded. Despite the bags under his eyes he looked like an overgrown boy.

"Wrightly!" Julia said, kissing him on both cheeks. "When did you get here?"

"I took an earlier flight from Detroit and I saw the reporters downstairs. They said something had—where is—?"

"This is Wrightly Waring, managing editor of *Car and Driver*," Julia told Imogen. She gave an apologetic smile, said, "Would you excuse us?" took his arm, and steered him into the main room of the suite. Cal tagged behind them and Imogen decided to take advantage of this half exodus to get rid of everyone else.

Benton broke off speaking as she approached. He looked up and gave her another of those smiles. "Let me introduce you to everyone. Sadie, Eros, Mother, Pierre, this is Imogen Page of the FBI."

Imogen shook hands. "I am glad to meet all of you," she said. Her voice in her ears sounded like a seven-year-old's practicing grown-up manners. She hated how insecure these people made her feel. Clearing her throat, she said, "I'll have a member of my staff interview each of you sometime in the course of the day. We don't want to inconvenience anyone, but it is very important we talk to all of you who knew Rosalind best. Right now, though, I am going to have to ask that everyone leave this room."

No one moved. Not the people standing with Benton. Not the police officers or the Bellagio security guards. No one.

It was like the horrible nightmare Imogen used to have where halfway through a sold-out performance of *Cymbeline* she discovered she was onstage in a training bra stuffed with old socks.

Then she realized that no one was looking at her. Every gaze had gone instinctively to Benton. He nodded, just barely, and without another sound everyone filed out of the room.

That did it. Imogen put her hands on her hips and looked up at him and said, "That includes you, Mr. Arbor. And you, Detective Eastly. I'll need the room empty before I can have my team get to work." She had no team, and nothing for them to do, but she wanted to be alone.

Benton stared down at her. "You are kicking us out." Statement, not question.

"Yes."

Benton's face went sincere. "Look, Ms. Page. I appreciate that you have come here all the way from—"

"Minneapolis," Imogen interjected. "On an airplane, with a goldfish, next to the Samoan Elvis."

Benton frowned. "Samoan Elvis?"

"WEWF—World Elvis Wrestling Federation—is in town," J.D. explained, not leaving his place against the wall.

Benton said, "I appreciate that you came here on an airplane with a fish and Elvis wrestlers, but I think there's been a mistake. This isn't a job for the Bureau. I have everything under control. I am specially trained in hostage search and—"

"This is not a hostage situation or a kidnapping."

Benton opened his mouth to speak but J.D. put up a hand to stop him. He pushed off the wall, saying, "Imogen Page. I've spent the past fifteen minutes trying to remember where I heard that name before. You're the one who broke the Connoisseur case."

"I was part of the team," Imogen answered.

"I read that you resigned from the Bureau."

Imogen was surprised that anyone had bothered to write about her resignation, much less read about it. "They asked me to come back for this."

Benton frowned. "For what? The Connoisseur was a serial killer, right? Is that your specialty?"

"Yes," Imogen replied. Her specialty. *Tonight serial killer over easy in a light bearnaise—*

"Then what—"

"If I am not mistaken," J.D. interrupted, "Special Agent Page is here because for some reason the feds think that Rosalind's disappearance has something to do with a different serial killer. The Hide-and-Seek Killer."

Benton went very still. "What do you mean?" He asked the question of Imogen, and for the first time she felt she had his undivided attention.

"I think Rosalind Carnow is the Hide-and-Seek Killer's next victim."

"No," Benton said, shaking his head. "She has been kidnapped."

"Has there been any ransom demand? Any concrete evidence to substantiate that this is a kidnapping?"

"No," Benton shot back. "Has there been anything to substantiate serial murder?"

Placing her carry-on bag carefully on the bed, Imogen extracted her copy of the collage Lex had left for her. She held it out to him and said, "I'm afraid there has."

CHAPTER 10

Standing as far from each other as they could and still see, Benton and J.D. looked hard at the collage.

It appeared to show the interior of a young boy's fantasy room from the early 1980s. Along the right side was a bed in the shape of a race car with race-car sheets. At the foot of the bed was a TV set with an Intellivision console hooked to it and the game Night Crawlers inserted. Next to that stood a set of shelves with a stereo, a plant, a geode, a Great Houdini brand magic set that promised in bold letters to *Amaze Your Friends*, and an Original Ouija game. Against the far wall was a desk above which hung a poster for the TV show *Emergency!* that showed a sign pointing the way to an intensive-care unit with a fire truck—California license plate **N390W1** registered through April, 1980—parked in front of it. Fuzzy dice hung improbably from the fire truck's rearview mirror. On the desk was a hardcover book, text illegible, open between pages eleven and twelve, with the slightly blurry words *Ford County Library* rubber-stamped in the upper margins. There was also a bottle of Liquid Paper, a scratch pad with the phrase *Audrie Lumber—Knot Your Normal Lumber Store* printed across the top but otherwise blank, a half-visible greeting card, and a Mead notebook.

Like the other collages before it, this one was made up of dozens of different pieces, carefully glued together from magazines and catalogs. The flavor of the clues seemed to Imogen to be about the same.

But there were two crucial differences. One of them she had discovered only that morning while sitting opposite Burt in the Bellagio security office and she was still not sure if she believed it. The other was unmistakable.

The previous collages all had a chalk outline that traced the way the corpse would be found. The outlines were disquieting, particularly coupled with the knowledge that the victims were subjected to the tortures that left them in their contorted positions before they died, but what this collage had was worse. Because there was no outline—there were outlines. Six of them. One, a head in profile, standing on the desk; two others, both with toes attached, on the bed; and three on the floor. Six outlines showing how they would find the six different pieces of Rosalind's dismembered body. That was what Lex had meant when he said the killer was escalating.

After a minute, Benton glanced up from the collage. "I don't see how this could possibly have anything to do with Rosalind."

"She is the only missing person whose name corresponds with the clues he's given us," Imogen said. "The car theme, for Carnow, is very strong with the bed and the sheets. And then there is this." She pointed to the greeting card on the desk. "It is a valentine. If you look closely you can make out the first words."

" 'Roses are red,' " J.D. read aloud. "That is where you get Rosalind."

"Why can't it be Violet?" Benton asked. "Violets are implied in the next line of the poem."

"Because we don't see the next line," Imogen explained. "And because no one with the name Violet has been reported missing."

"How do you know the victim is not someone who hasn't been reported yet?"

"We don't know that much about our killer, and his methods alter slightly every time he hits, but the one thing that has remained constant is that he has always chosen someone whose absence was noticed quickly. It is one of his conditions. He seems to choose as victims only people others care about or rely on."

Benton stared at the collage. "How do you know it is not"—he put his finger on the desk pad—"Audrie Lumber? Or someone named Audrie?"

"No one named Audrie or any word relating to lumber—tree, wood, twig, plant—is missing. Nor anyone with a name referring to geodes, stones, Houdini, magic, illusion, or night crawlers. The writing on the library book says 'Ford County Library,' and there are no Fords missing. Understood as another automotive reference, it also points back to Dr. Carnow."

Benton shook his head and indicated the stereo. "What about this? It is tuned to 87 and it says 'Dolby.' Reading the numbers as letters of the alphabet that could be Dolby, H. G. H. G. Dolby. Did you check that?"

Imogen sighed. "I checked it, but that is not what it says. 87 upside down is L8. Get it? Late? Dolby late. *Don't be late.* It's a pun. He loves things like that."

"How can you be so sure?" Benton said.

"Because I've been working on this killer for almost two years."

"And you haven't caught him. That hardly inspires confidence."

"I do not need your confidence, Mr. Arbor."

"No, you've got plenty of your own," Benton said. "Even if I accept that Rosalind is the only missing person in Nevada whose name corresponds to a pattern on some boy's sheets, how do you know his next victim will come from Vegas?"

Imogen pointed at the Mead notebook. It was one of the traditional kind, covered in blue fabric that invited scribbling on. Aside from the Mead logo it was blank, except in the middle, where there was a hangman's gallows. Next to it were eight spaces for letters, five of which had been filled in so it read:

_ O _ ERBOY

Below those letters was written the letter C, and hanging off the gallows was the round form of a head, indicating one wrong guess.

This had been the clue that got Imogen on the phone with Elgin at three A.M. "What does this spell to you?" she asked Benton now.

"I don't know."

"Loverboy," J.D. said, sounding it out.

"Right. These letters all correspond to the places where his other victims were found. Oakford, Illinois; Ellsworth, Oregon; Boston, Massachusetts; Ocala, Florida; and Yorba, California. O-E-B-O-Y. We don't know what the R is, but I would wager it was his first killing in this spree, before he thought of the collages. The C below the line and the head on the gallows show the Bureau's one wrong guess, on the last one, when they went to Chicago rather than going to Boston. I don't know how much you have been following this killer's cases, but one of the strange circumstances is that we can find no pattern for how he chooses where to strike. There is no parity between the victims, they are different ages and types, different sexes, from all over the country. Some were killed in small towns, others in cities, some in the North, others in the South. Usually when this happens there is some sort of seasonal pattern, either with the temperature or trade fairs, but we checked up on everything and got nowhere. Until now. Now we see that he has been spelling his name. The cheeky bastard is telling us who he is. Or who he thinks he is."

"And the missing letters are L and V. Las Vegas," Benton filled in. "But why couldn't they be two different places, two different killings? Lawndale and Venice, for example?"

"He would not be giving up his name if this were not his last killing. This is his signature, the final piece in his work of art, his last killing as Loverboy. After this he will change into something else. Probably"—her eye caught on the six chalk circles—"probably something worse." She looked at Benton. "This is our last chance to catch him before he mutates. It is also our best chance to find Dr. Carnow."

Benton studied the collage for a moment longer. He held it out to her. "That is very interesting," he said. "But I'll need to hear something far more concrete before I hand over any part of this investigation to the FBI."

"I beg your pardon?"

"The smallest news leak can be deadly in a kidnapping case, and I want to limit the number of people who have access to the details of our operation."

Imogen turned from him to J.D. "Are you the ranking officer?"

J.D. shook his head. "I would be happy to work with you, but you've got to talk with Mr. Arbor. He was put in charge this morning."

"How?" Imogen demanded.

"I know a few people," Benton told her.

Imogen clenched her fists. She wanted to punch this man more than she had wanted to punch anything in a long time. "My people are as trustworthy as yours."

"Nothing I have seen of the FBI's handing of kidnapping cases inspires any confidence at all," he said, his tone infuriatingly calm. "There are quite a lot of people who think the initials FBI stand for Fast Breaking Information."

"I assure you that no one on my team would share anything with the press."

"Right, because I'm not going to give them, or you, anything to share."

"You refuse to let me work on this?"

"Until I have more to go on than that"—he pointed to the collage—"yes."

"I could call my boss at Quantico."

"And I could call his boss in Washington. My cousin Julia, the one you met? She is his goddaughter."

"I don't care if you call 1-800-Jerkoff," Imogen heard herself saying. "This is my case. And it is not a kidnapping. If you treat it like one, you will be desperately sorry." As she spoke, Imogen saw that he was barely able to keep from laughing at her. "You want to know more? You want facts? I will give you facts. Fact one: there is a false panel at the back of Rosalind Carnow's armoire that leads to a construction channel and is how she was removed from the hotel without appearing on any security cameras. Fact two: this"—she pointed to markings written by hand in the top corner of the collage—"is the date you can write on Rosalind's death certificate if you don't let me get to work. Those are facts."

She was suddenly completely exhausted. She needed to get away, to be alone to think. Or sob. At least change Rex's water. She said, "I am leaving my men in control of the crime scene and giving you three hours to make up your mind. If after that time you still refuse to hand over everything you have, I'll have you arrested for obstructing a federal investigation."

Before he could actually laugh in her face she hugged her bag to her chest, stalked out of the room, muttered, "Bastard," under her breath, and closed—not slammed—the door of the suite behind her. Shoulders squared, chin up, holding her spine straight, she continued down the corridor until it rounded a corner. When she was out of sight of his suite, she slumped against the wall and pressed her palms into her eyes.

What the hell was she doing? Why couldn't she have been tactful? Smiled, been nice. She knew better than to let people like Benton Arbor get under her skin. Smug, condescending, entitled bastard-type people. She banged her head against the wall.

What she wanted, more than anything at that moment, was to turn around and run out of the Bellagio and pretend she'd never heard of Rosalind Carnow or Loverboy or the FBI. She wanted to be back on the beach with Sam in Hawaii; she wanted everything to go back to being perfect like it was then.

But Sam was gone and there she was, standing in a plush corridor in a Nevada hotel, acting like a fool.

And probably killing a goldfish.

She looked in her bag and saw that although he'd lost some water, Rex was still okay. When she looked up she wasn't alone. Enrique "Bugsy" Montoya was holding a handkerchief toward her. "You were stupendous, boss," he told her.

In the absence of Sam, Bugsy would have been her next choice for a companion, and she had told Elgin his assistance was one of her requirements for going back to work. He was not only a good investigator, he was also a solid friend, one of the few people she could stand to have close to her—in both a physical and professional sense. One of the few people she trusted. She stood on her toes to give him an unprofessional kiss on the cheek and wiped her eyes. "How did you get here so fast?"

"I was in L.A. for a family wedding when the call came, so I got the first flight up. You walked by me when you left the villa but you were distracted."

"I'm sorry I made you leave the wedding."

"I'm not. My mother and aunts had already asked me eighty-six times when it was going to be my turn to walk to the altar. I think that's about enough for a year. Plus, I would not for anything have missed the expression on Benton Arbor's face when you told him you were going to arrest him. I don't think anyone has ever said that to him before."

Imogen sighed. "I overreacted."

"No. He deserved it. From how he looked when I left, I'd bet he's still rooted to that place, staring in front of him."

"He's in there laughing at me."

"No way. Cowering. That's what he is doing."

"I should not have lost control."

"You only do that when someone gives you less respect than you deserve. I think it's healthy. Of course, there is your slight problem with rich people."

"I don't have a problem with rich people."

"Right. Anyway, you are the only person I know who seems most tightly in control at the times when you claim to be out of it."

"Super. That makes me sound deranged." Imogen was hating this assignment more every moment.

"Deranged? Would a deranged woman tell a world-famous millionaire with connections to the Pentagon and enough military decorations and clout to get himself appointed to the cabinet to call 1-800-Jerkoff?"

Imogen closed her eyes. "I did that, didn't I?"

"Yep. And let me tell you, it was stupendous."

Imogen groaned, tasting strawberry embarrassment. When she opened her eyes she said, "Bugsy, do you think the rooms here are expensive?"

"Yes. Very."

"Not in our budget?"

"Not in the least."

"Good. Get me a suite. And an order of French fries with really spicy chili."

"Already done, boss. Two bathrooms, a bedroom, and a living room in shades of blue, lavender, and green. Wait till you see it, it's amazing. I also took the precaution of bringing some of this along from L.A." He reached into his pocket and pulled out a small green bottle of Imogen's favorite habanero salsa. He'd worked with her enough to know that really spicy food was one of the few things that could subdue the slew of tastes that inundated her during an investigation.

She took his muscular arm in hers. "Bugsy, what would I do without you?"

"Muddle along. Come on. Your palace is on the thirty-fifth floor."

She was feeling better by the time they reached the elevator bank, but something made her hesitate as the doors slid open. Inside, her finger wavered over the large rectangular button that said CASINO. The casino was in the lobby, the lobby was freedom.

She could still leave. She could still turn around and walk right out the door, right out of Vegas, take her fish and head for the hills. She did not have to do this.

What, are you chicken, Page? Afraid to play?

She pushed the circle marked 35 and the elevator began to rise. She could not get the taste of licorice out of her mouth.

CHAPTER 11

The sound of dice knocking together drew the man in the well-tailored gray wool sport coat to the craps table. No one would recognize him as the same man who'd been outside the hotel hours earlier. The shirt, pants, shoes, wig, and glasses had all gone straight into the Bellagio incinerator and now there was just this handsome fellow, out for a good time. He smiled at the only other player there, a woman in the middle of her turn with ultrablond hair, and plunked down a stack of ten five-hundred-dollar chips on the Come line.

"That's a mighty big bet you're laying out there," the woman said with a Southern drawl. She leaned over, exposing a surgically rounded décolletage that he couldn't stop staring at. "You sure you can trust me with it?"

The man smiled in her direction but not right at her, because he didn't want to make eye contact. "We'll just have to see how lucky I am," he replied, perfectly copying her accent. He loved betting on the Come line. The Cum line.

"You here for a convention?" she asked, teasing the red Lucite dice in her hand with French-tipped nails.

The man shook his head. "No. Just to play. And you?"

"I'm looking for my fortune." She stroked the dice one last time and let them fly in a perfect arc. They hit the opposite side of the table and rebounded, coming to rest with the three and the four faceup. She'd rolled a seven, craps. He'd won five thousand dollars.

"I'd say you're mighty lucky," the woman told him, her drawl diminished in direct proportion to her losses.

"I'd say so too," the man agreed, smiling again. Actually, he'd been watching her and decided the odds of getting what he wanted were enough in his favor to make a shot worth it. He preferred to play games he could win. "Why don't you keep these"—he pushed two five-hundred-dollar chips toward her—"as thanks for handling the dice so well." Their fingers brushed as she reached for the chips and she licked her lips seductively.

It was a cum-on, he thought to himself. She was CUMING ON TO HIM. He laughed and she laughed too. He liked a woman who could laugh with him. It made him feel silly in the best way.

"Why don't you let me buy you a drink? So we could celebrate." He offered another winning smile, keeping his eyes on her boobs.

"I'd like that," she purred. "But why don't you come up to my room and have a drink with me there?"

CUM IN MY ROOM.

He hesitated for a moment. It was a little early for this kind of thing, and Mother told him to be careful. Said now was not the time to take any chances. But this wasn't a chance, this was E-Z. And today, with Imogen arriving, was his lucky day. He deserved to celebrate.

"I'll meet you up there." He took her room number on the thirty-fifth floor and watched her saunter toward the elevators. Ten minutes later, with a single rose in his hand, he appeared at her door.

"Knock, knock," he said toward the peephole. That was how it always started, how it always had to start.

"Who's there?" the drawl asked from inside.

"Abbot," he answered, pressing his lips to her hole. She was playing his game with him. He liked her a lot. She was a nice lady.

"Abbot who?" Still playing along.

"Abbot time you open the door," he said, and she did, laughing.

They laughed together, her silhouetted in the doorway. She was wearing a pale peach see-through thing that only went to her thighs and nothing else.

He could see everything she had, and it wasn't bad.

He chuckled at the rhyme and she smiled some more. She extended a hand into the space of her suite, parting the flimsy fabric of her robe so her entire front was visible and said, "Do you want to come in?"

What a question!

CHAPTER 12

It took Imogen a moment to figure out who she was when she opened her eyes. With her head propped on the arm of the couch she was facing an entire wall of floor-to-ceiling windows that overlooked the glittering Las Vegas Strip and the mountain-ringed desert beyond it. The couch itself was parallel to a huge television and divided the living room, which was the size of her last two apartments combined, into halves. Behind it was a bleached white circular table with upholstered chairs, a wet bar, and the door to her bedroom. The entire suite was coated in rich fabrics and milky marble floors, designed for luxury and comfort and pleasure. Nothing about it resembled anywhere Imogen Page would ever get to stay.

Except maybe the ice bucket Rex was now calling home, which was sitting in the middle of the coffee table.

Then her cell phone rang and reality snapped back into place. A voice she knew too well said, "Where the hell have you been, Imogen?"

"Good afternoon, Lex."

"No, it isn't. Do you know how I've spent my day so far?"

"On an oversold charter flight to a city you don't want to be in to undertake an investigation you want no part of at the behest of a man you don't respect? Oh, wait, that's my day," Imogen said. "Please, tell me all about yours."

Imogen could picture Lex white-knuckling his desk so he would not run his hand through his hair and mess it up. One of their problems when they had been together was his obsession with neatness.

"Are you done trying to be witty, Imogen?"

One of their problems.

Lex was going on. "We need to talk. I've had the phone glued to my ear since I got in. I would not have thought it possible, even for you, to alienate an entire police force in less than four hours, but I was wrong."

"I've told you before, you underestimate me."

"This is not a joke. Do you know how many calls from important people we've gotten today about you?"

"No, but I bet you were thrilled. You love talking to important people."

"One of them was a member of the cabinet."

"Is that why you called me? To tell me how much I am increasing the prestige of your Rolodex? Because if that's all, I am a little busy. I have to go arrest a recalcitrant millionaire. Good-bye, Lex."

"Imogen, Gigi, you—"

Imogen hung up on him but kept the phone at her ear as she looked at her watch. The second hand moved—*click, click, click, click*—

Ring.

"Four seconds, Lex. You are really losing your touch. If you keep this up your efficiency rating is going to go to hell."

There was a crackle of laughter on the other end of the phone and a male voice said, "I love your sense of humor, Imogen." It paused for a beat, then added, "Welcome to Las Vegas."

Imogen's throat went dry. It was not Lex. She pushed the automatic-trace button on her handset and demanded, "Who is this?"

"Your biggest fan. You looked tired but still wonderful this morning. Although I could wish you would wear slightly more feminine clothes. You have such a nice figure and your eyes would really look better with peach than all that black."

"Where are you?"

"Close by. *Very* close by."

At that moment there was a knock on the door of her suite and the line clicked dead.

Imogen stood, frozen, with the phone at her ear.

Knock, knock.

She forced herself to move to the door, her gun out and ready. "Who is it?"

"Ben."

"Ben who?"

Punch lines from a hundred stupid knock-knock jokes that Sam told when they were young bubbled through her mind—

Ben a long time, hasn't it, babe; Ben keeping yourself busy, I see; Ben waiting so long to kill you—

"Benton Arbor. You know, the bastard from the crime scene. Can I come in?"

Imogen looked through the peephole. She opened the door. As Benton walked in, he noticed the gun in her hand.

"You won't need that. I promise not to do anything untoward."

Imogen kept the gun in her hand. With her eyes she directed him into a chair opposite the couch. She stood and stared at him.

"Is something wrong?" Benton asked when the silence had lengthened.

"How did you find my room?"

"I asked one of the men downstairs." It was true, as far as it went. He had asked them. But they hadn't told him. Working with Imogen Page was a privilege no one was willing to risk by giving out information about her. At least, useful information. If you were interested in how she had solved the Martina Kidd murder case simply by having tea with a woman, or how she had single-handedly toppled a Colombian drug lord's empire by deciphering a code for INTERPOL, or how she tasted clues, or how many times she had beaten the deputy head of the FBI at chess, they were plenty forthcoming.

He'd gotten the pseudonym she was using—Lucretia Borgia—and her room number from the head of Bellagio security, who was a friend of J.D.'s, or wanted to be, and had some making up to do after that morning.

"You weren't kidding about the goldfish," he said.

"Why are you here?"

Benton took a deep breath. "I came to apologize. You were right; we found a passage where you said we would."

Imogen had been watching him, gauging him. Since the call, everyone she had met in Vegas was a suspect. *You looked tired but still wonderful this morning,* the caller had said. He had seen her, been near her. She could tell by the way his coat hung that Benton had a cell phone in his inside breast pocket. *Close by. Very close by.* He could have phoned from outside her door. She did not really think Benton Arbor was a serial killer, but she decided to test him. "He called me."

"What? Who?"

"Loverboy. He called me."

Benton came out of his chair. "Did he say anything about Rosalind? When did he call? Have you had it traced?"

She weighed his reaction. It was the right mix of concern, surprise, and pragmatism. It tasted genuine. "No. He called just before you knocked. He said he had been watching us, watching me, this morning." She paused. "Why didn't you come to Vegas with Dr. Carnow? What kept you away until yesterday?"

Benton's jaw tightened, then relaxed. She could tell that he did not like answering to someone else. She knew the feeling well, and there was a certain pleasure in knowing she had earned the right to inflict it on a man who had never had to work for it, a man who had been given power and authority on an antique silver platter.

"Rosalind wanted some time at the spa. She'd been working very hard and said she needed to clear her head. I had meetings in Detroit until yesterday morning, so it worked out well."

"That can be checked, you know. Your meetings in Detroit."

Benton stared at her, realizing belatedly that she'd been asking him for an alibi. "Don't be ridiculous. A deputy director of the FBI—your boss, Clarence Elgin—has certified me himself."

"The last killer I caught was the daughter of an Episcopal bishop, an esteemed professor of anthropology, and one of Clarence Elgin's frequent partners at national bridge conventions. They used to summer together when they were children."

"Do you trust anyone?"

"No."

His face looked like she'd slapped him. He said, "Fine. Check my meetings."

"I will." When he opened his mouth, probably to explain more about the credentials his money had bought him, Imogen interrupted. "Look, Mr. Arbor. I am trying to find a murderer and save your friend. You can either cooperate with me or get out of my way. I don't want your help and I don't need it." She glared at him.

"I would not be so sure about that," Benton retorted, glaring back.

They stood in the middle of her suite glaring at each other, two overgrown schoolyard bullies having a staring contest. Then Benton's expression changed, and he moved his eyes.

"I'm sorry, Ms. Page. I have handled this badly. I should let you do your job. I am unaccustomed to ceding command."

Imogen continued to stare at him.

"And, before, downstairs. I did not want to admit that there could be anything going on here besides kidnapping. That was bad enough, but the idea of Rosalind in the hands of a killer . . ." His voice trailed off. When she still did not speak he said, "Also, I am sorry about your brother."

Imogen shook herself. "What do you mean? How do you know about my brother?"

"I saw the obituary. I knew him slightly."

"How?"

"We were in ROTC together in college."

"Why?"

"Why?" he repeated.

"Why did you do ROTC? Why didn't you just have your father write a check for the tuition?"

"Are you this great with everyone or are you trying especially hard to be nice to me?"

Imogen appeared to think about that for a moment. "I think it is you," she replied flatly. And astonished herself by starting to laugh. She tried to hold it back, knew she should hold back. It was the most inappropriate kind of laughter, completely unprofessional, most likely to end in tears. But she couldn't stop.

And then Benton started laughing too, in the same way. When they were done, Benton blurted, "My father lost all our money and could not afford the tuition. That is why I did ROTC."

Imogen recognized the offering for what it was and reciprocated. "Our parents died when we were both young and our aunt thought college was a waste of money," she said.

Their eyes met and held again, but this time not with challenge. After another silence Benton went on. "Sam and I trained together— as much as anyone could be said to have trained with your brother. He was a legend, Sam Page. No one else was even in his class. I thought I was so great, going for the Army Rangers, Special Forces, but he made the rest of us look like amateurs. He broke every record ever set in basic training, you know, easily. And he was so modest about it. You would never have guessed he was an Olympic fencer."

Imogen nodded, her heart beating fast, filled with pride for Sam, to hear him spoken of that way. In her mind she saw him at the hospital, lifting his arms, and she had to press her lips together hard to keep them from trembling. She swallowed softly, said, "Thank you."

"You're welcome. It's the truth."

She said, "I am sorry about Dr. Carnow. We will find her. I promise you that."

"I know I can count on you. I am just afraid of what we will find."

Her mobile phone rang and they both jumped. Imogen grabbed it.

"We picked up your alert and got a trace on that call," Lex's voice said at the other end of the line.

Imogen frowned. Reporting on a routine phone trace wasn't something the director's left-hand man did.

"You're not going to like it, Gigi."

"I told you not to call me that. What did the trace say?"

"It was a cell phone, so even if we can triangulate its position when it called, there's little hope of finding out where it is now."

"I see." That was bad news, but not as bad as Lex had made it sound.

"There's more Gi—Imogen. The phone was registered to some-one. Someone you know."

"Who?"

"Professor Martina Kidd. The Connoisseur killer herself."

CHAPTER 13

Martina Kidd sent Imogen a holiday letter every year that described the twelve new ways she had devised to torture the special agent, were she ever to get out. They were extremely creative.

Imogen made her voice extra calm. "Are you telling me that Martina Kidd has escaped?"

"No," Lex said, dragging the syllable out to reassure her. "You know she's in max security. No way out."

"That might not stop her. But if she's not on the loose . . ."

"We don't know how she got the phone. We're looking into it. Possibly identity fraud of some kind. The woman is ingenious."

"You don't have to tell me that," Imogen said, thinking of the drawing that came with the last letter.

"I know. The thing is, we are fairly sure that there is a connection between Kidd and the Hide-and-Seek Kill—"

"Loverboy," Imogen interrupted.

"What?"

"His name is Loverboy. That doesn't matter. Look, I need to see Professor Kidd." She glanced at her watch. It was a quarter to one. Even if she could get on a flight to Ohio immediately, she would not arrive at White Haven Maximum Security Correctional Facility in time to get in to see the professor before visiting hours were over. "Can you make an appointment for me first thing tomorrow morning? I'll need you to call ahead to Dirk Best and arrange it so he can't stand in my way."

"I think you're jumping the gun a bit," Lex said, his voice measured.

"There is something you aren't telling me."

"No, something I *haven't* told you. In light of this development, the link between Kidd and the Hide-an—Loverboy, we have decided that you are not the right person for this case."

Imogen went very still. "I beg your pardon?"

"You know that Martina Kidd has it in for you. She makes no secret about it. What if she is using this Loverboy to get to you? That makes you a potential victim. And takes you out of the running as an investigator."

"You are taking me off the case?" Imogen repeated. Her mind flashed to what she had seen in the collage that morning. "You have no idea, no—"

She felt the phone being taken from her hands and the next moment heard a voice saying, "This is Benton Arbor. Who am I talking to?"

Pause.

"Right. Of course, at the director's house. Yes, I am Congresswoman Arbor's cousin. She is charming, isn't she? Yes. What is this I hear about you taking Imogen Page off the case?"

Pause. Benton turned to look at Imogen, who was staring at him with her fists clenched. He winked at her.

"I see what you are saying, but I disagree completely. I think she is the only one for the job. You certainly don't need me to tell you she's the best. I've been reading the file about her that your office sent over. I've seen your own reports."

Benton dodged as Imogen grabbed for the phone, saying, "They sent you my personnel file?"

Benton spoke not to her but to Lex, saying, "No, that won't be good enough. Look, Lex, if we take the date on the collage as day

zero, that gives us only thirteen days counting today to find this bastard. I don't think anyone besides Imogen Page can do it."

Benton listened for a while more, then covered the mouthpiece
and told Imogen, "I'm on hold. Did you know they play Muzak
when they put you on hold? I would have thought the FBI would
be— Yes, I'm still here. What is that? Really? Excellent, I'm sure
she'll agree to that. Hold on, I'll get her for you." He held out the
phone. "Lex wants to talk to you."

Imogen took it and turned her back to him. "What have I
agreed to?"

"That you will work with Mr. Arbor. He sounds like a reason-
able man, so that should not be a problem."

Imogen looked over her shoulder at Benton, who gave her a
tentative smile. She turned her back to him again and stared out the
window. "And if I don't?"

"We pull you off the case. There are a few other things here that
can use your attention. I would prefer that, actually, because—"

"I agree to your terms. I'll work with Mr. Arbor."

"I hope you know what you are doing, Gigi." Lex's voice sounded
genuinely worried.

Imogen looked at the dusty red mountains that circled the Las
Vegas valley like the walls of a gladiator's arena. The city spread before her, the stage set and waiting for her and Loverboy to fight it
out. If she could find him.

"I know exactly what I am doing," she lied, and hung up.

She contemplated the view for a moment longer before turning around. When she did, Benton was on the couch,
hunched over the collage. He looked up as she came toward him.

"Thank you," she said because she had to. She sat down on one
of the chairs facing the sofa.

"I don't want gratitude and I'm not going to try to use my connections to take control. I did it for Rosalind, not you. I believe
what I said. I think you are the only one who can find her. I've been

staring at this"—Benton indicated the collage—"for the past two hours, and I can't make heads or tails of half the things in it. I read your reports on the other collages, so I have an idea of how they work, but I'm still at a loss. Can you explain it?"

"Which part?"

"Start with this. I know we are looking for clues about where he is holding her. On the collage before this one, the Boston killing, you found them by interpreting the ISBN numbers on the back of a book as longitude and latitude markers. Could these be the same thing?" He put his finger on the poster from the show *Emergency!* that hung over the desk and pointed to the fire truck with the California license plate **N390W1**. "Could this indicate north thirty-nine degrees, west one degree?"

"Yes, but that's a place in the middle of the ocean off the coast of Spain. I already looked into that. Besides, it says something different." This was what she had discovered earlier that morning. She had decided not to tell anyone, because she knew what the upshot would be. But Lex was ready to pull her off the case, and sharing confidences built allies.

She said, "Do you see how the ICU sign seems to point to the license plate?" Benton nodded and she turned the collage upside down. "Now look at what the plate says."

Benton frowned at it. Upside down it looked like **1MO6EN**. He gave a low whistle. "It spells Imogen. ICU Imogen."

"Right. 'I see you, Imogen.' It's a message for me. He put me in his collage."

"Why?"

"To tell me he knows about me. To taunt me."

"To challenge you." He looked at her. "You were right, I am a bastard. If I weren't, I'd call Lex back and have you taken off the case because of this. He's got Rosalind, but he is obviously targeting you. I should not let you endanger your life this way."

"Mr. Arbor, you have absolutely no control over what I do with my life. The better you remember that, the better we'll get along."

Benton opened his mouth to say something, then shut it. His eyes were fixed on the wall opposite them but his hand rummaged in the pocket of his pants and came out with a pack of Juicy Fruit gum. He ripped the foil off three pieces, shoved them in his mouth, and began to chew savagely. He shook himself. "I'm sorry, that was rude of me. Would you like a piece?"

Imogen felt the corner of her mouth twitch in a smile. This, she imagined, was Benton Arbor's version of losing control. Not minding his manners. "No, thanks." She picked up her phone and started dialing. "I've got to go to Ohio tomorrow morning first thing," she explained, to cut the silence, as she waited for the call to connect with the Bureau travel office.

"Where in Ohio?"

"I guess I'll have to fly to Cleveland and rent a car. I don't expect there is a direct flight from here to Westport."

"Yes, there is. What time do you want to go?"

"What?"

"I need to file a flight plan. We can leave on my plane whenever you want."

"You have a plane?"

"Yes. When do you want to go?"

Imogen hung up the phone. A private plane. As the price for her soul, it beat the hell out of a case of Asti Spumanti.

CHAPTER 14

The most nervous Bugsy had ever been in his life, he thought, was the time he met Sam Page, Imogen's brother. More nervous than his exams at Quantico or when he came out to his grandmother during his father's birthday party. Of course, the five tequila shots had helped then. The time with Sam he was nervous because he was worried that the man would think him unworthy. Unworthy to be Imogen's protector, her friend. But Sam had given him a hug and told him how highly Imogen spoke of him and, right before they said good-bye, had said, "Thank you for standing by her."

"I'm just doing my job."

"That's not what Gigi says."

"You know how she is. Clueless." And they'd laughed. Because it was totally untrue. Except about herself.

Like how she did not even notice the effect she was having on her team that first night in Vegas, the way Tom, Harold, and Dannie (or, as Bugsy thought of them, Tom, Dick, and Harry, despite Dannie being short for Danielle), the three FBI agents Elgin sent, were watching her every move like at some moment she might create lightning. Bugsy loved watching them whisper to one another for fear of disturbing her as she paced in front of the blown-up version of the collage that was pinned to the wall. Next to the collage was a map of Las Vegas, and on a sheet of paper Imogen had begun a list of guesses based on street names from the map—Mead, Paradise for the pair of fuzzy dice on the fire truck, she explained, Audrie, Elm because of the lumber reference. Bugsy could sense her frustration, her tension, and he knew that it wasn't just because none of the street names felt right to her. He also knew with her in that mood her team could have made gorilla mating noises and she wouldn't have heard them.

After about an hour of her pacing and their whispering, there was a knock on the door and J.D. came in, wearing his slick-guy dark glasses, carrying a glass fishbowl. "I brought this for Rex," he said, holding it toward Imogen.

She said, "Thanks," without turning around.

He set the bowl down and said, "The forensics lab report just came back. The fibers in the construction channel match the ones in the dresser drawer. They were definitely from Rosalind's sweater."

"Of course they were." Again without turning around. "I told you they would be."

Bugsy would have guessed that behind the lenses of his glasses J.D.'s eyes showed surprise mixed in with lust. Not that you could see, but Imogen had that effect on men during an investigation, he knew.

He was watching J.D. try to organize his face when there was another knock and Benton came in. He was carrying a big fish tank, complete with little rocks on the bottom and an electric-pump filtration system. He started to say, "I brought this for Rex," then stopped when he spotted the fishbowl already on the table.

It took every moment of the special-agent training Bugsy had had at Quantico to keep him from cracking up at the way the two men looked at each other. Both of them coming in like they'd laid the golden egg, offering the moon and stars. Imogen not even noticing.

She never noticed that kind of thing, the way all the men work-ing a case with her would fall on their faces trying to get her atten-tion. He had not been on a single case where the other men on the team hadn't been totally smitten by her. One guy had been ready to leave his wife and kids; another, a D.A., was ready to sail off to Brazil with her just because she once mentioned she'd always wanted to cha-cha in Rio.

Despite all the offers—and some of them were from men Bugsy wouldn't have minded going out with—she remained stub-bornly single. The only times she seemed even moderately inter-ested in a guy, he was the kind you could see a mile away wouldn't last for her. She wouldn't admit to it, and maybe it wasn't con-scious, but she always dated the bad ones.

That gave J.D. an edge over Benton, Bugsy decided. Not that there was anything wrong with J.D.; he just didn't seem like the kind of guy you'd build a life with. More like a hot, torrid affair. Which he would have thought was good for Imogen at times, but not right now. Right now, he decided, she was too fragile. Only someone who knew her well would have been able to see it, but it scared him how vulnerable she seemed. Particularly with what she had planned for the next day.

At one A.M. Bugsy realized that Imogen had disappeared fifteen minutes earlier, and he decided to send everyone home. When the suite was empty he walked into her bedroom, empty, then spoke to the closed door of the bathroom.

"Boss? You okay?"

From inside, muffled: "Fine. Great."

"Everyone is gone. Do you want to come out?"

"No."

"Can I come in?"

Pause. "If you want to. The door is unlocked."

He walked in and found her sitting, fully clothed, knees un-der her chin in the empty bathtub. Rex, still in the ice bucket, was next to her, and she had a book in her hand. Her eyes and nose were red. As Bugsy pulled up the little chair from the vanity table and sat next to her he saw the book was *Grieving for Not-So-Dummies.*

She said, "I needed some time alone. Everyone out there talking, making so much noise."

He nodded. He would have hugged her but you didn't hug Imogen Page. He said, "Of course. Perfectly understandable." His eyes went to the pile of Kleenex on the floor next to the bathtub.

"I seem to have some allergies. And I think there's something wrong with me," she went on, opening the book and pointing to a chapter headed "Go Ahead, Get Angry!" "I don't feel the way they say I am supposed to."

"You can't grieve from a book."

"Why not? It says on the cover if I do the exercises inside, I'll be able to expedite my grieving and move on."

"That's not how it works."

"How do you know?"

"Remember when my grandmother died? What a mess I was?"

"You weren't a mess. You were anything but a mess. You cleaned everything in sight. My apartment has never been that spotless."

"Remember when I called you at four-thirty A.M. sobbing because I was out of Soft Scrub and Q-tips and my grout was still dirty?"

"Yes."

"That is what grieving is like. You can't lose a person who is important to you and not feel decimated inside. I'm not sure it's a good idea for you to be working again."

"What should I be doing? Knitting? Dusting Sam's plants? Letting Rosalind die?" Her voice got quieter. "If I can save Rosalind, then maybe I'll have made up for it."

He didn't ask, "Made up for what?" He knew her well enough to know what she was blaming herself for this time. He said, "You need to recognize that there was nothing you could do to save Sam. He was sick. He had—"

She stopped him. "I can't listen to that right now. I appreciate what you are trying to do, really, but can we put this off until after we find Rosalind? Then I promise I'll clean manically. Or do whatever you say. But not now. Okay?" When he nodded she said, "Did you mean it, that everyone is gone?"

"Yes. I thought they should get some sleep."

"But the collage is still out there. God, I hate that thing."

"I can take it down."

She shook her head. "It won't matter, I see it even when my eyes are closed. And you know the worst thing about it?"

"The Night Crawlers game?"

"Everything I need to save Rosalind is in there. Every clue. And I can't find it. Because my mind isn't sharp. Because of this stupid grieving." She threw *Grieving for Not-So-Dummies* out of the tub and smiled as it thwacked against the wall. Then she stood up.

"Fighting your emotions is only going to make them stronger."

"Did you get it from a comic book?" She climbed out of the tub and headed for the living room.

Bugsy stopped her right before she got there. It was time to talk about what was really worrying both of them. "Boss—are you sure you have to go see Martina Kidd tomorrow?"

"Positive."

"Can I come with you?"

"No. This is something I have to do alone."

"Why?"

"So no one can see how badly I screw it up." Trying to make it sound like a joke, but Bugsy knew it wasn't one. She walked to the table and took a Tootsie Pop from the box. Then she turned to him and said, "Hey, where did the fishbowl and fish tank come from?"

Clueless.

As he was leaving, Bugsy handed her his handkerchief. "For your allergies. Your nose will be red tomorrow if you keep using those Kleenexes in the bathroom. You don't want Martina Kidd to notice a thing like that."

She gave him a smile as they said good night, but he heard her start sobbing the minute the door closed behind him.

CHAPTER **15**

Late that night, driving home from the "office" with the lights of the Strip winking at him to his left, the man decided that the hard part wasn't staying focused on his job once it all started. He'd been doing that since the beginning, his games always taking place when he was on an assignment without anyone even suspecting.

The fact was, recently the game had begun to get boring. Or not boring, exactly, but the thrill was diminishing. The last time, with Louisa Greenway, he'd had to add a few things to keep it exciting, keep himself from killing her before the appointed day. He could have, of course, but that would not have been following the rules. And rules were what made a game. Without them, there was nothing.

That was why he'd invited Imogen earlier this time. Before it had just been him and whoever he was playing with. The FBI was out there, sure, but they were miles behind him. Now, on purpose, they were right there. He had made the first clues so easy Imogen couldn't miss them. He had wanted her close to him, the best of the best where he could watch her. But it was different than he thought it would be, and that was what was getting to him. For one thing, she seemed super sad, and he worried that would distract her. For another, she'd brought that fish with her.

The fish really bothered him. He tried not to let it, but it was like a little remnant of her brother, something that she could look at and get right then, boom, all teary eyed, thinking of Sam. He had seen it happen in front of him. He didn't want her mind on her brother, on anyone but himself. He had thought of different ways to kill it, but that wouldn't be nice. Still, if it looked at him funny, just once, he would have to do it.

What he needed to do, he realized as he got closer to "home," was make sure there was plenty to keep Imogen busy. Himself too. His little dalliance that afternoon had been nice. He'd have to consider doing that a few more times. And for Imogen, there was her field trip to Ohio tomorrow. After that, though, he wanted to keep her close to him. Not share her with Mother or anyone else.

He rolled to a stop at a red light. The streets in both directions were empty, so he could just have floored it and kept going, given himself a little thrill, but again, that was against the rules. Stoplights were stoplights. As he sat there, wondering why the reds in Vegas were five times as long as anywhere else, a woman and a boy stepped into the crosswalk, holding hands. The woman was young, probably in her mid-twenties, with a big poof of dark curly hair in a ponytail, wearing medical scrubs with pictures of lollipops on them. The boy, no older than ten, was in his pajamas, stumbling along half-asleep. The man looked at them and guessed the mom was a nurse at the hospital in the next block, working the night shift and picking her son up from his baby-sitter now. Pulling him out of sleep for the long bus ride home, maybe kissing his forehead and saying, "Wake up, honey bun, it's time."

The image made the man smile and feel a little silly. He rolled down his window, ignoring the green light, and said, "Ma'am? Can I offer you a free ride home? It looks like your boy is tired."

The woman hesitated. People were justifiably wary about taking rides from strangers. But when she looked at him he knew she would see that he wasn't exactly a stranger. That he looked familiar. And kind.

Like he was reading her mind he said, "You're a nurse over at

University Medical Center, aren't you?" Then lied "I think you might have helped my boy. Little guy, got a cast on his leg?"

The woman bit her lip, trying to remember.

"Doesn't matter," he assured her. "You must see so many patients. But it looks like you've had a long day, and the staff over there sure treated Tommy well. Figure I should help you all out if I can, return the favor as it were." Shit, he shouldn't have given a name. Too many details.

The woman was still searching her mind for nonexistent "Tommy," but her son was dragging on her arm, looking up at her.

"Can we, Mom?" the boy asked in his pathetic voice, giving a big showplace yawn. "Please?"

Manipulative little fucker, the man thought. He knew the boy just wanted a ride. Still, it worked. The mother smiled tentatively. "Are you sure? It's not far, but on the bus . . ."

"Positive. Hop in." He leaned across and threw open the passenger door and the mother got in, holding the boy on her lap.

"It's awfully nice of you, sir," she said as she gave him directions to her house. "You were right about the long day. I had a double shift."

"You do the work of angels over there," the man said, sounding even to himself like he was laying it on a bit thick.

But the woman smiled. "Thank you. It is nice to hear that. Sometimes you don't feel appreciated."

She rattled on but he wasn't listening, wondering instead if the boy had a father, one who took him out and threw balls to him on the sidewalk. One who yelled at him when he missed. Told him he was disgusting. One who liked to "spend time with Johnnie" twice a month and then the next day couldn't even bend over to tie his shoes he was so hungover. One who—

The woman's voice broke into his thoughts. She smiled, ruffled her son's hair, and said, "And so this is it. If you just turn right into the next driveway we'll be home."

"This driveway?" he said.

"Yes, and I can't thank you enough for the—"

The man hit the gas and sped by the turn she was pointing to, into the driveway of a pathetic-looking faux-Tudor apartment complex. Quickly, he glanced over and saw the first flush of panic in her cheeks. He saw her chin drop as she realized that she might have made a mistake—a grave mistake—getting into this car with the nice-looking stranger. He watched her swallow hard and smelled her sweat and started feeling *really* silly.

After a block he smiled to put her at her ease. He said, "Oops," then, "Sorry about that, I'm a bit of a speed demon," keeping it light. "Yep, I'm just a speed *demon*," he said, then slowed the car, not slow enough for her to get out—he saw her hand on the door handle—but slow enough to make a U-turn.

He could see she was close to tears, one hand with white knuckles clutching her son's pajama top, the other still on the door handle. With a flourish, he did a perfect ninety-degree turn into the driveway of Ye Olde Village Apartments and hit the brakes. Her hand was shaking so hard it slipped trying to get the door open. She didn't even realize he had it locked.

For ten seconds, the ten longest seconds of her life, he bet, he let her struggle with the door, seeing her house so close but not able to get to it, get away from him. Breathing in little gasps, her heart pounding so hard he could see the pulse in her neck. There were tears running down her face and onto the upholstery, and her son kept saying, "What's wrong, Mom?"

When he hit the unlock button, she almost pushed the boy onto the pavement struggling out of the seat. As she got out of the car he saw circles of moisture under her arms. She was sobbing, terrified, clutching the boy to her, not looking at the cab, running toward the second set of stairs on the left.

He waved jauntily at her and took off laughing. He knew she would want to put the whole thing out of her mind, never think of it again, so she wouldn't report it. Besides, what could she say?

Some cabbie offered her a free ride and then missed a turn? Yeah, not likely.

Even if it was a risk, it had been totally worth it. That one whiff of fear would be enough to hold him, for a little while. Still, he wanted to spice things up. He got out a piece of paper and a pen and started a list, leaning against the pad next to the steering wheel as he drove. Get clothes to dry cleaner. Pick up most recent security tapes. Krazy Glue. He put a question mark next to that one; it was an idea he had been working on, but he wasn't sure about it. What else? Maybe go to a pet store, buy one of those little treasure chests that go in fishbowls to leave for Imogen. He could decide later whether to put poison on it.

He pulled into his parking spot and was about to put the list into his breast pocket when he thought once again about Louisa Greenway, how he'd played with her. How fun it had been. Funny too.

He added one more item to the list.

12 days left!

Imogen could still sense the low hum of the airplane engine vibrating in her bones as she and Benton climbed out of their rented Ford Focus in front of the visitors' entrance of the White Haven Correctional Institute. At least, she told herself it was the vibration of the airplane that was making her knees feel wobbly.

Professor Martina Kidd. The Connoisseur. Imogen doubted there was a best way to handle the interview they were about to have, but she was sure that whatever she did would not be it. Lex maintained that it was Martina Kidd that had really doomed their romantic relationship, that Imogen had only used his infidelity with Carol as an excuse. Lex liked to spread responsibility out a bit, but there was something in what he said. It was only after her brush with Martina Kidd that Imogen had taken up boxing.

The morning was freezing. The cold sucked the color out of the entire landscape, leaving it a flat, dead sepia brown. The facility dated from the early part of the century, when they believed in building prisons with long redbrick walls punctured by pointy-roofed guard towers. These days the guards were replaced with cameras and the walls were surmounted with electrified barbed wire, but the whole thing still looked like a Victorian madhouse to Imogen.

Her eyes were glued to the snowy ground, not looking at the

walls. Mechanically, she noted the brand of a cigarette butt—Camel, fuchsia lipstick on the tip—poking out of the snow, the smudge of dirt from a motorcycle tire, the size of Benton's footprints.

You know what they say about men with big feet, a guffawing voice broke into her thoughts like an out-of-tune radio. She stopped, startled.

"Is something wrong?"

She felt her cheeks flush. "No. I just don't like coming here. Martina Kidd is difficult to talk to. And I had a slight disagreement with the warden a few years ago."

Dirk Best was an improbable warden. Hollywood handsome with a dark, closely cropped helmet of hair just going salt-and-pepper at the temples, a perpetual tan, and teeth that could have been an ad for whitening toothpaste. His eyes were lined just enough to make him look distinguished, and his grip, when he shook, had the solidity of a politician's. If he'd been able to keep his hands off of other men's women, he could have been governor, or so he liked to say. Imogen thought he stood a better chance as the host of Fantasy Island.

"Mr. Arbor. It is a real pleasure to meet you," Dirk boomed cordially as they entered the administration building. He nodded in Imogen's direction and mumbled, "Special Agent Page."

At least she did not have to guess whether he'd forgiven her.

As Dirk led them down the corridor that connected the administration wing to the rest of what Dirk called "the Campus," he and Benton discussed advances in the steering mechanism in the newest Arbor Motors cars, and Imogen did her best not to count the number of doors that slid closed and locked behind them.

Clang.

Concentrate on why you are here, she told herself. For an interview you don't want to do. With an audience you really don't want. She had told Benton she wanted to go in alone and he'd nodded. Then she'd explained her reasons and he'd nodded. She'd told him he could jeopardize the interview and he'd nodded. It was like talking to a Weeble. When she was done he said he'd let her run the interrogation—that was what he called it, like they were in a gangster movie; if he'd only known—but he was going to be there. She'd nodded.

Clang.

Only one more, Imogen knew. Dirk said, "Lex said you would be wanting a private interview with Martina, so I'll leave you here. Curtis will show you the rest of the way." He offered a hand to Benton. "It was a pleasure talking to you." And he turned back without acknowledging Imogen.

Curtis lumbered out of his seat at the guard station, pulling on his jacket. His keys jangled together as he led them down another linoleum corridor and through another gate.

Clang.

"Here we are, ladies and gentlemen. Welcome to cell block K, what we around here call the Zoo. Please keep your hands and arms away from the cages at all times. The animals can be dangerous."

CHAPTER **17**

"Imogen!" a voice shouted down the corridor. "Imogen, pick me!"

"That's Loretta," Curtis explained, the tour guide. "She sure has a thing for you, don't she?" he said to Imogen.

To Benton it looked like she didn't even hear. That was how she had been on the whole plane ride and the drive from the airport. In the air, when he'd asked her if there was anything he should know about her technique, any special signals they should have with each other for the interrogation, she'd just given him a look like he'd said something retarded and gone back to staring out the window. He had tried again in the rental car, asking, "Do you make a list of the questions you're going to ask during the interrogation? In your head?" Without looking at him she'd said, "No. Some *interrogations* go better if you wing it," in this weird voice. And that was that.

Wing it.

He decided she wasn't much of a conversationalist in the morning, but now, walking next to her, he felt her tense like an athlete before an event psyching herself out, and he decided maybe that was what she'd been doing. He couldn't wait to meet the person who could have that kind of effect on Imogen Page.

Still, he was shocked by his first glimpse of her.

His initial thought: It's that lady from *Murder She Wrote*.

Martina Kidd didn't exactly look like Angela Lansbury, but

close. She was thinner, to start with. Really she looked like the kind of sweet grandmother who sneaked you extra sugar cookies when you went to have tea at her house and didn't mind if you wanted to run outside to play on the tire swing she kept there just for you. She had gray hair done up in a slightly lopsided bun and was wearing gray plastic-framed glasses, bifocals, with some smudges on the lenses. She was in her early seventies, and if she hadn't been dressed in a prison uniform he could have pictured her in a flower-print dress with a Peter Pan collar, cardigan thrown over her shoulders, carrying a casserole to a church potluck. She had smile lines around her mouth and bright blue eyes, and as they approached she grinned and clapped her hands together and said, "Imogen, my dear child, what a wonderful surprise to see you," like she meant it.

Beside him, Imogen ground her teeth.

Martina beamed at them through the bars. "You are looking older, Imogen. Have you been taking care of yourself? I hope you are using that moisturizer with the SPF I told you about. You are prone to wrinkles around the eyes, like me. All that looking into people's souls, I suspect."

When Martina turned her gaze on him, Benton got a hint of what that meant. It was like how people described brain scans by aliens in tabloid stories, like she was probing him, looking for deficiencies. It took maybe two seconds. Her eyes still on him, she said, "Imogen, aren't you going to introduce me to your handsome friend?"

"Professor Kidd, this is Benton Arbor."

Benton wasn't sure what the protocol was in a situation like this. Imogen and Curtis had both told him not to get close enough to touch Martina, so he couldn't shake. And he wasn't sure "It's a pleasure to meet you" was quite right. He said, "I've heard a great deal about you, Professor Kidd."

"Please, call me Mother, everyone does," Martina said. "Everyone but our Imogen. Benton Arbor. What a treat to meet you in person."

"That is very kind of you," Benton said.

"Handsome and with manners. Arbor, like tree. You're a member of the family tree. What a delightful name. I love names with double meanings." She turned back to Imogen. "What have you done with your hair, Imogen? Are you still going to Supercuts? I told you last time we got together, it is worth the extra money to have a style, not just a cut. I wish you'd let it grow out a bit more. A slightly longer look would be so much more flattering. Don't you agree, Mr. Arbor?"

"I think Special Agent Page's hair is fine."

"Special Agent Page. We're so formal. He says your hair is 'fine,' Imogen, but from a man with his manners, you know that means it needs work. You could be such a pretty girl if you just kept your bangs out of your face and let the sides grow longer. Do you ever use those barrettes I gave you?"

"Sometimes."

"Fanny Fib-Teller! You know you can't lie to Mother. Now, dear, tell me about your poor brother's passing."

"Why don't we talk about why we are here first?"

"Please? Humor an old woman. Just a little about it. You know how I love all the little rituals and goings-on associated with death."

Benton was surprised when Imogen nodded and said, "The funeral was very simple, nothing fancy. Just Sam's friends."

Martina put up a hand. "No, no, no, my dear, that's not what I meant. Tell me from the beginning. Go back to his bedside. When he died. You were right there when he died, weren't you?" Clapping her hands over her mouth like a gleeful six-year-old on Christmas morning when Imogen nodded. "I knew it. Oh, I envy you." She leaned close, through the bars. "Did you hear that last gasp of breath?"

Benton felt like he was watching a prizefight, Martina circling around Imogen, trying to unsettle her, establish some kind of dominance by jabbing unexpectedly. Imogen taking a few hits but offering no defense, nothing. Holding back? Watching her swallow hard now, Benton felt himself gearing up to take over. Winging it was not working. He opened his mouth to step in, but Imogen spoke first.

She said, "Yes, I heard his last breath," her voice a bit shaky.

That was it. Benton cleared his throat and started to say, "I really think we should——" when Martina turned to look at him.

"Yes?" she said, giving him a smile. "What do you think, Mr. Arbor? Is it something about what Imogen was saying? Do you have any little comment to add?"

Her smile started to give him the creeps. He glanced at Imogen, clenching her jaw, remembered that he'd promised not to interfere. To Martina he said, "I——no."

Martina said, "As you like," then looked back at Imogen to say, "It really does rattle, doesn't it, that last breath? Tell Mother, has it been haunting you? Oh dear, I knew it would. You poor thing. Keeping you awake at night. Taunting you. Saying if you had only done more he'd still be alive." Pressing her sweet grandma face between the bars.

"Not exactly." Imogen cleared her throat. "Professor Kidd, we're here because——"

"Such a hurry, Imogen. You need to learn to take things more slowly. Not skimp on ceremonies of politeness and civility. Tell me, dear, did you find, as I always have, that the moment of death is a letdown? It's the rest of it that is pleasurable. But then they are gone and there's nothing else you can do to them. Or, in your case, for them."

Martina turned her old little-girl eyes on Benton. "You know, Mr. Arbor, Imogen saw her parents die too. Well, not die, probably, but she was the one to find their bodies. Weren't you, dear? Did you get to hear their last breaths? I can't remember."

"Maybe we can talk about this another time," Imogen said, sounding really rattled now.

"You did, that's right, I remember now. At least your mother's. When you cut her down. That image of you, poor sweet little girl, dragging a big heavy bar stool across the floor just to be tall enough to reach on your tippytoes up with the scissors to cut the cord your mother hanged herself with, try to save her. It's positively heartwarming. What a family scene. How long that must have taken, a little girl with only her blunt school scissors. Maybe if you'd been faster you could have rescued her. Or your father. The sound of a chair scraping across the wood floor, the sound of futility. I imagine it would be almost indelible. Do you ever hear that? Late at night? Sometimes wake up to it?"

"We've talked about this before, Professor Kidd."

"Yes, but my mind is so unreliable these days, I can't remember a thing." She leaned to one side to confide to Benton, "It's a touchy subject with her because she thinks she killed them. They would not have committed suicide if you'd been a better daughter, isn't that what you think, Imogen? Is that true about your brother too? Really astonishing when you think about it. So many people die on your watch. You remind me so much of myself, in my heyday."

"That's why I'm here. To try to stop another person from dying."

"Ah, making it all about work. I see the bloodhound is back on the scent. That is what they call Special Agent Page at the Bureau, you know, Mr. Arbor. The Bloodhound." Martina beckoned Benton forward. "Shall I tell you a curious thing? They seldom give nicknames to agents—they usually reserve them for killers. Do you suppose that means something? Do they know something we don't know?" Swiveling to Imogen. "I'm sorry. Remind Mother what you were saying. My mind strays so these days. I hope I didn't upset you, dear."

Imogen said, "No, you don't."

That made Martina laugh. "I'm glad you've still got your sense of humor. Lose that and where are you? Too much repression will hurt you. Don't you think so, Mr. Arbor? Can't you talk some sense into her?"

Benton, thinking there was maybe more going on here than he'd realized, looked at Imogen and said, "I'll try, Professor."

"Mother, dear. Call me Mother." Shaking her head now. "I do worry about her. Every day. Anyway, where were we?"

"I wanted to ask you about the case we are working on," Imogen said.

"The Hide-and-Seek Killer? I've read all about that in the papers. Delightful the way he has you on the run."

"We're calling him Loverboy now."

"Ah, you've found one of his secrets. That must please you. Why would you think I have anything to do with him?"

Imogen said, "We believe he's been in touch with you."

Martina pursed her lips together and cocked her head to one side. "Well, I will tell you, dear, it's possible he has been, but I get so much correspondence I might not even be aware of it. Did you know that a letter from me, to a stranger, sold on Ebay for four thousand dollars? Yes! It was one of the ones in which I describe a dream I had about you. Since then people write to me constantly. And they send me the sweetest things. I've begun making a scrapbook. Would you like to see it?"

"Perhaps another time." Imogen's shoulders sagged, her posture suddenly dejected and tired. She looked at Benton. "I told you it would never work to come here. That she wouldn't tell us anything."

It was on the tip of Benton's tongue to ask her what in the world she thought she was doing, did she think they were just going to leave, was this her idea of an interrogation, but then he saw something in her eyes. Something behind the dejection. He said, "I guess you were right."

Now she was talking to Martina. "Thank you for your time, Professor. Sorry to have bothered you. Good-bye." She reached into her bag like she was looking for something, and the magazine she had in there fell out, hitting the pavement with a thud.

Martina went very still. She whispered, "I-is that *Vogue?*"

Imogen picked it up and held it in her arms, mostly covering it. "Yes. British *Vogue.*"

Martina said, "Oh my *dear*," and Benton was almost sure she had tears in her eyes. "Is that for me?"

"Would you like it? I just got it to read on the plane."

That was a lie, Benton knew, but it had an incredible effect on Martina. As though Imogen had just scored a direct hit, Martina's eyes glazed over, her mouth sagged, and she whispered, "The plane. Read on the plane."

What the hell was going on here? Before he could even finish the thought, Martina snapped out of her trance and shot Imogen a coy smile, saying, "Well, aren't you Miss Sneaky Snake? I didn't think you still had it in you, my dear, but you do. You definitely do. You become more like Mother every day, knowing just how to gouge a person in the guts and laugh about it. I commend you. And"—she paused for effect—"that will stand you in good stead with Loverboy. He is a boy with a divine sense of humor."

Imogen didn't pause to savor what Benton felt was a victory. She said, "Why does Loverboy even need you?"

"Because I have certain expertise."

"In what? Scrapbooking?"

"Imogen, I believe you are making a joke. No, my dear, in you. In how to hurt you."

"So he's just milking you for information. That means you probably don't know anything about him."

"I know more than you do."

Imogen shifted her hold on the magazine so a bit more of the cover was showing between her coat sleeves, under the headline, *Have Yourself a Micromini Christmas!* "Prove it."

"Give me the magazine," Martina said.

"Tell me what you know."

"Did you bring the barrettes? I would love to see your face more. Can't you tuck your hair behind your ears? Very well. You only want to talk about Loverboy. Well, he's handsome. Has lovely penmanship. Smart. Fun-loving. And the first killing you know about—that isn't his first murder. He killed when he was younger."

"And?" Imogen said.

"Don't be greedy, my dear. He's a bit greedy. Or actually, more jealous. He doesn't like to share. Finding him won't be enough. You'll have to find her on your own. He would rather have her die than share her with you."

"Who?"

"Look who's being a coy carrot! Why, Imogen, the woman he's taken. Mr. Arbor's friend. Why don't you tuck your shirt in? I know it's the fashion to wear it out but you have such a nice tiny waist. Well, never mind. Do you have a photo of the woman?"

Benton looked at Imogen for instructions.

Martina tapped the bar of her cell impatiently. "You do. Come on, let me have a looksie, Mr. Arbor. Be a good boy. Surely you don't suspect I'll do anything vulgar with it? What if letting me see it will save her life?"

Benton took the photo from his jacket pocket and held it toward the bars. It was a picture he'd shot the previous summer. Rosalind and Jason had been visiting Julia and Cal on Nantucket, and Benton had flown up for the weekend. White-tipped waves mirrored the few clouds in the sky. Rosalind's eyes and Jason's were the same color as the sea as they squinted smiling into the lens.

Imogen had chosen the picture, she told him the night before, because it did not show any distracting body parts.

Martina tilted her head back so she was looking through the bottom of her bifocals and held the picture out straight in front of her, moving it back and forth until she got the right distance. She studied it for a moment, running her fingers over the glossy surface, and said to herself, "She has a son. Of course, of course." She stopped moving and stared into space, her head going slightly to one side in a way that made Benton think of a bird as she murmured, "Oh my, my, my. I am impressed."

Then she handed the photo back to Benton and said, "I can tell you one more thing. He likes to keep secrets. He was even keeping one from me."

"What?" Imogen asked. She moved her arms apart slightly so the cover model's legs were showing.

Martina's eyes were riveted. "Do you like her, Imogen? The woman he's taken?"

"I've never met her."

"I wonder, does that make it better or worse? Knowing her death will be your fault? Well, her torture and then, later, her death. I always liked to know the people I killed. It made it more . . . satisfying isn't quite the right word. Transcendent."

"Did he tell you he was going to torture her?" Imogen asked.

"At your brother's funeral, did everyone crowd around you, try to touch you? They did, didn't they? That must have been awful for you. I hope you wore a dress. With a smart hat. Although of course you didn't. Now, dear, if you please, I'll take the magazine."

"What did you mean when you said you were impressed?"

Martina stared at the magazine for a long few seconds, then dragged her eyes away. Covering a yawn with the back of one hand she said, "You're asking all the wrong questions today, Imogen. I find it wearing. I'm sorry, children, it has been a delightful interlude, but since it is clear you have no intention of giving me that magazine, the time has come for my confession. The truth is, I've just been playing with you. I don't know anything about him, this Loverboy. But a girl's got to have her bit of innocent fun. Plus, Loretta needed a little more time before she was done with her drawing of your ass, Imogen. She's been looking forward to this visit of yours for weeks. You have no idea how much."

Imogen said quietly, "For weeks? You knew I was coming?"

Martina tilted her head to the side, gave a tinkling little-girl laugh, and moved backward, toward the table in the middle of her cell. "Did I say that? You always put words in my mouth, my dear." She picked up a pencil and adjusted her glasses to focus on what looked like a book of puzzles lying open on the table. "If you are so eager to cram me full of words, why don't you work on this? I need a six-letter word for 'plagiarize.' "

"Good-bye, Professor Kidd," Imogen said, and started walking.

Loretta's voice chanting, "I love you, Imogen, I loveyouIloveyouIloveyou," followed Imogen and Benton out of cell block K.

At the guard station, Curtis and his partner grabbed the British *Vogue* the fed woman had dropped on a chair as she left and started flipping through it. Man, those women were hot. They were so distracted that they did not notice on the closed-circuit camera when Martina Kidd shoved a piece of paper into her bread roll before her tray was taken away. The tray was wheeled away on the orderly's cart to the kitchens, where it was picked up by a woman in a hairnet wearing pink lipstick and dumped into the garbage.

The roll went into her pocket.

That was what Imogen Page got for bringing last month's *Vogue*, Martina thought pleasantly to herself.

CHAPTER 18

They rode out of the parking lot in their rented car about a mile in silence until Imogen said to Benton, "Pull over. Now."

She was out the door before they stopped moving, skidding down the embankment away from him, toward a chain-link fence that separated the road from a neighborhood of houses. She kept going until she couldn't see the car anymore, and stood with her mittens looped through the links of the fence, watching her breath condense in the cold air and staring at the backyard of the house in front of her. Woodpile, birdbath covered in snow, garden gnome with a chipped hat, shovels lined up against the side of the house to dig the path out, doghouse with a broken roof. Signs of normal life. Normal people. She stuck her tongue out to let it get cold and numb and hopefully stop tasting like chlorine, desperation and fear with just a hint of metallic triumph mixed in.

What a great talent she had where loneliness was sour cherry, perfectly pleasant, but triumph, something you'd want to savor, tasted like rebar.

After a longer time than she'd expected, she heard Benton's footsteps behind her. He looked almost embarrassed approaching, and stopped a yard away, extending his hand, holding a napkin from the coffee place they'd pulled into that morning.

"I'm sorry," he said as she took it from him, looking like he really meant it, but Imogen had no idea why. "This was the only thing I could find."

"Why would I want a napkin?"

"I thought—I don't know."

"You thought I would be here sobbing? Or throwing up my breakfast?" She could see she had guessed right the second time. "You don't have a very high opinion of women, do you, Mr. Arbor?"

"That has nothing to do with it. It would be a common reaction to a stressful encounter with an adversary."

It was funny how puffed up he got when he was challenged, Imogen thought. "It's not my reaction."

"I see that now." He paused, unpuffing. "Look, I know why you are mad at me. I owe you an apology. In there with Martina Kidd. I—at first I didn't see what you were doing and I was skeptical. That's why I started to butt in. I shouldn't have."

"That is okay. I expected it."

"What?"

"You are not exactly the Enigma Code, Mr. Arbor. You believe that no one can do a job as well as you can. You were bound to question me, so I counted on you interfering. It made Martina feel like she had an ally. Like your doubt would help slice through any self-assurance I might have had left when she was done with her little walk through Imogen Page's memory morgue."

"You played me. You weren't really winging it."

"That upsets you? That I knew what I was doing?"

"No. Of course not. But you could have told me. We could have worked it out together."

"Why? I knew what I wanted to do and I knew what I wanted you to do."

"That's not very collegial."

"I don't work with colleagues."

"It was a risk. I could have reacted differently."

"No, you couldn't have."

"You are saying I am completely predictable?"

"Yes."

He clenched his jaw two times, then pulled out his cell phone and started dialing.

"Who are you calling?"

"1-800-Jerkoff," he said, pressing SEND.

"For you or for me?"

"I figure we can take turns."

Imogen had to work not to laugh. Then she stopped working. He had been nice, concerned about her, bringing her the napkin, and she had been a bitch. She said, "I was tense about our meeting with Martina, and when I'm like that I am not easy to work with. Or so Bugsy tells me."

"No way. I'd sue for libel."

"I know it. He's just oversensitive." It got silent. She looked through the fence again at the two-story house, identical to all the other two-story houses that backed up to the county road. She said, "Have you ever seen a bird in a birdbath?"

"Not this time of year."

"But any time of year? I mean, why do people have them? Do they even like birds?"

She felt Benton staring at her. He said, "I've never really thought about it," making it clear with his tone that he couldn't imagine why anyone would.

She was used to being looked at like that, even by Sam, like when she went through her phase of having to know how every magic trick they saw on TV was done. How could you cut a lady up in three pieces and then have her come out whole without a *single speck* of blood on her? It didn't make sense. Sam asking why she couldn't just think it was neat without knowing how it was done.

That wasn't how it worked, she explained. You had to know, keep digging until you understood it, so that no one could trick you.

But that will take all the fun out of it, Sam said.

Not to her. To her, knowing was fun. She'd had no idea back then that it was possible to know too much.

"They should latch their back door," she said aloud to Benton now, gesturing to the house.

"Okay."

"We should leave them a note. It's not safe to have that door unlatched. It's like an invitation."

"Why don't we just climb the fence and go on inside? Maybe carry the shovels. That will get the message across stronger, that there's something scary out there. Besides the strangers casing their house from the highway."

Imogen wondered what it felt like not to lock your doors. "Maybe."

"Was it some object in particular at that house you wanted? Want to point something out to me? I'll tell you right now, though, I'm not stealing the garden gnome. Not even if you beg."

She was thinking about it, about how they must not be afraid, when she realized what Benton said. "Why would I want to steal a garden gnome?"

"I don't know, you're the one who said to stop the car. No one likes a good side-of-the-rural-highway-in-the-freezing-cold stop more than I do, but if we're not breaking in, what are we doing here?"

She had to admit it was a good question. Stopping came from the same impulse that had led her to accept Dirk Best's, the warden's, invitation to lunch three years earlier. Wow, had that been a mistake. The impulse was okay, though, the need to remember that there were people who had lives that had no daily contact with kindly-looking grandmother types who murdered fifteen girls, sometimes sending their families thank-you cards with inspirational verses and a choice bit of the body as enclosures. People who didn't read autopsy reports with their breakfast. Who didn't have breakfast with a goldfish. She said, "I needed some fresh air. Martina Kidd has an unsettling effect on me."

"Me too. That interview was one of the weirdest experiences of my life. Are they always like that?"

Interview now, no longer *interrogation*, Imogen noticed. Benton Arbor was not exactly as predictable as she had said. Which she was not going to tell him. "Martina's questions vary, but the style is the same."

"The strangest thing to me is that even now I'm not sure what we learned. If we learned anything. Did we?"

"Yes. Despite what she tried to claim, the professor has been in touch with Loverboy."

"Because of what she said about him having killed when he was younger? I mean, she could not have known about that unless he told her himself."

"No, that's more a statistical certainty. The kind of thing Professor Kidd would know. He's too organized for these to have been his first."

"Then how do you know they have been in contact?"

"What she said at the end, about my coming, how she had known about it for weeks. That was true. She has a tell, a way of tilting her head when she is caught off guard. She did it when I pressed her."

"I saw that."

"I'm not sure what her knowing means except that they are communicating, and about me."

"Martina seems to know a lot about you."

"She claims I am her hobby. I would only be moderately surprised to learn that Elgin sent her my dossier. They still correspond. And, of course, there's Dirk Best, the friendly warden."

She sensed that Benton wanted to press for more information about that, but instead he asked, "Do you think anything else she told us was true?"

"What she said about him not giving Rosalind up unless we find her ourselves feels right to me. It's part of the game. But the only other time she seemed genuinely interested was when she looked at the photo. I'd like to take it, if you don't mind, to see if I can figure out why."

"Sure," Benton agreed, but he didn't hand it over. He said, "You seem to know a lot about her too. You made her tilt her head when you said you bought that magazine at the airport."

"For the airplane," Imogen corrected. "The plane was the key. Most killers have a hunting ground, a place they go to troll for their victims. Or as Martina called them, her dear children. She went looking for them on airplanes, sitting next to them on flights. You can imagine how she looked, the kindly grandmother reading *Chicken Soup for the Geriatric Soul* with a big magnifying glass and a bookmark with photos of her grandkids on it."

"She has grandchildren?"

"No, it was part of the act. To get people to trust her. Not seem suspicious. She always requested the middle seat, though, which should have seemed suspicious, a tip-off right there. Anyway, she would strike up a conversation, form a bond, invite them to her house for tea. They would go because she had a wonderful collection of whatever happened to be their personal hobby to share with them. She said. And then she would kill them."

"I'll have to remember never to speak with my seatmate on an airplane again," Benton said. "That is really sick."

"You don't even know what she did to them."

"I remember reading about it, but I can't recall the particulars."

"We didn't release any, but since you're fortunate enough to be part of this official investigation, I think I can divulge them." Imogen's gaze moved back to the fence. "She sliced away their eyes, tongues, and hands and then made a mold of their bodies and filled it with plaster to use as statuary in her garden. She discarded the bodies and the other pieces all over town. Except the pieces she popped into envelopes with thank-you notes and sent back to the families. She loves beauty but said those women had sullied theirs by their stupidity. Her way, they would be preserved for all time."

"How did you find her?"

"Through her lifelong friendship with Elgin. When we started working on the Connoisseur case, Elgin had an agent get in touch with Professor Kidd because the removal of the eyes, hands, and tongue gave the killings a sort of ritual feeling, and the professor's specialty was burial rites. Later, when I was put on the case, I went to follow up on something she had said. That was when we figured it out."

"How?"

"I went to her house to ask her to clarify something she had suggested about the killer, and we had our interview in her garden. She lived in her family's old house, it's really a mansion, and it has a sort of park around it. As we were talking, I remembered that she had misquoted an e. e. cummings poem to the last agent who interviewed her. The misquote had stuck with me, I couldn't get it out of my head. That happens to me sometimes. I was about to ask her what she'd meant and then I understood that she was the killer."

"Just like that?"

"Yes. She and the other agent had been discussing idols and the development of rituals around them, particularly death rituals, and Martina quoted, 'A pretty girl who naked is/is *not* worth a million statues.' But the line actually goes, 'A pretty girl who naked is/is worth a million statues.' She had inverted the meaning to make statues more valuable than live girls. I should have seen it earlier—we were sitting in a garden filled with statuary, all of female nudes. She had grown so cocky that she liked to show off. Anyway, she saw my eyes move and—" She stopped, her hand going to her temple. "I got away."

Benton said, "In the end, was it a ritual? The eyes, tongues, and hands?"

"No. That was only for convenience. Those are the body parts that really make a mess of things when you are covering a live person with molding compound. Everything else you can pretty much staple down without ruining the lines."

She saw the color drain from Benton's face. She offered him the napkin he'd given her. "Want this?"

He shook his head, reached into his pocket, and pulled out a pack of Juicy Fruit gum. He peeled off four pieces and handed her the pack. "Have as many as you need."

She supposed that in certain circumstances everyone got a bad taste in their mouth. She took one, hoping it would at least cover the taste of chlorine that had resurfaced. It didn't. "Wow, this is really not subtle. The sweetness."

"Yep, it's a great product. Did you know you can live on Juicy Fruit gum for a week if you're ever stranded without food? You can."

"Is that how you make all your gum decisions? Nutritional value?"

"No decisions. Always Juicy Fruit." He must have seen something in her expression because he said, "Got you. You didn't expect me to be a confirmed Juicy Fruit chewer. You see, I'm not as predictable as you think."

She rolled her eyes. "Would you like more proof of how predictable you are?"

"More than anything."

"Okay, I can predict your exact reaction to my next question."

"What will my *exact reaction* be?"

"You'll balk."

"I can already tell you you're wrong. I've never balked in my life."

She held out her hand and said, "May I please have the car keys? I'm driving."

CHAPTER 19

"Saying no is not balking," he told her.

"Why can't I drive? Is this some caveman thing about female drivers?"

"No, I just—I just don't like it when someone else is driving. Why do you need to drive?"

"The same reason you do, to feel in control. Besides, I want to get out of here and you drive too slow."

"I drive the speed limit."

"You drive like an old lady. I thought you were a race-car driver."

"I am. On a racetrack. This is a county road. In the snow. And a Ford Focus is not exactly—Where are you going?"

She had marched to the side of the road and put her thumb out.

Two minutes later the key chain flew through the air and landed with a clang over her thumb.

"Nice toss," she said.

"I spent a lot of time at carnivals as a kid. I'm freezing my ass off. Can we go?"

"Of course. I was just waiting for you."

They didn't talk much on the flight back, except when he turned to her and said, "You know, old ladies get to be *old* ladies because they drive the way they do," and she'd said, "In all this time, that's the best you could come up with?" But he'd made her laugh again, and she had to admit that Benton Arbor really was not that bad.

Imogen decided she'd let Benton drive once they landed in Vegas.

"They're only streets," she told him, informing him of her decision. "There's no danger of you getting mowed over."

"Gee, thanks." He pointed his 'sixty-six Thunderbird up Swenson, took a left on Flamingo, and headed for the side entrance of the Bellagio to avoid any reporters who might be waiting out front.

A valet parker came over as they pulled into the driveway, but Benton waved him away.

"Aren't you coming in?" she said.

"Later. I want to get over to the Garden to check on a few things."

"The Garden?"

"Our race-prep facility here. We had some problems a few months ago at the Speedway, so we moved into an old skating rink, the Ice Garden."

"What kind of problems?"

"Some sabotage. Someone tried to screw with one of our cars, which wouldn't have been a problem, if they hadn't also tried to screw with Cal. They didn't hurt him too badly, thank God, but we decided not to take any more chances. Besides the hysterics from Julia we'd have to deal with if anything happened to her precious husband, he is by far Arbor Motors' most valuable asset. Without him in engineering, our cars wouldn't stand a chance."

"I'd completely forgotten you were supposed to be here for the invitational. It's in two days, isn't it? And I've had you running all around the country."

"I offered. Actually, I think I insisted."

"There may be something to that. Still, you must have a lot to do."

"I just want to make sure the equipment is in top shape, since it's going to be a struggle for me to stay focused on the driving. It feels crazy to think of the race, with what Rosalind must be going through." Imogen saw his hands tighten on the steering wheel, and he wouldn't meet her eyes. He said, "Martina said Loverboy was going to torture Rosalind. Was that just a guess too? Like about him having killed when he was younger? Would he—"

Imogen reached out and put her hand on his arm. "Whatever he might be planning, he does not seem to harm his victims until just before he kills them. We're going to find her before that."

Her voice sounded tinny in her ears, wishful, but it must have sounded better to Benton. His grip on the steering wheel eased up and he nodded his head. "Right. We're going to find him before that."

It was amazing what people could believe when they needed to, Imogen thought.

CHAPTER 20

Imogen sat in the living room of her suite and stared at Rex in his fishbowl. Bugsy said that she needed to relax, that watching fish was supposed to be soothing. She checked the clock on the VCR. She'd been looking at him for three minutes and didn't feel soothed yet. She felt tense and pissed-off and worried. Scared. And a little sad.

Going up in the elevator to her room two hours earlier, her head had still been pounding from her conversation with Benton. What she'd told him about Loverboy not torturing his victims until just before he killed them was mostly true. Physically.

Or at least it had been until Louisa Greenway, his most recent victim. The one whose treatment was probably closest to what they could expect for Rosalind. The one whose torture appeared to have started a bit earlier in the cycle. Eight days earlier.

Which was four days from now, in Rosalind's case. Unless he was accelerating.

This was in Imogen's mind when she walked into her room, her mouth tasting like chlorine and lime, and found her team there, sitting in front of a whiteboard. On it they had made a list under the heading LOVERBOY PROFILE. It said:

Charming
Good-looking

Sense of humor
White male
Organized
Educated
Between thirty and forty
Sick fuck

She agreed with the last one unequivocally. The rest of the list, while probably true, didn't tell them anything, it was so general. Seeing how little they had to go on, all laid out nice and neat, made her feel like someone had punched her in the stomach.

"You forgot 'Good with glue and scissors' and 'Doesn't play well with other children,' " she'd said as she put her bag down, and was stupefied when Dannie rushed to write her suggestions on the board.

She'd had to explain to Dannie and the team that she was just kidding, trying to make a point. That while their profile was too generic to narrow the field, it could also be dangerous, creating blind spots in their thinking, making it too easy to overlook certain kinds of suspects who didn't fit any of the things they'd written down. Going on to explain that she didn't really believe in profiling, didn't see how a list would help them find the killer, this white male, thirty to forty, who had killed five people over eighteen months, who tortured them before they died, who was escalating and could right now be— She never got to say what he could be doing, because at that point Bugsy dragged her into the bedroom and closed the door and told her she needed to relax. And she'd asked how could she relax with a killer out there and a team of agents staring at her like they expected her to pull his name out of her armpit? What if she couldn't? What if she failed? What if they were too late?

So many people die on your watch, she heard Martina saying. *You remind me so much of myself, in my heyday.*

"We have twelve days," Bugsy reminded her.

"Do we?"

Bugsy had quickly assigned interviews to Tom, Dannie, and Harold, and hustled them out of the room. He'd asked if he could bring Imogen anything and she had said yes, the forensics report from Metro. And information about the Arbor Motors sabotage at the Speedway the previous year.

Bugsy shook his head. "I meant food."

"I'm not hungry."

"Look, boss, you don't think well when you are this tense. Spend some time staring at the fish," he said as he closed the door. "Talk to the fish. It will soothe you."

She'd sat and eaten Tootsie Pops and stared at the list instead. A list that read like a personals ad: "LOVERBOY: charming, good-looking white male, educated, successful, with a great sense of humor looking for . . ."

Looking for what? What was motivating him? If only she could figure out what was triggering him. Conventional profiling usually pointed to the loss of a job or the end of a relationship, but this guy was too organized, the intervals between his kills too random. It was as though he was always waiting, but waiting for what? For the right victims?

"But all the victims were different. They had nothing in common," she said aloud. Great, now she was talking to herself. Bugsy was right. She was so tense that she was losing it.

That was when she'd gone to stare at Rex. Eight and a quarter minutes now. She still did not feel soothed.

"Can you see this?" she said to Rex, and made a face at him. He didn't seem to notice. "What about this?" sticking her tongue out. No response. Making faces at fishes, that could be soothing. For about a minute.

She gave up relaxing and moved back to the table, flipping through the files until she came to Louisa Greenway's.

There was the report on the old house where she was found.

The two couples living in the apartments on the floor below did not know anything about the girl being held in the attic.

There was the report on Louisa's movements in the days before she was taken. They painted a portrait of a happy, normal girl about to enter high school as a junior. Gymnastics practice, diving, youth group, staying up too late to talk on the phone. Baby-sitting her twin brothers.

There was the report from the fibers team, which started with a list of her clothes. Like all the victims, she had been fully clothed when she was found, wearing the outfit she was taken in. And, as with all the others, her clothes had been washed. Loverboy dry-cleaned them. They had sent bulletins to all 126 of the laundry and dry-cleaning establishment owners around Vegas with a description of the outfit Rosalind Carnow was taken in, but there had to be hundreds of camel-colored crew-neck sweaters and pants sent to the cleaners each day, and Imogen was not hopeful. Despite the cleaning, Louisa's clothes had been gone over five times for telltale substances. The only thing not accounted for at the crime scene was a fine polyester thread found under the arm of her light cotton sweater. Reading about it always made Imogen faintly taste oranges.

Finally there was the medical examiner's report. Imogen skimmed this, not wanting to feel the words, not wanting to taste them. Louisa, the athlete. Louisa, whose flexibility had been—

Imogen stopped and put her hand to her mouth, frozen. The file had somehow gotten jumbled and the crime-scene photos had slipped into the middle of the ME's report. Oh God, she was not ready to face those yet.

Ha, ha, made you look!

It was that damn voice in her head again. This was how it always started, her connection with the killer. Obliquely, subtly, so that it took her a few days to realize that her reactions to things were not her own. To realize it had begun.

Imogen pushed Louisa Greenway's file away from her and

looked at the wall, but it was too late. That taste, that image was seared into her mind.

Louisa Greenway's face. Pretty green eyes. Pug nose dotted with freckles. Generous lips. Holes in her cheeks.

Holes the ME assured her had been made while Louisa was alive. A week before she'd died, actually.

With standard scissors.

The ME even knew what size. No, he had not sharpened them. Just stuck them through using brute force. But carefully. The holes were exactly even.

"Why?" she asked Rex. "Why would anyone do a thing like that?"

The fish stared at her.

"Is that soothing for you? Watching me?"

Bugsy didn't know what the hell he was talking about.

CHAPTER 21

"I've been waiting for you to interrogate me," Julia announced, breezing into Imogen's suite an hour later, her dog, Lancelot, wearing a monogrammed sweater, at her ankles.

Imogen looked up from the forensics report on Rosalind's room that J.D. had sent over. "I told one of my agents to—"

Julia waved that away. "Dannie? I sent her to see my colorist, Tori, at the salon. You should be arrested for letting that woman walk around with hair that color."

"She likes red hair," Imogen protested.

"Her hair was not red, it was orange. Anyway, that doesn't matter. What matters is that I have quite a lot of important information to impart to you, and I propose to do it over a drink at the bar."

Imogen hesitated.

"You have to talk to me. I am Rosalind's best friend," Julia said, and Imogen was struck again by the phrasing. Most people would have said, "Rosalind is my best friend," but Julia had stated it so that she was more important. A spoiled child needing attention.

"The best thing for Rosalind would probably be—" Imogen began. Julia cut her off.

"—for you to stay here. Yes, of course. But I have ulterior motives. Cal and Wrightly and Benton are at the Garden and they'll be there forever, and Sadie and Eros are locked away doing I can't even imagine what. That leaves me suffocating with Benton's mother,

Theresa, and her husband Insipid Pierre. If you abandon me to them you might have another homicide on your hands. And you would not want that, would you?"

Imogen admitted that she would not. And she was intrigued by the subtle taste of sour cherries—loneliness—she picked up from Julia's tone.

"Excellent. Then you see the only thing for it is to come have a drink."

"Do you ever *not* get your way?" Imogen asked as they waited for the elevator.

"It happens," Julia admitted, examining her reflection critically in the polished brass doors as they opened. "But most of the time, I do. I am very persuasive." She nuzzled her face into Lancelot's sweater. "Isn't that right, Little Ugly?"

"Is that what you call him?"

"Only when Cal isn't around. It makes him feel guilty. I wanted a dog but he's allergic to the hair, so we had to settle for Little Ugly. They say dog owners resemble their pets." She held the dog's smashed face up to hers and bared her teeth like it was doing. "What do you think?"

"Twins," Imogen confirmed.

Julia kept Lancelot under her arm as they made their way through the casino toward one of the lounges. They sat down, Julia on a wide couch with Lancelot in her lap, Imogen on a chair angled next to them. Behind them, Imogen could see the roulette wheel and some blackjack tables.

"You are younger than I am," Julia told Imogen, pulling her attention back. "Younger than me and Rosalind. Ros is two years older than I am, so she's thirty-six."

Imogen seized what she knew was a deliberate opening. "How did you and Rosalind become friends?"

"It was when I was dating J.D., at the end of my sophomore year of college. Ros and Benton were already an item then, and the four of us would go out sometimes. She was a little behind, because of having Jason, so she and I finished after J.D. and Benton left. We lived together for a year, the two of us and Jason. But that's not the important part. Don't ask me about that. Ask me when the last time was that I saw her."

"When was the last time you saw Rosalind?" Imogen repeated dutifully.

"Noon on Tuesday," Julia announced. "After that chambermaid says she saw her. So I was the last one."

"Where?"

"In the kitchen. I went to pour coffee for me and Cal, and she was there, throwing away the two bottles of champagne she'd drunk the night before."

"Did she usually drink that much on Monday nights?"

"Sometimes." Julia's eyes glittered. "This is the part you don't know yet. She liked to drink champagne when she was with someone."

"Wrightly Waring," Imogen said.

Julia looked crestfallen. "How did you know?"

Imogen shook her head. Julia did not need to hear that the crime-scene team had recovered fibers from Wrightly's tweed jacket in Rosalind's room. She said, "I thought Rosalind and Benton were a couple. How long had Rosalind and Wrightly been seeing each other?"

"I can't believe you knew." Julia pouted, trying to get the waitress's eye. "Rosalind started dating Wrightly about four months ago. Since then it's been—" Julia interrupted herself to order a bottle of champagne.

Imogen ordered a Shirley Temple with extra cherries and turned back to Julia.

Julia said, "You ordered a Shirley Temple."

"So?"

"No one does that."

"I like pink drinks."

Julia shook her head and stroked Lancelot's sweater. "Rosalind would like you," Julia said after a moment. "She wouldn't like the way Benton looks at you, but she'd like you."

Imogen ignored that. "Tell me about her relationships with Benton and Wrightly."

"Benton and Rosalind haven't been an item in ages. They let the press go on thinking it because it's convenient for both of them, but they haven't really been intimate since just after college. Not that she wouldn't want more."

"Then why won't she marry him?" Benton's mania for proposing to Rosalind made up the bulk of his FBI file.

Julia waited for the waitress to put down Imogen's drink and open her bottle of champagne and pour. She took a sip, nodded approvingly, and said, "She doesn't marry him because she is not a fool. Benton's got this problem with confusing being needed with love. It's not his fault—all the women in our family have perpetuated it. But Rosalind wants more than that. She wants someone who will share with her—share responsibility, share everything. What anyone would want. Benton sucks at sharing. He can't stand not being in control." Julia gulped champagne.

"I noticed. I almost had to wrestle him for the car keys this afternoon."

Julia put down her glass and stared at Imogen. "He let you drive? While he was in the car?"

"Not his car. Just a rental."

"No, no, *no*. You don't understand. That is historic. Benton never lets someone else drive. He won't do anything where he's not in control. No roller coasters. Not even elevators. That's why he flies his helicopter to work in Detroit and NYC, so he can take the roof stairs to our penthouse offices rather than having to ride the elevator up from the lobby." Imogen tasted a subtle shift in the other woman's posture and tone. The sour-cherry loneliness was back, but along with it Imogen tasted burned sugar. Tension, hostility. Julia said, "The tabloids all think it's glamour, but it's like some sort of sickness. An inability to let anyone else do anything. Anyone else have their own lives. I shouldn't complain. He's great for publicity, which makes my job easier. And I have a lot of respect for him. Sometimes, though . . ."

Imogen waited, but Julia left her thought hanging, saying instead, "Did you know he built Arbor Motors from scratch?" The burned sugar was gone.

"I thought it was America's second-oldest automobile company, and its proudest."

"You've read my press releases. What they leave out is the fifteen-year period where Benton's father Malcolm ran the company into the ground. Benton rebuilt it by sheer force of will and personality. But we are only barely holding on now—that is why this race is so important. If Benton and the cars show well, the company floats. If they don't . . ." She shrugged as she poured more champagne for herself, then settled back into the cushions.

"How did he react when Rosalind refused to marry him? For someone as used to getting his way as he is, that must have been hard."

"He understood. Tried to change. That was funny." Julia sat forward, confidentially. "Benton's idea of changing is to buy a new wardrobe. You know, 'Maybe if I wear navy blue I'll seem more open, more relaxed, less controlling.' "

"Did it work?"

Julia rolled her eyes. "I told you that you and Rosalind would get along, Imogen. She is not an idiot. Of course it didn't work. It probably prolonged their relationship a little because there was no way for Rosalind not to feel touched. But it didn't address the real problem."

"What are Rosalind and Wrightly like together?"

"Sweet. Wrightly doesn't just look like an overgrown boarding-school student, he is one, at least in love. And he's been in love with her since college. He and Cal were roommates at MIT, and the first time Wrightly met Rosalind, at a party, his mouth literally gaped open, like in a movie. They are really cute together. The day before she disappeared we'd all been out together, and there was a certain tenderness between them I hadn't seen before."

"Where were you?"

Julia smiled to herself. "We went to the Stratosphere. The tall hotel at the end of the Strip? Someone had told Rosalind that they have the world's highest roller coaster on the top, so she was determined to ride it. And Wrightly wanted to take a try on the bucking bronco they have in their arcade."

Imogen caught a taste of oranges. It disappeared. "Did you see anyone odd? Did Rosalind seem nervous or tense?"

"Anything but. She was happy. Well, a little nervous, but that was because she had decided she was going to tell Benton about Wrightly and she was worried about his reaction."

"Should she have been nervous?"

"I'm pretty sure Benton already knew. He and Wrightly had a meeting together last week and Wrightly came out muttering to himself. I could have killed Benton, because we need Wrightly to print reams of praise about our new line, but there wasn't anything I could do."

"Did you ask either of them what they discussed?"

"Not Benton. He would have gone all strong and silent. Wrightly moped a lot about how Benton didn't deserve Rosalind and suggested that Benton had said a few things, mostly about Rosalind's son, Jason, and making sure that Wrightly knew what he was getting into. Typical caveman stuff." Julia gave Imogen one of her disconcertingly direct gazes. "Benton's not a bad guy, though. Are you involved with anyone?"

"Do you enjoy asking indiscreet questions?"

"Don't you?"

Imogen worked to spear the ice in her glass with her straw. "No. I've found questions aren't usually the best ways to get answers."

"Oh." Julia paused, stymied. Said, "Well, you can ask me any you want. Go ahead—oh, here's one: ask me why I married Cal when I am still in love with J. D. Eastly."

"You're not in love with J.D.You care what he thinks of you, but you don't want to be with him." She did not add that Julia seemed almost afraid of him.

"You're right. But most people don't see that. Cal does, of course. AuntTheresa, Benton's mother, and my grandmother think I married Cal to upset them, and I let them go on believing that because it's delightful to confirm their opinion of me. It's a little disappointing that Cal has turned out so well, actually."

"But that isn't why you married him," Imogen prompted.

"No. I married him because he was the opposite of J.D. I'd known Cal forever, he was always around when we were growing up, since his parents worked for the company. But it was only once things with J.D. ended that I even looked at him sideways. And I've never been sorry."There was an almost rehearsed quality to Julia's words, but they did not taste like lies. And for the first time in the conversation, Imogen did not taste any loneliness. "Cal is lovely and uncomplicated, whereas J.D.—for one thing, he's too damn self-sufficient. Secretive. The way he wears those dark glasses all the time so you can't see what he's thinking. He can't open up or trust people. And he never laughs. No sense of humor. Especially not about himself. I'm probably partially responsible for that." Julia tipped the last of the champagne into her glass and said, "There are better ways to end an engagement than by phoning the groom on your wedding day from the Air France departure lounge."

Imogen was agog. "That is what you did?"

"Yes. You can dress it up pretty, but underneath it's still ugly." Julia stroked Lancelot's sweater. "Not that it mattered. I had this speech all ready, I'd been practicing it, but I didn't get more than two sentences into it before he said, 'That's okay, Jules. No problem.' No problem! Like I was breaking a date to go to the movies, not our wedding. The bastard." Julia picked up her glass to take a sip, then set it down hard. "Ah, speak of the devil—and I use the term advisedly."

Imogen followed Julia's gaze and saw J.D., Wrightly Waring, Cal, and Benton walk into the bar.

A man walks into a bar and says, "Ouch," a voice cut into Imogen's mind. She went very still, waiting. But there was nothing more. Just that one snippet, another bad joke.

A blond woman in a clinging peach dress walked toward the men. She might not have been pretty—it was hard to tell—but she moved in a way that made Imogen think of brash confidence, a way she'd always admired. As the blonde reached the group, she paused, smiled at Benton, and winked.

Imogen choked on an ice cube.

While she was coughing—boy, was she smooth—she saw J.D. look at his watch and veer away. The three others started toward the table she was sharing with Julia.

What do you call three men in a doorway? the voice cut in again.

At first there was nothing. No punch line. Then the voice said, *Stuck.*

It was a lousy riddle, but it made a good subtitle to where she was on the case. Stuck. Nowhere. And being a sop to the loneliness of the victim's purported best friend wasn't going to change that. She decided it was time for her to get back to her room.

Standing to leave she saw a man stop Benton, Cal, and Wrightly on the way to the table. He pointed at his two female companions, then at Benton. Benton nodded, knelt between the two women, and said something that caused them to giggle and beam at him while the man searched his pockets for a camera.

He was loving it, Imogen thought, a little disgusted. Was the man who had seemed so upset about Rosalind's abduction earlier that day in there somewhere, behind the smile? The winking women? She watched him pose, giving a perfect toothpaste-ad grin, and could tell he loved the attention, the adulation, the audience. The one-two-three smile for the camera, Mr. Arbor.

One-two-three smile!

Imogen saw white spots as if the flashbulb had gone off in her eyes, and had to reach out her hand for the arm of the chair to steady herself. She knew what the holes in Louisa's cheeks were for now.

Stuck.

Loverboy had been making Louisa smile. He had used the holes to stick fishing hooks through to make her smile. So she would be a good audience for his jokes.

Back in her room, she took a marker and on the PROFILE list wrote: *Needs positive attention.* It wasn't much, but it was a start. Something that didn't sound like personal ad material.

The next day she'd have one of her people start canvassing bait-and-tackle shops.

Loverboy was tired when he got home, but he couldn't wait to show Ros what he'd brought her.

He displayed them together. "Family value size," he read from the lasagna package. "And, ta-da, a movie! You and me. Family values. Dinner and a movie. Won't it be great?"

She was already in her recliner, so while the lasagna was heating, he put the tape in the player. He had to fast-forward and rewind a few times before he found the part he was looking for. It was from the previous day. It showed him going up to the lady's door, knocking, talking through the keyhole, being let in. Knock, talk, in, knock, talk, in.

The big old-fashioned timer dinged and he went to take the lasagna out of the oven. "Good home cooking," he said as he carried it in. He put the entire thing, bubbling, on the tray strapped to the front of Rosalind's recliner. "Eat up," he said.

Rosalind looked at him. Her eyes were the only things not taped closed on her face. Her hands were bound to the arms of the chair.

But he pretended not to see. He turned and scooted closer to the TV and watched the tape again. He was so gallant in it. Such a loverboy. He could talk his way into any hole.

That thought made him laugh. "Hey, Ros," he said, turning around to tell her. "Get—Why aren't you eating?"

Rosalind looked at him with questioning eyes.

"You aren't going to be ungrateful, are you?"

She shook her head. She'd had a lesson in ingratitude the day before and had Band-Aid- and Bactine-covered arms to show for it. She made herself think about her son, Jason. Her sweet boy. What would make a boy turn into a monster like this?

"I've never known you not to finish your dinner," Loverboy said, and his voice now was more like the man she knew, the man she'd known so many years. The man she'd— Don't think about that, she told herself.

"Come on, Ros," he said. He loomed over her. In one motion he ripped the tape off her mouth.

She did not even think to scream. She just put her head down and tried to eat whatever she could of the food in front of her. He stood there, watching her feed.

"Like a pig at a trough," he said, disgusted. "Look at you."

But she didn't care. She needed to eat to keep her strength up, keep her strength up so she could escape, escape so she could hold Jason one more time, so she could—

Eat.

"Is piggy-wiggy finished yet?" he taunted.

Rosalind kept eating.

"That's enough!" he said finally, jerking the lasagna away from her. "Shouldn't you be watching your figure?"

Rosalind said, "Could I have some water?"

He looked at her, as if startled by the sound of her voice, and she realized that she hadn't spoken since they arrived. He was suddenly subdued. He padded to the kitchen and came back with a glass of water that he held to her lips while she drank.

"Was that enough?" he asked tenderly.

Tenderly. Rosalind wanted to throw up.

"Yes. Thank you. That was a very good dinner."

Something flickered in his eyes for a moment that made him look like an even younger, sweeter boy. It disappeared when he looked at her sideways. "You're trying to fool me. You're trying to make me trust you so you can run away."

"No," Rosalind said evenly. "I was just giving you a compliment."

Why did this appear to throw him? Why did he frown, confused, at her? He said, "Knock, knock."

"Who is there?"

"Tom."

"Tom who?"

"Tomorrow we'll have Kentucky Fried Chicken!"

Rosalind didn't say anything. What could she say?

"You are supposed to laugh. That was a joke. Imogen would have laughed. She's got a good sense of humor."

"Who is Imogen?"

"My friend. My *girl*friend. Or at least, she will be soon."

"Where did you meet her?" How many times had she had conversations like this with Jason?

"She came to see me. She works for the FBI."

Rosalind's throat went dry. The FBI. They were looking for her. Oh thank God. "What does she do?"

"She is very important. She's looking for me. But she doesn't know it. She won't find me, will she, Ros? Because I'm only Loverboy for you. Only in here. I'm someone else for all the other ladies, and no one will ever figure it out."

Rosalind realized what was going on. Realized the futility of having the FBI there. No one would figure this out. No one could imagine it. "No, they won't," she said.

"Don't look like that," Loverboy scolded her. "It's funny. You are supposed to laugh."

Rosalind didn't move.

"Come on, Ros. Let us have a smile."

She couldn't. All she could think was how hopeless it was. How even the FBI would never guess.

"Do it," he said. His voice had changed. "Smile. Now."

She made herself think about Jason. About how when she got

out of here she was going to hug him for three months. About the trips they were going to take together. About how many times she was going to tell him she loved him. Her lips curved up.

"Oh, that's so pretty," Loverboy said. "Soooo pretty." His hand snaked out and slapped her. "Bitch. I know you weren't thinking about me. You were thinking about that other boy. You can't fake me out. I don't want his smile. Next time I want one of my own."

He got out the roll of duct tape and slapped some over her mouth again. Then he went back to watching himself on TV. Soon he was smiling again. He looked so good.

CHAPTER 25

11 days left!

The garbage truck inched like a snail up Melville Drive, leaving a trail of slime. The two men tossing in the trash weren't very good at it.

"Must be training day," Elise Herbert commented to her sister as she watched them from the window of their bungalow.

"What?" Betsy Herbert asked. She was ninety percent deaf.

"I said"—louder this time—"it must be training day."

"Oh." Betsy nodded. "I'd like that."

Elise rolled her eyes at her sister and continued to peer at the two men. She didn't like the way they were going about things. Salvador and José, the regular men, were tidy and courteous. These two were horribly noisy.

Seated in the beat-up purple Nissan with the self-tinted windows that Bugsy had borrowed from one of the valets at the hotel, Imogen spotted Elise frowning in the window of the house to the left of 1112 Melville. Melville was a street of modest one-story houses, nearly identical except for the colors and whatever "improvements" had been made by their owners to the front yards. Elise Herbert's lawn had a white windmill in the middle and a collection of terra-cotta rabbits, posed in well-tended flower beds. The front yard of 1112, by contrast, consisted of a rusted wheel, a chain-link fence, and clumps of dry grass. The house was painted beige

with dingy yellow trim, and the windows were dark, whether because its inhabitants weren't up yet or because their curtains were
drawn was impossible to tell. How anyone could sleep through the
racket the two Metro officers dressed as garbage men were making
was a mystery to Imogen, but she'd been up for three hours and was
jittery with excitement and convenience-store coffee.

It was now 7:23.

"Hi, Gigi," Sally Tagashi had said too jovially when she called at
4:14 A.M. from Washington, D.C. "I hope I'm waking you."

Sally was one of Imogen's closest friends at the Bureau, one of
the few people she tolerated calling her Gigi, and a visual-materials
specialist. Imogen adored her. But not at four A.M. "It's your lucky
day," she said into the phone, pushing herself into a somewhat upright position. "I went to bed an hour ago."

"Good, that means I beat the cops out there."

"On what?"

"The text of your killer's book," Sally said. "In the collage. I've
got it. I know what it is. *Moby Dick*. I've got the edition and the pub-
lisher too. I'm faxing you focused copies of the two pages."

"How did you do it?"

"Magic. But I've got a friend in the Metro imaging department
and he said they were close, so I was afraid they'd beat me. I could
barely wait to call."

"*Did* you wait to call?"

"Fifteen minutes. But now I'm going home to bed. I worked on
it all night."

Imogen ripped the pages from her fax machine as they came in,
and read them waiting for her room-service coffee to arrive. After
two passes, she was disappointed. Pages eleven and twelve of this
edition weren't even the text of the novel. They were the middle of
a scholarly introduction to Melville.

Maybe he hadn't intended for them to read the words. It seemed
like such a deliberately taunting clue, but maybe he was only interested

in the rubber-stamped markings that said *Ford County Library*. To confirm the car theme. Or—

Imogen went and stood in front of the map of Vegas. She became so engrossed that the room-service waiter had to knock three times before she heard him. Her eyes roved over the streets and street names, now almost as familiar to her as her résumé. Sahara, Riviera, Desert Inn, Sands, Flamingo, Tropicana, the names of famous hotels, some of them still there, others long gone. Then others, names of early settlers and where they were from, Swenson, Maryland, Oakey, Mead, Melville, Charleston—

Melville. Her eye circled back to it. *Moby Dick*. By Herman Melville.

She picked up the phone. "Hi, Bugsy, did I wake you?" she said, too excited to care that she was repeating the dialogue she'd just had. "I need a car. Inconspicuous, quick."

Bugsy was a more polite audience than she had been. He said simply, "Got it, boss. Meet me downstairs in half an hour."

Getting Benton was harder. She got no answer on his cell phone. When she called the villa, Sadie answered.

"I'm sorry to wake you, but I urgently need to speak to Benton."

"Oh, you didn't wake me, love," Sadie assured her. "We haven't been to sleep yet. But I don't know—"

"Tell them you're busy, honey," a male voice suggested throatily in the background.

Sadie gave a low laugh and said into the phone, "Ms. Page, I'm not—"

"Sadie is occupied right now," Eros said, taking the phone. "She must make love to me. Good-bye, person."

Click.

Imogen decided she would stop at the villa on her way to the car. She dialed J.D.'s cell phone as she waited for the elevator, got forwarded to his police department voice mail, and left a message. Was she the only one working on the case who answered her damn phone? Glancing at her watch she saw it was only 4:45 A.M. But still.

Benton himself opened the door of the villa on the first ring. He was wearing the clothes he'd worn the day before and did not look like he'd changed out of them. "What are you doing here?" he asked, sounding more surprised than upset, blinking at Imogen through a pair of small glasses.

She'd never seen him in glasses before.

"We have a good lead on Rosalind's location," she told him, explaining about the book. "I obviously want more than that before we go ahead, but it's the most exciting news we've gotten. I——" Why had she come barreling into his room before five A.M., before she'd even confirmed that there was a house at that address? She was like a television-commercial child on Christmas morning. "I just wanted to keep you in the loop."

Benton rubbed his hand over his chin and its day's growth of beard. "Are you going there now?"

"Yes. I want to see what it's like. If it could work."

"I just got home from the Garden, but the valet should still have my car up. Come——"

Imogen interrupted him. "I don't want too many people over there yet in case he is watching. Actually, what would be more helpful is if you could try to reach J.D. and his team. I'd like to have everyone in my room in forty minutes for a meeting."

"Aye-aye, Captain," Benton said, saluting her.

She blushed. "I didn't mean——"

He waved it aside. "Forty minutes. Go find Rosalind."

Imogen's first impression of the house at 1112 Melville was that it was perfect—for Loverboy anyway—and that was only confirmed as the morning went on and information filtered in.

By 5:20 A.M. J.D. had found out that 1112 Melville was privately owned but managed by a company whose secretary wanted nothing more than to do him favors. It turned over a lot, she told him, but they'd rented the place a month before to Mr. Joe Smith.

"Not John Smith, anyway," one of J.D.'s men pointed out. "This guy has a real imagination."

As in Boston, the neighbors on either side were elderly, and two of them were hard of hearing.

But as Imogen discovered after the meeting, while she was watching the garbage truck lumber by the house, at least one of the neighbors was very much alert.

That was part of what they'd hoped to learn with the noisy garbage truck, who was in the house, who was paying attention. Elise Hubert could be a useful source of information on the people next door.

And, of course, there was the trash itself.

The truck had reached the end of the street. Imogen looked over at Benton, who was slouched in the driver's seat of the Nissan. He was wearing sunglasses, and he looked like he was asleep.

"Great," she muttered to herself.

He sat straight up and his jaw came unclenched and she realized he had not been sleeping. He had been struggling with being locked inside the car instead of outside doing things.

"I hate this," he told her.

"I know. But we can't do anything—"

"Right, right. The truck is finished. Can we get the hell out of here now?"

Imogen nodded and he pulled the car away from the curb. There was no way to know what would happen if Loverboy identified them. Her team was already being fitted with red "Census Taker" windbreakers for their canvass of the neighbors.

If they were going to do this right, if they were going to get Rosalind out alive, they would need a SWAT team and a warrant. And before they could have either of those, they needed evidence that this really was Loverboy's hideout, and that Rosalind was there.

Benton followed the garbage truck to a minimart parking lot, where the cops handed the keys back to Salvador and José to continue their route, and gave Imogen five bags of trash.

Four of them were easily eliminated as coming from the neighbors' houses. The remaining one was the smallest, and contained a receipt from a drugstore for makeup, a video rental coupon, two empty bottles of soda, a box of Marani's Best Family-style macaroni and cheese, and the wrappers from two McDonald's Happy Meals.

The Hide-and-Seek Killer had fed his third victim, Kaylee, McDonald's Happy Meals.

It wasn't proof, but it was something.

By ten A.M. they had more bits and pieces in place. Yes, Joe Smith was a youngish man, not younger than twenty-three, not older than forty. No one had seen a girl with him, but Elsie had occasionally heard "girlish noises" from the house next door upon which she did not wish to elaborate.

"Talking?"

"Sometimes."

"Screams?"

"Not exactly."

"Groans?"

"I would not know anything about that."

"Did it sound like the person was suffering?"

"I'll say."

"How long did this go on?"

"An hour or two at a time. Usually at night. It only started recently."

"Visitors?"

"I couldn't say for certain. They could go around the other side of the house. There is a gate in the fence over there."

Benton, J.D., and Imogen sat around the table in her suite and reviewed what they had. Imogen was sucking on a Tootsie Pop, using the candy to blot out minor tastes so the major ones would be easier to distinguish. That morning she wanted desperately to taste hickory, the taste she'd had when she got the other clues right, when she'd found the other Loverboy houses. But rather than bringing it into focus, the Tootsie Pop was just making its absence more obvious. There wasn't even a glimmer. Something was not right.

Reports from agents in surveillance positions said that there was definitely a woman in the house, that she was not moving but seemed to be seated or bound into a chair. So far they hadn't glimpsed "Joe Smith," but there was one room they couldn't see into.

J.D. said, "I'm not sure I can get a warrant for the SWAT team with only this to go on."

"Did you really try?" Benton challenged him. "Don't you have any pull? What the hell good does it do to be the head of the violent crimes task force if you can't even get a warrant?"

Imogen saw J.D.'s jaw clench. Very slowly, he reached up and slid his dark glasses off. It was the first time she'd seen him without them and she was surprised. Without them he looked about ten years younger and incredibly vulnerable, had the most open, candid eyes she'd ever seen. It was as though you could see clear into his mind. And what Imogen saw was pain. He looked right at Benton and said, "You are not the only person who cares about Rosalind, and you are not the only one working his ass off on this case. I don't give a fuck if you respect me, but you have got to trust that I am doing everything I can. For Rosalind."

Benton didn't say anything. He nodded slowly.

J.D. put his glasses back on and turned to Imogen. "Can you get a warrant?"

She thought about it before answering. "I might be able to, maybe, but I'm not sure. I'm not convinced this is our man. Our house."

"Why not?" Benton asked. She could sense frustration, but he was keeping it in check.

"I don't know. It's just not quite—"

Benton's frustration broke loose. "Shit, Imogen, what do you want? A sign on the doorbell? A welcome mat?"

"I want more than this. Everyone in America eats at McDonald's. Everyone drinks Coke. This could be anything. I don't want to mount a SWAT operation and endanger agents' lives and possibly the lives of innocent civilians without more."

"What about Rosalind's life?" Benton asked quietly.

"We still have time," Imogen pointed out. "We still have eleven days."

Benton studied his hands like he was wondering how they could be so useless. "I keep thinking about the six circles on the collage and what Martina Kidd said. About how he's going to torture her." He looked at Imogen. "You're right that we have time. But that gives him time too. What do you think he's doing with it? What do you think he's doing to Rosalind right now?"

Imogen's mind fixated on the holes in Louisa Greenway's cheeks. The words of the ME's report—*wounds show signs of healing. Best guess for time of puncture is eight days before death*—flashed in her mind.

J.D. stepped in, saying, "I agree that we don't want to put anyone needlessly at risk, but if there is a chance we can spare Rosalind one day of torture, we have to take it. A warrant gives us that chance."

Benton pointed to the LOVERBOY PROFILE list. "Your team has made a good start there, but those are all just guesses. Right now we could be on to something concrete. I don't want to lose it."

Hell, now they were tag-teaming her. She liked it better when they were fighting. Their posture was identical, both sitting with their forearms on the table, leaning forward. It was called mirroring, Imogen knew, and it meant they were in agreement.

At that moment she would have called it bullying.

"If we had anything else—" Benton said.

"But we're stuck," J.D. finished.

Stuck.

God, she hated that word.

Imogen tossed the Tootsie Pop into the trash, put her elbows on the table, and leaned forward. "You alert the SWAT team. I'll find a way to get a warrant."

It was noon.

CHAPTER 24

The SWAT team began deploying in a strip mall parking lot a quarter of a mile from the operations site at 12:50. The shopping center was slated for destruction to make way for a housing development, so most of the tenants had long since left. This gave the patrons of Rick's Ball and Stick an unobstructed ringside seat all to themselves.

At first they moved their stools under the awning and sat drinking beer and watching as the SWAT guys practiced their maneuvers, waiting for something exciting to happen. But Benton had stayed at the Bellagio to oversee things there, and J.D. had disappeared down to the Department of Records to get a blueprint of the house for the team to plan its entry, so there weren't even any celebrities to hold their attention. There were jokes about the guys' dopey outfits, of course, but jokes about how many SWAT guys it took to screw in a lightbulb—or screw Anna Lightbulb—stopped being so funny when one of the SWAT guys in question demonstrated the accuracy of his firearm on the neck of a bottle of beer en route to someone's mouth.

After two hours they dragged their stools back inside and returned to darts.

In her suite at the Bellagio, Imogen was calling in every favor she had to get a warrant.

"No, we have nothing concrete, but the circumstances—"

"No, I would not want you to lose your job—"

"No, a negotiator is no good because we don't know what he would do to her if he knew we were out there—"

"No, I am not kidding, I do still have that note you wrote about the director—"

"Yes, I swear if you— Hold on."

Dannie was holding the hotel phone out to her.

"Where the hell is my goddamned warrant?" the SWAT coordinator boomed at Imogen when she took it.

"I'm working on it," she said.

"My men are ready and in position. I don't want to blow this because some asshole in Washington wanted a long lunch."

"I'll get your warrant. I promise."

She called Benton and J.D. to see if either of them had anything more she could use, got bounced into voice mail both times, and decided it was time to bite the bullet. She swallowed hard and dialed her least-favorite number.

"Hi, Lex, it's Imogen. Got a minute?" She knew Lex had the pull it would take, but she also knew he'd only do it if he thought it was his idea.

Slumped on the couch, her elbows on her knees, head down, she gave him a report about what had happened so far that day, ending it saying, "I don't know, I'm beginning to think it might be better to let this go. Or just let the Vegas cops deal with it."

He took the bait. Imogen smiled to herself as Lex launched into a lecture on interagency rivalry.

She interjected an "I agree, of course, but—" and one, "No, you're right, we wouldn't want that," winding it up with, "I don't know, it seems pretty impossible. Still, I guess if someone knew the right people—" At that point, Lex said he'd find a way to get them their warrant. As she said good-bye, promising to stay right by her phone, she could already hear him flipping through his Rolodex, getting ready to make a few calls.

She hung up with a sigh. Tom, Dannie, and Harold all looked at her.

She nodded and put up a hand. "It's not definite, but . . ."

"But we're going to get it," Tom said.

"I think so."

"Good," Bugsy said, putting down the hotel phone and coming to join them. "Because that was the SWAT commander again. He called to say the eagle had returned to the nest."

Imogen frowned. "What?"

"The suspect just went inside."

"Honey, I'm home!" Loverboy sang out as he came into what he liked to think of as the family room. He smiled at her. "How are you today, Ros? Did you miss me?"

Rosalind blinked her eyes in reply.

"Silly me, I forgot about the tape on your mouth." He put two bags on the floor and bounced over to the recliner. He stopped short. Rosalind probably expected him to rip it off, like he had the other times. This time, though, he reached into his pocket and pulled out a knife.

Her eyes watched the blade flick open.

"Stay very still, Ros," he cautioned as he inserted the tip of the blade into the tape. He was having trouble keeping his hand level. If he lost control just once—just once!—he could cut her lips off. Oh, that was a lot of responsibility.

Very slowly he sawed a hole in the middle of the tape. He stood back to survey his work. Not bad.

"We're going to give you a makeover today," he told her. He grabbed the bags he had brought with him and dragged them toward the chair. The smell of fried chicken hit Rosalind like a tropical breeze.

Loverboy reached into the bag for a drumstick and started gnawing on it. "This stuff is so good," he told Rosalind. "Want a bite?"

She nodded.

He pulled off a tiny piece and shoved it through the hole in the tape. "How was that?"

"More," she tried to say.

"What?"

"More."

Loverboy began to laugh. "You sound just like a seal, Ros. 'Moooh, mooh, mooh.' You could do impressions."

Rosalind tried to get him to look at her but he turned away. "Besides, there's no time for you to eat now," he said. "We've got to make you up pretty. Time to give you a whole new look."

When he turned back, he was holding a long pair of scissors.

When he was just about ready to leave, Loverboy bent over Rosalind and kissed her forehead. "Sorry to eat and run," he told her, "but I've got a date. Do I look okay?"

Ros didn't move. Not even her eyes. He really couldn't blame her, he guessed. She had passed out right at the very beginning, an hour ago, and hadn't come to yet. It was too bad, because she didn't get a chance to see how pretty she looked once he was done.

He gave himself a once-over in the mirror to make sure there was no blood on him. Sure he was all clean, he carefully stepped over the trip wires that ran to the explosives under Rosalind's chair and out the door. It was easy to avoid them if you knew where to step, but if you didn't—well, then, things could get *messy*.

He whistled as he walked down the corridor. He was in a great mood. Everything was going so well.

CHAPTER 26

She was already naked between the sheets when he came in, her Barbie-doll breasts making twin alps. He had been feeling tense and on edge all day, and when her phone call came he knew this was exactly what he needed, but he had about a dozen other things to be doing. He looked at his watch. He had seventeen minutes.

"Howdy, partner," she drawled. "How's cows?"

"Busy. I can't stay."

She pulled him to her with a French-manicured hand. "I know. But I can't seem to stay away from you."

He smiled despite himself.

"I've only got a few minutes myself," she said, "so don't waste time. These are coming off." She reached up and slipped his dark glasses off with one hand. With the other she unzipped his pants, rolled him onto her palm, and teased him toward her mouth with the tips of her nails.

His hands went to her nipples, dark and the size of silver dollars, then farther down, and they were really at it. He liked being with her, no lies. No "I love you," no promises, no disappointments. Just "Wanna fuck?" and "See you later." Everything a man could want.

Some men.

When they were done he went into the bathroom and took a quick shower, then started running a bath for her.

She lay on her side in the bed, watching him dress. "I'm not sure this is a good idea, what we're doing," she told him.

He looked at her in the mirror. "I'm sure it's not."

"I mean it. I wonder if this should be the last time."

Putting his glasses back on he moved over to her, kissed her lips, and let his hand rest on her neck. "If that's what you want, just say the word."

CHAPTER 27

Two Metro police officers in yellow bike shirts turned back the residents of Melville Drive as they began to filter home from work around dusk. On the rooftops of the empty and emptying houses, FBI sharpshooters appeared, little black shapes against the encroaching darkness. In the minimall parking lot, the SWAT team was attracting the attention of the Rick's Ball and Stick night shift. Everything was in place. Everybody was ready.

"Where the hell have you been?" Imogen demanded as her team and J.D. pulled into the shopping mall parking lot simultaneously.

J.D. pointed to the passenger seat of his car. The scent of KFC wafted out from the buckets stacked there and every officer in the parking lot was suddenly gathered around him.

"I was buying undivided attention. Can't have a SWAT operation without KFC." He lowered his voice and added confidentially, "Actually, I didn't have to buy it. I convinced them to give it to me for free."

"Why aren't you taking it out?" Imogen asked, suddenly ravenous.

"The KFC is for *after* the operation," he explained as if she were slow. "Otherwise it makes your gun hand greasy."

When J.D. had finished his briefing and handed it off to the SWAT commander to begin the deployment, he came over and stood next to her. "You can sneak a piece of chicken now if you want," he whispered. "When the boys get at it, it goes pretty fast."

Gun hand, Imogen thought. She swallowed and said, "Thanks, I think I'll wait until I see how this turns out."

"Do you want to go over with the team?"

She nodded. "I'll stay behind the lines but I want to be nearby when they go in."

It was dark when they got to Melville. There were no lights on in the buildings on either side of 1112, and the streetlight right in front of the house had been disabled. But more than anything, it was quiet.

No skin showed on the six operators who would penetrate the room. They wore all black, down to their goggles and gloves. Against the asphalt of the street, they were nearly invisible.

Imogen counted ten snipers and guessed there were probably a few more. Hostage rescue was the most difficult job a SWAT team did, Imogen knew, but this SWAT commander had done his job well. His team was ready. Everything was perfect.

A tiny, metallic *ping* reached her ears through the night. This was it. They were going in. Please let it all go right.

That was her last thought before the world exploded into blinding white light.

CHAPTER 28

Imogen had known what to expect. She'd trained with flash-bang grenades and knew all about lag, about the way the brightness and the noise overloaded the senses. It was the key to the rescue attempt, the three-second window when the hostage taker would be overwhelmed and could be disabled. But even though she was ready for it, knew all about it, the explosion of the stun grenade shook her out of all thought. For a few moments she could not think or breathe or see or hear. Her consciousness came spilling back in and she heard the walkie-talkie of the SWAT commander crackle to life with the message, "We've got them both. All clear!"

And then, against all regulations, Imogen heard the operative start to laugh.

Imogen couldn't blame him when she stepped over the welcome mat in front of the bungalow door and saw why. Against one wall was a man, about her own age, handcuffed, with his pants around his ankles. Duct-taped to a recliner was a naked and hard-used blowup doll with an elaborate wig and a lot of makeup. The recliner faced a TV that was playing a nature video about otters. A dozen other animal videos were lined up against the wall.

J.D. took in the room without saying anything. He and Imogen did not make eye contact. There was nothing to communicate. They had been wrong.

It was over, at least this attempt. Incredibly, no one had gotten killed. Even Joe Smith was fine—or would be, when he was allowed to change his underwear. So why didn't Imogen feel any better?

Benton pushed his way into the room and said, "Where is she?"

J.D. shook his head. It was all Benton needed to see.

"Where were you?" Imogen asked him.

"Someone forgot to tell the cops that I was not a civilian," Benton hissed, looking at her.

"Talk to J.D.," she said. "I had nothing to do with Metro."

"I'm sorry, Benton," J.D. said. "I thought I took care of it, but I must have forgotten."

Benton wasn't letting up. "I tried to call you but you didn't answer. I've been standing out there wondering what the hell was going on for almost two hours."

"I said I'm sorry. It was a mistake."

Benton nodded to himself, then said, "The place is swarming with press. That's how I got in. I don't know which of you thought it would be a good idea to alert the networks, but—"

It was one thing to have made a mistake. It was another to have made it on national television. Imogen turned to J.D. "I thought we agreed, no press."

"So did I."

"My people didn't leak."

"Neither did mine."

"This is a fun game, children," Benton said, "but it's not going to get us anywhere."

J.D.'s second in command, a woman Imogen had been introduced to that afternoon as Rachel, approached them from the window. "Mr. Arbor is not exaggerating. Everyone's out there. I bet they picked it up off the police scanners."

"Or from someone in Bellagio security," Bugsy suggested, coming over to flank Imogen.

"I don't care where they came from," Imogen said. "I want them gone. Now."

J.D. and Rachel exchanged looks. "Meth lab?" she asked.

"Meth lab," he said. To Imogen he explained, "We use the same kind of deployment when we bust drug labs, but we do it often enough that no one wants to write about it. When the press hear it was just a standard raid like a hundred others, they should evaporate."

Imogen nodded and didn't say anything. She stood to one side of the window facing the street, and watched as Rachel came out and crossed the dead lawn toward the reporters.

The cameras and questions sounded to Imogen like feeding time at the aquarium she and Sam had visited in Hawaii—snapping jaws hungry for fresh meat. She shivered and turned away from the window.

"I want to know who leaked, and how," she said to Bugsy. "They're going to pay for this."

She felt Benton's eyes on her and she swung toward him, defiant. But he was just staring out the window at the press.

He said, "I think Bugsy's right. Bellagio security is the best place to start." Then, "If you will excuse me, I'll see you at your suite in a few minutes."

J.D. gave Imogen a ride back to the hotel. It was the first time they'd been together, just the two of them, and Imogen felt a little awkward. It was because of seeing him without his glasses on earlier that day, she realized. It had felt like seeing someone naked.

She noticed a baseball mitt and one of those baseball jackets, a royal blue one, scrunched behind the driver's seat and said, "Do you coach a team?"

He shook his head. "No. I just travel around the country giving speeches. Stay in school. Don't do drugs. Don't get girls pregnant, that kind of thing. The glove and jacket are more of a costume now than anything."

"What about a hat? I thought all baseball players wore their hats until they died. Got buried in them. But I haven't seen you in one."

"My ex-wife liked the cap too much."

"You were married?"

"For a little while. You sound surprised."

"It's just—you seem more the bachelor type." It was true, she realized, but not because he wasn't presentable. Because he seemed tired. Deep inside. Like he'd been putting on an act, doing a show, all by himself for years.

He said, "What about you? Have you ever been married?"

"No," she said, and it felt a little like a failure. After a moment she said, "Do you think we made a mistake today on Melville? Going in like that?"

"You really asking my opinion, or just trying to change the subject?"

"Opinion."

"No, I don't. If there was any chance Rosalind was there, we had to take it." She felt his eyes on her. "You don't believe that."

"I had a bad feeling in my stomach, which I ignored. But I would have had a worse one if Rosalind ended up dead."

"Must be hard for you with Benton, both trying to take responsibility for everything. How are you dividing that up?"

"You really don't like him. Why not?"

"I saw him cheat at cards once and deny it." She looked at him, thinking he was making a joke, but he wasn't.

As they were riding up in the elevator to her room, he said, "Be careful with Benton. He has a way of making people belong to him."

CHAPTER 29

Imogen didn't have time to think about J.D.'s strange warning because she could practically hear Lex shouting through the phone lines from the corridor outside her room.

"Why did you turn your cell phone off—" he started, then switched gears to "Do you know what I had to do to get that warrant for you?" It went on from there, no surprises, a little louder than she would have liked. J.D. and Rachel had followed her in and were standing together on the opposite side of the room, talking in low tones. She tried to catch what they were saying but Lex's voice hummed on.

"—middle of a game . . . butter up a prosecutor . . . embarrass me—"

Imogen turned to study the map while he spoke, wondering if she could cross off Melville. Wondering why she had ignored all her instincts that told her this was a bad idea.

"And if you think my name on the warrant for some cheap drug lab bust—" she tuned in to hear Lex saying, and had to fight hard against the urge to tell Lex that no one would recognize his name so he didn't have to worry.

Her fax machine started spewing out papers and she moved toward it, amazed that Lex managed to both fax and berate her on the phone at the same time. But the cover sheet said *Las Vegas*

Metro Police Department. Not for her. She motioned J.D. to the fax machine.

Lex was still talking. "Not only that, but I also had to cancel a dinner at Morton's to help you with this, and you know——"

Ah, Imogen thought, now we've mined the real matter. Lex had been inconvenienced. Lex had been so seduced by the idea of a big SWAT operation, lots of burly men in black suits, all doing it because he ordered them to, because of his name on a warrant, that he'd missed dinner at one of Washington's best steakhouses. No doubt at someone else's expense.

Imogen was getting ready to say something appropriately apologetic when she turned and caught sight of J.D.'s face. Instead she said, "Great, Lex, I'll call you back," and hung up.

"What's wrong?" she asked.

"This is a crime-scene report," he said, holding out the fax. "Only homicide hasn't gotten any calls that fit this description, and the case-file number doesn't exist."

"It's probably a hoax," Rachel said as she read it over.

"Weird hoax," J.D. said. "We should check it out. Rachel, take someone with you and run up to this address."

"3600 Las Vegas Boulevard, room 3518." Rachel copied the address, then looked up. "That's this hotel."

Imogen moved to the door and pointed. "Room 3518 is just down the hall."

"I hope this is a hoax," J.D. said.

It took J.D. less than five minutes to convince security to unlock the door of 3518 rather than waiting for a warrant. The room was neat, the bed tousled, the strangled woman's body floating in the bathtub, just as the report had promised it would be. It was not a hoax.

"What are you doing in——" Benton started, just arriving. He broke off when he got to the bathroom. "Oh. Oh God."

Imogen looked from him to the corpse. "That's the woman who winked at you yesterday at the bar. Care to tell us her name?"

"I don't know anything about her," Benton protested. "I'd never seen her before."

"Do women frequently throw themselves at you that way in public?"

"It happens," Benton stated, not bragging about it, just a fact.

"Benton is a very well known personality," J.D. pointed out.

Imogen turned away. She did not want a lecture on Benton Arbor's celebrity, even in the ironic tone J.D. was giving it. She wanted to take in as much of the crime scene as she could before a crowd arrived. She had just noticed one detail of the crime scene, a smell, that hadn't been mentioned in the faxed report when she heard J.D. saying, "I'll get some homicide detectives down here," and turned back.

"No," she said, shaking her head. "It was Loverboy. He did this."

"Just because the fax was sent to your room?" J.D. asked. "That's a little premature."

"I'm telling you," Imogen insisted. "It was him."

"Why?" Benton wanted to know.

Bugsy walked in and handed Imogen three sheets of paper. "Your fax machine ran out of paper before it was done," Bugsy explained. "These printed when I refilled it."

The top two were a continuation of the "crime scene" report. The last one had a hangman's gallows in the middle of it. Below it were twelve empty spaces. Below that, in the place for wrong guesses, someone had scrawled *1112 Melville*.

On the gallows was a circle for a head.

"This is why," she said.

Benton looked over her shoulder and said, "What does it mean?"

Before she could answer, the crime-scene unit arrived. She said to the lead analyst, "I need you to go over this place with a microscope. And take a sample of the perfume from the bed. I want to know what kind it is, and if it matches anything in the room."

The woman nodded and got to work.

Then Imogen turned back to Benton. She pointed at the hangman's gallows. "You want to know what it means? It's a threat. He's telling us that every time we guess wrong, someone will die. He's telling us that this is our fault."

She hoped her voice sounded normal. Her ears were ringing.

CHAPTER 30

"Ms. Page. Imogen——" Benton followed her back to her room.

"Don't talk to me."

"Look, I understand that you are upset, but——"

Imogen swung on him. "You understand nothing. That woman in there is dead because of me."

"Because of Loverboy."

"If I hadn't agreed to get the warrant——"

"We made that decision together, you, me, and J.D."

"How can you be so cool about this?"

"Not cool, just realistic. You cannot blame yourself for every person who dies."

"If I had done my job better, this would not have happened."

"That's not true. If you go on like that, where does it end? Are you responsible for every homicide in America because you haven't caught the killer?"

"If I had understood I could have prevented this."

"Understood what?" Benton threw up his arms. "Talking to you is like talking to a brick wall. Do you ever listen to anyone else?"

"When they say something worth listening to. That woman died because of a decision I made. Period. You know what? I don't want to argue with you. I want to work. We can talk philosophy another time."

She turned as Bugsy came into the room. "Anything?"

"We've started canvassing downstairs, dealers, bartenders, that kind of thing. And I went down to get the security video for this hallway during the past four hours, but they said they'd already sent it up. Is it here?"

"No."

"They said someone from Metro came and got it. I'll go ask next door." He looked from Imogen to Benton uneasily. "Unless you need me."

Imogen shook her head and he left.

"This Melville Drive operation was wrong from the start. I could feel it and I let it go on." She blew air from her mouth.

"At least we have another crime scene. Another body to work on. More evidence," Benton pointed out.

Imogen's stomach tightened. Not because she disagreed, but because he was right. Just like the press, she thrived on someone else's misfortune.

She felt filthy all over. She'd been up for almost nineteen hours. She could use a stiff drink, a long shower, and sleep. She glanced at Benton and saw that he looked as beat as she did. And he had a race the next day.

"Why don't you go to bed?" she said.

"And leave you to maul yourself with guilt?"

"Pretty much."

Before Benton could object, the Metro team came through the door.

"News?" J.D. said.

"Nothing here," Imogen said.

"No. I meant, anyone want to see how we played on the news?" He took the remote control and flipped the TV on.

Imogen stood off to one side, cupping her elbows with her palms. A news conference with the sheriff in which he announced an end to organized crime in Las Vegas—prompting a slew of "disorganized crime" jokes from the Metro cops—opened the program, but their "meth lab bust" got second billing.

"I thought you said it was so routine that no one would cover it," Imogen said to J.D.

"They shouldn't have. Must have been a particularly boring day here in Vegas."

Rachel handled the questions well, Imogen thought, even the direct ones such as "What was Imogen Page of the FBI doing at a small-time drug bust?" and "We've heard rumors that this is linked to the Rosalind Carnow disappearance." Imogen was about to breathe a sigh of relief when the cameras went wild and shifted onto a new target, and it was clear why the network was running the piece.

Benton stood there, his expression grim, as befitted a man whose girlfriend was being held by a serial killer. He hit every note just right, talked about how hard the last few days had been for him, how much he was looking forward to his race the next day.

"What are *you* doing at a meth lab bust, Mr. Arbor?"

Good question, Imogen thought.

"I came for the KFC. Always have KFC at SWAT operations. 'Bye, everyone." A wave and a tense smile and he disappeared into his shiny Thunderbird.

That was why he'd shown up so long after them at the hotel. That was what he'd been doing downstairs at the crime scene when they pulled away. Imogen had wondered how she and J.D. had been able to evade the press, but she understood now. Benton had wanted the limelight all to himself.

No wonder he couldn't feel bad about the woman next door's death. It would mean more publicity for him. More attention from the cameras. More chances to see himself on TV.

Keeping her voice low so that all the officers in the room wouldn't hear, she swung toward Benton and said, "What did you think you were doing out there? Were you trying to advertise our connection to the raid?"

"I was trying to change the subject."

"You sure were. Benton Arbor to the rescue. Thank you ever so much." Imogen was seething.

Benton said, "I wanted you to be able to leave without having to deal with the press."

"Everyone talks about how charmingly controlling you are—oh my, he won't go in elevators. But you are not simply controlling, Mr. Arbor. You have, like, a pathological need to be worshiped. To be noticed. This whole thing, Rosalind's disappearance, the death of the woman next door, it's all some big publicity opportunity for you, isn't it? To get that good-looking face on the cover of another tabloid."

She thought she saw Benton flinch. He said, "Publicity opportunity? Are you listening? I was trying to *help* you. So you and J.D. could get away without being hounded."

"The sad thing is, I think he believes it," J.D. said.

"I think you're right." Imogen glared. "You do, don't you, Mr. Arbor? Think you are so selfless, just trying to help. Because nothing can work without your assistance. When what you really want is for people to rely on you. So you can be the center of attention and adulation."

Benton raised his voice. "At least I don't lash out at people for no reason just because I feel like I screwed up my job." By this time, all the officers and her team had turned to stare at them. "You need to get your priorities straight, Ms. Page. All you've done the past twenty minutes is say 'I'm responsible,' 'I this,' 'I that,' or 'You're an asshole,' 'You this,' 'You that.' This isn't about you or about me, about the job you are or are not doing. It's about Rosalind. And if you'd stop wasting time feeling guilty and keep your mind on that, we would stand a chance of saving her."

Imogen moved to the door of the suite and held it open. "Thank you for all your help today, everyone. I don't think there is anything else for us to do now. Good night."

She did not slam the door behind the last person. But when she turned around her fists were clenched. Even reminding herself of the twitch in Benton's jaw could not make her feel victorious.

"He was not right," she told Rex, who was swimming around the fancy tank Benton had brought. "That was not what I was doing. Lashing out. Thinking about myself."

The fish stared at her.

He has a way of making people belong to him, J.D. had said, and she started to wonder if it extended to fish. She decided to move Rex out of his swank digs and into J.D.'s fishbowl in the morning.

As she lay in bed trying to sleep, her mind kept coming back to one image in particular—the welcome mat in front of Joe Smith's apartment. That poor man. He'd probably never welcomed anyone in before in his life, and suddenly he had more visitors than he'd bargained for. Unwelcome visitors.

Her mind flipped to another welcome mat—

"Don't step on that, your shoes are dirty. That's only for *invited* guests."

"Yes, Aunt Caroline."

—and tasting sour cherry, she fell into a fitful sleep and dreamed that Sam and her parents were having a wonderful time. Without her.

CHAPTER 31

Frankie Valli singing "Oh What a Night" blasted from the speakers of the car parked in the corner of the top floor of the Rio parking lot. The man behind the wheel sang along, really feeling the lyrics tonight. Oh what a night!

He moved his head back and forth to the beat and looked at the view. He thought this spot had the best view of Vegas, the city lights spread out in front of him like a playland, all those people down there near him, but not around him. Not close enough to touch him.

He was feeling so good, so amped, that he decided to give himself a treat. Usually the rule was that he could only look at the book at the beginning and the end, but things were going so well he decided to make an exception. An exception wasn't the same as cheating. He hated cheaters because they ignored the rules or broke them. An exception was stretching a rule, which was okay because it didn't ruin the game.

It was the same if your opponent made a mistake. Like in a sports game, if a player for the other team tripped, it was not against the rules to take advantage of that and make them pay for it. That was what he had done tonight after Imogen's mistake, and it felt great. He thought of it as collaboration, letting Imogen have some say in how things went, even if she didn't know it. It raised the stakes for both of them. It was certainly true that he was feeling everything ten hundred times stronger this time than before, but whether that was because of Imogen or because he'd finally found the ultimate victim, he didn't know.

Rosalind made the *best* noises.

Carefully he lifted the scrapbook from the seat next to him and flipped through it until he found the page he wanted, the one he'd been thinking about that day. It had a gold-colored piece of newsprint on it, photos of a pretty girl, some boys. A group shot with him, fifteen years old, in the back. And in the center, a picture of a roller coaster with the words *Big (Bad) Bess* beneath it.

It was taken the summer he'd worked at a carnival, one of those traveling ones that set up in empty fields outside. He used to go in early, sneaking in illegally through the shrub border so no one would see him. He'd always gone to visit Big Bess, the largest roller coaster, but he wouldn't get on. He'd use his key from work and go through the maintenance door, getting underneath the big machine.

He especially liked to go after the bad dinners with his father. The ones that started with his father saying, "Pay attention to me," or "I'll slap you silly if you don't look me in the eye," or "You are a disgusting shit," working himself into a frenzy until the red-labeled bottle sailed through the air and crashed against the wall.

When he was younger he had tried to understand why his father was always so insistent on him looking at his eyes. It didn't make sense, so he'd used a grapefruit spoon to take the eyes out of Snookie, the next-door neighbor's cat, and see if he could find what was behind them. Maybe cat's eyes were different, but as far as he could tell the only thing inside Snookie's eyes was goo and stringy cords. Once he knew that, knew how it was like Jell-O back there, it was even harder to look his father in the eye. He'd always thought Jell-O was gross.

Most times when his father got like that the bottle just hit the wall, but this one time that summer it hit the TV and broke it. He remembered turning to face his father, and felt his cheeks go pink. That always happened when he was feeling silly, that and the sensation that his senses were all in overdrive, he could hear everything, see everything, particles of dust in the air, practically smell each molecule. This time he remembered the sound of pushing his chair back away from the table, lifting his plate and carrying it to the sink.

"What do you think you are doing?" his father demanded.

He stared at his father's shoes, old black leather lace-ups with mud on the left toe. He said, "I've got to go to work."

"Can't you see I'm talking to you? You can't leave! Look at me when I talk to you."

The silliness was spreading. Be careful, he told himself. C-A-R-E-F-U-L. "Sorry, Dad."

He had reached to take away the untouched plate in front of his father but the man made a grab for his wrist. He twisted it hard. "You're not even my son, are you? You're a freak. A freak!"

Being touched like this made him *so* silly. When he had been younger, what his father was doing hurt, but the boy now towered over the man. He brushed the hand off his wrist as if it were a fly. He took his father's plate and set it in the sink.

Dishes done, he changed into overalls, fastened his tool belt around his hips, and went to the door.

"Good-bye, Dad. I should be back around midnight."

"Goddamn you," his father said. "I hate you. You're trying to drive me into an early grave."

"Have a nice evening," he said, because you were always supposed to be polite. The door closed behind him with its familiar *knock knock*.

Like usual, he'd headed straight for Big Bess. He crawled beneath her to lie down in his favorite spot, under the third left-hand curve. It was the sharpest, so it was where the girls always screamed the loudest. Sometimes boys screamed there, too, but they denied it later. He loved to hear them. It was his special place, and he saved it for when he was feeling very silly. He would slide his hand inside his overalls and let the screams wash over him, watch the machine whirl above him, around him, slide back and forth on top of him, down and around, down and around, until he felt like he would explode.

That night, as though Bess knew he was upset, a rectangular card came fluttering down from between the tracks onto his stomach right as he lay down. It said *Esmeralda's Prophecy* across the top, and then *The path to happiness lies before you. You shall have all that you desire. Insert another quarter and I will tell you more.*

He knew it was destiny that the card fell down to him. If it had gotten caught in the tracks it could have jammed the gears, maybe even derailed a car. But it hadn't. It had landed right on him. A gift, a special message.

He had just crawled out from under the roller coaster and was dusting himself off, making sure he had not left a spot on the front of his overalls, when he heard the footsteps behind him.

"Oh look, it's Mopey Dick. Visiting your girlfriend, Mopey?" a voice sneered.

Only one person called him Mopey Dick. It had started when he'd admitted in English class that Moby Dick was his favorite book. He liked to think of the whale. But it wasn't cool to have a favorite book, or at least not one with such a provocative title, and Charles Tooley had branded him with the nickname that very day.

If it had been anyone else, the nickname would have gone away, but not Charley Tooley. Charley lived in a big house with a mother and a father and a sister and always had the coolest records and the latest clothes. Tonight he was wearing a T-shirt and bright white Vans sneakers. He had a rust-colored Members Only jacket tied around his waist.

Members Only. The boy loved the sound of that.

"Hi, Charley," he said. The silliness was gone. He felt totally in control. "Did you have a nice summer?"

"Better than yours, I bet. What were you doing under there? Jacking off?"

He didn't blush, even though the circle of girls and boys around Charley tittered. He was careful. No one could have known.

"Yes, it was great. You should try it."

"I don't need to, Mopey. I've got a real girlfriend." Charley reached out and pulled Bethany Samson toward him. She was pretty in a pinched way, but mostly she was graceful. When she grew up she was going to be a dancer; everyone said so. He himself had been dreaming about kissing her for two years.

"Hi, Bethany."

"Hi," she said.

She had tiny eyes, so you didn't really have to look at them, and really pretty hair and she smelled nice. He'd love to watch her hair swing around as she rode on the roller coaster. "Why don't you all go on Big Bess?" the boy asked. "On me. Unless you're chicken."

Charley said, "I don't need your generosity, Mopey. My dad's not a drunk loser."

The boy looked Charley up and down and made fists with his hands. He watched Charley's ears and the sides of his neck go red. The Members Only jacket would look terrible on him like that.

Charley said, "I'm not chicken, Mopey," he began. "If you want to pay me to ride your girlfriend, I won't say no."

"Charley," Bethany objected, but Charley shut her up with a hard squeeze to her arm.

"Come on, hon. We're going on Big Bess."

"The rules say you have to leave anything that could fall off or dangle out here," the boy told them. "If anything gets on the tracks, it gums up the works."

"Listen to him, talking about the rules. What a priss," Charley said, but the boy knew he was just doing it to make himself seem bigger. Charley needed to learn about politeness.

Pockets were emptied, sweaters tossed aside, and the boy watched as the Members Only jacket got hung on a peg of its own. Charley and his gang spent the time they were waiting in line pushing each other, while the girls who were with them giggled nervously. Bethany once looked shyly at the boy and gave him a little smile, and he knew that she would rather be with him than Charley.

But even she didn't notice when he left to go to check in for work at the maintenance trailer.

It was the week after that when the crash happened. The boy waited nearby until they got on, to be sure, then went back to his job at the ring-toss booth across the fairground. Far enough away to have a good view, but close enough to hear the screams. He heard Charley's, heard Big Bess's. And over them all, Bethany's. Her scream was special. Just for him.

It was her last. As the local papers reported the next day and for weeks afterward, Bethany Samson, the only survivor of the Big Bess derailment, was paralyzed from the neck down and could neither speak nor move. Her doctors were confident that after a year or so of intensive physical therapy, she would be able to swallow on her own. Usually.

It was a great tragedy for a local girl with such a promising future. That was his favorite line from the article.

An inquest was undertaken, but no one could find any explanation for why the roller coaster flew off the track like that, apart from a few shreds of one of those cards that the Esmeralda fortune-telling machine spit out. The inquest did not report that there was no sign of Charley Tooley's Members Only jacket either.

The carnival never came back after that year. Bethany's father became rich from the lawsuit and was now living in a nice house in Maui with his new family. He never visited his daughter, who was in an institution in Boston near her grandparents.

She'd had one visitor recently, though. A handsome man who made all the nurses titter and say, "Isn't that . . . ?" Bethany didn't show any sign of recognition, but, of course, he was all grown-up now and looked different than he had all those years ago. He'd been in the area, feeling celebratory, and thought of her and couldn't resist. He'd brought her a present and everything. And he'd given her a kiss.

After all, he owed her for the jacket. And for the crucial lesson

he'd learned that day: the closer you were to the screaming, the better it sounded. That's what he'd been thinking about all day.

He closed his eyes on the lights spread out in front of him and let
his fingers trace the letters on the front of his scrapbook. F-A-M-I-L-Y-
R-E-M-E-M-B-R-A-N-C-E-S. He was a lucky boy. He had so much
to remember that the album was getting full. There were still a few
blank pages but not many. And in two days, there would be one less.

Unless Imogen started making more mistakes. Then things could
go faster.

10 days left!!

"She went by Marielle, but her real name was Mary-Ellen Wycliffe, thirty-four, most recent address a P.O. box in Texas. The hotel will deny it, but it looks like she was here working the conventioneers. Pick them up at the tables, make a deal over drinks, then up to her room."

"Any I.D.s from the dealers?" Imogen asked the police detective, a woman a little older than she was.

"A few saw her, mostly playing craps, but none of them noticed her companions. Those were the night shift, though, and the casino tends to be busier at that time. We've just started canvassing the day shift."

Imogen thanked the woman and went back to the medical examiner's preliminary report. Marielle had been dead between one and four hours when they found her. She had taken part in consensual intercourse right before she died, possibly even while she was dying, during which she'd gotten a hickey. There were no signs of struggle, nothing under her fingernails, no signs of any filtered-off debris in the bathwater. The cause of death was strangling by hand. She was placed in the tub after her death.

"About all I can tell you about this guy," the ME told Imogen, "is that he's got strong hands."

The crime-scene lab technician gave Imogen his report over the phone. He sounded like he was in his sixties, and he had a slight accent. Imogen looked at his card—Gianni Basso. "My family is from Bologna," he said, pausing for a deep smoker's cough, "and anytime we have leftovers we throw them all together in a dish with some pasta and béchamel and make a pasticcio. That's what you've got here—the leftovers of a lot of hard nights."

There were dozens of fingerprints, all of which would be run through the databases but none of which would probably yield anything. The only item of interest were a few grains of powder stuck in the carpet beneath a slight indentation indicating a footprint.

"What kind of powder?" Imogen asked.

"We're still running some tests. It looks like synthetic sweetener with something else."

"Could it have been a drug he used to subdue the victim?"

"I don't think so. Still, I wouldn't put it in my pasticcio if I could help it. I got a match on the perfume too. It's called Poison."

"Of course it is," Imogen said. It would be.

"Been around for a while. We didn't find any in the vic's room, so your guy might have brought it with him."

"Thanks."

Around lunchtime, with her team gathered in her suite, they got a break. One of the craps dealers not only remembered Marielle, but also her companion. "Good-looking guy, brown hair, tall," *Gordon Taylor, Boise, ID,* explained, seated opposite Imogen at the big table that was her command center. "Wearing sunglasses. Nice jacket. I noticed the jacket because it's the kind of thing you see in magazines, 'What the well-dressed man is wearing on his yacht this winter.' It was a light-colored sport coat. Very European. Anyway, he and this lady hit it off right away. If she wasn't a working girl, then that guy was smooth. A charmer. Not two seconds and they're making plans for a drink in her room."

At least they'd gotten the "charming" and "good-looking" parts of their Loverboy profile right. "What day was that?"

"I was off yesterday and the day before, so it must have been Thursday."

The day Imogen arrived. She did not even have to tell Bugsy to bring her the security tape of her hallway from that day. He was already out the door.

"Could you recognize the man again? Pick him out of a lineup?"

The dealer shrugged. "I could try. I was looking at his clothes more than his face."

"Keep your eyes open for him in the casino and get in touch with one of us if you see him."

"Will do," Gordon said. He glanced at the TV. "Hey, is that the invitational?"

"Yeah," Tom said. He, Harold, and Dannie were sitting in front of it having lunch. "It hasn't started yet."

"I hope Benton Arbor wins. I've got a fifty riding on him. Great guy. Always tips big."

Imogen crunched a Tootsie Pop. Was it not possible for her to go through a day without someone pledging their undying love for Benton Arbor in her vicinity? She sat down in a chair with her back to the TV and started going over the old case files. Marielle's killing was an aberration for Loverboy. None of the other victims had shown signs of sexual relations. The fact that Marielle had not struggled as her throat was crushed meant she was not afraid, that she had expected nothing of the kind from this man. She had gone to her room to have sex with him. This was even more telling if she had been a prostitute—women who made their living that way tended to be more careful with their companions.

The perfume was odd too. He'd been so meticulous with the other killings, leaving no trace behind. But if he had brought Poison with him—was it a trigger? Was it just the name that turned him on?

The two different kinds of killings suggested a split in Loverboy's personality. On the one hand he was rigorously organized and controlled; on the other, the same man, but slightly undone. It was as if the effort of control required for the Loverboy killings took its toll and he had to find another outlet. As if he were acting a part.

Unless his murder of Marielle had simply been a way to punish Imogen.

Imogen closed her eyes and rubbed her temples with her fingertips. She needed to know if there had been others killed like Marielle. If there were others, it was part of his pathology, not something special he had done just for her.

There was only one way to know. She made herself dial the number of the Boston Police Department before she could chicken out.

A man's voice on the other end of the phone answered. "Homicide, Detective Reginald Nottingham."

"Hi, Reggie? It's Imogen. I'm glad to see you're still working Sundays."

A beat. The voice, going husky, said, "Finally. I knew you would wake up and see that life without me is incomplete."

"You are absolutely right." Imogen laughed. "And all I need to complete it is for you to do me a favor."

"Sexual or professional?"

Imogen rolled her eyes.

"I hear you rolling your eyes. That's how well I know you."

"Reggie, do you remember the Louisa Greenway case last June?"

"Of course. It was the last time you were here in Boston—the last time I had a happy moment."

"Right. Could you do some looking around for me to see if there were any other unsolved homicides at around the same time?" Reggie snorted with the derision of an overworked cop, and Imogen rushed to elaborate. "Any others involving women, probably under forty, who had recently had sex but were killed with no sign of struggle. Possibly killed during sex, possibly dumped in water, possibly with a hickey. Possibly with traces of Poison perfume on the sheets. I'm not sure how specific to get."

"You don't want much, do you?"

"I'll return the favor sometime."

"Now you're talking. I'll see what I can find and call back. We're a little busy here right now but I'll fit this in for you. Or rather, your favors."

Imogen hung up and glanced at the television. She had never watched professional racing before, but from the jammed grandstands she might be the only person in America to have missed it. The invitational was not, as she had imagined, a single race, but an entire day of racing involving different categories of cars. She looked at the schedule at the bottom of the TV screen and saw that Benton's race was the last of the day, after at least a dozen others. Her eyes began scanning the crowd. The speedway was packed with people, most of them families, and all of them cheering and laughing and smiling.

Smiling.

She started flipping frantically through the dossiers of Loverboy's victims with one hand, making a list with the other.

Rosalind Carnow had ridden on the Stratosphere roller coaster the day before she disappeared.

Benny Woolworth, the Oakwood victim, had tokens in his pocket from a video arcade.

Steve Simon of Ecton had been moonlighting as a security guard at the Crocodile County Fairgrounds for four weeks, in order to buy his two sons mountain bikes for Christmas, before he failed to return home one night.

And Kaylee Banks had attended a birthday party for her younger cousin at a miniature golf course two weekends before she was taken.

That meant four of the six victims had been to amusement sites, places where people went to have a good time, right before the killer struck them. Places where people smiled. Could that be his hunting ground?

Buried deep in the file on Pauline Dodd, Imogen found more

suggestive evidence. Pauline's bedside table contained a stack of paper tickets, like the kind you won at a carnival.

She would have to have someone call Pauline Dodd's sister, with whom the girl had lived, and ask if she had been to a carnival. They had buried her over a year ago. It seemed cruel to reopen the wounds, but Imogen had no choice.

The only victim unaccounted for was Louisa Greenway. Imogen reread every word of her file but came up with nothing.

Just a thread.

Imogen called the FBI crime lab and asked to speak to someone in fibers.

"Can you tell me what this"—she read the scientific name of the polyester thread found on Louisa's clothing—"would come off of? Or, better, could it have come from a stuffed animal?"

"Maybe. But not a fancy one. We're definitely not talking FAO Schwarz."

"One from a carnival?"

"Yeah, that would probably be about right. No promises, obviously, unless I'd seen the fiber and the animal, but I think you're on the right track."

Imogen realized, as she hung up, that her mouth was filled with the taste of oranges.

She looked up and saw Bugsy come in carrying the tape from the security office. "Bugsy, I need— Bugsy, are you listening to me?"

He turned away from the television. "Sorry, boss. I just wanted to make sure I hadn't missed the race."

"Probably not for another ten minutes," Dannie assured him.

"Bugsy, I need maps of about a thirty-mile radius from where each of Loverboy's other bodies were found, and on them I want all of you to mark any places where people go for fun."

"Motels?" Bugsy suggested.

"*Family* fun," Imogen corrected. "You know, arcades, bowling alleys, miniature golf. Amusement parks."

"Movie theaters?"

"No, too many."

Bugsy glanced at the television again. "Racetracks?"

"Sure. And carnivals."

"Some carnivals are seasonal," Tom pointed out. "It would be hard to get all of those."

"Check for around the dates of the murders. Or, even better, just circle fairgrounds."

Imogen was buzzing with nervous energy. She was on to something, but had no idea what. She should call Louisa Greenway's parents and ask them if their daughter—or even one of their sons—had brought home a cheap stuffed animal before the girl disappeared, but she couldn't bring herself to do it. She wanted to stretch out the possibility that what she was thinking might be true for as long as she could.

She took a red Tootsie Pop from the box on the table and parked herself in front of the collage. Her eyes roved over it, from object to object: bed, television, Intellivision console, Night Crawlers game, stereo, geode, Original Ouija board, Great Houdini Magic Set, *Emergency!* poster, desk, Audrie Lumber notepad, Ford County Library book (*Moby Dick*), Liquid Paper, valentine, Mead notebook. Next to it she'd taped up Loverboy's most recent hangman's gallows. Somewhere in that collage there were the twelve letters that spelled Rosalind's location. Somewhere.

Groans emanating simultaneously from the television set and from Tom at her elbow pulled her attention from the collage.

"He's fallen behind." Tom pointed out Benton's chrome-and-yellow car on the television. "He was up in the first lap but now he slowed down."

"He's just trying to trick them," Harold told Tom confidently. Harold's admiration for Benton had been growing at an exponential rate. "You know, make him think he is slower than he is so they'll eat his dust. He told me all about it. It's strategy."

"I hope you're right," Dannie said, abandoning all pretense of working and moving over to the couch in front of the TV. Soon they were all sitting there, eyes glued to the screen.

Imogen gnawed her Tootsie Pop down to the stick without realizing it.

"This is it," Harold murmured, and they all leaned closer. Three cars in a tight pack approached the final bend of the motor speedway in a dizzying blur.

"He's moving to the inside," Dannie shouted.

"He's not going to make it—wait—" Tom said excitedly.

All five of them sat spellbound watching as he edged into the inside of the turn. His nose edged between two cars. It was close. It was damn close. It was—

He was in front.

"He's going to do it," Tom yelled.

"He's pulling it off," Harold cheered.

"Come on, come on, come on," Dannie hollered, jumping up and down.

Imogen's heart was racing. She found herself on her feet, craning her neck at the TV as if it would improve her view, holding her breath—

Then jumping up and down and cheering with her team as the finish flag dropped behind Benton's bumper.

It was absurd. She didn't care how he did. Yet when he climbed out of his car, smiling and waving at the crowd, she found herself, alongside Tom, Harold, and Dannie, smiling and waving back. At the television.

She was just happy for him, she told herself. For how he must be feeling. A job well done. Success.

Her phone rang fifteen minutes later. "Imogen? It's Julia."

"Congratulations."

"Were you watching? I'm calling because we've taken over the Fontana lounge tonight to celebrate and I wanted to invite you and the rest of your hardworking staff. I know you are all busy and believe me, none of us feel like a party either, but the head of our stockholders just called and said that if we don't capitalize on this win and show it's business as usual despite our little personal problems—that's what he called them, the asshole—we are going to be looking at a hostile takeover in the morning. The truth is, I am trying to get as many warm bodies there as I can. I know that's not the most elegant invite, but at least it's honest. Is there any chance any of you could come? It would really help us out. And the band is going to be good, so at least we can work out our frustrations salsa-ing like mad. Things should start around seven."

Imogen was delivering the news to her team when her phone rang again. Bugsy got it. He handed it to her.

"Are you having a party out there?" the caller demanded. "It sounds crazy."

Imogen snapped back to work. "Reggie, please be calling to tell me you found something."

"Will you give me the best years of your life?"

"Those are long gone. What is it?"

"I found a listing for a vic, around the same time as your Greenway murder, one who matches what you described. Sex, no violence, strangling, found in bathtub. This one doesn't have a hickey. But someone doused her sheets in Poison."

Imogen kissed the phone. This was a break. Marielle was not an aberration and she didn't die just because of a mistake Imogen had made. "Can you send me the file? And a list of the evidence found on the body?"

"Yeah, but it will take a few days. We're short-staffed."

"How many days?"

"Three or four. If I rush it." He paused. "Of course, if you wanted to fly to Boston and have dinner with me tomorrow, you could see the file as soon as you got here."

Imogen looked at her watch. It was 4:30 in the afternoon. Even if there were a flight leaving in an hour, she wouldn't get to Boston until two A.M. local time. "What time do you get in?"

"Nine, but I'll push it to seven for you."

"I'll see you then."

"I'll make a dinner reservation."

Imogen hung up and turned to Bugsy. "Get me on the first plane to Boston and make an appointment for me to see Louisa Greenway's parents the day after tomorrow."

Bugsy disappeared with the phone. When he came back he said, "First direct flight out is at midnight. It gets you in at sixty-thirty tomorrow morning."

"There's nothing sooner?"

"You could change airplanes three times and arrive at eight A.M. if you'd rather," Bugsy told her. "Besides, this way you get to come to the party."

"I am not going to a party," she said, appalled.

"You know you owe me a mamba, boss," Bugsy told her. "From the agency Christmas fete last year. A mamba and a rumba. And you could use the stress release."

That was low. Bugsy was one of the few people who knew Imogen's secret: She loved to dance. It allowed her a kind of single-minded concentration that cleared her head unlike almost anything else. It was the only time she did not mind being close to another body. It was the only thing she would unabashedly admit that she was good at. And Bugsy, who had made it to the quarterfinals of the men's Latin dance championships two years earlier, was even better.

There was really nothing for her to do until she had seen the evidence she hoped she would find in Boston, at least nothing that would occupy the entire time before her flight left. She gave in, put her hair behind her ears, and said, "You'd better wear comfortable shoes, because just for that, you are going to spend a full hour on your feet."

Bugsy stood back to examine her. "You've got a lead, don't you?"

"If I'm lucky."

"Maybe we should skip the dancing, go play the tables."

"It's not that good a lead."

CHAPTER 34

The party was great, at least until Julia came over to steal Bugsy from her. "You two dancing are amazing to watch," she said, then leaned over and whispered to Imogen, "Go ask Benton to dance. Please? He's been watching you all night."

Imogen tried to sound sincere as she said, "I really wish I could, but I've got some work to do before my flight leaves," and ducked out, heading for her room.

She sat down on the couch and began watching the security tape from the day of her arrival that Bugsy had found, people parading up and down her hallway. She saw Marielle Wycliffe come out of her room in the morning, but she didn't come back and no one went in.

"Look at my posture," she said to Rex. "And can you believe no one told me I had a big white mark on my jacket all day?"

Rex blew a bubble that she decided meant he agreed with her.

Apart from her slouching and the fact that she'd been practically walking around with a KICK ME sign on her back, there was nothing else on the tape to notice. She put it back in its envelope, picked up her overnight bag, and was about to leave the suite when she thought of something.

She got the tape out and ran it through again. And again. The time stamp was right. But there was something missing, she was certain of it. Because Benton had come to her room that day, the first day of the investigation, to apologize. He had talked to Lex. But he wasn't on the tape.

Someone had edited it.

She called down to Bellagio security and cringed when her friend Burt from Eureka, CA, answered the phone. Of course, Sunday night late duty. It had to be the worst shift besides dealing with recalcitrant FBI agents.

"I'm sorry to bother you, Burt, but can you tell me who checked out the tape for Thursday before my assistant?"

She heard the sound of Burt putting down his pencil—she wondered how far he'd gotten on his word-search book—and typing on his computer terminal. One-fingered, it sounded like. He came back on.

"That tape was checked out to Peter Bembo on Friday," he said. "Returned Saturday A.M."

"Peter Bembo?" Imogen stared at the receiver. "Don't you ask for any identification before handing out the security tapes?"

"Of course." Burt sounded stiff. "Whoever's on the desk checks it out. And there's a note here says that Peter Bembo was from Metro."

"Can you give me the home phone number of the man who was on the desk when the tape was checked out?"

"Sure could," Burt said, "but wouldn't do you any good. Grouse is down in Cabo fishing. Won a vacation on a charter boat or something like that. He won't be back until next Monday."

"Thanks, Burt."

Imogen hung up and spent a minute sorting through the tastes in her mouth, trying to make her hands stop shaking. Peter Bembo, Imogen knew, was not from Metro. He was not even from the current millennium. Peter—Pietro—Bembo was historically said to have been Lucretia Borgia's lover in the sixteenth century. Pietro Bembo was Lucretia Borgia's loverboy. And Lucretia Borgia was the name she had registered under in the hotel.

That was a good one. Loverboy was flaunting himself at her, showing her how close he could get, how funny he was. Making a big joke.

But maybe he'd made a mistake too. She picked up her phone and dialed.

CHAPTER 35

It had been Hungry-Man family-style dinner night for Loverboy and Rosalind. He'd taken the tape off her mouth and she had wolfed down the Salisbury steak and mashed potatoes and peas so fast he'd begun running around the room making slurping sounds and calling her Hoover, like the vacuum cleaner.

The food had almost come back up again when he held the mirror up for her to see herself. She had never been good around blood, and the blood caked around the holes he had driven through her ears was an unfortunate match in color for the meat she'd just eaten.

"I knew you'd look better with pierced ears," he told her, twisting one of the small gold studs he'd put in, until she winced.

"I think it might be infected," she said.

He looked serious. "You could be right, Hoover. I'm sorry, I mean *Dr.* Hoover. We'd better do something about that when I get home."

He left, turning off the lights. Only the tiny red blip of the smoke detector pierced the room. When he came back four hours later he was sweaty and exultant. He was also carrying in his hand an enormous bottle of industrial-strength household cleaner. "Look what I got!" he said, holding it up proudly. "Look what good care I'm taking of you. This has ammonia in it," he explained. "It should fix you right up."

"I don't think that is the right thing for my ears," Rosalind told him. "You aren't supposed to put that on open sores."

"Why not?"

She looked at him, aghast. He knew this. She even remembered the time, years ago, that they had emptied out a cupboard of cleaning supplies together in the apartment she shared with Julia so Jason— *Don't think about that,* she cautioned herself. He was not the same man. She spoke as if she were speaking to a child. "Because it is highly toxic. It is not good for me. Or for you to touch." And it would hurt like all hell, she added to herself.

His face changed, aged, grew stony. "You're lying. That's not why you don't want me to do it. It's because you're afraid it's going to be ouchy."

Rosalind did not deny it.

"Haven't you learned about lying to me yet?" he asked her. "You lied to me when you smiled, and now you lied to me about this."

"I wasn't lying."

He pasted on an expression of mock pensiveness, his finger at his chin. "Hmm, let's see, I wonder if I believe that?" He leaned in right next to her face and yelled, "NOT!"

He stayed there, letting her smell his breath, see up close the lines, skin, eyes, nose, lips she'd looked at so often, so happily, over so many years. Had this monster been hiding under there all that time?

His cell phone rang, breaking the silence with the opening chords of "Take Me Out to the Ball Game." He looked at the display and a huge smile cracked across his face.

He stood up and tucked in his shirt before answering. "Hello. I had a feeling you'd be calling," he boomed. As he spoke, he moistened a cotton ball with the industrial cleaner. He balanced the phone between his cheek and his shoulder and, looking in Rosalind's direction, mouthed the word *liar.*

Then he reached for her ear. He didn't even put his hand over her mouth as she screamed in agony.

9 days left!

Corrina Orville had left her office at Boston Custom Liquor and Wine at 5:30 P.M. on June 28, like she did every day. It was a Thursday and like every Thursday, she stopped for a drink at L'Enoteca, a small, upscale wine bar with plate-glass windows that fronted onto Tremont Street. Thursday was poetry night there, and while she wasn't willing to read any of her work, she enjoyed listening to others'. One day, she promised, she'd get up the guts to take the stool and spout off. She was known to the other regular poets as Bacchus, the god of wine, because she was the wholesaler who provided L'Enoteca with its wares.

L'Enoteca was not only one of her clients, but also near her apartment. In fact, it was equidistant between her apartment—where she was found murdered in her bathtub—and the apartment in which Loverboy had held Louisa Greenway. That much Imogen had been able to learn during her first half hour with the Corrina Orville file in the overheated interrogation room Reggie had lined up for her use. She still had no idea where Corrina Orville had encountered her killer, how he'd talked his way into her room, or why the woman hadn't struggled.

She was pretty sure it was Loverboy. The killing was exactly the same, Poison perfume on the sheets and none in the apartment, sex accompanied by strangling, victim dumped in the bathtub at the end. Was it a ritual? Did he do it to clean his traces off the victim? Or could it be a subtle, playful way of advertising that all the murders led back to him?

You're going to take a bath on this one, Page.

No one at L'Enoteca had seen Corrina talk to a stranger, and they were sure that she hadn't left with a man. One of the poets, Max Y. Bolash, suggested that Corrina was a lesbian and would never have gone home with a man, but interviews with two others revealed Max's unrequited crush on Corrina. Max, unfortunately, had an alibi for Corrina's murder. And he had been unequivocally in Boston the past two weeks, ruling him out as a suspect in Rosalind's disappearance or Marielle Wycliffe's death in Las Vegas. In fact, the idea of ever setting foot in Las Vegas gave him "head-to-foot skeevy boils," he told Imogen on the phone.

None of her friends remembered her wearing Poison ever, either.

The only other interesting item she found on the case summary was a penciled note that said simply *Susan K.* The department secretary, Vickie, had confirmed that it was the scrawl of Clive Ross, the detective who had worked the original case, but had no idea what it meant. Clive Ross had retired three months earlier and was now living in Florida. Vickie gave Imogen the number, but when she dialed it she got an answering machine advising her in a jolly voice that "Clive and Paula have set sail for seven seas to celebrate their golden wedding anniversary" and would not be back for another four days. A picture of Clive based on his voice—slightly overweight, wearing a goofy Hawaiian shirt and shorts, laughing a lot—formed in her mind, and Imogen was jealous. Of the cruise. Of Paula.

She left a message.

Finally, she flipped to the evidence lists. Nothing on Corrina's shoes provided any clue about where she had been. All the fibers on her skirt and sweater set were indigenous to her house. The only thing in the list that caught Imogen's eye was a book of matches from the Four Seasons hotel. One of Corrina's coworkers admitted to detectives that she and Corrina had occasionally closed the office early and slipped down the street to the hotel for a drink when no one was around, so the matches could have been taken then. Interviews with the bartenders had turned up no evidence that Corrina had been in the night she was killed, but Imogen decided to try again.

She was acting half on impulse and half on logic. If Loverboy had not been the man who met Marielle at the craps table and got invited up to her room, there would have been no reason for the security tape to be edited. This meeting took place four days before Marielle was killed. What if he had acted the same way in Boston? What if he hadn't killed Corrina until their second meeting? The detectives had really only asked the bartenders at the Four Seasons if they had seen Corrina the day of her death. Imogen was ready to bet she had met her killer there before that.

Imogen knew she was in trouble when the first thing she was told was that the hotel had no bar.

"There is no place for people to have cocktails?" she asked, astonished.

"Oh," the woman at the dark-wood reception counter said. "Cocktails. Yes. For that, there is the Bristol Lounge."

It only got worse from there.

"I really cannot speak to you," the hair-sprayed-spit-polished-creased-trousered lounge waiter told Imogen tersely. He refused to even exchange a word with her inside the lounge, and, instead, they were huddled in a corner of the wood-paneled lobby, opposite the concierge's desk. He did not sit down in one of the green leather sofas, as if to underscore that they would not be speaking long. "People share things with me at the bar when I mix their drinks that they would not share elsewhere. They trust me. What happens in the lounge, as in the rest of the hotel, is protected information."

"Protected by whom?" Imogen asked.

"You have heard of attorney-client privilege? Or the sanctity of the confessional? It is the same for me."

"In what sense?" Imogen asked. "Have you been ordained?" She would not have been surprised to have him answer yes.

But he merely regarded her as if her question were ridiculous. "Our guests' trust is the most valuable commodity we have. And we preserve it by protecting their privacy."

"I think they would trust you to cooperate with law enforcement officials," Imogen told him. Imogen could have sworn he was about to tell her that he was above the law when a voice behind her made her mouth taste sweet.

"Ah, Mr. Arbor. So good to see you again," the concierge said.

Imogen turned very slowly and saw Benton looking at her. He nodded, hesitated, took a step forward, and said, "Don't jump to any conclusions. I am here for work. To make everything look just like normal." Sounding tired now, like he hated it.

She said, "Why didn't you tell me you were coming to Boston?"

"Why didn't you tell me?"

There was no rebuke in his tone, but there could have been. She should have told him. He was nominally supervising her investigation. She decided to change the subject. "What work?"

"Our winter track is just outside of Boston. You can check that if you want to."

"I will," she said.

"I figured. Now, if you'll excuse me—" He went back to the concierge's desk and started conferring intensely.

The lounge waiter had taken advantage of the interruption to disappear back into his holy of holies, leaving Imogen standing alone in the corner of the fancy hotel lobby. She decided she liked Vegas better, because at least there she could lurk behind the slot machines. Here her aloneness, her out-of-placeness, glared.

She was walking across the thick Persian carpet to the discreet brass-and-mahogany reception counter to see if she could contrive a meeting with the manager when the man himself emerged from a well-concealed door to greet her.

"Lars, our head lounge attendant, just told me you had been in.

I am terribly sorry he gave you a hard time. He would be happy to answer all your questions. He was just"—the manager sought for a word—"misguided."

Imogen could not keep the amusement out of her eyes. She did not dare ask directly if Benton had somehow affected the new "Welcome, FBI" attitude she was sensing, even from the head lounge attendant, because if he had she would have had to feel bad about accepting it. Better to pretend he had nothing to do with it. But she knew how she could test it without really letting herself know for certain.

"Thank you so much Mr."—she looked at his name tag—"Richeleau. I was wondering. Your hotel is so beautiful. Is there any chance you have a room available tonight?"

"As a matter of fact we do. It's a suite, but of course, for a member of the FBI, we offer a special price."

Damn Benton, she thought. Damn him for being helpful and useful in an unobtrusive way even though he was exhausted and under stress. Imogen wondered if he had specified the suite or if that was just an accident. "Thank you," she said against all her better judgment. "That will be perfect."

She went into the Bristol Lounge, took a stool at the long wooden plank that anywhere else would have been called a bar, and gave Lars the third degree. It was the least she could do after all the trouble Benton had gone to. And she did learn something interesting. Three days before she was killed, a woman "possibly" resembling Corrina Orville had been having a drink with a friend at one of the tables that looked out on the Boston Common. It was not busy yet, so Lars had been waiting on the tables as well as taking care of the bar. Her friend left abruptly and Corrina stayed to pay the bill. But a "tall, dark, and handsome" (Lars's words) stranger had paid instead and they had become engaged in conversation. Lars was not sure, because he did not make a habit of listening in on other people's conversations, but he thought the man might have mentioned something about being in publishing in New York. He and the woman seemed to be discussing poetry, which Lars noticed only because he himself was a poet. If it were not for that, he certainly never would have eavesdropped, but he did think he heard them say something about going around the corner, to Pignoli, for dinner. No, they did not say anything about going to her place, but Lars would not have been surprised, because the woman seemed eager to show the man her work. Only her work? Well, she did not seem displeased with the man's company.

Of course, he would *never* eavesdrop on the hotel's guests, so he wasn't certain.

CHAPTER 37

Imogen managed to convince Reggie to change their dinner reservation to Pignoli, but none of the waiters remembered anyone like Corrina Orville or Lars's tall, dark, and handsome stranger dining together in June.

Conversation between her and Reggie was somewhat hampered by her distraction and his insistence to inch closer to her every time she inched away. Tall, dark, and handsome could easily have described Reggie. She remembered the crush she'd had on him when she had been in Boston working on Louisa Greenway follow-up. Heavy flirting, a lot of good chemistry. Remembered how excited she had been when she had introduced him to Sam. But as the case petered out she discovered that the attraction had been driven by the intensity of the investigation, not anything real. Her crush disappeared when the last of the paperwork was done, and although Reggie called a few times after that with suggestions of weekend getaways, Imogen always apologetically found she was too busy with work. One day the calls stopped.

Sam had not been impressed with Reggie. "He's like one of those Easy-Bake cakes," Sam had said after meeting him. "Nice package, a cinch to make, but never as good as you want it to be. And smaller. Have you noticed that? Always smaller than you hoped."

Imogen laughed to herself at the memory, and Reggie, taking

this as a good sign, slid his hand all the way up her thigh and whispered, "Your place or mine?"

"Are you still living with your ex-wife?"

"Good point. Yours."

She removed his hand. "I'm afraid not."

"Look what I brought," he said, sliding a thin box of condoms onto the table. "That way you can't go all ice princess and make excuses the way you did last time."

Imogen grabbed them and shoved them into her purse. She could feel her cheeks flaming. "No."

"Why not, Gigi?"

"I don't want to."

"Are you seeing anyone?"

"No."

"So what's to stop us? We're not talking about a life commitment. We'll be great together, I know it. You know it. Come on, why not? Just a little fun."

Sam's voice was again in her head. "I wish just once you would date someone hard. Someone who would know the difference between what you are giving him and what you are capable of, and would demand more."

"I don't want to be with someone who demands more. I like the kinds of relationships I have," she had replied. They were lying on their backs, head-to-head, on the beach in Hawaii, looking up at the night sky. Lying in more ways than one.

"Look, Gigi, emotions don't kill people—"

"—people with psychoses kill people," she had finished his sentence. "I don't want to talk about this right now, Sammie. We can talk about it later."

But they hadn't. Later was too late. Because Sam was gone.

Reggie's tongue was in her ear.

Imogen pulled away. "I said no, Reggie," she told him.

He looked at her, still not getting it, she could tell. He gave her a lazy smile, said, "Okay. But you can't blame me for trying. I mean, you call out of the blue talking about favors, then fly here at the drop of a hat—"

"That was for an investigation." She knew she shouldn't have called him. Knew it.

"Sure," Reggie said, nodding smugly. "Right. I get it now. Well, if it's all business, let's let the Bureau pick up the check for dinner."

Was this how Loverboy had behaved with Corrina Orville? Imogen wondered, and decided it wasn't. She had the sense that he was suave and a good judge of people's reactions. He would never have missed the cues she was sending out. He would do everything he could to make himself appealing, carefully constructing a persona that would make his companion like him.

Like him. Maybe that was why he did not kill them on their first date—because he wanted to be sure they liked him before he did it. To prove to himself that they'd fallen for his act, prove that he was smarter than they were? Or was delaying the killing simply an exercise in self-control? A way to show himself that he did not have to kill them if he did not want to?

No. It was more complicated than that.

Distracted, she paid the check, and agreed to let Reggie walk her the three blocks back to the hotel. They were almost there when he turned and pushed her into a recessed doorway.

His mouth pressed hers and his hands moved over her coat as he whispered, "Come on, baby," hotly in her ear.

"Reggie, *stop.*"

He shoved his hand up under her jacket until he found the zipper on her pants. He pressed his erection against her thigh and whispered, "Let's do it right here. I know you were just freaked out with all the people around in the restaurant. You've always been a priss."

"That's not—"

His fingers were on her waistband, touching the silk of her underwear. Touching her skin. Inching down. He panted, "Let yourself go. You know you want to, Gigi."

Imogen socked him in the jaw.

CHAPTER 38

She was standing there, staring at Reggie's unconscious body and rubbing her wrist, when Benton came up behind her.

He said, "Nice shot."

"I wish he hadn't gone down so easily. I would have liked to hit him a few more times."

She was making light of it, but he could see she was trembling. What he really wanted to do was pull her to him, wrap her in his arms, hold her tight until she stopped shaking, but he sensed that there was a fifty-fifty chance she'd slug him too. Maybe more like eighty-twenty. Anything to prove she wasn't weak. So he just stood there.

He had spent the entire plane ride to Boston reading over her personnel files. He'd memorized parts of them, favorite lines, like *almost no one more unsuitable to working with a team* and *best agent to come through the Bureau in decades.* He liked her letter of resignation too, where she told her boss in a P.S. to get a new toupee. He'd bet the man had.

He had realized, staring out the window at thirty thousand feet and seeing only her face, that was the thing about Imogen Page. You wanted to strangle her. But you wanted to make her happy more.

He said, "If you want to take another shot at him now, I won't tell."

"No. That wouldn't be fair." She looked at him now. "Can we go somewhere and get a drink? Not at the hotel. Someplace seedier."

And there was that damn thought again, the one that had drawn him to read her files, the one he'd been determined to talk himself out of. The one he'd had when she pulled a gun on him and when she'd insisted on driving and when she'd told him his jokes stank but laughed anyway. The thought that Imogen Page was someone who could make him want to compromise. Everything.

He said, "Sure. I know just the place."

The decor of the Iguana Café was early Tijuana. It had dusty crepe-paper flags hanging from the ceiling, patches of sawdust ground into the floor, and smelled like old beer.

"Is this seedy enough for you?" he asked her as they walked in.

She looked around and nodded happily. "Perfect."

In a few hours, Benton knew, the place would be filled with college students, but right now there were only two other customers in there, sitting at opposite ends of the bar staring as a woman on television demonstrated a fantastic new concept in mopping. The waitress was watching too, leaning back, elbows on the bar, her hand rubbing a nicotine patch on her upper arm. She looked over her shoulder at Imogen and Benton as they came in, said, "Whatdyouwant," one word, then gestured them toward one of the scarred wooden booths that lined the wall.

As they waited for their order—two bourbon-and-waters and a bowl of ice—Imogen flexed and unflexed her hand. She said, "I wonder if I should send someone to look at Reggie."

"Who? The cops?"

She started to laugh, and through it Benton could see the effort she was making to hold herself together. He said, "He'll be fine. Plus, he deserved it."

"How do you know?"

"I watched him with you at dinner. No, I was not following you.

I was seated at the table behind you having a meeting. You can check if you want. It was with two boat designers."

"Is Arbor Motors branching out into boats?"

"No. Julia says we need more of a luxury presence. More than just my 'lovely face on the cover of another tabloid.' " He saw her wince slightly, thought, Good, then went on, saying, "We're thinking of commissioning a boat for the Americas Cup race. *The Courtesan.*"

"That's a nice name."

Their drinks came. Benton nodded at her hand as she put it into the ice and said, "What did you do to him, anyway?"

"Left jab."

"Nice. Unexpected from a righty."

"Exactly."

"Where did you learn that?"

"Recess. With a little help from a boxing coach in D.C. named Big Fat Joe. Where did you learn that ankle twist you pulled on me the morning we met?"

"You mean when you arrested me?"

"Tried to. Yes."

"Army Rangers. It rarely comes in so handy. I'm out of practice."

"You did a nice job," she told him like she meant it. And gave him a smile.

Do not say anything you are going to regret, he warned himself. He looked away from her and said, "Apart from getting some quality time with your friend out there, was your trip productive?"

She nodded and he listened as she told him about the other dead woman, her theory about Loverboy meeting them more than once, about amusement parks and family fun and how she was going to see Louisa Greenway's parents the next day to see if she could back the idea up.

He leaned forward. "Wait, what if that's it?"

"What?"

"I keep thinking about Martina looking at the photo of Rosalind

and Jason, tilting her head. She said, "She has a son. Of course."
What if Loverboy is making a family? I don't know if it works with
the others he's taken, but Louisa had brothers, right? Her obituary
said something like 'survived by her parents and two brothers,' I
think. So what if she were the sister in this family?"

Her eyes moved past him and she said, "Steve Simon had two
children. He could be the father. Benny Woolworth took his nephews
out every Wednesday night, including the Wednesday before he
disappeared."

"Uncle," Benton supplied.

"And Pauline Dodd had been out with her sister and her sister's
children Christmas shopping."

"Aunt."

"Father, sister, aunt, uncle."

"What about the brother?"

"No." Imogen shook her head. "The other victim was a girl.
Kaylee. She lived with her aunt and uncle and their two children—
Oh. She was a cousin."

"Which makes Rosalind the mother."

She nodded slowly and used her index finger to put her hair behind her ear. "Yes. Maybe why he saved her for last. That is really
good. It tastes right. And it goes with an idea I was working on the
other day, about how the victims themselves trigger him. I had as-
sumed all the family connections were just to ensure that the victims would be missed, but your explanation is much more solid.
Thank you."

She smiled at him again.

He said, "Where do the Greenways live?"

"Somerville. Do you want to come with me to see them?"

"I've got an appointment in Cambridge tomorrow morning.
Somerville is on the way. I'll drive you over—if you'll let me. Want
to meet for breakfast at seven-thirty?"

"Breakfast at seven-thirty will be perfect."

They got the check and, despite his insistence on paying, split it. The walk back to the hotel was quiet. At the elevator bank Benton said good night to her, kept himself from saying half a dozen other things he would be sorry about in the morning, and was heading for the stairs, willing himself not to turn around, when he felt her hand on his arm.

She said, "Wait, Mr. Arbor. Before you go, I owe you an apology from the other day."

Now he had to turn around. He said, "I don't think I heard that quite right. Can you repeat it?"

She rolled her eyes. "It was not all my fault, though. You may somehow have found a way to be the head of this investigation, which I still don't understand, but you cannot talk to me the way you did in front of other people. My team and the police. And you should have told me you were going to stay and talk to the press, or at least told me afterward. You said you were trying to protect me, but you need to understand that I neither need nor want your protection."

"Is this the apology?"

"Yes. Because you are right. I did lash out. Because I felt like I messed up. Your yelling at me didn't make it any better, or that whole thing acting like I couldn't take care of myself, but everything you said was right. I was so focused on feeling bad that I wasn't focusing on the job. Since Sam died my head has been a mess and I haven't been as sharp as I should be, but now I am, or I'm going to be. I'm just going to push all this—" Looking up at him now, her cheeks were flushed. She bit her lip, "Sorry, I'm babbling."

"Is it my turn?"

"Are you going to accept my apology?"

"Yeah, I think so. To encourage you in the habit." She narrowed her eyes but gestured with her hand for him to go ahead. He said, "I can't imagine what you're going through after losing your brother, it sounds like you two were very close and you need to grieve and I respect that."

"No, I'm done. I'm fine now. I grieved yesterday and—"

"That's weird, I thought it was my turn."

"Right."

"It was unfair of me to talk to you the way I did, particularly while J.D. and the others were there. Although you started it."

"That's different because—"

He tilted his head to one side. She stopped talking.

He said, "The stress of the race and of thinking about what could be going on for Rosalind. It got to me and I lost control. I never wanted to give the impression you couldn't take care of yourself. That stunt with the press was wrong. I really was trying to get you out of there because you seemed so tense, but I could have done it a better way. A different way than putting myself in front of them."

"Yes, like you could have rammed into one of their cars. Created a diversion. Or you could have sent—"

Benton stopped trying. Trying not to say what was really on his mind. "Let me ask you something, Ms. Page."

"If I know the definition of 'your turn'?"

"If, when this is all over, I could take you dancing."

Her jaw almost hung open. "You want to go dancing with me?"

"Dinner too. Take you on a date."

He saw her mind working, trying to come up with reasons it wasn't a good idea to let anyone be close to her. She said, "I don't think that's advisable. I mean, of course, I'm flattered and that's very sweet of you—"

"I'm not sweet."

"Right. But whatever you're feeling, it's just about the case. Your feelings will go away. So I really think—"

"Two dates."

"What? Why two dates?"

"Because I hope that will be enough."

"For what?"

"Are you chicken?"

Now her jaw really did drop. "No, I am not chicken to go on a date with you. I'm just trying to say——"

The elevator doors opened and Benton held them until she stepped inside. He said, "Good. That's settled. Good night, Ms. Page. See you at seven-thirty." And he left.

Imogen stood in the elevator for a second as the doors slid closed, totally stunned. Then she hit the number of her floor hard. She could not wait to get to her room and call Sam and tell him about her date with Easy-Bake Reggie and especially about Benton Arbor——who was not bad-looking, especially when he was tired, and much nicer than you would think and smarter too——asking her out, even if it was just because of the investigation. Benton Arbor.

She was fumbling her plastic key in the lock on her room door when it hit her. Sam was dead. SAM WAS DEAD.

She closed the door behind her and collapsed.

For one instant, with Benton, her world had felt back in balance and she had forgotten, but it crashed down around her again with all the pain of a Band-Aid being ripped off a half-healed wound. The tingling excitement she'd felt turned to a chill that started in her arms and slithered through her entire body. Bleakness and loneliness. And failure. Sam was dead.

She fell asleep clutching her knees to her chest in the corner of her room and sobbing for her brother and Marielle Wycliffe and Corrina Orville and all the others who had died, and worrying that she was not good enough to make it stop.

CHAPTER 39

He sat himself down at a table in the back corner where he could see the whole lounge in one glance and waited for the waitress to come over. It was fairly early by Vegas standards, so the place was less than half-full, just a handful of couples scattered at the small tables and pretty quiet. A good place to sit and figure some things out. He needed to clear his head from wondering what Benton and Imogen were doing in Boston. Wondering what was really going on with the investigation. Hoping that Imogen had taken his hint and was staying away from Benton, that she understood that getting involved with him would be a big mistake. Bad things happened when people made mistakes.

The waitress came by and he ordered without thinking about it. Only when she gave him a funny look and said, "A Coke with cherry syrup in it?" did he realize what he said, asking for a cherry Coke, and that told him how he was really feeling. Sometimes he needed outside things like that to make what was going on inside clear to him. Too many years of repression, he'd bet Rosalind would say, and she would probably be right.

He started thinking about Rosalind—was she awake, was she thinking about him, how many bad things could happen to her before time ran out—about all the things he planned to do with her. Experiences he wanted to share with her. Things from his past, to help her understand.

He wondered what she would say if he told her about the cherry Coke, made it like a story, Hey, Ros, once there was this boy who drank cherry Coke. Forty-two of them, one each month his father was at the medium-security lockup. Should have been sixty months, but the man lied his way out, discharged on good behavior. Incredible.

Tell her about taking the bus out to the "facility," sitting in the visiting room, letting his father give him a bear hug, push his hair around, punch him in the stomach to make sure he was in shape. The visit going okay until his dad started in with the game stuff, was he practicing, tell me about your averages, how's the arm, tell the coach to call me.

Sure, Dad.

There was always a TV in the visiting room and it was all he could do not to watch it, stare at it whatever it was—beer ad, talk show, cartoon—anything better than having to watch his dad as he arranged his face for lying. Be out of here in a few months, Sergi tells me, his father would say. The appeal is going well, Sergi says we got them on a technicality. Always trying to sneak around the rules, bend them. Sergi, a lawyer who worked out of a storefront on Main Street that he shared with a shoe-shine guy. The shoe-shine guy always seemed to have more clients.

Sure, Dad.

If he was lucky the visits were quick and ended before his father started riding him for being uncommunicative, then for being sullen, finally started yelling at him, telling him he was an ungrateful bastard, didn't he know he'd done it all for him, that he was in there, in prison, right now just so his son could—

I never asked you to rob banks, Dad. I never wanted a father who was a criminal. What would Mom say?

You have no right to talk about your mother.

Say to Rosalind there, What could you do? The man had issues. Showing her that he was totally over it. Then tell her how after the visit, he'd walk a mile and a half to the ice-cream parlor across from the bus stop to clear his mind—maybe not tell her how he'd wish someone would come by, make a mean comment, so he could beat the shit out of them—and have a cherry Coke. He always wanted a sundae, but they cost three dollars more. Describe it to her, the old-time feel of the place, red vinyl booths, black-and-white linoleum checkerboard floor, long counter with round stools where he would sit and pretend he was someone else, not a kid who'd just visited his father, his only parent, in the medium-security prison down the road, but a kid from a fifties TV show with a father and mother and dog and paper route.

Wasn't it weird, he'd say to her, what you dreamed of being as a kid, compared to where you ended up? The way little things could change your whole destiny. All I ever wanted was a perfect family like that.

Thinking about that, wondering what Rosalind would say, he gazed across the empty floor of the lounge and noticed Cal Harwood and Wrightly Waring pass by the entrance to the lounge, then saw Wrightly spot him.

Damn.

He watched Wrightly say something to Cal, probably, "Go on, I'll catch up in a moment," then walk unsteadily toward him, until he came to a stop against the table, braced himself against the edge, leaned forward, and said, "How can you just sit there at a time like this?"

He smelled like a barrel of Jack Daniel's.

Wrightly now launching into how nervous he was, how upset, desperate, wanting to know what was going on, no one willing to tell him a thing. Sounding like a fly buzzing around, not shutting up. It made him wonder how Wrightly had lived as long as he had, being this annoying.

He'd nod or say, "I don't know," or "You're right," but really he was still thinking about Rosalind, wondering how she would react to his story about the lonely boy and the cherry Coke who had dreamed of having someone who was his, someone who loved only him. If she would understand that she was the one he wanted to build his family with now. Imagining her smiling at the end of it and saying—

Wrightly's face was in his face. "Have you been listening to me? What I've been telling you?"

Man, Wrightly's neck looked like it was made to be wrung. He made himself keep his hands under the table and say, "Yes. You think the FBI is overlooking something."

"Not overlooking. I think there is a cover-up going on. Maybe Benton is covering this up, I think he hates Rosalind because she and I— I don't know. There's just too much that doesn't make sense. There's got to be more evidence out there, and someone has got to make them find it before—" Wrightly stopped and wiped his eyes on the back of his sleeve, almost falling over, then looked up and said, "Dammit, why are you just sitting there staring at me? I thought you of all people would understand and be as worried as I am."

"Why me of all people?" He said it very quietly.

Wrightly backed up. "Because you're a friend of Rosalind's. Ease up, that's all I meant."

He gave Wrightly a long stare through his dark glasses and said, "You don't know anything about me or the state of my thoughts. Rosalind is on my mind day and night."

Which was the truth.

Then he stood up, dropped a twenty on the table, and said, "I've got to go. I'll see what I can find out, but I don't want you mentioning this to anyone. Not your concern. And nothing about me and Rosalind. Got it?"

Wrightly nodded and slumped into the booth. "Sure, J.D., whatever you say."

only 8 days left!!

What Imogen remembered most about the Greenways from her last visit were Mrs. Greenway's hands. For hours as they talked Cynthia Greenway would lean forward, staring at her own hands as they clenched and unclenched, as if she did not understand how they had gotten there.

"Stop that, Cynthia," Arthur Greenway would mutter every few minutes, every fewer minutes as the interviews wore on. "Dammit, Cynthia, you're driving me crazy."

Cynthia's hands would unclench for a moment, and Arthur would disappear into the fluorescent-lit kitchen. Imogen would be left sitting alone with Cynthia, who would try to smile and say, "You have to excuse Arthur. He is taking this very badly." The same words every time.

Then Arthur would come back, eyes glassier, reeking slightly more of Scotch, and the scene would begin again.

Imogen had visited the Greenways five times to interview them about their daughter after she was killed, in the hopes of getting information that could help them catch the killer before he struck again. The last time she arrived, Cynthia Greenway opened the door by herself. She had a black eye.

"You'll have to excuse Arthur today," she said with the same glued-on smile. "He—he had to go."

The woman had collapsed sobbing into her arms. Imogen had

called child services and the welfare department and listened to Cynthia explain that Arthur had not meant to push her, that she hit her eye when she fell, that it had been an accident, just an accident, really. When Louisa's minister came, a woman no older than herself, Imogen had left guiltily. Guilty for how glad she felt to leave. Guilty that she never wanted to go back. She realized now as she stood on the top step listening to Benton's motor running on the street below and waited for the door to open that she was terrified of what she would find.

Loverboy's making a family, Benton had said, and she thought he was right. But he could just as easily have been trying to destroy one. How does a family recover from losing a loved one? How could a family recover from something like Loverboy?

When Arthur Greenway opened the door she almost did not recognize him. Instead of asking her in, he stepped outside the house and closed the door behind him. She was looking at him, but his eyes seemed unable to find her.

"Before you go in, Ms. Page, there is something I want to tell you. I—Cynthia and I—" He looked at her now. "Thank you for helping her. Last year. I just went crazy with all this. I'd never done anything like that to her before and—" He shook his head and his cheeks went red, but not from drinking. "I want you to know that I'm getting help now. We all are. But mostly I wanted to thank you. I don't know what she would have done that day without you."

Imogen was stunned. Arthur Greenway blurred in front of her as her eyes filled with tears. She hoped like hell Benton was not watching. "You are welcome. I am so glad that—that you are working things out."

Arthur nodded. "Me too. What is a family for if not to help survive something like this? It's the most important thing. I can't believe I almost let it go." He looked away politely as Imogen wiped her eyes on her coat sleeve. "Guess we'd better go inside. They are waiting for you."

"They" were Cynthia Greenway and the twins, Neil and Billy. They were all standing in the living room just off the foyer, motion-less, when Imogen stepped in. Cynthia Greenway broke the tableau, rushed forward and hugged her.

Imogen, only a little stiff, hugged her back. This was hardly the same woman she had met the previous summer.

They put her in the seat of honor, opposite the couch. There was a dab of furniture polish between the molding and the glass in-lay on the coffee table, and Imogen was sure they had cleaned the house for her arrival. She did not think anyone had ever done that for her before. She dragged her eyes from it and looked at the Greenways in front of her. Cynthia and Arthur were holding hands.

Why did everything make her want to cry that morning?

Cynthia spoke first. "I wanted to call you so many times. To tell you thank you. But——"

Imogen shook her head. "You have nothing to thank me for. Whatever has happened, you two have done it."

"We four," Arthur corrected, smiling at the twins sitting on the floor next to the coffee table. "Your office asked if the boys could be here and, anyway, they wanted to see you too. We let them stay out of school this morning."

Imogen was at a loss. She sat in the tall-backed guest-of-honor chair and wished she were anywhere else than at the center of this kind circle of people whose happiness she was going to shred by bringing up something they were better off forgetting.

"You don't have to be afraid to talk about Louisa," Billy, the twin nearest to her, said. "We talk about her all the time."

Arthur smiled at him. "It's true. It's the best way to keep her memory alive."

Imogen sought blindly for something in her emotional lexicon that made sense of this, of this desire to remember rather than lock away, push down, forget, pretend never happened. She had a strange, terrifying urge to tell them about Sam and how much she missed him and what joy he had brought to her life and how sometimes she had dreams, these dreams about him that were so real that when she woke up for an instant—

Once that started, there was no end.

She said, "Louisa would be proud of you for what you have done."

"Louisa would want us to help. That was what she believed in," Cynthia said quietly. "Tell us how we can help you, Ms. Page."

Imogen plunged in. "I was wondering if Louisa brought home a stuffed animal, like the kind you win at a carnival, before she disappeared."

Arthur and Cynthia looked at each other, and Billy and Neil screwed up their faces in a pantomime of thinking.

"No," Arthur said finally, and Cynthia shook her head too. "I just packed up her things into boxes last month, and I would have remembered if there was anything like that."

Imogen tried not to show her disappointment on her face. She had known it was wrong to cling to that one thread, the one hope that Louisa too had been to a carnival and the Greenways had forgotten, somehow, to mention it earlier. She had known it was wrong, but she had done it anyway. "I know we went over her movements the week before she was taken several times when I was out in July, but would you mind if I asked again?"

Four heads shook.

Imogen reached into her bag and took out the pad of paper on which she'd made notes about Louisa's activities. It had been summer vacation and Louisa had been baby-sitting her brothers during the day while their parents were at work, until they all went to sleep-away camp in July. She had earned five dollars per hour, which she had faithfully deposited in her college savings account every week.

Imogen could not imagine how you kept two ten-year-old boys occupied all day.

"When Louisa was watching you, did you stay home the whole time?" she asked the twins.

Billy answered. "No way. We always did something fun."

"Not always fun," Neil corrected. "We had to go to the library a lot."

"I like the library."

"You would, loser."

Imogen smiled. "Besides the library, where did you go?"

"We had swimming lessons Monday, Wednesday, and Friday," Neil said. "I'm in the red group. That's the highest one."

"Yeah, and youth group on Thursdays at the church," Billy added.

"When you had swimming or youth group, did Louisa stay with you?"

"She was on the diving team, so she had practice too," Neil explained. "But she was there with us at church. All the kids are together but they do different things depending on what they like."

Imogen led them through soccer practice, trips to the library, Frisbee at the park. No strangers talked to them and they never went to any carnivals or arcades or movies or racetracks, and they were always home by five when Cynthia got home from work. The family spent weekends together, often going to visit friends on the shore. They had been planning to do that the weekend before Louisa disappeared, but all three kids had come down with colds so they stayed home.

Imogen looked over her notes again, praying that something would catch her eye. She asked, simply to feel thorough, "How did you get colds?"

"Yes," Arthur said, teasing his boys. "Tell Ms. Page about that."

Neil and Billy suddenly looked sheepish. "We had a snowball fight," Neil said cryptically.

"In June?" Imogen asked.

Billy opted for a full disclosure. "It was at the end of our sno-cone sale. You know, to raise money for the youth group's annual trip? After it was over there was still a lot of ice left and—"

"—and it was the kind that is perfect for snowball making," Neil put in.

"So we made snowballs and threw them at the girls."

"And then they threw them back at us."

"And then—"

Imogen nodded. "Where was this?"

"At the Somerville five-K run. We had our booth at the end. We thought maybe the runners would want to have sno cones because it was so hot."

"Were there other booths?" Imogen's heart was suddenly pounding.

The boys shrugged but Cynthia said, "A few. It's a real community event. Lots of people turn out to run in the race and lots more just to watch. At first only the local merchants set anything up, but this year there were a few commercial things."

"Commercial things?"

"The kind they have at carnivals," Billy offered. "Like ring toss."

"And Strongest Man," Neil said. "You know, where you use a hammer and try to hit a bell to show who has the biggest muscles. That was the most fun."

"Did you win when you played?"

Neil looked chagrined. "No, but I'm going to next year. I'm going to lift weights. There was a Pokémon toy I really wanted."

Imogen barely resisted the urge to kiss both boys, and only managed to because she knew that if she did, Neil and Billy would never be allowed near another ring toss again. The Greenways were strong, incredibly strong, but they could not be blamed for keeping their boys away from what Imogen was now fairly confident was the kind of place Louisa had met her killer. Louisa had not come home with a stuffed animal, but Imogen now thought that the killer had. The idea that if she could find the origin of the thread, the stuffed animal, she would find the killer was lodged in her head along with the taste of oranges, and she could not shake it.

The ringing of the doorbell interrupted her thoughts and spared her the awkwardness of having to make up more questions. She had learned what she had come for.

"I think that is my ride," she said as Arthur went to open the door.

"Hi, I'm Ben—"

"You're Benton Arbor!" Neil said, peering around his father with eyes like UFOs. "You're famous! Dad, that's Benton Arbor. Benton Arbor's at our house!"

Arthur moved to one side but the expression on his face was almost as comical as Neil's. "Please come in, sir. It is an honor to have you here."

Benton looked large and sheepish and handsome in the foyer of the house as Arthur and Neil told him about having watched him on TV just two days before. He nodded and smiled and apologized when they said he'd had them really worried for a few minutes. Neil almost exploded when Benton promised him a private tour next time they were doing tests on the Boston track.

While Neil ran around the house in raptures, Benton introduced himself to Cynthia Greenway and finally turned to Imogen and said, "If you aren't ready, I can wait in the car."

Imogen felt like a sixteen-year-old being picked up for a date from her parents' house.

"No," she stammered. "No, I think we are done." She went to Cynthia Greenway and took the woman's hands in hers without thinking about it. "It makes me so happy to see you, your family like this. Thank you for meeting with me today."

They moved to the door, but before they reached it Neil appeared, carrying an album and a pen.

He shifted from one foot to the other and finally blurted, "Um, Mr. Arbor, can I have your autograph?"

When Benton handed it back to him, his mouth gaped. "He wrote 'To my friend Neil,' " he read aloud. "The boys at school are never going to believe this. Thank you, sir, thank you."

Benton was so good at being famous, Imogen thought, but for the first time it did not rankle her. She turned to look for her scarf and found that Billy was holding it, and an album like Neil's, out to her.

"Could I have *your* autograph, Ms. Page?" he asked shyly.

"Mine?"

Billy nodded. "When I grow up, I want to be an FBI agent just like you."

Don't be just like me, she wanted to tell him. For the fourth time that morning, the world swam in front of Imogen's eyes and she found her hands were not steady. Her first autograph ever and it was going to be illegible.

After another round of good-byes, Imogen and Benton finally managed to leave.

"It looks like your errand went well," Benton said as he started the engine of the rental car.

"Yes." She looked at him. There was something wrong with his expression. "Where did you go?"

"Just to visit the garage I used to work at when I was in college, Robby T's. I always like to make sure they're not seeing a lot of our cars."

"Are they?"

"Fortunately, no." He was frowning as he drove and seemed to be searching for something. "The Greenways weren't what I was expecting," he said.

"What do you mean?"

He was pensive for a moment. "I guess I thought that any family who had lost a child would be decimated."

Imogen tasted something besides surprise in the tone of his voice. Something like oversweet envy. She didn't know what it was and was about to ask about it when he seemed to find whatever he had been looking for. He turned the car into a parking lot and pulled into a space.

She peered through the front wind-shield and saw a Korean bar. "What are we doing here?"

"I'm afraid I have some news you aren't going to like, Imogen."

The sense of dread she had felt standing on the front steps of the Greenways' house reasserted itself, squeezing her stomach.

"What has happened?"

"This." He was holding up a tabloid with that day's date in the corner. Across the front, under the announcement "*Global Weekly News* Exclusive Interview," the headline blared:

"LOVERBOY SPEAKS: 'IMOGEN PAGE IS MY GIRLFRIEND.' "

CHAPTER 41

Imogen held the paper in her hand for a moment without opening it, her eyes on the flashing green neon sign for Korean beer in front of them. "Is it a real interview?" she asked him finally.

"Read it and see what you think. I would not put it past the *Global Weekly News* to make something like this up but on the other hand, it has often been my experience that the tabs have the most accurate news because they're less squeamish than the big leagues."

She opened to the second page and started reading.

A KILLER SPEAKS
By Leslie Lite

Global Weekly News star reporter Leslie Lite was granted an exclusive interview with the man the FBI is now calling Loverboy. At the request of Loverboy, this telephone interview is reprinted here in its entirety.

Loverboy: *I had a feeling you'd be calling.*
LL: *Thank you for granting this interview.*
Loverboy: *You're welcome, Leslie. Professor Kidd tells me you are very beautiful. Is that true?*

LL: *I would rather talk about you, Mr.——*

Loverboy: *You can call me Loverboy. That's one word, not two. What are you wearing?*

LL: *What are you wearing?*

Loverboy: *Wouldn't you like to know. Hey, here is someone who wants to say hi to you.*

(Confused background noises)

LL: *What is that?*

Loverboy: (Laughing) *Not what. Who. That is Rosalind Carnow.*

LL: *May I speak with Dr. Carnow?*

Loverboy: *Hang on, I'll see. Ros, do you want to talk to Leslie?*

(More confused noises)

Loverboy: *Sorry, she says she is busy.*

LL: *What are you doing to Dr. Carnow?*

Loverboy: *Right now? I'm just cleaning her up. I want her to look just right.*

LL: *For what?*

Loverboy: *For when Imogen Page gets to meet her.*

LL: *Who is Imogen Page?*

Loverboy: *Imogen Page is my girlfriend. My special friend. She works for the FBI.*

LL: *When will she meet Dr. Carnow?*

Loverboy: *When the time is right. Imogen knows.*

LL: *Tell me about yourself, Loverboy.*

Loverboy: *I'm a charming, good-looking white male between thirty and forty who is organized and educated. Also, I like to eat fish.*

LL: *Me too.*

Loverboy: *Goldfish. Raw.*

LL: *I see. Do you have any hobbies? Special activities you enjoy?*

Loverboy: *Long walks on the beach, candlelit dinners, drives through the mountains, romantic picnics. You know, the usual.*

LL: *You sound like the perfect date.*

Loverboy: *You got it. Basically, I like to see everyone around me happy. Isn't that right, Ros? What, Ros? I can't hear you.*

(Confused noise)

LL: *I guess the question everyone would like to have answered is, Why are you killing these people?*

Loverboy: *Torturing them first. Then killing them. Get it right, Leslie.*

LL: *I'm sorry I—*

Loverboy: *Because I can. Wouldn't you? I mean, if you could get away with it? Ask Professor Kidd. She's my instructor. She knows all about it. Plus, they all deserve it.*

LL: *Why?*

Loverboy: *They're liars. Every one of them. Hey, you're going to print all of this, aren't you?*

LL: *Of course. We might have to edit—*

Loverboy: *No editing.*

LL: *But you will sound better if—*

Loverboy: *I'll tell you this, Leslie Lite. You print this the way I told it to you, every word of it, and all the sounds too, or I'll come and cut off your titties right in front of your face. And you know the best part? You won't even know it was me until it's too late. You'd come home with me in a heartbeat if I asked you to. Any woman would. Have you got that? Just wait until you see what I'm going to do to Rosalind. Stop squirming, Ros. Look, I gotta run. Ciao for now.*

This reporter subsequently visited Professor Kidd, known as the Connoisseur, in her cell in White Haven Correctional Facility in Ohio. After listening to the tape transcribed above, the professor made this comment about Loverboy:

"He is a very talented boy. He knows what he wants. And the FBI is going to have a hard time catching him."

To the question of how she knew Loverboy she replied simply, "Those who cannot do, teach."

When asked if she were conducting the investigation, what she would do, she said, "Whatever Imogen Page is doing." She added, "I'd try to find out how he transported Rosalind Carnow's body from the Bellagio."

But employees at White Haven Correctional, where some of this nation's most dangerous criminals are held, offered a different opinion. "Takes a man to catch a man," one prison official who asked to remain anonymous said. "Get Imogen Page off the case and put on someone with some real muscle."

On one side was a photo of Imogen that looked to her as though it had been snapped at Sam's funeral, with the caption, "Takes a man to catch a man?" beneath it. On the other side was a picture of Martina Kidd, smiling, and the words, "I believe in Imogen!"

"Imogen, I——" Benton started to say, but she shook her head once, hard.

"Don't talk to me. He read off our profile list to show he'd been in my room, then threatened my fish. The goddamned bastard——" She was dialing as she spoke and cut off when Bugsy answered. "Bugsy, it's me. It's about Rex, is he—— What? Oh. No, he didn't tell me." She slowly turned to look at Benton. He kept his eyes aimed straight out the window, hands at ten and two like a driving-school mannequin. He felt her gloved hand touch his arm and she said, "Thank you. For calling to find out if Rex was okay."

He shrugged. "It was the only thing I could think of to do."

Their eyes locked for a moment and he saw that the article was having the same effect on her that it'd had on him, so he looked back out the window, trying to give her some privacy. He heard her take three deep breaths and say into the phone, "Bugsy, are you still there? I need to find out how Leslie Lite got in touch with Loverboy. I want her tapes. And I want to interview her. On the phone, if necessary, but in person would be—" Silence. Then, "So no one knows where she is?" More silence. "Wait, do you still have her editor on the other line? Ask him if Leslie wears pink and if she smokes Camels."

The silence was longer this time. Benton watched her out of the corner of his eye so she wouldn't feel it. She slouched, phone pressed against her ear, forehead against the window, drawing dots with her fingertips. He said, "Do you think we can use the fact that he was in your room, saw that profile list, to find him?"

Imogen shook her head. "There are so many people in and out of there, delivery people, room service, it could be any of them. And he made it so obvious, telling Leslie to print exactly what he said, that he must be pretty confident we won't pick him out. I'll get someone to go over the security tapes, but I doubt we'll find—" She broke off, listened for a second, tucked her hair behind her ear, and said into the phone, "No, and I would look stupid in a cape. But I do know where she is. Hang on a second." Turning to Benton to say, "Do you have your plane here?"

He shook his head. "No, I flew commercially. I didn't like the weather reports. I can drive you to the airport if you want."

Imogen went back to her phone. "Bugsy, get me two seats on the next flight from Boston to Cleveland."

When she'd ended the call, Benton asked, "We're going back to Ohio?" Suave, not emphasizing the *we*, afraid to make any assumptions.

She didn't look at him but said, "Yes. We are."

And his heart started to beat faster. What an idiot. He said, "What do you think Leslie can tell us?"

"I'm not sure, but she's the only person we know who has communicated directly with Loverboy. Maybe there's something on the tape, or in her interview with Martina. Or maybe there's nothing." Her voice cracked at the end, and it was only then that Benton saw just what it was costing her to stay so composed. She put the heels of her hands over her eyes and took a ragged breath. "I can't stand this."

He shifted the car into first and said, "I know," wishing there was something he could do to help. Adding, "So if you're psychic, does that mean I'm not really predictable? That it's you?"

In his peripheral vision he caught half a smile from her, just a little one, but he knew he'd done his job. She said, "More driving, less talking, Mr. Arbor. I think a horse and buggy just passed us."

CHAPTER 42

Imogen knew the sign they pulled up next to said, *Luxury Adult Living,* but it was barely legible in the darkness because one of the bulbs had burned out and someone had painted the letter C over the first two letters of *adult.* Looking at the place, Imogen thought, Luxury Cult Living was more apt anyway.

White stuccoed buildings with sloping roofs and built-in balconies rose up on all sides around the parking lot. Partially closed vertical blinds let out strips of light from the windows of the second-story condo in front of them, making her think of prison bars. Or maybe it was just her memory of the last time she had been here.

"Is this the part where you tell me why we're here?" Benton asked, craning his neck to look over the wide dashboard of the rental car. They had arrived on the heels of the World Tupperware Congress, the woman behind the Hertz counter at the Cleveland airport told him apologetically, and the only car that was left was a forest green Lincoln Continental.

"They must call it that because it's as big as a continent," Imogen had said when Benton pulled up in front of her. They had engaged in a brief battle of wills over who would drive—her line: "You have two options, Mr. Arbor: move over or get in the back. I want to get there before dawn"; his line: "No way"—and she now addressed him where he sat on the passenger side of the green velour front seat.

"This is Dirk the Dick's secret hideaway," she said. "The prison warden." She realized her fingers were tapping on the steering wheel like she was nervous, which she wasn't. At all. She twined her fingers together.

Benton said, "I don't want to know how you know that, do I?"

"No."

"And you think Leslie Lite is in there?"

"I'm nearly positive."

"How do you know?"

"I saw a cigarette butt outside the prison the day we went there. It had pink lipstick on it, but it was the wrong time of day for any of the female employees to have had a break, so I remembered it."

"A cigarette butt. That's why we are here."

Imogen looked at him sharply, but he wasn't making fun of her. She tasted more amusement than doubt.

He said, "That would explain her access to Martina Kidd."

"Among other things."

"Okay. Let me see if I can guess what you have in mind. You go up alone and confront Dirk. Meantime I just sort of loiter around down here in case someone decides they need a little late-night air and accidentally leans too far out a window."

"Exactly." It was not a long drop from the window to the snow-covered grass outside. Imogen knew, she'd done it once herself.

Dirk opened the door only after she'd been knocking for about a minute. He was wearing what seemed to be an air force uniform complete with cap, but his shirt was undone and his shoes were missing. He looked like he'd had a few.

His first reaction was surprise, but it did not last long. "Imogen Page. Did seeing me the other day make you realize what a mistake you made when you ran off?"

"Oh yes," Imogen agreed. She found she was having trouble keeping a straight face. She had been furious ever since Benton had shown her the tabloid in Somerville, but somehow seeing Dirk standing there, wearing some kind of costume, drained her fury. She said, "Aren't you going to invite me in?"

Dirk looked over his shoulder and back at her. He shrugged. "Sure."

"That is hardly a warm welcome," Imogen chastised him.

"It's just that—"

She slithered past him and went straight to the bedroom. "It's awfully cold to have the window open, don't you think?" she said, shutting it.

Dirk was frowning. "Far be it from me to say you are unwelcome here, Imogen, but after our last encounter—"

"Yes, I noticed your warm welcome the other day, Dirk. Or should I just call you 'a prison official who prefers to remain anonymous'?"

Dirk's expression changed. "Why are you here?"

"I have a few questions for you. And your girlfriend."

"I'm not answering any of your questions. I don't want anything to do with you. Do you know how much trouble you caused me? How hard it was to explain the bruises you gave me last time to my wife?"

"You couldn't just tell her it was because you were trying to have nonconsensual intercourse with someone and she had to fight to get away?"

"Nonconsensual? You wanted it, Imogen. You had lunch with me. You came back here with me."

"I took your lunch invitation because I was too shaken up by my meeting with Martina Kidd to drive myself to the airport. Afterward you told me we were going someplace where we could not be overheard to discuss Martina's security."

"You're not an idiot. You knew what was going on. You didn't really want to *talk*."

"No, *you* didn't want to talk." But even the memory of that afternoon, of the moment when Dirk disappeared to "get some papers" only to reappear wearing nothing but a velvet smoking jacket, a Mad Hatter hat, and silk boxers with *Eat Me* embroidered on the crotch, the moment when he'd said, *I thought we could take a trip to Wonderland together*, and she had cracked up and learned all too clearly that he was dead serious, now seemed only farcical and maybe a little sad. And reminded Imogen yet again of what a fool she was around men. She said, "I'm sorry to hear you had such a hard time explaining your injuries from that day to your wife, because I'm afraid it will be much harder for you to explain why you've been fired."

"What do you mean?"

"Your disciplinary board hearing. Selling prisoner access in exchange for sex."

"You and I never had sex."

"I wasn't talking about me, Dirk."

"Then I don't know what you *are* talking about."

Imogen stooped to pick up a lizard-skin bag dyed hot pink. She took a billfold from inside it and read, " 'Leslie Lite, investigative reporter, Global Weekly News, Incorporated.' That is what I am talking about."

Squeals erupted from behind them and Benton appeared in the doorway of the bedroom. His arms were wrapped around a very pretty blonde with slightly smudged pink lipstick.

"That is my purse, those are my possessions, and what you are doing is illegal," the blonde announced as she struggled, and her objections carried extra weight because she was wearing a Wonder Woman costume. Right down to the small gold crown, matching bracelets, and red vinyl boots. It looked good on her, Imogen noticed, despite the pink lipstick. Dirk's tastes had definitely improved since he tried to get her into bed.

Whatever animosity Imogen had felt toward Leslie Lite vanished the moment she saw her outfit. Now all she wanted was her information.

"I apologize for bursting in on you and Dirk like this, Leslie," Imogen said sincerely. "But we need to talk to you. I can arrest you if I have to, but I would rather not."

"You can't arrest me. You don't have a warrant," Leslie said, more Wonder Woman by the second.

"I do, actually." Imogen pulled paper from her coat and waved it in front of Leslie and Dirk. "So you have a choice. You can voluntarily tell us everything and hand over the cassettes and notes you made from your interviews with Loverboy and Martina Kidd. Or we can handcuff you."

"Do you think the cuffs will fit over her bullet-deflecting bracelets?" Benton asked.

Leslie turned to glare at Benton, but he ignored her and said to Imogen, "What do you want me to do with her?"

"I think you can let her hands go. For now."

Leslie's first act of freedom was to stomp over to Dirk and kick him in the shin with her shiny red boots. "You did this," she hissed at him. "You told her where to find me. You've been talking about her all night. I should have known that you would call her and tell her about me to try to worm your way back into—"

Dirk was emphatically denying it, but it wasn't doing any good.

Imogen interrupted. "Leslie, work with us. You've already gotten your two exclusive interviews. It's the coup of the century, your career is made. Now help *us*. Help us stop this madman."

Despite using her most persuasive arguments, including the fact that Leslie wouldn't last a minute in jail in her Wonder Woman outfit, it still took Imogen ten minutes to get the woman to agree to hand over everything. Even then, Imogen was not convinced they had it all.

Back in their rental car, the heater hissing out a combination of hot air and boiling drops of water, Benton looked at her and said, "What would you have done if she asked to see the warrant, Special Agent Page?"

He sounded angry. Imogen tried to look innocent. "Shown it to her."

"I'm sure she would have found the Danny's Pizza take-out menu very compelling reading. Dammit, Imogen, the fashion police had more legal grounds to make an arrest in there tonight than we did."

"Why are you pissed at me? It worked, didn't it? They had— I'm sorry, did you say the fashion police?" She frowned, rewinding the conversation in her head. "You did. You said—"

And their eyes met and she cracked up and then neither of them could speak because they were both laughing too hard.

Leslie Lite pushed Dirk out of the way to look down at the parking lot as she tugged on her Lycra running pants. "Aren't they gone yet?" she said impatiently, touching up her pink lipstick. "I want to get out of here. What are they doing anyway? The windows are all steamed up."

"I can only guess," Dirk said, thinking of the spacious dimensions of a town car's backseat, and his voice held more envy than malice.

CHAPTER 43

An hour later, eyes glued on the different scars that covered the table in Benton's Motel 8 room, they were no longer laughing.

Norm Rocks!

Marco & Sonia
$$\begin{array}{r} 2\ good \\ +\ 2\ be \\ \hline 4\ gotten \end{array}$$

They had listened to Leslie Lite's interview with Loverboy first. Neither of them recognized the voice, which did not surprise them, because they expected a criminal as clever as Loverboy would disguise it. The tape had been accurately transcribed in the paper, apart from the mentions of "confused noises." The noises, on the tape, were not confused. They were screams.

Imogen and Benton did not look at each other afterward and did not speak.

Imogen set the screams apart in her mind—they might have been anything; he might have been making them up; they sounded so real; they were probably fake—and concentrated on what she tasted in Loverboy's voice. He was cocky and confident. And young-sounding. She felt she had definitely been on the right track when she thought he needed attention. He was playing, playing a game.

Playing house. With his pretend family.

But where the hell was his house?

Imogen looked at Benton. "I need to listen to the tape again. Do you want—"

Without a word, he got up and went through the door that connected to her room, shutting it behind him. She replayed the tape, listening closely not to the words or the screams, but to the noises behind them. She thought that once or twice she heard something that sounded like machinery. And two other times something that sounded like an airplane.

She was hanging up her phone when Benton came back in. She tried not to look at him too closely. The hair near his ears and around his hairline was wet and he smelled faintly of soap. "I used one of your towels," he said, and his voice sounded normal. "You can take one of mine instead if you want. Or use a piece of sandpaper. It's about the same consistency."

Imogen nodded, her finger tracing the graffiti on the table.

$$\begin{array}{r} 2\ good \\ +\ 2\ be \\ \hline 4\ gotten \end{array}$$

She knew what she had to do. It was wrong to just not talk about the screams, to pretend they weren't there, but she did not know how to start. She said, "Benton, I—"

He shook his head. "No. I don't want to. Who were you on the phone with?"

"Bugsy. A guy who manages a gas station called the FBI number in Vegas to report a taxi parked behind his place, been there a few days. We're following it up."

"Do you think it's what Loverboy used to transport Rosalind?"

"Who knows? A taxi would certainly blend in at a hotel. But it's a long shot, could be completely unrelated. In the meantime, I asked him to work something out so that we can borrow the Metro audio lab when we get back to analyze the tape. There are noises in the background that we could use to figure out where he was calling from."

"If that is Rosalind on the tape, we would know where he's holding her."

Imogen hated and was grateful for how controlled he was. "Exactly. They are also tracing the number Martina gave Leslie for Loverboy, but I'd be surprised if it led them anywhere more interesting than the bottom of a drainage ditch." She got up and paced around. "At Dirk's I felt sorry for her, but now, having heard that, I am furious. If she had come to us with that tape Sunday night when it was made, or better yet with the phone number whenever she first got it, we could have traced the call or at least followed it up and maybe found him. She willfully put a woman's life at greater risk and hampered an investigation. I asked Bugsy to look into how many ways we can prosecute her."

"Do you really hate journalists or are you just trying to displace your frustration and sense of impotence without screaming at me because you don't think I can handle it?"

She stopped pacing and stood looking out the window at nothing, rubbing her arms with her palms. Finally she said, "Both."

"You are right. I couldn't handle it. Thank you."

She did not face him, just nodded.

"Do you believe her story?" Benton asked her back. "About getting the messages from inside his bread? Why not just have her go there and talk to him?"

"What fun would that have been? Dirk Best's greatest problem is that he is a man with a lot of imagination trapped in a very boring job. All his affairs are a way to make believe he's got an exciting life. The thing with the bread fits perfectly." She moved to the table. "I guess we should listen to Leslie's interview with Martina Kidd. Her reluctance to hand it over makes me very curious."

"It makes me queasy," Benton said.

Imogen sat down and emptied the disintegrating paper cup of coffee in front of her. She made a face. "I think it's your coffee that is making you queasy. Did you ask them for the dregs of the pot?"

"Yesterday's pot. I like my coffee well done. It reminds me of college. When I worked at Robby T's, coffee wasn't any good unless it was at least a day old." He sighed, sat down next to her, and said, "Enough stalling. Are you ready?"

"Yes."

Benton slipped the tape into the boom box he had "rented" from the motel manager and hit PLAY.

CHAPTER 44

Leslie's voice crackled on the bad speakers, saying, "Interview with Martina Kidd, the Connoisseur, by Leslie Lite. Good morning, Professor Kidd."

"Good morning, my dear. Thank you for coming. Call me Mother."

"Thank you for taking the time to talk to me, Mother. You have heard the Loverboy tape. What do you think?"

"I think Loverboy is a very talented boy. He knows what he wants. And the FBI is going to have a hard time catching him."

"Is it true that you two have a relationship?"

"What a question. Pretty and smart. Truth is how you see it, dear."

"How do you know Loverboy?"

"Those who can't do, teach."

"Do you mean that you are telling him what to do?"

"And what not to do. With a bright boy like him, that is even more important. His self-control is so flimsy. Left to his own devices he'd—Well, I can't go into it."

"How do you and Loverboy communicate?"

"I'm afraid our communication is a trade secret, my dear. Is there a special gentleman in your life, Leslie? You can tell me."

"Professor Kidd, I would like to stay focused on Loverboy."

"Mother, dear. Of course. I'm sorry. It's just that I get so few visitors of your caliber. Charming young women. Have you met Imogen Page?"

"The FBI agent? No. But that is one of my questions. If you were conducting the investigation, what would you do?"

"I would do whatever Imogen Page is doing. She and I see eye to eye on most things."

"Would you give her any advice?"

"Yes, but she wouldn't take it." The sound of two chuckles. Benton looked over at Imogen and saw her roll her eyes.

Martina's voice went on. "I would try to find out how he transported Rosalind Carnow's body from the Bellagio. I think she will find that interesting."

"How do you know so much about Loverboy?"

"I know a great deal about a great many things, my dear. Your perfume, for example. It's Calvin Klein's Obsession, isn't it?"

"Yes. That is remarkable."

"It's nothing. You know, the knockoffs of that scent are particularly good. You could try them and save yourself some money."

"Thank you." A pause.

Imogen said, "Martina's working on her. I bet Leslie has to look at her notes to remember her next question."

And sure enough, Benton heard the sound of paper being flipped. Then Leslie said, "Are you the mastermind behind these crimes, Prof—Mother?"

"Oh, dear, what a phrase. Mastermind. Are you master of your mind, Leslie? Are any of us?"

"I guess—I don't know. Tell me, how did you get that number you gave me? The number to call Loverboy?"

"I wish I could, Leslie."

"It would mean a lot to me."

"I'm sorry."

"I understand."

"You understand?" Imogen said to the tape, sitting forward. Then bringing her hand to her mouth and saying, "Oh no. I have a feeling I know why Leslie didn't want us to hear this."

Benton asked, "Why?"

Imogen said, "Listen. It will be soon."

More back and forth chitchat, and then Martina said, "You have beautiful hair, Leslie."

There was a silence, in which the recorder picked up the sound of Leslie shifting in her chair.

Leslie said, "Thank you."

Martina's voice: "Have you ever considered wearing it up? It would be gorgeous pinned up in a chignon."

"No, I—" Leslie cleared her throat. "How do you know Lover-boy, Mother?"

"How does anyone know anyone? I propose a trade, Leslie of the Lovely Hair. I will answer your question if you would be kind enough to give a message to Imogen Page for me."

"I told you, I don't know Imogen Page."

"You will."

"What message?"

"Do you use Clairol color on your hair? Or L'Oréal?"

"I don't see how that can possibly—"

"Humor me, dear child. What harm can it possibly do? Tell me, do you color your hair at home? Over the sink? Or in the bathtub?"

A tight, nervous chuckle. "In the sink, usually."

"It must be messy."

"Well, not so bad once you are used to it."

Benton looked over at Imogen and saw she had her head in her hands. "What?" he started to ask, but she just pointed at the tape player.

Martina said, "What were we talking about?"

"You were asking me to take a message to Imogen Page."

"That is right." A pause. "I wonder if I dare."

"What?"

"Dare to ask you—could I touch your hair? Would you deign to humor a lonely old lady that much?"

"You want to touch my hair?"

"Oh, I knew it was too much to ask."

"No, of course."

"It's so beautiful."

Sound of chair being pushed back, papers and recorder being set down, high-heeled footsteps.

"Beautiful," Martina's voice murmured. "So soft."

There was a scream and the sound of something hitting metal hard. Next a crazy staccato like high heels vibrating on the ground, and the heavy thudding of the guard's footsteps. Over it all Martina laughing and Leslie's voice, "Help me! She's strangling me with my hair! Help—"

Imogen sighed, said, "Poor woman," and reached out to turn the recorder off.

Benton stopped her. "Wait. There's still a little more of the tape."

The sounds of confusion continued, with a clatter like someone stepped on the recorder. Then came Leslie's voice, shrill, shouting hysterically, "You are evil, Professor Kidd. You deserve to rot here forever."

And finally Martina's voice, clear atop the din. "You knew exactly what was going to happen, didn't you, Imogen, dear? Just like I knew that you would be listening to this right now. We are so much alike. I hope you enjoyed it as much as I did. Sweet dreams."

Benton reached out fast and clicked the tape recorder off. "I'm sorry. I had no idea that would be on there."

Imogen shook her head. "She had to get the last word. She would not have been happy otherwise."

The room got quiet except for the sound of traffic outside. Benton sat and stared at the greenish-brown carpet, feeling terrible. He said, "Is that why you told me not to get too close to her when we went there?"

"Yes. She's much stronger than she looks. And once she's fooled you into believing that she is harmless and sweet, anything is possible."

"What did you think of the tape?" he asked. "Apart from that stuff at the end. Do you think there is anything useful? Do you think it means she really is controlling Loverboy?"

"I'm not sure. She could be bluffing. It is only logical that Loverboy would have used a car or truck, something inconspicuous like a delivery van, to transport Rosalind from the Bellagio, so it could have been a guess on Martina's part. As always with her, it could be either. What do you think?"

"Do you really want my opinion?"

"Yes."

"When we first met you said Martina Kidd was a bridge player, right?"

Imogen nodded.

"I'd say she's trying a finesse. Trying to make us think she's in a stronger position than she is. I could be wrong, but I don't think she's got all the cards she pretends to be holding."

"You play bridge."

"Not anymore, if I can help it. I played too much in college. I know what you are thinking, rich boys sitting around in tweeds drinking Pimm's and playing cards. But that is not how it was. It was my job."

"You were a bridge pro?"

"More like a bridge gigolo."

He saw her nod slightly. She said, "J.D. told me he saw you cheat at cards once and deny it. Was it playing bridge?"

That guy really needs a life, Benton thought. Said, "What happened was, the woman I was playing with, my client, wanted to lose and told me to throw the game. She thought it would give the guy we were playing against enough confidence to ask her to marry him. You play how your clients tell you to. That's why you get paid."

"You cheated to lose?"

"It wasn't cheating, it was just playing badly. J.D. was playing with the other man and they won. He got a lot of money, probably. I can't believe he's still talking about it, it was years ago. He is never satisfied. I've never met anyone more competitive than him. I get the feeling he even sees this investigation as a competition, or he would, if you weren't involved."

"Yeah, I'm some big help."

"That's the least of what you've done."

She gave one of her half smiles and he was suddenly incredibly aware of the smell of her, citrus shampoo and wet wool and Chap Stick. Aware of wanting to pull her toward him and whisper in her ear that he was falling in love with her and listen to her laugh and try to talk him out of it. Aware of wanting very much to kiss her, thinking maybe it would be okay, maybe she felt it too—

She said, "I think it is time for me to go to sleep." She got up from the table and walked toward the door that connected their two rooms. "Good night, Benton."

Maybe not.

He said, "Good night. Breakfast at seven-thirty?"

"Sure."

She had her hand on the knobs when he blurted, "I just have to know. I did not want to ask you this but I can't get it out of my mind. The time you went to Dirk's house, did you wear the Wonder Wom—"

"No. It was not like that."

"Oh." Pause. "It would have suited you."

She rolled her eyes and shut the door behind her.

CHAPTER 45

J.D. drove home with one hand on the wheel and the window down, letting the cold night air clear his head a little. He'd been at one of his community service performances, all dressed up in his baseball jacket and glove, standing in front of a group of eleven-year-olds, telling them to be good, respect their parents, work hard, dreams could come true, like his to be a ballplayer, then a cop. Hating himself.

He heard Imogen's voice now, asking, "Why don't you wear a baseball cap?" and in his mind saw the bonfire he'd made with them when he quit. In the backyard of the big beige stucco house he and Marcie had, in the fire pit that the realtor had told them was "great fun, especially for families." He could picture Marcie coming out on the balcony above it, holding her white silk robe together, hearing her before seeing her because of the way her mules clicked on the "artisan-made" Spanish tile.

"What are you doing?" she'd shrieked.

"I quit!" He'd yelled it up to her, smiling, feeling great, his arms outstretched, beer in one hand. "Come down and have a cold one with me."

"You're insane. You've gone insane."

"No, baby, I've never felt better."

When he came out of the bedroom the next day he'd found her

sitting on the couch, clutching a charred cap in her hands and crying, saying over and over again, "But you looked so cute in this."

And he'd realized—like an idiot, getting it only then—that what she loved wasn't him, it was being married to a ballplayer. Which was only fair, since, in all honesty, what he had fallen in love with about her were her breasts. He had been young and horny and stupid, but they were gorgeous, not huge but a mouthful, and seemed to know where they were going always. Made her look perky and purposeful even when she was pouting, which was almost all the time after he quit, lying on the couch and flipping channels on the television and giving him her cheek when he tried to kiss her.

Finally one day he said, Honey, we need to talk, and she put the TV on mute as he tried to explain it to her, how it had always been his father's dream that he be a ballplayer. That he'd done it thinking it would make his father proud, even after he died. But it got so he hated the game, hated everything about it. Couldn't stand the commentators thinking they were so smart, dubbing him the "base robber" like his namesake, John Dillinger, America's most famous bank robber. His father's hero. What a thing to call your son.

He went into baseball to make his father proud, he explained. Quit and made himself feel better.

That was the idea, anyway. It turned out that quitting was just the opposite of playing, not something he was doing for himself, something he was not doing for his father. So he joined the police force. That, finally, was for him.

"Are you sure?" Marcie had asked when he told her.

"Are you sure?" Damn how that had rankled him. It bugged him more than it should have. Are you sure? That one question making the whole thing start to unravel. Piece by piece until the day Marcie said, "I'm leaving. And just so you know, my boobs are fake."

And he thought, that summed it all up perfectly, their relationship, even him becoming a cop. Young, stupid, and horny. Or at least idealistic.

The justice he was working for, the laws he wanted to uphold, all fake. Two years on the force, watching cases get thrown out on technicalities or guys who beat their kids go free because the kids were too scared to testify or murderers getting parole only to murder again, taught him that. Every night the police scanner full of stories that just proved it, that the cheaters, the ones with the least respect for the rules, understood them the best, and always won. Cheaters like Benton Arbor.

He was listening to the scanner now as he drove and almost hit a pole when the litany of loitering and pickpocket complaints was interrupted by a priority bulletin that a surveillance unit was needed at a gas station to watch an abandoned taxi. "Do not approach," the scanner said. "Covert surveillance only, by order of the FBI. Possible connection to the Loverboy case."

He hit the brakes, made a U-turn across four lanes of traffic, and stepped on the gas. If Imogen thought he was going to sit on something like the taxi and wait, she was a sick fuck herself, just like she'd written on her profile board. The car was there, filled with clues, information. Evidence.

And with her and Benton dicking around in Ohio, wasting time, he was the one in charge.

He pulled into the gas station and immediately spotted an unmarked patrol car across the street. Some covert surveillance. He crossed over and leaned in when one of the officers rolled down the window.

"You two can move on," he told them. "I've got it covered."

"You sure, sir?"

"Positive. You called for a criminalistics team yet?"

"No. The feds said—"

"Fuck the feds. You radio in for criminalistics, I'm going to go check out the car."

"Yes, sir." No one liked taking orders from the FBI.

It would take the crime-scene unit a minimum of ten, maximum of fifteen minutes to get there, J.D. calculated. He went over to the taxi, walked around it, then opened the door and slid behind the steering wheel. Pulling the sleeve of his jacket over his hand so he wouldn't leave fingerprints, he flipped down the visor—nothing— then leaned across and opened the glove compartment.

He let out a long breath when he saw what was in there and reached in. No one needed to know about that little item, he decided, grabbing it and slipping it into his pocket. Thinking, it was a very good thing he'd come here.

He was leaning against the outside of the car when the criminalistics van pulled up.

"You touch anything inside?" Ned Blight, the criminalist heading the team, asked him.

"It was unlocked so I thought I'd look around. Why, that a problem?" Making a joke. "No, Ned, I wasn't born yesterday."

"Okay, funny guy. Mind if I get my team in there?"

"All yours." Which meant he couldn't tell them about the body in the trunk either. That was okay. They'd find it themselves, kind of a special surprise. "I want your report on my desk first thing in the morning."

"Course you do. I wasn't born yesterday either," Ned said.

7 days left! Uh-oh!

Dirk Best was not in that morning, his secretary told them apologetically, but he had called in instructions that Imogen and Benton were to be taken to Martina Kidd right away.

And then taken the hell out of there as fast as possible. "Call me when they leave, Nancy," he'd said, before slamming the phone down.

Imogen didn't really care as long as he'd done what he promised, moved Martina out of her cell and into one of the interrogation rooms. They would have this interview sitting opposite each other across a table. When Benton overheard her requesting that Martina's hands and legs be manacled he'd asked, Is that really necessary? And she'd had to remind him about the tape they'd listened to the night before.

Imogen felt like her thoughts were coming to her from a long distance. The clanging of the gates behind her was not oppressive this time, but somehow sad, almost mournful. They had only a week left to catch Loverboy, and they were no closer than they had been. The papers that morning had made that only too clear.

Instead of going past the guard station this time they made the left turn and walked down a corridor that led to a solid white door. Next to the door was a one-way mirror through which she could see Martina.

Pulling into the parking lot Benton had asked, "Are we winging

it again?" and she'd smiled, despite everything. Now, standing outside the room, he said, "Do you want to go in alone?"

And she surprised herself by saying, "No."

As they walked in, Martina said brightly, "Did you know, Mr.
Arbor, that the average human tongue is only four inches long? Its
reach is much farther, though. After all, mine brought you today.
Please sit down, my dears. I'm sorry I can't offer you any refresh-
ments, but you know how this place is."

They sat down side by side facing Martina, who scrutinized them
both before saying, "It is such a pleasure to see you both. And you've
gone to some trouble, arranging this lovely room. You must want
something very important from me."

Imogen tried to look even wearier than she felt. She said, "I'm
not going to play games with you today, Professor Kidd. We are here
to learn how you and Loverboy are communicating."

"In exchange for?"

Imogen set three magazines on the table and indicated the far-
thest one with her index finger. "This came Federal Express from
Rome. It's next month's."

Martina reached toward it, but it was just out of the range of
her manacled hands. She gave Imogen a fast, mean look, then leaned
back in her seat and said, "If we're playing show-and-tell, what about
that lovely article in the paper this morning? Curtis showed it to
me. What was the headline? 'Loverboy's Latest.' About that nice taxi
driver they found dead in Las Vegas."

Imogen tasted lime. Chlorine. Everything bad.

Follow your plan, she told herself. Still, in her mind she could
see some of the photos that had accompanied the article in that
morning's national papers. Two in particular: the first, a picture of
an ordinary-looking man in his forties, smiling, standing by a BBQ
and wearing an apron that said, *Will Work for Beer (and Hugs);* the second, the empty trunk of his taxicab where his body had been found.

She'd gotten the call from J.D. before she saw the article, the phone waking her at 6:15. She couldn't believe what he was telling her. Even now it pissed her off all over again.

"Why the hell did you move the car?" she had asked. "Why not leave it where it was in case he came back for it and use it to trap him?"

"I had a choice," J.D. said in his unreadable, flat voice. "I could sit on the car and wait for him. Or I could have it brought in and gone over inch by inch. The guy who works at the gas station said it had been parked in the same place for three days. He only called it in after he read the tabloid story. I decided our man wasn't coming back for it and we needed the evidence."

"You don't know he wasn't coming back. If you had left it, we could have had him *and* the car."

"Or we could have had nothing until it was too late. I made a judgment call. I decided the sooner we could get a forensics team into the car the better, and there is nothing we can do about it now."

"You run it for prints? Blood?"

"That never would have occurred to me. Thank you so much for the suggestion." His voice still flat, but he was being sarcastic.

And she deserved it. She was being dumb, letting her anger get in the way of her brain. She had sat with the receiver pressed to her ear, her forehead against her hand in the dark room. What J.D. had done was not wrong, she knew. It was simply not how she would have handled things. But that did not matter anymore. She asked, "Have you found any useful evidence? Anything to link the cab conclusively to our case?"

"I'm not sure. There was a rectangular card clipped to the notepad next to the steering wheel that read, 'Don't like my driving? Call 1-800-Jerkoff.' Does that sound familiar to you? It reminded me of something you said the first day you arrived."

And she'd felt dumber and more angry. Furious. And had to push all of that—the fact that the cabdriver who had picked her up at the airport was the killer, the fact that he had likely been targeting her, the fact that her investigation was not really hers to run—from her mind. She was here to listen to Martina.

Who was saying, "Did you read about that poor soul? He drove that cab seven days a week to keep his wife in dialysis treatments and his children in tennis shoes. A good man. A great man. A great American. And now he is dead." Martina shook her head. "Who killed him? You did, Imogen. If it weren't for you, he would still be alive."

"If it weren't for those meddling kids and that damn dog," Imogen heard Benton mutter next her, a quote from *Scooby-Doo*, and almost laughed. It stole some of the drama from Martina's pronouncements, even if they were still partly true.

But she didn't laugh and she didn't say anything.

Martina waited for a response and, getting none, said, "What about Marielle Wycliffe? You killed her. You're responsible for both deaths, you know, Imogen. And all the others. Because you could have stopped them. Every day that passes without you finding Loverboy is a testament to your stupidity, and every person who dies because of it is as much your victim as his."

Imogen didn't say anything.

"Are you giving me the silent treatment, dear? Have you really become that childish?"

Imogen kept her mouth closed.

"You are wasting your time, Imogen. And mine. I'm not going to tell you anything else. I've already given you plenty to find Loverboy. It's an old story, my dear, and only your blindness keeps you from seeing it."

They sat in silence for a few moments until Martina brought her hands down hard on the top of the table. "I want to go back to my cell."

No one moved or spoke.

Martina said, "You think the pleasure of your company during this unauthorized visit means you can just demand answers from me and then stare? In exchange for a few paltry magazines?"

"We have authorization," Benton started to say, but stopped when Imogen shook her head slowly.

She pushed her hair behind her ear and said to him, "Professor Kidd doesn't mean from the warden. She means authorized by Loverboy."

Martina smiled. "She speaks! Very good. Yes, you were his little gift to me last time, but this time I made you come all on my own. Tell me, Imogen, have you figured out what the R in Loverboy stands for yet?"

Imogen just looked at Martina.

"You haven't, have you? It's nearly the centerpiece of the word."

There was a tap on the door and Curtis came in. He made a sign to Imogen, who pushed her chair away from the table. Benton did the same.

Martina looked up at them, genuinely confused. "That is all?" She clicked her tongue. "Where has civility gone? I suppose after all of this, you won't even leave those magazines because I haven't done what you wanted. Such a selfish generation, yours."

Imogen said, "Actually, you can have them, Professor Kidd."

Martina tilted her head to one side. "Why?"

Imogen smiled. "When I was here last time you told me I was asking all the wrong questions. This time you are."

"Aren't we coy! What do you mean, dear?"

Imogen ignored her and said to Curtis, "All done?"

"Yes, ma'am."

Martina said, "What games are you playing with Mother, you naughty children? Come back here and tell me."

At the door Imogen stopped. "You shouldn't have been asking what I brought you, Professor Kidd. You should have asked what I can take away. Good-bye."

CHAPTER 47

The boxes of papers they had confiscated from Martina Kidd's cell sat in front of the empty seat between them on the flight back to Vegas, and Imogen sat as far from them—and Benton—as possible.

The papers held their only chance of learning how Martina had been communicating with their killer, and what he had said. When Imogen had finally managed to get Dirk on the phone, at four that afternoon, she had agreed not to mention anything to the disciplinary committee if he would honestly tell her how Martina was talking to Loverboy. Dirk had sworn up and down that he had nothing to do with it, and she believed him. There had been cowardice in his voice.

That meant that they were in touch more subtly, and the only way to figure out how was to go through Martina's papers minutely. There were several notes from journalists requesting interviews, which they would follow up, and there were quite a few letters from Elgin, Imogen's boss. But according to the postal log, all the letters were there and accounted for and none of them seemed incriminating.

Which left as possibilities only the contents of the cardboard box with the fake wood graining below her. The box contained some clippings from different fashion magazines, all over a year old, every American Association of Bridge Players newsletter printed since Martina's imprisonment, and two books of collected *New York Times* crossword puzzles.

"Games," Imogen said. "More damn games."

Benton looked at her. "What?"

"Sorry, I was thinking out loud. Or not thinking."

Benton nodded. "I didn't want to interrupt you before, you seemed deep in thought but I was wondering. You learned something during the interview, didn't you?"

"What makes you say that?"

"You have a tell just like Martina does."

She frowned at him. "I do not."

"Yes, you do. You push your hair behind your ear when you are excited."

"I do?" She caught herself doing it. "I guess I did get something, but not much. Just confirmation of what I suspected, that Loverboy sent us to see Martina that first time we went. And that it wasn't just to show his control. That he did it because Martina asked."

"Why?"

"Payback is my best guess. But I don't know for what. Hopefully something in one of those boxes will help."

"She told Leslie Lite that there was nothing in her papers."

"She also told Leslie that she was a charming girl."

Benton glanced at the scratches on his hands Leslie had inflicted the night before. "Good point."

Imogen looked at his tray table, which was covered with papers. "What are you doing?"

"Bridge problems. I'm not as brave as you are."

"Brave?"

"I didn't want to think. But now I'm stuck. I can't find the next newsletter to check the solution to the problem I'm working on."

"Do you think it's missing? On purpose?"

"It could be."

"Is it the only one?"

"So far."

Imogen got it then. That he had not really just been doing bridge problems, that he was sifting through the evidence, and she felt completely exhausted. She did not want to believe that a missing bridge newsletter had anything to do with the case. Not another quirky clue, not another game. She sighed and reached for the air phone.

"I'll have Bugsy request a copy from their headquarters," she said.

"I hope they get it soon. I hate not knowing if I am right."

"You're Benton Arbor. I thought you always knew you were right."

Benton chuckled. "Do you really think I am that pompous?"

"No," Imogen admitted. "Not anymore."

"Progress," Benton declared, rubbing his hands together. "Two champagnes please, stewardess."

When it came, they toasted to progress.

Neither of them mentioned it, but it was lousy champagne.

CHAPTER 48

Only six days left, J.D. kept repeating to himself as he drove the long way to his place. As of the next morning, there would be only six more days.

He was sitting at Rachel's desk, using her computer, when she came over to tell him that Imogen had called from the plane saying she and Benton were going to come by there when they landed to look at the files on the taxi. Was there anything he wanted her to hold on to? And he'd said no, show them everything. Not telling her he'd already taken away anything he didn't want them to see.

Then he'd grabbed his keys and gotten the hell out of there.

He was not in the mood to see either of them yet, go through explaining his behavior again, talk about the car. He was so damn tired of having to justify himself to everyone, make excuses. Juggle what was going on inside him with what was going on around him.

And then there was Wrightly Waring, hounding him on the phone, asking for progress reports, driving him crazy with his questions. He didn't deserve Rosalind.

Heading across town on Flamingo he remembered when Rosalind had called him to tell him about Wrightly. He'd said, "Hold on," gone and put his hand through the wall, and come back. "What were you saying?"

She explained that Wrightly wouldn't upset Benton, that she could have a normal, calm life with him. "That's all I want, J.D."

"I can give you that."

"No, you can't. You're not peaceful and I'm not peaceful with you."

"I thought you liked that."

"I do. I did. I loved it. But I can't live that way."

He'd squeezed his eyes closed, remembering: Santa Barbara, that white cottage at the beach . . .

It was a friend's house right on the sand, the place deserted because it was winter, just the two of them. They'd had a week together, one-on-one, the best seven days of his life. He'd felt terrific, and so in love. She'd felt it too. Only she was nervous. Nervous that Benton would be upset.

Him asking, "Who the hell cares what Benton thinks? If you love me, who cares?"

She said, "I love him too. And he's done so much for me. For Jason. I can't."

Benton "Fuck You" Arbor.

Martha's Vineyard, sneaking into Cal and Julia's house in the fall . . .

Lying on their king-size bed under the down comforter, listening to rain outside. She said, "The problem with you and Benton is that you are too much alike."

"Never say that," he told her. Joking. Running his finger along the side of her ear, her head on his chest listening to his heartbeat, his hand tracing the length of her spine. He'd never been happier.

"Really. You both have to be the boss. And two bosses never get along."

"I don't want to boss you around," he said. "I just want to love you. You can boss me around."

"I'm not talking about with me, I'm talking about with the world. You two are almost primitive, staking a claim, marking territory, and protecting it fiercely."

"If you're talking about your heart, you're right. I would do anything to protect that. I want to be with you forever."

And she'd looked at him with that sad expression on her face and put her fingers on his lips and said, "Let's just enjoy what we have right now."

The inn in Arlington, Virginia, just around the corner from her house . . .

Making love, holding each other like they couldn't let go, eyes open, desperate. And he'd said to her, "Does Benton make you feel this good?" and felt her freeze. "What? I'm just asking."

She pulled away and sat up on one elbow. "J.D., this isn't healthy. For either of us. It's getting so that this isn't about me or about us, it's about him."

"That's what it's always been about. You trying to get revenge on him for not loving you enough. Don't think I don't know it." Lashing out on purpose to hurt her.

He still remembered the expression on her face. And the way he wanted to get on his knees and apologize. Cry and beg her forgiveness. Tell her he didn't know what had come over him, that he was so consumed with jealousy and wanting her and love.

But he couldn't. He just heard his father's voice in his head, his dad saying, "You'll never change, you'll always be a disappointment."

And Marcie saying, "Count on you to always do the wrong thing. Throw everything good away."

So he sat there and watched Rosalind pack, blaming Benton Arbor for it. All of it. Watched her walk out of his life like Marcie and his mother and every other woman. Choose someone else. Some other man.

And he'd wished more than anything that he could do it all over. From the beginning. Learn to be better. Learn to be the boy, the man they chose. The man they loved and wanted to stay with. The man Rosalind wanted to stay with.

Six more days. He hoped he could hold it together that long.

CHAPTER 49

Imogen and Benton went straight from the airport to the police station, where they were shown into a beige conference room and handed the preliminary reports from the taxicab that Loverboy had used. There were no prints inside or outside of the car, no hairs, no empty cups with DNA on them, no clues at all that could help them identify the killer. No evidence.

At least there was no blood in the cab either.

"Come on, I'll give you a ride back to the hotel," Benton offered at 11:30, but Imogen refused.

She pointed to the files scattered over the table. "I want to go over these one more time."

"You've already been over them five times." Benton's tone was exasperated. "What are you looking for?"

"I don't know. But there is something here. Something I'm missing."

"I can't tell if you are determined to find something so that impounding the taxi won't have been a waste, or if you are determined not to so you can blame J.D. for making a mistake."

"We shouldn't have gone to Ohio. It took too long and gave us too little."

"I disagree, and besides, we couldn't have known that without going."

"Maybe. Look, I don't have time to talk about this right now."

Benton leaned over the table toward her. "Why are you punishing yourself?"

"I'm not."

"Yes, you are. You cannot hold yourself responsible for everything that happens."

"This is my case. I *am* responsible." She took a deep breath, stifled a yawn, and said, "I am not asking you to stay here, Mr. Arbor. In fact, I would prefer it if you got out of my way and let me do my job. I'm tired of having you around watching me all the time. I feel like I'm being baby-sat." Some part of her knew she was lashing out at him, but she couldn't stop herself.

Benton shook his head, said, "Fine," and left the conference room. He did not ask her if she wanted to have breakfast with him at 7:30 the next morning, she noticed. Good. That phase of their relationship was over. She'd known whatever feelings he thought he had for her would disappear.

She spread the crime-scene photos of the cab's interior over the table and looked them over once again. Something in the cab was different from when she'd ridden in it. The taste it evoked was less lemony and had an undertone of pepper. Something had changed, but she could not figure out what. She'd had a tune going through her head for the past hour that she could almost but not quite identify. It hovered just outside her reach, on the tip of her tongue. Just like the answer to the collage. Just like the killer whose taxi she had ridden in. She almost but not quite knew everything, but the gulf between the two might as well have been a boiling sea of magma with the success she was having bridging it.

An hour later, as she was sitting there, letting the images blur together in her head, there was a knock on the door and J.D.'s assistant Rachel came in.

She tossed another manila folder on the table, saying, "This just came from the forensics lab. They said they missed it the first time through."

Imogen flipped it open. There was a photo of the latch of the glove compartment enlarged five times. In the corner, barely visible, was a tiny royal blue fiber. The report attached to the photo said it was a polyester blend. Another thread. She said, "What was the taxi driver wearing when you found his body?"

"Green shirt," Rachel said. "So this fiber could have come from something Loverboy was wearing."

"Or it could have been there for months."

Rachel nodded. "We'll have someone go to the cabdriver's house tomorrow and look over his things. Unless his wife has already gotten rid of them."

So many people die on your watch, Imogen heard Martina saying, and wanted to bang her head on the table, make it stop.

Rachel yawned. "I'm going to take off to try to get some sleep. Can I give you a ride home? I'm heading in that direction."

Home, Imogen thought. Meaning the Bellagio. That was some home. She felt like leaving now would be giving up, betraying Rosalind, but she was also exhausted. And she had a strange need to see Rex, make sure he was okay. She looked around the Metro interrogation room, looked at the same things she had been looking at for hours, and yawned herself. She nodded at Rachel. "That would be great. I'd love a ride home."

As they drove toward the hotel Imogen looked out at the lights and asked herself which ones belonged to Loverboy. What he was doing to Rosalind.

And where she'd recently seen something royal blue.

CHAPTER **50**

He was standing somewhere near her, behind her, when Rosalind woke up in the dark, bound to the bed. She was disoriented from the sedatives he had been giving her and had no idea how long she had been asleep. From the sick emptiness in her stomach she thought it might have been a long time. She was wide-awake now.

He was not moving, but she could smell him. Sense him. Feel his eyes on her.

"Mommy?" he said in a little voice. Rosalind went completely cold. "Mommy, are you awake?"

Rosalind lay still. This was new, but she should have seen it all along, she realized. Should have understood what the ear piercing and the hair in curlers and the lipstick slathered on her mouth meant. He was making her into his mother.

It was new and it was horrible. Because she knew exactly how her captor felt about his mother. Inside the blue velour housecoat he'd dressed her in, her body broke into a cold sweat.

"Mommy, I know you are awake," he said. His voice was tighter now, the way it got before he punished her.

"I am," Rosalind tried to say through the tape over her mouth. It came out like a croak.

"I had a bad dream, Mommy."

I had a bad dream, Mommy. How many times had she had this

dialogue with Jason? *Mommy, I had a bad dream. Mommy, I'm scared. Mommy, there's a monster under the bed. Mommy—*

No! Rosalind's mind screamed as she remembered how it ended, what came next. *No, no, not—*

"Mommy, can I sleep in bed with you?" Loverboy said.

Rosalind wanted to cry, but her eyes were so dry nothing came out. Until now there had been no hint of anything sexual, but she had been dreading this. The idea of having his hands on her like that, his—

No, she tried to cry out. But of course, she couldn't say anything.

He climbed next to her in the small double bed and slid under the covers. Rosalind tensed every muscle in her body, waiting. She would do whatever she could to prevent this, she swore. It would not matter what punishment she got.

A minute passed.

Five minutes.

Nothing happened.

Ten minutes.

She rolled her head over as far as she could. For the first time she let herself really look at him. She was not sure if what she was seeing was better or worse than she had imagined.

His beard had begun to grow in and he still wore his button-down shirt. He looked like a grown-up. But he was clutching a blanket against his closed eyes. He was humming a nursery tune Rosalind knew too well.

And he was sucking his thumb.

Mommy, Mommy, there's a monster in my bed! Rosalind wanted to yell. But she couldn't.

It didn't matter anyway, she realized. No one ever believed you when you said that. And there was no one to hear her scream.

Please, she thought, *please just kill me now.*

6 days left!

Imogen woke before it was light out with the taste of chalk in her mouth and the image of a taxi driver's fingers reaching out to her. Brushing her palm. Not wearing gloves.

"Hold on to that," he said. "You'll want it later."

It took her a moment to realize what she was remembering. When she did, her throat went dry. She spilled the contents of her wallet over the comforter on her bed and gently sifted through them until she found it. The taxi receipt from the morning of her arrival.

Holding it by the corner, she dialed Bugsy. The racing of her heart almost drowned out the unidentified tune that was still, inexplicably, running through her head.

Bugsy's voice on the other end of the line was groggy. "Good morning, boss. Sleep much? I mean, well?"

She said, "Great. Listen, how soon can you be up here with some crystal iodine and a camera?"

"Ten minutes. Maybe sooner if I don't brush my hair."

"Don't brush your hair," Imogen ordered, and hung up.

CHAPTER 52

Her captor showed only a trace of the previous night's insecurity when Rosalind woke that morning. She did not know what kind of pills he was giving her, but they left her dazed. By the time she was fully awake, he had already taped her hands behind her and her feet together and moved her to the recliner. Now he was standing in front of her holding a steaming mug that smelled like hot chocolate, like home at Christmastime with Jason.

Don't think about that, she ordered herself.

"If I take the tape off your mouth, will you scream at me for sucking my thumb?" he asked, keeping the mug in front of her.

That was the beginning of Rosalind's understanding. He had not been keeping her mouth covered so she couldn't shout for help, she realized in that moment, but so she couldn't shout at *him*. He was afraid of being disciplined and scolded. He was playing at being a naughty boy and he wanted her to be nice to him.

To be maternal.

"Promise not to yell?" he asked.

She nodded.

He took the tape off, gently this time, and fed her the hot chocolate in small gulps. Lumps of powder still floated on the surface and it was too watery, but it felt like magic on her throat. As she drank, she studied him. He looked different. There were dark circles under his eyes and his hands were unsteady. She decided to take a chance. Pretend he is Jason, she told herself. Pretend he is your son and you love him.

"Has someone been mean to you?" she asked. His hands trembled so much he nearly dropped the mug in her lap.

"How did you know?"

"You look worried."

He stared at her. "Are you trying to trick me?"

"No, I need you."

"To take care of you. You sure do."

"I sure do," Rosalind agreed, remembering how repeating Jason's words used to work to calm him down when he was younger and having a tantrum. "So I would not want to trick you."

"You'd better not," he cautioned. "That wouldn't be nice. My other mother tricked me."

"What do you mean?"

"She tricked me and said she liked me and she took my car away."

Rosalind's eyes searched his face. Could he really be this demented? Did he believe what he was saying? And if he did, why didn't anyone else notice how sick he was?

"What kind of car was it?" she asked.

"Don't you remember? You rode in it with me. It was a taxi. It was NICE. And Mother was jealous. So she told the newslady about it and it had to go to the police before I was ready. And now I've got to find a new set of wheels." He looked away from her and his face and voice changed. Became more grown-up and more menacing. "She betrayed me. It was a silly thing to do. But I'll show her. She'll be sorry when she sees what I'm going to do to Imog—what I'm going to do."

Rosalind wanted to bring back the safer personality. Pretend you love him, she reminded herself. "That is good hot chocolate. Thank you. Do you think I could have some toast too? I'm hungry."

The boyish expression returned. "Not toast. Sundaes! We're having sundaes for breakfast!" He shook a finger at her. "I know that's not what you are supposed to have for breakfast, but remember you said you wouldn't yell at me."

"Of course not," Rosalind assured him, swallowing down nausea. "You can have sundaes for breakfast on a special occasion."

He looked at her with wary surprise at first, then started to giggle. He kept it up as he fed her three huge scoops of vanilla ice cream, five spoonfuls of Cool Whip. She gagged on every other bite and that made him laugh more.

"I'm taking good care of you, aren't I?" he asked. She smiled through the taste of sweet plastic in her mouth. "Only the best for you, Ros. See, this is even *real* Cool Whip dessert topping, not the fake kind. Nothing fake here. Oh wait, but I forgot——" He ran away and came back with a squirt bottle of Sam Strawberry's Special Syrup. "Open up!" he told her and, pulling her head back by the hair until her lips opened, poured a long shot of it into her mouth.

That was more than her too-long-empty stomach could take. She did her best but she could not keep from retching. Instinct took over and she struggled to turn her head away, sending the strawberry syrup spilling across the front of her housecoat, into her lap.

He went completely still. All but the hand holding the pink plastic bottle of syrup upside down. Strong adult fingers closed tightly around that, and the rest of the thick red sauce oozed out to puddle on the floor at Rosalind's feet. When the bottle was empty, he let it drop. It fell with a dull splatter into the mess.

"I worked hard to get that food for you," he said. His voice was eerily calm. "It was your fault if you got sick." The calmness began to break apart. "Your ate too fast. You were bad. You shouldn't have done that."

Rosalind nodded, hoping to appease him. "You are right. I ate too fast. I should not have done that."

"Look at this mess. You'll have to clean it up," he told her. "You have only yourself to blame."

"I know. It was my fault."

He was not listening. She was not even sure he was seeing her as he sneered right into her face and said, his voice harsh, angry, "You disgust me. You're a disgusting little shit."

"That's not true." She backed as far into the recliner as she could, but he leaned in closer.

"You're a disgrace to the family. Look at yourself." He rubbed the syrup from his hand on the sleeve of her housecoat obsessively, as if he were trying to clean off blood. "Look at you. Disgusting. A fucking pig. You eat like a pig and now you look like a pig. Covered in filth," he snarled. "Oink, oink, oink, piggy wiggy. Who the hell do you think you are? Are you too good for my food?"

His personality had shifted, Rosalind understood. He was no longer the playful boy; now he was the punishing parent. Rosalind took a deep breath. *Pretend he is your son. Reclaim the parental role.* "Calm down, love," she said. "It's all right. Calm down."

"Calm down?" He jumped into the puddle of strawberry syrup, splattering both of them with it. "Calm down? You want me to calm down." Now he was leaning over her, his hands gripping her shoulders. "You fucking ruined my life, you ungrateful little shit. I hate you. I. Hate. You." His teeth gnashed in front of her nose.

Rosalind forced herself not to flinch. Not to show any sign of the revulsion she felt. She said, "I don't hate you."

"Yes, you do," he screamed in her face. "Yes, you fucking do. You are faking. You want to get away from me. You want to leave me. Everyone does."

Rosalind did not move. "That is not true."

He wavered, confused for a moment, hovering between personalities. He shouted, "You fucking ruined my life, you ungrateful little shit."

Rosalind's voice was easy, unhurried. "You already said that, love. It is not true. I am grateful to you."

"Shut up. You are lying. Look at me when I talk to you."

"I'm not lying. I need you. If you were not here, I would have starved to death." Please, Rosalind prayed, please let it work. "I need you," she repeated.

His face was so close to hers that his eyes merged into one great opening that stared, unblinking. She felt like she was being studied by some monstrous Cyclops for signs of lies, of disgust. He let go of her shoulders and pulled slightly away and was the man again. The man-boy-monster.

"I'll slap you silly if you're lying," he said, but the threat had been drained out of him. "I mean it."

"I know," Rosalind assured him. Pushing all her hatred for him into the smallest corner of her mind, she forced herself to smile.

He took two steps backward, away from her fast, as if she had shouted at him. From that safe distance he stared at her, his head cocked to one side. His face was a mask of confusion.

He rubbed his left arm with his right hand, smearing red syrup all over his shirt, but not really noticing. A muscle twitched in his neck. After a minute had passed, he opened his mouth. In a plaintive voice, small, young, he said, "What do you call a boat with your whole family on it?"

Damned, Rosalind thought. She kept smiling. "I don't know."

"The Kin Ship! Get it? The kinship?" He took a step toward her. "That's funny, huh, Ros?"

"Yes."

"I learned it from a Dixie cup. A real one, not a fake one. That's how you can tell, you know. Fake ones don't have riddles."

Pixie cups, Jason called them. "Mom, why do we always have to have the pixie cups with the flowers on them?" he'd asked. "Why can't we have the ones with the jokes? Those are cool."

Rosalind had wondered where Jason had gotten that idea.

"Now it's your turn, Ros. You tell me a joke."

The relief Rosalind had been feeling slipped away. She had always been lousy at remembering jokes. He knew that. She groped around desperately in her well of memories but all she came up with was Jason—the first time Jason's eyes focused on hers, the time he came home from school with the class lizard, his concern that she would not know how to take care of herself when he went away to camp at the age of ten, the time they went sailing last summer at the house in Nantucket, when they made cookies for—

"Well, Ros? Tell me a joke." He was standing, watching her expectantly. His tone contained the first blush of menace.

Come on, Rosalind, she admonished herself. *Come on, come*— "Why did the cookie go to the psychiatrist?" she blurted.

He made the exaggerated shrug of a ten-year-old aping adult mannerisms. "Why?"

Rosalind hesitated, then said, with a smile she hoped looked genuine, "Because he was only half-baked."

"Only half-baked," he repeated. "Only half-baked! That's funny, Ros. That's a good joke!" He laughed and Rosalind exhaled out her tension. It was the only joke she could think of, but once she'd begun she had realized that he might take the punch line the wrong way. But he did not seem to. He was just looking at her and chuckling to himself and—

He sprang at her and pulled the knife from his pocket in a single motion. He was not laughing as he pressed the blade against her throat. His lips whispered in her ear, "I'm not crazy, you know, Rosalind. I'm not half-baked. I'm no freak."

Rosalind heard his breathing, deep and fast and ragged, loud in her head. "I know," she said, trying to keep her voice light. The knife did not move from her throat. "Of course I know that. I mean, would I have told that joke if I thought you were?"

His breathing slowed but was still uneven. "I guess not. No." He kept the knife at her throat, but moved so he was kneeling in front of her. His breath covered her face. "You really do need me? Don't lie."

"I really do." Rosalind said. She put as much feeling into it as she could.

"The others, I just wanted them to like me, you know. I just wanted to take care of them, but they wouldn't let me. They made me feel silly. You will let me take care of you, though, won't you?"

The knife poked a little harder. His eyes were watching her, reading every sign of possible betrayal. Almost aching for a sign.

Rosalind kept her expression neutral. "Yes, I will let you."

The knife slashed downward, slicing the duct tape holding her feet bound together. For the first time since he had taken her captive, she could move her legs. She looked down at them, stunned, then up at him.

The knife was gone, back in his pocket. Instead of the blade she was looking at the naughty boy again. He smiled at her. "I've got to go out for a little while. Got some errands to do. Grown-up errands. But don't break anything and don't go anywhere while I'm gone, 'k?"

"Okay," Rosalind said.

"I mean it. I'm trusting you."

"Okay," she said again, already wondering what she was going to use to pick the lock on the door.

As if reading her mind he said, "I'm not locking the door or anything, because I trust you. But you should know that there are motion detectors all around and if you open the door even an itsy bit, four nail guns will shoot at you."

He had slipped on his jacket as he was talking, and with the strawberry stain on his shirt covered he now stood in front of her looking like a grown-up again. A grown man. A normal grown man. It took Rosalind a moment to synchronize what she was seeing and what she was hearing.

"Nail guns?" she finally asked.

"Oh, don't worry. You won't die right away. At first, until you lose enough blood, you will just be in a lot of pain. It will ring my cell phone, so I'll know you need me, but I might not get back in time to save you. Then again, I might. Anyway, I know you're not going to try to leave because you promised. And you don't want to know the punishment for people who break their promises, do you?"

Rosalind shook her head.

"I didn't think so. Well, 'bye for now!"

The sound of the door shutting behind him, shutting and not locking, was torment worse than any physical pain he could inflict, and Rosalind thought he knew it. For the first half hour her head replayed the click of the door for her over and over again, the sound of it shutting followed by silence. The silence of no bolt being slid home, no lock being engaged, click-silence that was invitation and damnation at once. She knelt in front of the knob as if it were a sacred object and rested her head against it and wept.

She could open it right now. She could be free right now. Free of the torment. Free of the pain. She could open the door and walk out to her death—

I might not get back in time to save you. Then again, I might.

—or worse.

CHAPTER 53

Walking around the Grand Canal Shoppes at the Venetian, he didn't feel like that other man; he felt like Loverboy. Earlier he'd try to only let himself go with Rosalind, and he'd come to a place like this and hardly notice anything. But now, only six days to go, he could feel himself being Loverboy, being a little silly, more of the time. When he felt silly it was like everything was totally in focus. Like the way he was noticing how pretty all the Shoppes were. He really liked it here. Everyone was so happy. And the double P in *Shoppes* made him think of his you-know-what. A teenage girl with red hair halfway down her back wearing a denim miniskirt and tight white T-shirt that let her nipples show passed him by, and he could tell she was thinking about his pee-pee too.

But he was not at the Shoppes for that. He was shopping for a present for Rosalind. For being so NICE that morning.

He had walked by Carlton's Cutlery in the Grand Canal Shoppes a lot of times before, but he'd never gone in. It wasn't good to be too noticeable. He was smart like that. He knew that the population of Vegas was so mobile that if you went somewhere even just two times you were practically a regular and people remembered you. This was his first trip inside the shop, and boy, *was* it a trip. Looking around at the rows and rows of knives and other sharp objects, he thought they should change the name to Carlton's Cut-ery.

"You got something to cut, we've got something for you to cut it with, that's our motto," the jovial man behind the glass display case told him.

Loverboy tried a smile but he could not meet the man's eyes. He could tell that the man wanted him to look at him, to pay attention to him, but he didn't want to. No way. The man's nose was red and the veins on his cheeks showed pink around his pores. A drunk, Loverboy thought with disgust. He could even smell it. Probably been taking a walk with Johnnie already that morning, just like his father.

Just like his father when he wanted to yell at him, to tell him he was——

Loverboy's eyes snapped up to the salesman's face and he demanded, "What? Did you say something?"

The man just stood there, smiling. He shook his head. "No, sir. Not a word. Are you browsing or is there something in particular you are looking for?"

Loverboy shook his head and slid his eyes back to the knives in the glass display case between them. The man hadn't said anything to him, he assured himself as he stared at the cold blades. Looking at them made him feel calm. There were dozens of them in every shape and length and breadth. The recessed lighting of the store made the metal shine with exciting menace. He felt in control again.

A whole store filled with things for cutting! Oh boy, that was good. And if he wasn't supposed to use them, why would they sell them right there in the Shoppes? Where anyone could get them? Even good boys like him?

He considered his needs. He would get Rosalind a present but he would only show it to her if she had been really good. He should definitely buy something good and sharp. Sharp enough so that one single pass would be enough. He would not want it to get caught on anything, especially not at the end when timing was crucial. Timing and cleanliness. The cuts had to be clean.

Loverboy held his finger over the glass case of knives, careful not to touch the surface, not to leave a print. "Is this the best one you have?" he asked, indicating the most expensive.

"That'd be the top of the line. They call it the Lizzie Borden. You know, after the girl who murdered her father and—"

"I'll take it," Loverboy said, interrupting him.

CHAPTER 54

Sunk deep in the beige velveteen backseat of the taxi-cab, Imogen closed her eyes and sorted through the flavors.

Metal. Lemon. Peanuts.

It had taken her fifteen minutes to get to the impound lot from the time she got the phone call saying the taxi was ready for her. It was not exactly that she had been waiting by the phone.

Liar.

She had been. Waiting. All damn day. Waiting as the adrenaline rush of watching the fingerprint come up right in the middle of the taxi receipt as they fumed it with the iodine crystals at six that morning faded. Waiting for the technical report on the Loverboy phone interview tape (not ready). Waiting for Benton to come over or call and ask her what progress she'd made (didn't happen). Waiting for J.D. to return her calls (nothing). Waiting to understand why the killings went in two-week cycles (no clue). Waiting for the crime-scene squad to put everything back in the taxi so she could sit in it and try to figure out something. Anything.

Waiting for Loverboy to kill Rosalind.

The metallic taste in the backseat of the taxi was fingerprint powder, she knew, so she ignored it. The lemon was one she remembered from her cab ride the first time. The peanut taste, new, but very faint. Had it been left by the crime-scene squad or the killer?

A flare of anger at how badly everything about the taxi had been mismanaged sparked inside her, but she pushed it down. Emotions had flavors too. She needed to keep her palate clear.

She breathed deeply, sampling taste and smell alone. She opened her eyes. Although she wore her dark glasses, the flavors on her tongue became instantly more complex with her eyes open. They fixed on the brown stain on the seat to the left of her thigh. The crime squad said it was chocolate ice cream, but she could not shake the idea that it was dried blood.

A familiar chalky taste slid over the tartness of the lemon, clicking like a memory into place, but there was a peppery pricking on the edges of her tongue. She turned her head slowly from left to right, letting the flavors creep in. The pepper was stronger near the driver's side of the crowded dashboard. Tom had interviewed the taxi driver's wife, who said the collection of toys glued and suction-cupped there had not belonged to her husband. Loverboy had brought them. A little audience all for himself, Imogen guessed. She forced herself to study each toy in turn, Elvis, NASA Barbie, the Smurf, the hula girl. She leaned forward, shifting the balance of the car slightly, and the three dogs began wagging their tails in unison, eager to please. But none of it registered. She sat back and closed her eyes, dredging up any detail of her trip in the taxi.

Why hadn't she paid more attention?

She remembered looking out the window at the many skylines of the city. Remembered trying to ignore all the banal advice he was giving her. Remembered the tail of dark hair that she now thought was a wig brushing the collar of his Members Only jacket.

Come on, come on. She dragged partial thoughts from her memory. The collar of his jacket was frayed, she recalled. What about the cuffs? Did she even look at his hands on the steering wheel? Did she—

Steering wheel. Notepad. She opened her eyes and the taste of pepper flooded her mouth. That was the difference. When she rode in the car the paper on the notepad had been blank under the *Don't like my driving? Call 1-800-Jerkoff* sign. Now the pad was covered over with a page ripped out of a word-search book.

Deliberately? Another game?

Word Hide-'n'-Seek.

She thought of *Burt, Eureka, CA*, in the Bellagio security office, with his word searches. But he could not be Loverboy because he could not have driven her taxi that morning and met her in the security office.

One of the crime-scene analysts, Larry, had even mentioned the word search found in the taxi, she realized. "Is your guy stupid or something? He did it all wrong. He didn't find any of the words he was supposed to. Doesn't look like he even tried."

Imogen sandwiched herself in the gap between the front seats and looked at the paper. Larry was right. The words that had been circled weren't the ones listed at the bottom of the page to be found. Most of them weren't even words. XYREEN. CUBWLAI. NONOQ.

It was completely haphazard. Was he losing it? Losing control? Or did it mean—

Her eyes began to pick out the letters between the circled words, the letters that remained. Reading between the lines.

Reaching behind her, she rummaged in her bag until she found a pen. With the cap in her mouth she copied the letters as they appeared onto her left palm.

YO USH OU LD NTH AVE
TA K ENM YC A RN OW
S O MEO N EMU STP AY

Imogen copied the letters onto a scrap of paper in her lap. When she was finished she read: "YOU SHOULDN'T HAVE TAKEN MY CAR NOW SOMEONE MUST PAY."

Only during her second pass through it did Imogen become

aware of the regular ticking noise, like the sound of a timer, coming from somewhere behind her.

Someone must pay.

Ticking like a bomb.

Imogen sprang to the door and had her fingers on the lock when the ticking stopped.

Rachel's face filled the window. "Bugsy said I could find you here. The tech guys are ready to report on the reporter's interview tape for you," she said.

The ticking had just been footsteps, Imogen told herself. Just the sound of Rachel's heels on the cement of the impound lot. She swallowed hard.

Rachel looked at her. "Are you all right? Is something wrong?"

"No," Imogen assured her.

Liar, liar, pants on fire, sang the killer's voice in her head. She looked down at the note that was clutched in her white knuckles.

SOMEONE MUST PAY.

If not her, then who?

CHAPTER 55

The night before Rosalind had longed for death but now, given the chance to embrace it, she could not do it. It was not simply because of her desire to see Jason again. Not simply because she was stronger than that.

She realized, sitting cross-legged in the middle of the floor, unable to wipe the tears from her cheeks because her hands were bound behind her, that it was because now she had a ray of hope. She was going to get the hell out of here and see that he got—

What he had coming to him!

—help. When understanding came it made her cry harder, from a sick sort of joy or from a sick horror at what she felt herself becoming, she was not sure. Finally she stood awkwardly and began pacing around the room.

Leaving her alone, with the door unlocked, was a test, just like all the other little tests before it, she realized. He was always testing, testing to see if she hated him, testing to see if she lied to him. If she was "a faker." When he believed her, believed that she really cared about him, he treated her better. It was what had happened that morning.

The strawberry syrup soaked through the fabric of the blue velour housecoat and dried in sticky pink patches of itchiness on her arms and feet, but she did not care. He wanted her to be nice to him, to like him. He was looking for positive feedback, and even the most subtle disagreement could send him spinning out of control. He almost seemed to crave the excuse. The thing to do was keep him happy, keep him feeling confident and loved. Showing him that she had stayed this time, had not even tried to escape, would be a good start.

She had to keep her feet moving in order to stop herself from going to the door.

She would stay only until she could find a way to get out other than the door. As she moved, her eyes roamed the blank white walls. They were clean, as if they had been painted recently. All four walls were identical, the same size, the same color, except the one with the door in it. The unlocked door. The waiting door. The just-one-turn-and-you're-free door—

Don't look at that!

—the death door.

There had to be another way out. She banged her head against all four walls of the room to test for hollowness but found they were solid. No hidden passages like the one he'd used to get her out of her hotel. The floor was carpeted from one side to another in a blue-brown industrial carpet that smelled dusty. Beneath it she guessed was concrete. The television plugged into an outlet that came out of the floor and was pushed against the middle of the wall with the door in it, with the two genuine La-Z-Boy recliners facing it. Hers was red vinyl. His was blue velvet. "Like a throne," he'd told her. "Like I'm a prince."

She shuddered at the memory.

The double bed with its restraints jutted out of the wall next to the TV. On the opposite wall was a drafting table with a drawer, a desk light, and an office chair. She had not seen him open the drawer but once, when she floated into consciousness during her first days there, she'd seen him looking over a large book. She suspected he kept it locked in the drawer. Next to the desk was the kiddie potty he'd brought in for her to use.

That recalled moments she preferred not to remember.

She perched on the edge of the recliner—she'd spent too much time in it to go back willingly—and scanned the room. There was something she had seen when she had been drugged and strapped to the bed. Her eyes moved to the bed, to the ceiling above it where the smoke detector perpetually flashed its red beacon.

That was when she spotted it. It had been painted over but it was still visible. Next to the smoke detector was the rectangular outline of a board. Screws held it into the ceiling at all four corners and in the middle of each side. Eight screws in all.

Furiously she pushed the recliner toward the wall with her knees until it was underneath the rectangle and climbed on top of it. It threatened to tip over but rocked against the wall and remained steady. Standing on the seat she might be able to reach the screws if her hands were not bound behind her, she saw. Standing on the arm she would definitely be in range.

If her hands were not bound behind her.

If she had anything to use to unscrew them.

Still, it was something. Something possible. Her heart was beating with adrenaline. The crucial thing was not to let him know she'd seen it. Not to let him know she'd thought of it.

She climbed off the arm of the recliner and leaned against it again to catch her breath. Her legs felt shaky with excitement and also weakness. She did not think she was getting enough to eat. And the medicine he insisted on giving her seemed—

The sound of someone whistling quietly outside the door broke into her thoughts. Whistling the song he'd been humming the night before. Whistling getting closer, now matched with footsteps. Whistling that had to be him. Oh God, he was back and the chair was near the wall and—

Using all her remaining strength she leaned her body against the wall and shoved the recliner back toward its position. She was checking to make sure she had it in exactly the right place when she saw the faint white line on the back of its red vinyl upholstery. It must have brushed against the wall, against the chalky paint. *Shit shit shit,* she thought, rubbing against it furiously with her thigh. The whistling was getting closer, each of his footsteps were audible now. It wasn't working. She could not rub hard enough. *Shit shit—*

She turned around and used her nails on the place where she thought the spot was. Twisting her eyes over her shoulder she saw the mark was gone. Almost. Enough.

She looked at the wall. If you peered right at it, there was a slight mark at the same level. But you would only notice it if you were looking for it, she decided. And she would see to it that he had no reason to look.

Footsteps right outside. She heard the sound of a switch being flipped. The doorknob began to turn with painful slowness. *Please don't let him notice the wall don't look at it please—*

Skidding back into the recliner she saw that the side of her housecoat was covered in white powder. She shifted slightly so she was sitting on it, glad that with her hands bound behind her he could not see the white powder that had to be caught in her nails.

The door opened.

Loverboy, carrying three shopping bags, stepped inside and smiled at her. "Hi, Ros, I'm home!" he yelled, louder than necessary. He seemed pumped up, excited. Scary.

Rosalind swallowed. "I'm glad." In her peripheral vision the mark on the wall beckoned to her like a huge flag. *Don't look!* she told herself. "Did your errands go well?"

He had stopped two steps into the room and was looking around, checking. His eyes roved from the bed to the walls, past the mark, across the floor, up to her face. Apparently satisfied, he set down the shopping bags and closed the door behind him. This time he did lock it. "Did you miss me, Ros?" he asked.

He had not noticed, Rosalind told herself. If he had noticed he would have reacted. "Yes. It's lonely here when you are gone."

He smiled, a genuine-looking smile that made Rosalind's stomach go tight. "Really? What did you do?"

"I"—*DON'T LOOK AT THE WALL*—"I wanted to watch TV but I could not figure out how to turn it on."

It was the right answer. "You wanted to watch TV? Me too! I should have left you the remote control. I just wasn't thinking."

"That is okay. Maybe we can watch TV together?"

He looked at her with wonderment and joy. "I would love that. But not right now. Right now I have a present for you. For being so good."

"I don't want a present," Rosalind assured him.

"Oh yes, you do. Look!" He held up two of the shopping bags. One of them was plain yellow. On the other were the words *Carlton's Cutlery*. From the plain yellow bag he withdrew a nightgown and a matching robe.

"Real silk," he told her, brushing it against her cheek. "You can put them on later to replace the ones you messed up, but you'd better not ruin them again. That's not the best part, though. This is the best part."

Rosalind could have sworn that for a moment his eyes went to the wall with the mark on it, but nothing in his face changed as he reached into the Carlton's Cutlery bag, so she figured she had been wrong.

His hand came out holding a small leather portfolio about the size and dimensions of a travel wallet. Slowly, like a lover prolonging the moment of seduction, he slid open the zipper that went all the way around it and held it open in front of her.

"Ta-da!" he announced proudly. "A nail file, a scissors, a cuticle pusher, two sets of clippers, and tweezers!"

Rosalind knew that what he was holding out in front of her was a manicure set. But in her mind all she really saw was a pocket-sized set of instruments of torture.

"We're going to have fun this afternoon, aren't we, Ros? Oh boy, am I going to take good care of you! Sit forward and let's see those hands." He took the larger pair of clippers from the set and, pasting on a plastic smile, said, "Now, will it be blood red or flesh-colored nails today, ma'am?"

"I don't—" Rosalind began.

His face went very still. His jaw twitched.

"Let me see your hands, Rosalind," he said quietly. "LET ME SEE YOUR GODDAMNED HANDS RIGHT NOW!"

CHAPTER 56

Peter Brompton, head of the audio-visual forensics lab for Metro, wheeled himself over to a computer console and hit keys and said to Imogen, "Okay, now listen to it again, this time with the voice turned off."

She nodded and held the headphones more tightly to her ears. At first she heard nothing. A low rumble. Nothing. Another low rumble.

She looked at Peter. "What is that?"

"That, Ms. Page, is a clue." He put on a pair of reading glasses and leaned over a pad. "Eleven-fifty-eight P.M., Southwest Airlines flight 2430. Twelve-oh-six A.M., America West flight 57," he read out. "They register on the tape almost as soon as they took off, which means that wherever the interview was given is very close to the airport."

"Of course, the airport is in the middle of the city," Rachel, standing behind them in the audio booth, pointed out. "So that doesn't narrow things that much."

"It narrows them to the east side," Peter corrected. "We can narrow it to within a mile of the airport on any side. And there's more." He swung the wheelchair back to the bank of audio equipment and turned a dial. "Tell me what you hear this time," he said, nodding to Imogen.

She slipped the headphones back on and waited. This time she heard a groaning sound followed by a slow crash. She frowned for a moment. "Garbage truck."

"Very good," Pete commended. "Emptying a Dumpster."

"Where do they collect the garbage at midnight?" she asked.

Rachel's answer was not encouraging. "All over Vegas. There's less traffic at midnight. A lot of roadwork and other city services are done then."

"True, my dear," Pete stepped in, "but not in residential neighborhoods." He smiled. Imogen, catching his meaning, smiled back.

She turned to Rachel. "How long will it take you to get me a list of all the Dumpsters on the east side of the city within a mile of the airport, along with their emptying schedules?"

"It might take a while. First of all, that includes many of the Strip hotels, which each have multiple Dumpsters. Plus, waste management for the city is privately contracted and there are a few different companies. They tend to be a little reticent about working with the cops. I think it comes from a history of being Mafia owned."

"Who did J.D. call to get us access to that garbage truck last week?" Imogen asked. "Could we get them to help us?"

Rachel shook her head. " I don't know who that was and I don't seem to be able to get the boss on his phone today. As soon as I do, I'll ask him. Service has been flukey recently."

"I noticed. I've been trying since this morning."

"I'll give it another shot. In the meantime, I'll start calling around and putting as much in motion as I can."

Rachel disappeared out the door and Imogen felt Peter Brompton's eyes on her. "There is one thing you have not asked me about, Ms. Page."

"I know. I was"—*summoning up the courage,* Imogen thought. She said—"waiting."

"Are you ready now?"

Imogen nodded.

"The screams in the background of the tape are human. And, as well as I can ascertain by matching their pitch and tenor with the voice-mail messages you got me, they were made by Rosalind Carnow."

Imogen exhaled slowly. She said, as much to herself as to Peter, "At least now we have an idea of where she is being held."

"Yes. You might just be closing in on Loverboy's hideout."

That was when Imogen realized the name of the song, the song that had been running through her head for the past twenty-four hours. It was "Ring around the Rosie."

Six days left. Six days when anything—

SOMEONE MUST PAY.

—could happen.

"Yes. We might just be closing in on Loverboy."

Please let that be true.

And that was when it hit her. What she had seen that was royal blue, like the thread that had been caught in the glove compartment latch.

It was J.D.'s baseball jacket.

She dialed his number and got kicked into voice mail again.

CHAPTER 57

Loverboy could NOT stop laughing. Being with Rosalind today was making him feel so SILLY. "I still can't believe you thought I was serious," he said, wiping his eyes on the back of his cuff. "Oh God, Ros, you totally should have seen your face. Man, it was priceless. You looked so scared. But you didn't believe I was actually going to pull your nails out, did you? I mean, *sheesh*. What do you think I am? Crazy?"

"No," she said, voice tight. "Of course not."

"Right." He was still chuckling. "Only someone not normal would do what you were thinking. Not me. I'm normal. I'm not a freak."

"Right. You are not a freak," Rosalind repeated. She sounded like she believed it too.

Boy, was it hard to keep his hands steady while holding hers. The nail file was like a little knife, and there were those tiny scissors. Everything so dainty. "I'm afraid I'll have to lock all of these up in my desk drawer when I leave," he told her as he sliced away her cuticles. "I wouldn't want you to hurt yourself while I am gone."

"Thank you," she said. Her voice quavered a little bit. He wondered if he was hurting her. There was blood around her nails, but that was probably normal.

"You are going to look so pretty when I am done with you, Ros."

"Yes," she agreed. Added, "Too bad my hair is such a mess."

His hand stopped moving. He squinted at her. "What?"

He saw her swallow. She said, "I just thought that maybe, if you pinned my hair back, I would look better." She smiled.

His eyes flickered from the smile to her gaze. "For who?"

"For you," she said. And she meant it. He could tell. His mommy wanted to look pretty for him. He reached out and twisted one of the gold studs in the ear holes he'd made. She winced.

"Did that hurt, Ros?"

"Yes. It did."

He studied her. "You want me to give you hairpins? To look pretty? For me?"

"Yes."

She said it in the same truth-telling voice she used when she said he'd hurt her by turning her earring.

That was when he really started feeling silly. Feeling so silly. The pressure was building, building inside him. He had to stop the manicure and sit back for a moment. The other knife was in the bag just behind him. He knew that this was the time to be careful, but when he got to feeling THAT silly—

It was only Wednesday. There was still so long to wait. Soon it would all happen. But not soon enough. He would have to stop spending so much time with Rosalind. He would have to start rationing himself. But he needed an outlet. NOW. He needed to be inside a woman.

The thought made him blush, and he brought his hands up to his eyes, peering between his fingers at Rosalind. Did Mommy know what he had been thinking? He hoped not. Boy, did he. But she was making him so silly. It was her own fault. Asking for hairpins. Oh HOW she liked him.

He needed to blow off some steam, bad. He remembered the girl he'd seen at the Penis Mall, the one with the titties and the long red hair. And he knew just what he needed to do. He reached for his phone, scrolled through his phone book, and pushed SEND.

"Where are you going?" Rosalind asked him as he got ready to leave.

"I've got a date, Mommy. Now, open wide."

"Why?"

"It's time for your medicine."

"I don't want—"

His hand squeezed her nostrils closed until her mouth opened, and he wrenched her head back by her hair, laying the tranquilizers onto her tongue. "If you don't swallow those will taste NASTY," he admonished her, and watched until the pills went down her throat. He waited five minutes to make sure they were working, then hauled her to the bed, waggled his fingers at her, picked up the bag with the knife in it, and shut the door behind him.

Rosalind fought against the unconsciousness for as long as she could, but almost instantly it overtook her. *Remember two* she told herself. *Remember—*

She fell into oblivious sleep.

A drink, a Fred Astaire–Ginger Rogers movie, and a huge plate of chili fries, Imogen thought. Then decided she could even skip the movie, make the drink a double. That was what she wanted more than anything in the world at that moment.

That and one of those automatic door-lock disablers so she could break into J.D.'s car, if she could find it, and check to see if there were any snags on his baseball jacket without him knowing.

What she had were Tom, Harold, and Dannie staring at her, practically crawling down each other's throats, everyone tense and moderately to very miserable. She looked around the table at her team and wondered if she should suggest they all take a few minutes to make faces at her fish, relax a little.

And she hadn't even told them about the message she found in the taxi. They were on edge enough without some kind of death threat hanging over them. Tom and Harold had almost come to blows because one of them had used blue pen to circle the location of racetracks near Loverboy's killings and the other had used green.

"We agreed on blue."

"You just picked up a pen and said, 'This one,' and I said, 'Yes.' It looked green to me."

"Are you color-blind all of a sudden? This looks green?"

It was a waste anyway, because they'd been able to pinpoint the places where Loverboy had found his victims and none of them were racetracks.

Dannie seemed distracted and kept looking at her watch. Imogen had to ask her twice if any progress had been made identifying the fingerprint they had found on the taxi receipt, only to receive a flustered, "I'm not sure, I'll look into it," in reply. She had gotten the same answer when she asked if there had been any news about other women killed like Marielle and Corrina.

There was always a soft spot in any case, Imogen knew, a moment when the regular plodding progress that good investigation required became frustrating for the people working on it. An investigation like this one was bound to be even worse—it seemed to go on forever but it had a definitive deadline. Usually when the FBI got involved, they were there after the crime had been committed, after the victim was dead. This time they knew that saving Rosalind's life rested on their shoulders. And that they had only a week left to do it.

She wished she could stop hearing Rosalind's screams in her head.

She was just giving her team assignments—Dannie to stay on the dead women, Tom and Harold to try to pinpoint the Dumpster she heard being emptied based on the time between the two flights—when the phone rang. Bugsy took it in her bedroom and when he came out she could tell by his face he had something.

Imogen looked at Dannie, Harold, and Tom and said, "I know it's not much to go on, but the only way we're going to get this guy is through attention to detail. I really believe that. Pay attention to everything."

The door closed behind them and she said to Bugsy, "Spill."

"I guess my poker face isn't working today." He pulled out his wallet and tossed it to her. "This is yours."

"Why?"

"Remember the other night, right before you went to Boston, when you called and told me to find out who knew about the pseudonym you used to register at the hotel? And when I told you pretty much everyone as far as I could tell, you demanded that I have someone scan all the database searches originating in Las Vegas to see if anyone had looked for information about Lucretia Borgia or Pietro Bembo? And I said that if we could even do it, which was questionable and probably illegal, the chances of it yielding anything were minuscule, and if it did, I'd give you a million dollars?"

"Yes."

"I don't have a million dollars. You can have whatever is in there."

Imogen sat forward. "Who?"

"At first the closest we could get was that a search had been done from the Metro homicide offices. But thanks to the Patriot Act, they managed to narrow it."

"J. D. Eastly," Imogen said.

"No. He doesn't have a computer, one of those guys who says he doesn't believe in them."

Imogen didn't bother to hide her disappointment. "Oh."

"But his assistant, Rachel, has a computer. And it was used for the search. At a time when she was off duty." He looked at her. "What do we do now?"

"Nothing overt. We can't let him know." She reached for the phone and started dialing. When Lex answered she said, "I need a surveillance team. The best. And I need it now."

CHAPTER 59

Loverboy stood at the window of his room at the Fun Motel and stared at the housekeeping maid slowly pushing her laundry cart around the balcony that lined the second floor. There were two of them, Marysol and Connie, one for each level. It was like watching a race, only neither of them could see the other one, see who was winning. The inhabitants of the Fun Motel slept late, so they worked from four in the afternoon on. This evening Marysol, on his floor, was faster. He was glad; he liked Marysol better, liked the way when she finished early she undid the top two buttons on her uniform and sat at the end of the walkway fanning herself. It didn't matter what they did as long as they finished all the rooms before Eddie came in the Western Linen Service van and picked up the cart full of dirty sheets. Dirty from all the fun people had there.

Loverboy liked the slow, regular activity at the Fun Motel. He felt like he belonged there, was part of the family. He went there whenever he could, to get away, think a little. Every day Marysol and Connie would smile at him. Every day they cleaned his room. Every day they walked right by him, sometimes Marysol giving him this flirty look like she'd like to get him in bed. Every day. But they never would have guessed who he was. Not them, not the other guests at the motel, not the people on the buses that zoomed by. Every one of them knew his name from the newspaper. Every one of them would like to GET THEIR HANDS on him. But none of them knew him for real! It made him feel so SILLY. So powerful.

He knew everything. He knew where Imogen had spent most of her day. He wondered what she found. Had she seen his note in the taxi? The others wouldn't get it, but she would, for sure. Imogen was smart. He really liked her.

As he thought about Imogen, he looked at the tower of the Stratosphere looming over the roof of the motel, tall like a huge penis, with a roller coaster at its tip. Family fun right at the top! Take a ride on me! Just knowing there was a roller coaster up there made him calmer. He could swear he could almost hear the screams from it. And even if he couldn't, no one would be able to hear anyone screaming from his room.

God, he was powerful.

Like how he had made Rosalind do whatever he wanted. She had been so NICE to him that afternoon. She even wanted to make her hair pretty for him. She was such a good mommy. She really liked him. She really—

Disgusting little shit.

SHE DID! She said it. He'd tested her and—

You're a bad boy.

NO! Rosalind liked him. She had always liked him. And now she extra did.

You believed her? You believed her even though—

SHUT UP! He was breathing hard and he had begun to sweat under his arms. That was bad. He would be dirty when his date got there. He had to calm himself down. Stay calm.

He counted the doors of the rooms, calculated how long it would take Marysol to finish tonight. Counting and calculating always helped him feel better. When his breathing had slowed, he reached into the Carlton's Cutlery bag and let his fingers rest on his new knife. His Lizzie Borden. One swipe with that would be enough, he thought. *Just one swipe, with my new knife,* he repeated to himself. It was almost a rhyme. Pretty funny, he thought.

This last week was always the hardest. This part, when they were nice to him. When they liked him. It was when he started to feel the sillies almost all the time. It was also his favorite part, but it required him to use all his control.

He saw his date drive into the parking lot.

All his CUNT-rol, he corrected, and giggled to himself. He put the knife away next to the bed and made sure he was ready. He loved staying at the Fun Motel. Loved the way that the F of the sign blinked on and off, so half the time it said *un Motel*. No one would think to look for him there. The only problem was that it had no bathtub, only a shower. But he would make do. He was flexible. He could adapt. He was—

A freak!

—easygoing.

He watched her get out of her car and look around. As she tilted back her head to check the numbers, the afternoon sunlight flashed off her hair. It was really pretty. He'd been wanting a red-head since he saw that other girl that morning at the Shoppes.

She had pretended to be shy and unsure, pretended she had work to do, when he first called, but he had known all along that she would come. She liked him. He knew that from the other night at the party. She would come. And he would CUM.

Boy, was he feeling FRESH!

He calculated that it would take her a minute and fifty-eight seconds to get to the room. Two minutes later he heard her footsteps in the hallway outside the door. Slow but okay. He would not let himself stand right next to the door until she knocked. He had to stay calm, stay in control. Always in control on the first date.

He loved the first date. Getting to know someone. Getting them to trust you. To like you.

This time it was the girl's turn to talk into the hole. His heart was beating hard and fast as her footsteps slowed, stopped. *This was it!*

Knock, knock.

He sprinted to the door but kept it closed. "Who's there?" he asked, his lips nearly touching the peephole.

"It's me."

He felt his cheeks get hot. She was not doing it right. That was not how it went. She was supposed to say her name, not, "It's me." Didn't she know the joke? SHE WAS MESSING EVERYTHING UP!

"Me who?" he asked, trying to keep the edge out of his voice. She was going to screw it all up. She was—

"Danielle," she said.

He exhaled. His blood slowed. That was better. In his mind he heard the punch line to the joke: *Dan yelled and yelled and yelled but no one came to help her before she died.*

But out loud he said, "I'm so glad you could get away, Dannie." He opened the door and smiled at her.

She blushed a little. "I'm so glad you could al—"

He put up a hand to silence her and looked deep into her eyes. "Let's not talk about that. Let's talk about us."

"About us?"

"About how well I am going to treat you this afternoon," he said, pulling her into his arms.

She came willingly. Just like they always did. He was the master. He was in CUNTROL!

CHAPTER 60

Imogen leaned her elbows on the balustrade that lined the lake in front of the Bellagio and stared across it toward the Eiffel Tower. Against the blue-black night sky, French flags waved from the sides of a building that was half the Paris Opera house and half the Louvre, smashed together down the middle. Las Vegas had no respect for history, for monuments. It mashed them together and had its way with them, laughing the whole time. And she liked the city for it. For its irreverence and freedom. It was not afraid of reinventing itself. Of taking chances.

It was a city for chances. For risks.

If you were allowed to take them. That afternoon she had felt like she was onto something, explaining to Lex what she needed. An outside team to watch J.D., someone he wouldn't spot, because she could not risk alerting him if he was Loverboy. Got it? and Lex had said, "Have you lost your mind, Imogen?"

Not the best start.

"Tell me again what you have on Detective Eastly," he'd said in his bored voice. The one that meant he was probably filing his nails as they talked.

"It's a hunch more than anything. But the thread we found in the taxi might match a jacket I know he has. And——"

"Are you listening to yourself? A hunch? Might match? And that computer search thing you described is not only illegal, it's almost impossible. Do you have any evidence of a prior relationship between them? Something that soured?"

"No. But he dated her best friend."

"Has he been in the other places where the killings happened?"

"I don't know, and you know damn well I can't find out without a warrant. But he travels all the time. Doing public-service events."

"He does public service."

"Don't tell me that means he's not a serial killer. John Wayne Gacy dressed up as a clown and—"

"I know about Gacy. But you need to give me more than that he travels."

"I don't have more. Just a gut feeling. And the fact that he doesn't answer his phone for long stretches, disappears."

"He's not the only one who doesn't always answer his phone." Lex's version of a funny joke. He said, "I am not sending you to investigate the head of the Violent Crimes Task Force on a hunch. Besides, my sources tell me he has no sense of humor and isn't charming, so he doesn't even fit the profile your own team worked up."

She really hated profiles. "Lex, I really think—"

"I am not interested in what you think. I'm interested in what you know. Proof."

"How can I get proof if you won't let me look into it?"

"Listen to yourself. You are getting so desperate that you're picking the first guy you see. And you sound like shit. If this is the best you can do for a suspect, perhaps I should be sending someone else in. Perhaps I should come myself."

"I thought this was my investigation."

"It is. Yours to lose. Do you understand?"

"Yes. I'll stop looking at J.D."

"Good."

So now she was trying to make herself think of something else. Asking herself all the unanswered questions from the investigation.

Why did Loverboy hold his victims for two weeks? What went in two-week cycles? That was half a moon cycle, half a tidal cycle, but she doubted Loverboy's timing had anything to do with the natural world. Judging from his collages, he was fascinated with manufactured things, things with labels.

That thought touched off a burst of peanut in the back corner of Imogen's tongue, but it disappeared as fast as it had come.

Two weeks.

A joke her mother told her once slid into her mind—

What's the difference between a good haircut and a bad haircut?

Two weeks.

—but she was pretty sure this was not about a haircut. Love affairs and engagements could last two weeks. Or less, where she was concerned. She'd managed to scare off Benton in less than two days.

Now wondering how you would get a piece of fabric caught in the clasp of a glove compartment. The best she could think of was if you had a sleeve pulled all the way down. The way you would if you were trying to avoid leaving any fingerprints. Which you would only want to do if you were hiding the fact that you'd been in the car.

Have you lost your mind, Imogen? She heard Lex's voice in her head and made herself stop. What if he had a point? What if she was focusing too much energy on a bunch of hazy suspicions, wasting more precious time? The thread was probably a fluke. And if it wasn't, if it meant—

Whatever it meant, she didn't want to alert anyone. Anyone who could take retaliatory action against Rosalind if she made a mistake.

A voice behind her said, "Hi, Imogen," and her heart began to pound.

She turned around. "Hi, Benton."

"Bugsy told me I'd find you down here. Are you watching the fountain?"

"I'm waiting for it to come on." More waiting. She turned back toward the water and he leaned on the railing next to her, facing her. "Where have you been all day?" she asked. She meant it to sound casual. It came out like a rebuke.

"Last night I got the feeling you wanted me to stay out of your way, so I did."

She nodded and stared out over the water, searching for the right thing to say. She couldn't find it. She said, "The copy of your bridge newsletter came."

"Oh, great." Benton did not even seem to be paying attention. He was looking behind her.

"You can come by the suite and get it."

"Ok. I'll come by tomorrow. Unless you need me to get it out of your hair now?"

"No," Imogen said. She shrugged. "Whenever you want is fine."

A series of metal circles began to rise from the surface of the lake in preparation for the fountain show.

Benton glanced over his shoulder and saw them. "It looks like the music is going to start. I'll leave you to watch. I just wanted to see—see how you were doing. Good night." He straightened up and moved toward the lobby.

"Good night." It was on the tip of her tongue. *Say it, dammit, just do it,* she told herself. *What the hell are you so afraid of? Take a chance.* She turned around and began, "Benton, do you want to have breakfas—"

But he was gone.

It was better that way anyway. Better gone now than after they'd found Rosalind.

Or didn't find Rosalind.

Remember that, she warned herself. *Remember what could happen. What probably will happen. And stop thinking about him.*

Behind Imogen, the fountains in the lake exploded with a thunderclap, and the first strains of "Hey Big Spender" drifted from the speakers. People strayed from the walkways to the balustrade, crowding near her to see better. Right next to her a couple in their

late teens twined their arms around one another and kissed, oblivious to the water show. On the other side a French couple in their
seventies held hands and bobbed their heads in time to the music.
Imogen slid out from between them and walked, head down, back
into the hotel. It was 10:45 and she felt tired. Tired of everything.

She retraced her steps through the lobby and across the casino.
A crowd gathered around the craps table burst into cheers and a
woman in a silver-sequined tank top raised her arms with double Vs
of victory. "Pay up!" she called to the dealer as he counted her
money.

SOMEONE MUST PAY, Imogen saw again.

Who? she wanted to know. When?

"Imogen, come have a drink with us!" Julia said, swerving toward
Imogen and grabbing her by the arm. Lancelot, wearing green angora
with ruffles around the legs, growled mildly under Julia's other arm,
and more forcefully as Sadie and her young husband Eros strolled up
and joined them.

"I can't," Imogen said, barely resisting the urge to shake Julia's
hand off. God, she wanted to get to bed.

"Please come have a drink," Julia pleaded. She leaned close to
Imogen. "Don't leave me alone with them. Benton and Cal are deep
in car talk, so if you don't come I won't have anyone to chat with.
Sadie and Eros will be making out at the table before we've even
ordered."

"I'm sorry, Julia, I'm exhausted."

Julia pouted and asked a few more times before she finally let it
go. Imogen was heading straight for the elevators when Wrightly
Waring grabbed her from behind a potted plant. This was getting
worse every minute. He said, "I've got to talk to you, Ms. Page."

"Here?"

"I don't know when I'll get another chance. There's something
you should know. Something about—" He broke off abruptly, his
eyes looking over her shoulder.

Imogen turned around and spotted J. D. Eastly coming across

the casino toward them. When she turned back to Wrightly, his face had lost all its color. She said, "Are you all right?"

He nodded stiffly, said, "Fine. Never mind, I've got to go," and took off just as J.D. came up to her.

"I was on my way to your room to see you," he said. "Rachel tells me you wanted to talk to me."

"I did. Why haven't you been returning my calls?"

"My phone's been acting up. I told Rachel to give you anything you needed. Was there some problem?"

"No, she did that, it's just——"

"Oh, and I'm already on the Dumpster schedule. Excellent idea, by the way. Was there something else you wanted to ask me about?"

Yes, she wanted to say. Did you tamper with the evidence in the taxi? Are you Loverboy? Am I wrong about you? She said, "No, nothing else."

"You sure?" Was he taunting her? Or was she really getting delusional?

"Positive." She thought she saw Benton moving toward them across the casino and her heart began to beat faster again. Then she realized it was just Julia's husband Cal coming to corral Wrightly Waring into the bar. That was bad——now she was seeing Benton everywhere. She needed to get to sleep.

She said, "Good night, Detective Eastly," slid past him into the elevator and punched the DOOR CLOSE button furiously before anyone else could get in with her.

Loverboy watched her stalk to the elevators and really felt for her. She had looked so tense when the Bitch tried to make her have drinks, and now she looked sad. Poor Imogen, having such a hard day. Maybe he should help her.

Maybe he should get her a present! Oh yes, a reminder that he cared about her. That he was thinking about her as much as she was thinking about him. It was an excellent idea.

"I really need to talk to you," someone near him said. "This is important."

That's what you think, sucker, Loverboy thought. *Buzz, buzz, buzz.* He had REALLY important stuff to think about. Like whether Imogen's present should be alive or dead.

Or something in between.

only 5 days left!

Imogen opened her eyes when she heard the knocking on her door. She glanced at the clock, saw that it was exactly seven in the morning, early for Benton, slid a robe on over Sam's flying-toaster pajamas, and went to answer it.

Cal Harwood, Julia's husband, stood blinking in the corridor.

"Come in," Imogen invited, closing the door behind him. "What can I do for you?" She heard the brusqueness in her voice and pretended it was not because she had thought it might be someone else.

"I woke you up, didn't I?" Cal said, embarrassed. With his perfectly pressed clothes and hair just barely wet from his shower, he was like a walking indictment of Imogen for sleeping in too long.

"No, no, I was up," Imogen lied. She tried a smile. "I was just in bed, thinking."

"I would not have come so early but I've got to get to the Garden. I came by the other day to talk to you but you weren't here."

Imogen batted his apology away. "I'm sorry. Can I offer you some coffee?"

"No, I don't drink coffee."

Imogen laughed at herself. "That's good, actually, because I don't have any. I'm sorry to be so unprepared. Sit down. Was there something specific you wanted to talk about?"

"I only came because Julia said I should tell you. It's probably not important. I can come back—"

"No, please. What is it?"

Cal gave her a shy smile. "It's a little embarrassing, really, that I know this. It's what Julia calls my geeky side."

"I'm all geeky sides."

Cal laughed. "Thanks, that makes me feel better. Anyway, the thing is, there's something wrong with the *Emergency!* poster."

"With the *Emergency!* poster," Imogen repeated.

"Yes. The one in the collage the killer sent." He pointed at the wall where the collage was hanging. "Because the show went off the air in 1977. September third, actually. But the fire engine in the *Emergency!* poster is registered 1980. April. See, that can't be right."

Imogen looked from him to the collage and back again. Her first, ungenerous thought was that he had come to her room at seven A.M. to tell her about the cancellation date of a TV cop show. But it *could* mean something. Anything could mean something. God, she was tired of this case. "Thank you. That is very helpful."

Cal looked bemused. "I knew I should not have come. I just thought that maybe, if the mistake was intentional, it could be a clue or something, like the killer's birthday. Probably the picture of the poster he used was just a counterfeit, though. I'm really sorry I bothered you. I told Julia—"

"No, really." Imogen tried to sound convincing. "It probably is important. Thank you."

Cal stood up. "You're being nice, but I feel horrible."

"Don't. Every detail matters," Imogen said. She repeated versions of this three times before she was finally able to close the door behind him.

She was still wearing her pajama top and only had time to get one leg of her pants on before there was another knock at the door. She reknotted the cord of her robe and pasted on another bright smile and opened it.

"Hi." Benton held out a cup of coffee and a waxed paper bag. "I brought breakfast."

Imogen's heart began to beat hard but her smile disappeared. She took the coffee and walked back into the room.

"Boy, I've never felt so welcome in my life," Benton said.

She put her fake smile back on and he pretended to wince. "Okay, forget it."

"I thought you were Cal," Imogen explained.

"No wonder he was running away with his tail between his legs. You look scary when you do that."

"Don't any of you ever sleep?" she demanded.

"Not when we could be helping you. Nice pj's, by the way," Benton added.

Imogen ignored him. She opened the pastry bag he handed her. Remembering why he had probably come, she pushed a Xeroxed pile of papers toward him. "Here is your bridge newsletter."

Benton's eyes lit up. "Thanks." He sat down and was immediately lost in it.

Imogen took a bite of the croissant he'd brought her and went into her bedroom to get dressed. When she came out, Benton was still working on his bridge problem. She envied his concentration. Unrolling the croissant from the middle, she moved to stand in front of the collage and stared at it. *Say something!* she demanded, but it stared back silently. Her eyes slid from the collage to the list of objects in it she had written up the previous day while waiting for the phone to ring. The assortment was—

She saw something she hadn't seen before.

Loverboy was extremely brand-conscious. Some of the objects were generic, but many of them had large, obvious labels. Imogen moved to his list of characteristics and wrote: *Poor family in rich neighborhood.*

Benton looked up to see what she had done. "What does that mean?" he asked.

"Look at the collage. Only someone who grew up coveting the things he saw on TV, the things that other kids had, would be this brand-savvy. Look how many of the items in the collage are labeled.

There's the Intellivision with its Night Crawlers game, the Great Houdini Magic Set, and the *Original* Ouija board," she pointed out, putting her hand on each item in turn. "Even his book has a label, from the Ford County Library. And on the desk he's got not generic correctional fluid but Liquid Paper, not a nothing notepad but one from Audrie Lumber, and a Mead notebook, its brand clearly visible. To top it all off there's the *Emergency!* poster. Which, Cal informed me this morning, is a phony."

"Your idea is that someone who had all those things would never be attracted to them or think to use them."

Imogen nodded. She stopped abruptly and said to herself, "Members Only."

"What?"

"His jacket. When he drove me in the cab, he was wearing a Members Only jacket. Maybe that's the key," she said, talking fast and unfurling what was left of her croissant. "It is more than just wanting possessions. It's like they buy membership in society. They define you. Let you fit in. If you have real stuff, you are real. Normal." She paused and her forehead scrunched. "And maybe it's not just about appearance. Maybe the names themselves mean something. Intellivision is like 'intelligent.' Night Crawler—he certainly does live in the dark shadows. He's like a Great Houdini the way he can make his victims disappear, and he knows their futures like the Ouija board. He's—"

"As hard to hold on to as Liquid Paper?" Benton asked, not critically, just curious.

For a fleeting instant she had the same hint of peanuts she had tasted in the cab the day before; then it was gone, along with her enthusiasm. What Benton had delicately implied was right. Her conclusion was specious at best—especially if what Cal said was true, and the killer hadn't even bothered to get a real *Emergency!* poster. And, really, what good did it do to know that Loverboy had probably worn hand-me-downs? Where did that get them?

Her eyes kept returning to the word *Emergency!*

Emergency!

That was where. Right back at the beginning. She was so frustrated, frustrated with herself and frustrated with Benton for poking holes in her idea, that she shredded what remained of her croissant into tiny pieces and dropped them into the trash.

Knock, knock sounded at the door.

"Who is it?" Imogen growled. She was not in the mood for any more visitors.

"Julia."

Unexpected punch lines surged into Imogen's mind. *Julia know the way to San Jose? Julia wanna go out with me? Julia—*

Imogen swung open the door. "Yes?"

Julia smiled at her cordially. "Good morning. Hi, Benton. Have either of you two seen Wrightly Waring?"

"No," Imogen said flatly.

Benton shook his head and added, "I thought he was meeting Cal at the Garden."

"He was supposed to but he did not show up," Julia explained. "I wanted him to do a piece on the night-vision feature of the X75."

"Oh," Benton said, clearly itching to get back to his bridge problem.

"Oh," Imogen said, not knowing or caring what the X75 was.

Julia nodded. "All right, well, I'll just go throw myself off a building or something,"

"Okay," Imogen and Benton replied in unison.

Julia had been gone only three minutes when the next knock came. "Who is it?" Imogen asked.

"Dannie."

Imogen opened the door and motioned her in but Dannie shook her head. "I'm going over to Metro's forensics lab. One of the techs there said he would show me how to access their local computer systems to look for unsolved female murders around the times of Loverboy's other kills," she explained. "But I wanted to stop in before I left to apologize for being so distracted yesterday."

"That's okay. This case is taking its toll on everyone," Imogen said. She had to work hard to keep impatience from her voice.

Dannie nodded. "Anyway, I just got the report on the fingerprint from the taxi receipt."

Imogen's impatience vanished. "And? Was there a match?" Behind her she heard Benton put his pencil down.

Dannie nodded, but did not look pleased. "There is a match. The print is Rosalind Carnow's. And the way it appears, right in the center, makes it look like he must have made her touch the paper especially to give it to you. Covering his tracks from the beginning."

"Or wanting to make sure we found the taxi. Wanting to make sure we were doing our job."

Imogen was so furious after that, after she realized the killer was just leading them around, that she could not speak. When the next person rapped hesitantly on the door five minutes later, she threw it open and demanded, "What?"

The startled bellboy took two steps backward before asking, "Are you Imogen Page?"

"Yes."

"These are for you." He shoved a large bouquet of roses into her arms. "Sign here, please."

Imogen walked slowly into the room and put the flowers on the table and hunted around for the card. Slipping it out of the envelope, she read: *Julia want to lose another one?* She turned it over and saw:

Ha, ha. See you in five days! Can't wait.
Your,
LOVERBOY.

CHAPTER 62

"The flowers sent to Ms. Page?" the concierge on the phone repeated crisply. "They had been charged to one of the villas, and the message was phoned in with them. Yes, Mr. Benton Arbor's villa. About an hour ago. Good-bye."

Imogen hung up and looked at Benton.

"I was here an hour ago."

She nodded. "But Julia wasn't. Yet someone knew she would be coming." She dialed another number.

"I don't know why I went to look for Wrightly in your room, Imogen," Julia, half-covered in grape-seed mud, told her over the phone from her treatment table in the spa. "It seemed like the natural place. Everyone is always up there—until they get thrown out."

Imogen sighed. She dialed again.

"Sure," the FBI head of graphology told her. "I'll have one of my guys look at the syntax of your card as soon as possible. Will two weeks be quick enough?"

Imogen was not sure whether she wanted to throw her phone, herself, or the flowers against the wall when Bugsy came in and said, "Nice roses. Hothouse, but nice."

The roses went.

Bugsy said, "I've got a present for you. Two of them."

"I don't want any more presents."

"The first one comes from Metro, actually. They found a carabiner, one of those things you use for rock climbing? It was wedged
behind the backseat of the taxi. And it has a partial print on it."

"Great. A partial print."

Benton looked up from the table and said, "Won't that come in
handy when we go to trial?"

Imogen glared at him. He went back to his bridge problem.

Bugsy said, "Okay, that might not have been so great, but you'll
like this other present, I promise."

"I already told you—" Imogen started to say when her phone
rang. "What?" she demanded.

"Is this Imogen Page? Of the FBI?"

Imogen's heart skipped. She recognized the voice from an outgoing answering machine message in Florida she had heard days earlier. "Is this Detective Clive Ross?"

"Ex-detective," the man corrected. "Beach bum now."

"I'm envious, sir," Imogen told him honestly.

"Don't be. It ain't good unless you earn it. Sounds to me, from
what I'm seeing in the papers, you're earning it pretty hard. Tough
case, it looks like."

"Very," Imogen agreed.

"Don't know if I'll be able to help you, but I'd gladly do my
best. On the answering machine you said you wanted to ask about
an old case of mine. From what I've read, I bet it's the Corrina
Orville case."

"How did you—"

"I was a detective once too, you know. Plus, the secretary in the
department in Boston, Vickie? She told me you'd had the file out."

He'd done his homework, making sure she was legit. Imogen
decided she would like Detective Ross. "It wasn't actually the file
that interested me so much as a note you made. It was in the margin
of one of the pages. I've got a copy and can fax it to you if you
want."

"No need. I know what it said. 'Susan K,' right?"

"Yes. What did it mean?"

"Nothing concrete, really. But that case, the Corrina Orville one? It reminded me of what happened to another girl. Susan Kellogg. I tried following it up, but didn't get anywhere. And then I retired and—"

"Can you tell me about the Kellogg case? I can get the file from Boston but it will take a few days and my contact there is—"

"—probably not eager to help you," Detective Ross finished the sentence for her. "Yep, Vickie told me that Reg came in with a swollen jaw the day after his date with you. Nice work. That boy is entirely too big for his britches."

Imogen was blushing from the roots of her hair to her toes. "I didn't mean—"

"You kidding? All the women up there want your autograph. In fact, I already told Vickie to send you the file. But all the same I'll give you the particulars now. It's an old case, sixteen, maybe seventeen years ago. Sad." He paused to take a sip of something and Imogen heard ice clinking in his glass. "Susan Kellogg was a Wellesley student, a junior. Pretty girl, at least until someone decided to strangle her and leave her floating in the Charles River. What was strange about her case, what made me think of it in relation to the Orville girl, was that both of them were killed, strangled, *after* sex. There was no sign of struggle or rape. And no sign of drugs. He took them home, had his way with them, then killed them, and all the while they were happy as clams. That's not normal, you know."

"No," Imogen agreed. "Did you find who did it?"

"Never solved. We looked at her boyfriend for a while, a Harvard student, but he came up clean. The case stuck with me, though. You know how they do. And when I saw the Orville girl—" He sighed. "There was one difference. The first one, Susan Kellogg? She had a hickey. Orville didn't. Did this new one, down where you are?"

"I'm afraid we're holding that," Imogen said, feeling bad. "I know it's been a long time, but do you possibly remember the name of that Harvard student? The one you looked at for the murder?"

"You bet. Funny name. John Dillinger Eastly. Imagine naming your kid after a bank robber."

Imogen put the phone down and stood, with her hand still on the receiver, staring at the wall until Bugsy said, "Well?"

She looked at him. "Our guy was suspected of murdering his girlfriend when he was in college. Strangled her, gave her a hickey, left her body in the water. Sound familiar?"

Bugsy nodded slowly.

"Who?" Benton asked. "Who was on the phone?"

Imogen kept her eyes on Bugsy. "It would be quite a clue, wouldn't it? If only we were allowed to act on it." She crossed her arms. "I'd do anything to get my hands on him right now. Of course, first I'd have to find him. What do you think the chances are that he's in his office?"

"None," Bugsy said, standing up from the place on the floor where he'd been picking up flowers. "He's at an abandoned arcade on Industrial Road. The Kool Daze Fun Center."

Now Imogen was staring. "For real? How do you know?"

Benton said, "What are you two talking about?"

Ignoring him, Bugsy said, "Remember I told you I had another present? What if I told you he has groupies? The type who like to follow him around. Sit in cars outside places. They want to learn everything about him. Huge fans. Two in particular. Who would have guessed he had such a following among FBI agents from L.A.?"

She said, "You got your friends to come up here and pull surveillance duty for kicks?"

"You haven't met these guys. And it's not surveillance. They are just very rabid fans."

Benton cleared his throat. "Can someone please tell me what the hell we're talking about?"

Imogen looked at Benton like she'd forgotten he was there. "Do you know how to disable a car alarm?"

"I don't know what you think my job at Arbor Motors is—"

"Do you?"

"Yes. Why?"

"You can come," Imogen said. "If you promise not to kill him."

"Who?" Benton asked, but he was talking to their backs.

CHAPTER 63

Bugsy parked the car across from a beige cinder-block building that had KOOL DAZE FUN CENTER with a clown face painted on the side in fading letters, partially covered by a Dumpster.

"Looks more like a haunted house than a fun center," Benton said, hoping one of them would explain what they were doing there, but they just got out of the car and walked to an ice-cream truck parked a few feet up the curb.

Now they were stopping for ice cream?

Two guys wearing little white paper hats who looked to Benton like their combined age couldn't be more than thirty-two leaned out the order window. One of them, sporting thick black-rimmed glasses, said, "What'll it be, kids? We're running a special on Astro Pops."

"Imogen, meet Wylie and Nate, two of the Bureau's finest out of L.A. Wylie's the one in the glasses. Guys, this is Imogen Page. Oh, and Benton Arbor."

These were FBI agents? Were they recruiting from Sunday schools now? Benton wondered.

"It's great to meet you, Special Agent Page," Nate said.

"Bugsy's told us so much about you," Wylie chimed in. "It's a total honor." Then looking at Benton. "Uh, you too, sir."

Imogen shook hands with them and said, "Any activity?"

"No." This was Wylie. "Unfortunately, on such short notice we couldn't get the best audio hookup, so we're not hearing much from inside, with all the bricks, but no one has gone in or come out since last night, and no cell calls. I bet the reception in there is lousy."

Imogen said, "Where's his car?"

"Parked around the back. There are no windows, so as long as he doesn't come out we can move around pretty freely."

Imogen turned to Benton, said, "You're on," and started across the street.

He followed her. "Is this the part where you tell me what we are doing here, who this is, and why you want into their car?"

"Nope."

But she didn't need to answer, because he figured it out, some of it anyway, when he saw the car. Arbor Motors X37 in black with the plate PLAYBAL. "This is J. D. Eastly's car," he said.

"Yes, and I think J. D. Eastly might be Loverboy." She was peering in the windows. She turned away and said, "Damn. It's not there."

"What?" Benton asked, shell-shocked by what she'd said.

"I was looking for—"

She was interrupted by a loud scream.

Bugsy, Wylie, and Nate ran over from the truck. Imogen said, "It came from inside the building. Fan out. If you see any way to get in, take it."

She was shaking as she walked, gun drawn, around the far side of the building. She stayed near the bricks, trying to listen for sounds over the pounding of her heart. Halfway down her side she came to a door. Reaching out with her gun she tapped it. It moved. It was unlocked.

She tapped against it harder, once, and it swung open and stayed. She listened, heard nothing, and stepped into the doorway.

It took a moment for her eyes to adjust to the darkness. She was standing at the edge of a large, windowless room. Rectangular forms, covered with plastic tarps, that from the outlines looked like pinball machines lined the wall in front of her. The wall to her left had an enlarged version of the collage on it, with the six circles painted a dark color. Next to it stood a white board with the words *LOVER-BOY PROFILE* on it, copied from the one in her room. She turned her head to look to the right and was looking down the muzzle of a gun.

"Special Agent Page," J. D. Eastly said. He was not wearing his glasses and his eyes looked cold. "What a surprise."

Imogen swallowed. "Where is she?"

"She? You mean, Rosalind?" J.D. shook his head. "It looks like you've made another mistake."

From behind him, Imogen heard a scream. This one was much louder.

CHAPTER 64

The scream was followed by the sound of breaking glass. J.D.'s head jerked toward it, and Imogen hit him with an uppercut to the jaw. Staggering, he dropped the gun and moved toward the room the screams were coming from, then stopped when Wylie and Nate came out of the door. They were carrying a boom box with them. Over the screaming came the sound of a man's voice now saying, "Sorry, she says she is busy." And Imogen realized what it was. The tape Leslie had made of her interview with Loverboy.

"Turn that off," Imogen said.

Nate pushed a button and they were standing in silence.

Imogen turned to J.D. "Do you always answer the door with a gun?"

"In this neighborhood. Do you always break into private property?"

"The door was unlocked."

Benton and Bugsy came in then and Benton said, "Where is she?"

Imogen shook her head, pointed to the boom box. "I made a mistake. But search back there."

Rubbing his jaw, J.D. said, "When you came in you asked for Rosalind. You don't think that I'm—" breaking off.

Imogen turned when Bugsy and Benton came out of the adjoining room, giving her the sign for all-clear. She said to J.D., "Tell me why I shouldn't."

J.D. stood with his eyes closed for a long time, breathing deep. From his posture, Imogen tasted a combination of anger, confusion, and, surprisingly, fear. When he opened them he said, "I don't know how to explain this. You don't understand. I've been going out of my mind about this. Look." And flipped on the light.

Imogen saw that she'd been right about the pinball machines, the collage, and the whiteboard, but had missed a skee ball layout at the back of the room. And the two dozen file boxes stacked around the edges, the smaller versions of the other collages tacked up on corkboards, and the piles of folders. An impromptu command center.

"What is all this?" Benton asked.

"My other office, sort of. It's where I come to think."

Benton bent to look at one of the file boxes. "*Benton 'Fuck You' Arbor,*" he read aloud. "Nice. I didn't know you cared."

J.D. said, "Don't let it go to your head."

Imogen was walking around, looking at the files and boxes and pads of paper with notes on them. "You didn't like the way I was running the investigation, so you started one of your own."

"It wasn't that, it has nothing to do with you, what you're doing. I just needed—"

"To have more control," Imogen finished for him. "Right. No wonder you and Benton don't get along. You are way too much alike."

"That's what Rosalind says too," J.D. told her.

"She's always been good with insults," Benton said. He stared hard at J.D. "You know, she told me about you."

J.D. looked surprised. "She did?"

Imogen cut in. "Later. Right now I want to know why you were listening to the tape."

"See if we missed anything," J.D. said. "If I could pick out any sounds that might help." He paused. "And also to make it real. What is happening to Rosalind. Sometimes I just——" He swallowed. "I'm having a really hard time with this. I blew it with her but I always thought I'd get another chance and now——" He broke off. "I always hoped, you know, if something happened to someone I cared about I'd be the strong one." Glancing at Benton. "But that's not me. Clearly, since you thought I was the one hurting her. Why? Why would you think that?"

Imogen almost wanted to turn away, not look at this man who seemed to be shedding layers of confidence in front of them. Glancing at the file boxes she said, "Remember Susan Kellogg?"

J.D. nodded. "Of course." Then saying it with a different tone: "Oh, of course."

Benton frowned. "Why are you asking about someone J.D. dated in college?"

"Don't you remember what happened to her?" J.D. said. "It was while you were away, dealing with your father's estate. She died. The police thought it was murder. They talked to me a few times, even took a dental impression. And found me innocent." The last phrase was directed at Imogen.

"What does that have to do with Rosalind?" Benton asked.

Imogen said, "I suspect that she was killed by the same person who killed Marielle Wycliffe and Corrina Orville and who is holding Rosalind. I thought it was suggestive that the main suspect in her death was also on hand now."

"That's why we're here?" Benton asked.

"Because of that. Because the same person has had complete access to our investigation, as well as all the people——living and dead—— in it. He is conveniently unreachable ninety percent of the time, including during the hours that Marielle was killed. The security tape that would have had the killer's face on it was checked out by 'Pietro Bembo,' a name he researched on the Web, and altered. And no one has ever bothered to ask him for a confirmable alibi." She looked at J.D. "Do you have one?"

He inhaled deeply. "Yes. But I would really appreciate it if this could be checked out quietly. I was with Marcie DeLonghi."

Imogen said, "Carlo DeLonghi's wife? The mobster? The one under investigation by your department right now?"

J.D. nodded.

"If it got out to the wrong people you would both be dead."

"At least dead."

Benton said, "J.D., you never stop blowing my mind. What you don't know"—turning to Imogen now—"is that Marcie DeLonghi used to be Marcie Eastly. She's J.D.'s ex-wife."

Imogen was moving around the room but she stopped and looked at J.D. "You say you're in love with Rosalind but you're having an affair with your ex-wife?"

J.D. clenched his jaw. "It's a long story. I've been doing some soul-searching." When Benton laughed he glared at him. Reaching for a pad and pen he wrote a phone number down, and pushed it across the table. "That's Marcie's number. I was with her when Marielle was killed, right before the SWAT operation, and probably most of the other times you were trying to call. We ended it. You can make the inquiries however you want, but for her sake I'd appreciate it if you could be discreet. I know she'll be able to give you the exact times and dates of our get-togethers. They tend to correspond pretty exactly with her husband's business trips and lawyer meetings."

Imogen nodded at Bugsy, who took the number and flipped open his cell phone.

J.D. said, "The service in here is bad. That's part of the reason it's hard to reach me. You might want to step outside."

Bugsy left and Imogen said, "There is one other thing. Why didn't you tell anyone you searched the taxi before the crime-scene unit arrived?"

"What are you talking about?"

"Don't bullshit me, J.D." She lifted his blue baseball jacket from a chair and carried it toward him. "A fiber that came from right here"—she held the right sleeve in front of him, pointing at a snag in the fabric—"was found lodged in the clasp of the glove compartment in the taxi the killer used. Everything else can be explained away, but not that. What were you looking for in there?"

J.D. put up his hands in surrender. "You're good." He reached into his pocket and pulled out his wallet, opened it, and removed a photo. He held it out so she could see. It was a picture of her, the one from her FBI identification card, and it had a heart drawn around it in ballpoint pen. Smudges showed it had been dusted for prints.

J.D. said, "The funny thing is, I took it because I didn't want you to get sidetracked. Freaked out that he was watching you too. I just wanted everyone to stay focused on Rosalind. You two were running all over, far from here and—I guess I just sort of lost it. And now it's actually sidetracked you more."

"Yes, it did." Imogen was furious but it was hard to be mad at J.D., the man practically decomposing in front of them. He wasn't looking at her, listening to her. His eyes were on Benton.

J.D. said to him, "You don't think I deserve her. Rosalind."

Benton seemed to mull it over. He said, "What I think is that she deserves someone who cares about her as much as you say you do. But also someone she can count on. And I don't get why, if you really love her, you are fucking around with your ex-wife. Seriously, why?"

"Because I lost Rosalind. And I wanted to blame you, but it was my fault. So I was just proving to myself what an asshole I am."

Benton said, "Oh. If you need any help, I can tell you what an asshole I think you are."

"Thanks, I think I have it covered."

Benton nodded. "You told me on the first day of the investigation that this was about her, not us. I think we should keep it that way."

"I agree."

Silence. Then Wylie, still in his ice-cream suit, said, "So, Mr. Eastly, this place yours? Pinball machines and everything?"

"Yeah, I inherited it from the first guy I arrested."

How nice, Imogen thought, listening to them talk. For some

reason it pissed her off, their camaraderie, and she moved to stare at the collage. Her investigation was at a standstill. Her prime suspect, if her ragtag collection of suspicions about J. D. Eastly could even have made him that, was gone. The only fingerprint she'd found turned out to belong to the victim. There were six hundred Dumpsters within a one-mile radius of the airport serviced by thirteen different waste management companies, five of whom had just sent their night supervisors on vacation.

Every lead felt dead. Worse, she knew, the leads were just window-dressing, just her spinning her wheels. Because everything she needed to find Rosalind was staring her in the face. And she could not see it.

What, are you stupid, Page? Can't solve a simple little riddle?

They all died because of you.

Knock, knock.

Don't screw this up, Page.

She drove her fingernails into her palm. Only five days left. There was no more time for mistakes.

Without looking at any of them she said, "I'm leaving. I'll see you back at the hotel," and walked out to the car.

She was gunning the engine, about to pull out when Benton knocked on the passenger window of her car. When she rolled it down he said, "I'm coming with you."

"I need to be alone."

He reached in, popped the lock, opened the door.

She said, "I can't be responsible for what I might say if you get into the car. I'm feeling like I messed up again."

"I'll take that risk." He buckled his seat belt.

She stepped on it.

Benton was watching her as she drove, her jaw set, her hand gripping the wheel. Almost as tightly as he was gripping the armrest. He said, "Imogen——"

"Don't. Don't say it. I know, I'm beaten. I was a fool to think I could do this on my own. I'll call Lex and have him send someone better."

"There is no one better."

"Stop it. That's not true. I made another mistake, and if we're lucky the news won't get to Loverboy, but if I'm not he'll find out and do something. To Rosalind. Someone better wouldn't have let that happen. Someone better would have figured out what the collage means." A car honked as she cut in front of it.

"Someone better might not even have made it to Vegas by now. Would not even have known about Rosalind. And we'd just be sitting here wondering why the kidnappers weren't calling."

"Right." She shook her head. "I'm no good. I can't even think straight anymore. Rosalind, you, the case, you deserve better."

"Do you know what your problem is, Special Agent Page?"

Imogen put up a hand to silence him, changing lanes one-handed without slowing down. "Please, Benton. I really do not think I can handle any—"

"You've been working too hard and people keep interrupting you and you barely ate breakfast and you're spending all day stuck in a place with no real air and lousy chili fries," Benton said, ignoring her. "Lucky for you, I happen to have the solution to at least that last problem."

"What?"

"I know a place with the best chili fries in the world. Really, really spicy. *And* fresh air and privacy, so you can think. I'll take you for lunch."

He could see she was interested, but fighting it. She said, "Where is it?"

"L.A."

"You want me to go to L.A. for lunch?" She swerved to avoid a pedicab, almost taking out two pedestrians. Benton thought she might have been aiming for them. "No way."

"Why not? Just a minute ago you were going to quit. I would rather have you in L.A. trying to sort this out than leaving. Or driving. You have your team doing all the door-to-door stuff here. All you need is the collage, to study it, right? We can take that with us."

He saw her thinking about it, tapping her fingers impatiently on the steering wheel as they waited for a light to change. "I have an appointment at one with the medical examiner to go over the cabdriver's body."

"That's okay, I have a few things to do here too. We'll leave after your appointment and fly down. The weather is great. Instead of lunch, we'll make it an early dinner. Afterward, I'll bring you right back. It is less than an hour each way."

"Are you crazy, Benton?"

"Look, I want you on this case. I want you one hundred percent on this case. And it's not happening here. Sometimes when I am stuck on a problem, going somewhere without distractions, somewhere different, helps me." He'd been dead serious, but now he got a gleam in his eye. "Besides, can you think of a better way to guarantee that a new lead will come up in the investigation than leaving town for a few hours?"

She took the turn into the Bellagio driveway on two tires but she slowed down well before pulling into the valet area. Benton decided that was progress.

CHAPTER 65

"Ros, Ros wake up!" Loverboy boomed in Rosalind's ear.

Rosalind felt like she was being dragged back from a great distance. For a moment she could not remember where she was. His face came into focus hanging right over hers, and it was completely clear.

"Hi," she said. *Smile at him. Make him feel at ease.* Her mouth tasted stale and her head ached. She smiled. "What time is it?"

"Pizza time! Mamma Celeste Deluxe Family Style!" he announced. "Now come on, lazybones! Don't make me do all the work!" He pulled her into a sitting position in bed, and turned her so that her feet were touching the ground.

She realized they were unbound again but her arms were still taped at the wrists. As he led her from the bed to the recliner she realized that something else was different too.

She was wearing the new nightgown he'd bought her the day before. He must have changed it while she was passed out.

Which meant he had to have seen the white marks on the back of the other one. The marks from leaning against the wall underneath the panel, looking for an escape route.

But he did not seem to be bothered. If anything, as he tucked the blanket around her in the recliner and began to riffle through the grocery bag near the door, he seemed calmer, more relaxed today than before.

"Did you have a good date?" she asked.

He looked up from the frozen pizza box he had been reading. "Date? Oh, yesterday. Yeah, it was great."

"What did you do?"

"Mommmm," he said in the tone of an exasperated teenager. "You don't expect me to tell you THAT, do you?"

"No," Rosalind agreed. Realized she really did not want to know.

"Right. Now are you ready? I've got to meet someone and I'm sort of short on time so you'll have to eat fast." He ripped open the pizza box.

"Do you have another date?"

"Is that any of your business?" he teased her. Then said, no longer teasing, "Maybe. Why? It's not like you care."

Rosalind heard his tone begin to seesaw between relaxed and tense. She shook her head. "That's not true. It is very boring here when you're not around. And"—her eye caught the TV—"and I hoped we could watch TV together tonight."

He looked from her to the TV, then back at her again. "That would be nice," he said. His voice was so sincerely wistful that for a moment Rosalind felt sorry for him.

Something horrible had made him this way. Something horrible and scary. She had thought she knew his history, but she realized now that you could never really know what went on behind the doors of anyone else's house when they were growing up. She said, as genuinely as she could, "It would be nice."

"Yep, but not tonight," he told her, matter-of-fact again. "I don't want anyone saying I'm a mama's boy." He pulled the pizza out of the vacuum-packed plastic bag and held it in front of her. "Eat up, Ros."

She stared from it to him. "It's frozen."

"It's frozen," he mimicked. "So? I should tell you this is your last meal for a while. Are you going to eat it or not?"

His eyes began to glaze over the way they did when he got angry. Rosalind knew that if she hesitated even a moment longer, he would take the food away.

At the very least, take the food away.

She opened her mouth and bit as hard as she could into the frozen crust. A huge piece cracked off and a square of frozen green pepper fell into her lap.

A corner jammed itself against her palate, poking the back of her throat. "Uh cah heeeew ich," she tried to say. Her arms flailed behind her. "Uh cah heew ich."

"Come on, Ros, we don't have time for your stupid games."

"Uh hoooaking."

"You're choking?" He stared at her. "You don't want your food?"

"Helll," Rosalind pleaded. "Pleeeeh helll muh."

Loverboy took the shard of pizza from her mouth and shook his head at her. "Why did you take such a big piece, Ros?" he scolded. "Bit off more than you could chew, didn't you?"

She gulped and nodded as she breathed hard. "I did. I'm sorry. I was just—just so excited to have pizza."

Why did that mollify him? Why did he suddenly look so happy? "Pizza's your favorite, isn't it, Ros? I knew it."

"One of them," she agreed. "It's one of yours too, isn't it?"

He nodded and began carefully breaking the pizza into smaller pieces. "Open up," he said, and tossed one into her mouth.

Rosalind managed to eat half the pizza that way. Her jaw ached with the effort of chewing the frozen crust and she felt cold, but at least she wasn't hungry. She was just swallowing the last bite when he said, "Ooh, I forgot! I have ANOTHER present for you."

The bite almost came back up. "Another one? Why?" she asked. This is it, she told herself. He saw the white paint and now he will punish me.

But when he reached into his coat pocket he pulled out a blue card with twenty bobby pins on it. "I bought you hairpins, like you asked for. Too bad we don't have time to play with them now. I'll leave them on the desk where you can look at them, though. So you can try to decide how you want me to pin you up."

Rosalind did not feel cold anymore. Her jaw did not ache. She could barely keep herself from weeping. Hairpins. When she asked for them she had been worried that he would remember the summer Jason became fascinated with locks, but she had to take the chance. It was her only chance. And he had brought them to her.

He had brought her an escape route.

"Time for your medicine," he told her, holding three tranquilizer capsules in his hand. She had learned to gauge how long he was going to be gone by the number of pills he gave her. Three meant a long time, which suited her well. She opened her mouth and let him put them in.

"Swallow," he ordered, and she did. He pinched her nose together to make her open her mouth so he could look around and poke under her tongue to be sure.

"Very good, Ros. You have really been very, very good today."

"Thank you," she said, careful not to move too much so the pills would not be too far down her throat. "So have you."

He stopped and stood motionless, staring at her after she said that and for a moment she thought she had made a mistake. But something clicked inside him and he smiled hugely. "I know. I am a good boy. I always am. 'Bye for now, Ros! See you soon!"

No, Rosalind thought. *No, you sick bastard, you won't.*

She managed to throw up only two of the three pills, but even if she slept a little, she should still have time for what she needed to do.

CHAPTER 66

Seven hours later, sitting on the end of the Santa Monica pier sucking chili from her fingertips with the cool wind off the ocean flapping around her ears, Imogen was thinking that Benton was right. Her mind felt alive again, away from what was going on in Las Vegas.

She glanced at the small copy of the collage anchored between the two of them under their Slurpees and the bottle of habanero salsa Benton had conned off Bugsy.

Sort of away from what was going on in Las Vegas.

Imogen slipped it out from under the Slurpees and stared at it. She looked out at the sea. She was getting closer. She could taste it. Closer, but not close enough.

He said, "I read in one of your files that sometimes you feel like you're thinking the same thoughts as the killer. What's that like?"

"It's like having Martina Kidd in my head all the time. Reminding me that there's not much that separates me from her."

"That's bullshit. What you love about your job is the challenge of unearthing the killer. What a killer loves is killing. You may think the same thoughts, but to opposite ends. It's a crucial difference."

Imogen was not sure what she was tasting at that moment, but it was new and it made her uncomfortable. She reached for the habanero sauce.

"What happened to your parents, Imogen?"

She took a moment to dot the sauce on a fingertip and suck it off before answering. "They committed suicide. I told you. Or Martina did."

"But why do you blame yourself?"

"I don't really. Not anymore." They sat in silence. "Oh hell, I do, you're right. It's because I started it. I was the one who saw the notice in the newspaper."

"Newspaper?"

"Tabloid. At the supermarket. It was about my father. He had once been sort of famous as a movie idol, but by the time I was born he was just doing theater. My mother was thirty-five years younger than he was. They met when she was eighteen and playing Ophelia opposite his Claudius in *Hamlet* at the Ashland Shakespeare Festival. Anyway, it must have been a slow gossip week, because one of the tabloids ran a story about my father on the cover. It said he had a gay lover. I didn't know what that was but it sounded nice. 'Gay' like happy. Love. So I asked my mother." Two beats of silence. "It did not sound as nice to her."

"Was it true?"

"Probably. You're the one who told me the tabloids always tell the truth. But my mother didn't know. Or didn't want to know. So she told my father she was going to commit suicide. And he, to prove to her how much he loved her, decided to do it with her."

"Are you kidding?"

"They were both actors. It made sense to them. Maybe my father had played Othello one too many times. Anyway, it was a fabulously dramatic exit." That was what love was, Imogen reminded herself. She remembered the way Julia talked about sharing everything with another person. The idea left Imogen cold.

"You do know that was not your fault, right?" Benton asked. "I mean, you've had therapy to address that?"

"Oh yes. Intellectually I'm all clear with it."

"And emotionally?"

"Emotionally I think I'm still about seven years old."

"Probably not ideal, but it will go perfectly with what I have planned next. Come on." Benton seized her by the hand and pulled her after him. They stopped in front of the Strongest Man booth. It looked like a prop from a 1940s movie, with a big mallet and a worn leather pad and a bell at the top of a meter that would say how hard you hit.

Benton handed the man two dollar bills and said, "Do you want to go first?"

"Uh, no. Go ahead."

He stepped onto the platform, picked up the mallet, and swung, hitting the bell at five hundred. Then he held the hammer out to Imogen. "Now you try."

"No, I won't get it."

He leaned close to her and looked very grave, like he was imparting ancient wisdom. "There is a little-known secret. It has nothing to do with arm strength, it's all in how strong your hands are. How hard you squeeze."

Imogen gripped the mallet hard and sent the ball flying up to three hundred.

"Try again. Close your eyes this time," Benton said, and for some reason she did. Stood on the platform and closed her eyes. "Feel the power of the force."

She opened one eye to look at him and he pressed his lips together. Then she took a deep breath, squeezed as hard as she could, and whammed the mallet down.

The bell rang. And for some reason she felt great.

"Told you you could do it," Benton said, repeating that after he showed her his secret tricks for the ring toss and skee ball.

"I saved the best for last," he said, and held open the door of the merry-go-round. He did not let her choose her own horse, but made her get onto a feisty white mare. He perched on a gray pony. They had gone around a few times before she noticed a plaque on the wall thanking Arbor Motors for the restoration of the horses and the mechanism. When she asked Benton about it he shrugged and said, "It's the merry-go-round they used in the movie *The Sting*. I couldn't let it get run-down. Besides, it's pretty great, isn't it?"

"Yes. It is pretty great." How many multimillionaire CEOs of auto companies had ever used the phrase *pretty great*? Imogen wondered.

They went on three times, the first two at Benton's insistence, the last time at hers. By then Imogen could see how two dates with him would be enough. Enough to make you want more. A lot more.

For someone else, she reminded herself.

It was dusk when they walked down the pier to the parking lot where they had left Benton's L.A. car, a 'sixty-nine Bel Air convertible. The sky was pink-orange and the ocean somewhere between gray and blue. Imogen grabbed Benton's arm and pulled him toward her and kissed him.

CHAPTER 67

When they separated, Benton was speechless but his eyes were the same color as the ocean.

Imogen, almost as surprised as he was, put her hands to her lips. "I should not have done that."

"Not if you want me to wait until the end of the investigation to pursue you."

"I do. It was just the perfect moment for it."

"It was," Benton agreed. "You can do it again if you want. I'll keep my eyes closed."

Imogen shook her head. "Benton, if this goes wrong, if we don't get him before——"

"You'll get him," Benton told her.

"No. Listen to me. If I don't, you are going to hate me. No matter how you feel about me now. You are going to hate me more than you ever thought you could hate anyone."

"Not possible," Benton told her, unconcerned. He unlocked her door and held it open for her. When she was in he slid into the driver's side.

Imogen's neck was craned to catch a last glimpse of the beach when Benton said, "Do you mind if we make one last stop before we go back to Vegas?" She shook her head and as they drove, listening to Tom Jones, top down, along the beach in the fading twilight Imogen felt oddly, inappropriately, at peace.

"Sam loved Tom Jones," she said, looking out to sea.

"I know," Benton said. "We talked about it during training. He said that his sister liked him too."

"Sam talked about me?"

"All the time. His brilliant younger sister who skipped third grade and went on to win a full scholarship to the University of Chicago. Plus a research position."

"It wasn't that big a deal," Imogen said. "They gave out two of them."

Benton opened his mouth to point out that two out of a freshman class of one thousand was a very big deal, but he knew she wouldn't listen. Instead he said quietly, "It was a big deal to him. He was proud of you." He heard a sharp intake of breath and looked over at her quickly. "I'm sorry, I didn't mean to upset you."

Imogen touched the corner of her eye and shook her head. "You didn't. It is nice to hear people talk about him. It makes him feel more—makes him feel closer."

They drove in silence for a few minutes until Benton took a right turn into an alley, waited for a gate to slide open, and pulled the car into a covered parking area.

"Where are we?" Imogen asked.

"My house."

"But you live in Detroit and New York City."

"No. I work in Detroit and New York City and I have apartments there and that is where I do all my entertaining. This is my house."

As he spoke he punched in a security code and a door clicked open. Imogen noticed that the mat in front of the door said, *Home Sweet Home,* in curly writing at odds with the sleek modernity of the structure.

They entered a huge glass-fronted room with double-high ceilings that looked right out onto the beach. The floor was bleached oak and all the chairs and couches were covered in smoky suede and framed by sandstone planters filled with spiky bamboo. They were all arranged around a square fire pit that extended from inside the room onto the terrace outside and was filled with smooth black stones. On one wall, which ran to an open kitchen, there were ten drawings, each in its own square black frame, each with the words, *Happy birthday Benton! Love, Jason,* scrawled across the bottom in increasingly more grown-up handwriting. The house was absolutely restful, ordered, peaceful, and yet intensely personal. It was not what Imogen would have expected. It tasted to her like the perfect balance of sweet and sour, heavy and light.

Benton handed her a bottle of water and, sliding open one of the enormous front windows, climbed up the stairs that ran along the fire pit onto the terrace. The railing was solid, clear glass topped with steel. He leaned his elbows on it and looked out across the bike path, over the sand at the sea.

"This place is wonderful, Benton," Imogen said, coming to join him.

He smiled. "I like it. I don't get here very often, but whenever I do, anything bothering me just seems to slip away. It always clears my head."

"I can see that."

They stood next to each other, not touching, sipping water and staring at the ocean and thinking their own thoughts for half an hour as the sun went down. When it was just a beam of light on the horizon Benton said, "I knew it would be good."

"What?"

"Being quiet with you. Vegas is so loud all the time it's hard to tell." He leaned on one arm and faced her. "We could spend the night here."

Imogen looked at him warily.

"That's not what I meant," he said. "There is a guest room."

She continued to study him in silence.

"I'm not going to lie to you, Imogen," he went on. "I would like to go to bed with you. And wake up with you. And maybe spend the rest of my life with you. But I would rather have nothing than just your company between the sheets. I want a lot more than that from you, and I am willing to wait until after the investigation is finished to convince you that you want that too. I am not used to being patient, but I'm good at it when I have to be. Don't think, though, that when this is all over I am going to just let you slip away. As soon as you give me leave I am going to pursue you like you've never been pursued before."

"I'm good at hiding."

"I have noticed. But I'm very good at hide-and-seek."

Imogen's mind grappled onto the words Hide-and-Seek, shutting off her other thoughts. Hide-and-Seek. Work. Safe. Good. She said to Benton, "I told you about my childhood. Now tell me about yours."

Looking back out to sea he said, "You've seen my FBI file."

"Yes. Man who commutes to work in helicopters, who's been engaged to two princesses—"

"Just one, and that was only for show," he interrupted her. "Artemis really wanted to marry a horse breeder named Rolf, but she knew her mother, Queen Patrice, would never approve it. There was only one person Queen Patrice disliked more than Rolf, and that was me, because— That doesn't matter. Anyway, Artemis figured that if she announced she and I were engaged, when we called it off her mother would be so relieved that she would welcome Rolf with open arms into the family."

"Did it work?"

"Don't you read the tabloids? Bad question. Sorry."

Imogen shook her head at his apology, but looked at him seriously. "Doesn't it bother you to be followed around by those people? By the press? To have everything you do documented?"

"No. Despite your parents' experience, the press can be your ally if you play them right. It's just a public persona. And it's good for sales and stockholder confidence. Plus, if I disappeared someone would be bound to notice. At least, that's what I tell myself."

Imogen considered this. "Okay, you were only *almost* engaged to one princess. And you fly a helicopter to work. Julia says it's because you're too controlling to take an elevator. Is that true?"

"Sort of. I don't like elevators."

"Why not?"

"I was trapped in one once. It was—unpleasant." He scrounged in the pockets of his jeans and came out with a pack of Juicy Fruit. "Want a piece?"

Imogen shook her head as he folded two sticks into his mouth.

"How did you get out?"

"It is a long story. Some building-maintenance people found me finally."

"How long were you stuck?"

"An awfully long time," Benton said. His tone made it clear he wasn't saying anything else.

Imogen looked for another way in. "Your dossier doesn't say much about you when you were younger except that you lived with your father outside of New York City. What was that like?"

"Cold."

"Do you mean lonely?"

"I mean cold. My father managed to blow most of his fortune, but he didn't want anyone to know he was broke. So we had to keep living in the family mansion, this huge house, even though we couldn't afford to heat it. Only my father's study was heated, and kids weren't allowed in there. I spent most of my time in the kitchen with the servants because we had to keep a butler and a cook and a chauffeur for appearance's sake."

"How old were you when your parents divorced?"

"Ten. A little past ten. It was just after my tenth birthday." He paused. "After that it was just my father and me. Just the men."

Imogen tasted discomfort from him. "Did you see your mother often?"

"Not then. She was always away. On a cruise or a world tour. She had money of her own and married more of it."

"What about your father? Did he date?"

That made Benton laugh. "No. The only women my father had time for were the bitches who gave birth to the greyhounds that ran at the dog park."

"He gambled?"

"When he had money. Once I was older, I was able to control it."

"Didn't he have a company to run?"

"After a certain point, the company was better off without him. When my mother left, my father became strange. He managed to alienate the rest of our family, so they were just thrilled to watch him run Arbor Motors into the ground. Family fun, Arbor style. That's what ruined my father. He needed an audience, and as his power and influence slipped away, he had to stoop lower to get one."

"Benton, the other day, when I said what I did about the way you are with the press and—"

"You were right. I do like to be the center of attention. To be needed. But I was right too. You strike out at others when you are feeling bad. "

"That's one of my better habits. You should know the bad ones."

"I intend to," he said. He looked out to sea. "We were talking about my father. He reacted a little like you when he felt bad, only he didn't just lash out, he got paranoid. His paranoia got worse and he decided that everyone at the office was ganging up on him behind his back, so he wouldn't go there anymore. That was when he started spending his days at the dog track. He got a whole new audience there, mostly men in slick suits. At first he only saw these new friends at the track, but later they came to the house. I'd be trotted in to perform for them."

"What did you do?"

"Card tricks mainly. Three-card monte sometimes."

Imogen faced him. "You performed magic tricks for your father's loan sharks?"

"Yep. I've got quick hands." He waved his fingers at her. "I think my father's master plan was to convince them not to kill him because he had such a promising son."

"Did it work?"

"Either that or the fact that I would hand them some of my mother's jewelry as they left for payments."

"You make it sound so jolly."

"It was, sort of. As you like to mention, I don't mind attention and I rarely got any from my father. And he was less prone to one of his moods when there were other people around. Plus, it was not like I was going to wear the jewelry. My mother had left it behind, with everything else, because she did not want it anymore. It was good training too. I learned how to read an audience. Comes in handy at stockholders meetings."

"Julia says you rebuilt Arbor motors single-handedly."

"Oh sure. Never believe a publicist. It was me and about nine hundred other people. And Cal. He is invaluable. My mother and grandmother were not thrilled when Julia decided to marry him. I guess they thought he was below her, but I personally was overjoyed. Not only does he make her happy, which is no mean feat, but it also meant that no one would be able to woo him away. He would be worth several million dollars to any of our competitors."

"Don't you have the same training?"

"More or less. We both have an engineering background, although he went to MIT while I only went to Harvard, but that's what makes him so remarkable. What he does goes beyond training. I had to learn everything, but it all comes naturally to him. When we worked at the garage together during college, a car would pull in for service and, just listening to it as it parked, he could guess what was wrong. And he never made a mistake—we used to bet on it. He's kind of like you with killers."

He brought it up casually. It was the first time anyone had mentioned it that way, in passing. Even Sam had never done that. He'd been too nervous about upsetting her. But Benton acted as if it were normal that she could think like bad people. As if she were normal.

"Okay," Imogen said.

"Okay?"

"Okay, we can spend the night. Me in the guest room."

Benton gave her a crooked smile. "It is an honor to have you as my guest, Imogen Page."

"It's an honor to be your guest." Guest was safe.

CHAPTER 68

Night had fallen while they were talking and the bike path in front of the patio cleared out. A woman Rollerbladed by behind a large woolly dog; then there was silence. The houses around Benton's were dark.

"Want to go for a walk on the beach?" he asked.

"Isn't it dangerous?"

"Not with your left jab."

They both changed into sweatshirts and sweatpants—his huge on Imogen—and headed out barefoot onto the beach. Occasionally they would exchange a word but mostly they just walked next to each other listening to the ocean. After nearly an hour they turned back. When they were about even with Benton's house he stopped.

He looked her up and down. "Are you ready?"

"For what?"

"A swim. It's the traditional end to a walk on the beach." He was out of his sweatshirt and sweatpants and into the surf in a flash of lightning. "Oh boy, that feels great," he called out to her. "Come on. No, don't think about it, just do it."

Imogen stood hesitating on the shore. The water tickling her toes was arctic. "It's February," she pointed out to him. "It's too cold for swimming."

He cupped his hand over his ear, and shouted, "What? Come on, it's great! Trust me!"

Imogen retreated up the shore, stripped off her clothes, and ran in after him. She stopped abruptly. "Oh God, oh God, this is freezing," she yelled as the water splashed her knees.

Benton, a head floating on the surf in front of her, cackled. "I made you get in, I made you."

She just looked at him, adult to immature boy. "But I'm not in. You are."

The cackling stopped. "Are you chicken?"

"That isn't going to work this time."

"You mean I got into this freezing water for nothing?"

"Yes."

"Oh man."

He sounded so sad, and so much like a disappointed boy, that Imogen dove in and swam toward him.

"That's better, isn't it?" he asked her as her head spluttered to the surface.

"No. This is deadly."

"I told you you'd be glad."

"I'm not glad."

"Yes, you are. And so am I." Benton bopped over, kissed her fast on the cheek, and disappeared.

"Benton?"

Nothing. It was suddenly very cold.

"Benton?"

Something brushed against Imogen's ankle.

"Benton!" she called out to sea.

"Right here," a voice behind her shouted. She turned and saw him standing on the shore. Moonlight glittered over his naked body.

It was quite a body. It appeared that there was a lot to be said for taking the stairs. For all her self-control, Imogen was normal, and a normal woman faced with a body like that might—

No, she told herself.

Benton held his sweatshirt out to her like a towel as she walked up the sloping shore and wrapped her in it. When she'd stopped shivering, he put it on. He pretended to look modestly away so she could get dressed.

"I see you peeking," she told him as she climbed back into his sweatpants and sweatshirt. She had never felt more like a teenager in her life. Especially when she was a teenager.

"You looked too."

"I did," Imogen admitted.

"Well?"

"Are you asking for compliments?"

"No, I just want to know if you find me disgusting."

Imogen thought about it. "No."

Benton's grin was huge. "Excellent."

She looked at him and thought about how much Sam would like him. Would like him for her. How much she liked him for her.

Benton must have seen her face change. He said, "What's wrong?"

"I was thinking about my brother." She swallowed and stared at the ocean. "He would have—"

She could not make the words come. The lump in her throat—not there a second ago, now everywhere—was huge, enormous. She gulped it back, hard, and then the words did come, no stopping, pouring out. "Do you know what the last thing was that Sam wanted? The very last thing that he asked for?"

Benton shook his head, not even sure she was addressing him.

"Well, he couldn't ask," Imogen said, slapping away her tears. "He couldn't really speak. But he kept . . . he kept . . . Oh God—"

The syllables were wrenched from her. Benton went and put his arms around her. "It's okay," he whispered into her hair. "It's okay."

She shook her head into his chest and balled fistsful of his sweatshirt. "At the end, he kept raising up his arms in a circle, and I didn't know what it meant. I tried everything. Everything I could think of. Except the right thing. All he wanted was a hug. That was what the circle meant, it was a hug. All he wanted was for me to hold him. And I didn't figure it out. And he died."

Imogen was sobbing, crying harder than she ever cried. The

thought of Sam, dying cold and alone because she had been too stupid, too selfish to know what he wanted, wrenched through her entire body. At the ultimate critical moment, her understanding had failed her. She was no good. She was impotent. "I didn't figure it out and he died," she repeated, pulling out of Benton's arms. "Don't you see? That's what is going to happen to Rosalind. I'm not going to figure it out and she's going to die."

"No," Benton told her. "It is not just you. It's all of us. A team. And we are going to figure it out."

"How? I'm stuck. I've stared at that collage until I see pieces of it everywhere and I can't find the right answer."

"You will. We will. There's still time." He gathered her back into his arms. "There's still time."

They stood on the beach like that for a long time before turning and heading back. Neither of them noticed the homeless man hunkered down low behind the garbage can as they made their way up the beach to Benton's house.

"Do you want to fly back to Vegas tonight?" he asked when they had dusted off their feet and were standing on the terrace.

Imogen thought about it. "No. You are right, it is too noisy there. I feel like my thoughts are clearer now. I want to go to bed, though. I feel a little fragile."

She could not believe the things she was telling this man. Benton reached out and touched her hair and she did not mind. "You don't look it. Come on, I'll show you your room."

He led her up a set of Lucite stairs to a bluish-white corridor that ended in a floor-to-ceiling window. On either side of the corridor was a single door. "That's my room." Benton indicated the door on the left. "That's your room." He pointed to the right. "And the balcony, which you can't really see in the dark, runs across the front of the house. If you follow it around you'll get to an outdoor shower if you want to rinse off from your swim. It's actually nicer in the morning, though. Of course, there's a regular shower in your room."

"Thanks," Imogen said.

"Thanks," Benton repeated.

He was halfway down the stairs when she did it. She took a deep breath and said, "Breakfast at seven-thirty?"

"Yes," he called back. She could hear the smile in his voice.

Imogen stayed up late listening to the ocean and thinking about Benton.

But not as late as Benton stayed up thinking about her.

CHAPTER 69

At two A.M., with a stinging neck and aching knees, after hours of false starts that felt like an eternity, Rosalind rolled onto her back on the dusty carpet of her prison and wept. The bobby pin slid from her mouth to the floor but she did not care. She did not need it anymore.

She'd picked the lock on his desk drawer. Now all she needed was to get the zipper on the manicure set open. Then she would be free.

She fell asleep.

4 days left!

Benton woke abruptly with the knowledge that he was being watched. He'd left the sliding glass doors of his bedroom open the night before so he could hear the ocean. Now there was someone standing there.

He reached for his glasses and something to use as a weapon. Saw it was Imogen in the door, and put down the water bottle. She was wearing the terry-cloth robe he had put in her bedroom for her, but it was too long and dragged on the ground like a train. She was barefoot and her hair was a mess and he'd never seen a sexier woman in his life.

"Hi," he said. Glanced at his clock. It was only a quarter past six. "It's a little early for breakfast."

She nodded.

"Are you okay?" he asked.

She nodded again. Took a deep breath. And said, "I was wondering if you wanted to take a shower with me."

Then somehow they were together, standing wrapped around each other in the middle of his bedroom floor and she was saying, Benton I can't stop thinking about you and he was saying, I don't want you to not ever, and she said, Your socks don't match, and he said, I love you Imogen and whatever you are going to say you are wrong.

Holding her face in his hands to say, "I do love you."

She looked at him and said, "I never thought the best day of my life would be in the middle of a murder investigation," and then, "I can't believe I just told you that," and he couldn't stop kissing her.

His hands slid under her robe and touched her naked skin, and she made a little noise that made him want to keep touching her everywhere. She wasn't wearing any panties, and when he pushed the robe off of her saw she wasn't wearing anything at all and he almost lost it right there, her looking up at him through lashes giving him a mock foxy look and then cracking up, cracking him up.

They were on the bed.

She pulled herself up so she was even with his ear and said, "Knock, knock," as her hand moved down his chest, toward his crotch.

"A man could get hurt with what you're doing," he told her as her hand circled his penis.

"That's not your line," she said, her finger tracing the length of him.

He squeezed out, "Who's there?"

"Fido."

"Fido who?"

She climbed astride him and said, "Fidon't get to have you inside me soon, Benton Arbor, I am going to explode."

Benton pulled her so she was lying still on top of him. "Did you make that up right now?"

"Yes." She pawed his chest. "And I meant it. Woof-woof."

"That has got to be the worst knock-knock joke ever created."

She moved her hips against him. "Let's see you do better."

"Not now. Later. Much lat— Damn."

"What is wrong?"

"Protection," Benton said. "This is so unexpected that I hadn't even thought about it. I don't have—"

"Don't move," Imogen ordered, climbing off of him. She slipped through his bedroom door and came back a minute later holding a box of condoms. "I hadn't thought of it either, but Reggie had."

"I'll have to write him a thank-you note."

She climbed on top of him and ripped one of the foil packages open with her teeth, which almost made Benton come right there. Moving down his body, she knelt in front of his penis, put the condom in her mouth, and slid it all the way down.

Benton thought he was a goner but held on, and then he was inside her and their eyes were locked and he said, I've never felt— and she said, Me either. Not like this. Then her eyes closed and she was making the little noises again, sometimes saying his name, and he wanted to hold on to it, this moment, this feeling, forever.

He stopped moving.

Her eyes came open slowly. "What are you—"

"Knock, knock," he said.

"No," she shook her head. "Not *now*."

"Knock, knock," he insisted.

"Who's there?"

"Ida."

"Ida?" Imogen repeated.

"That's not your line—"

"Ida who?" she corrected.

Benton smiled triumphantly. "Ida slow down if you want this to last more than another twenty seconds."

Imogen stared at him in disbelief and struggled to push down her laughter and failed. She collapsed on his chest, saying, "That was terrible," and laughing even more.

He was laughing almost as hard as she was. "I know. I made it up right on the spot."

Soon they were both crying they were laughing so hard, and then laughter gave way to moans and they were panting and gasping and clinging together. Arms and legs twined together, the pressure between them mounted until they were both making a lot of noise, and she said, "Oh God," and Benton said her name over and over again.

Afterward, they lay tangled together chuckling, holding hands. Benton pushed her hair off her forehead and let his hand rest on her cheek. "You aren't going to regret this."

"I know." Her eyes shifted to the clock. "It's almost time for breakfast. Now do you want to take a shower with me?"

He kissed her, and without taking his lips from hers picked her up, walked into the bathroom for two towels, and carried her outside. Her back pressed against the wall of the shower and his leg came up beneath her, anchoring her as he adjusted the water. Imogen felt one of his hands groping for something along the wall, and the sound of Tom Jones singing "She's a Lady" filtered into the shower.

They danced under the shower with Tom Jones singing over the sound of the Pacific Ocean, and the sun rising to the east behind them and whispered to each other and both felt spectacular. Then they dressed, grabbed a quick breakfast, and flew back to Vegas.

"What do you taste when we are making love?" Benton asked as his plane taxied to its parking spot at the Vegas airport.

Imogen blushed. "Really?"

"Yes."

"Juicy Fruit gum."

"I thought you didn't like the way that tasted."

"I do now."

CHAPTER **71**

Benton and Imogen managed to keep their hands off each other as they walked through the lobby, barely, but when they got to the empty elevator bank Benton pulled Imogen into his arms and kissed her. He was still kissing her when the doors of the elevator opened, and when they closed, and reopened on the thirty-fifth floor. He kept kissing her all the way to the door of her room.

They stopped there and looked at each other in silence for an instant. A flicker of discovery crossed Imogen's face and she said, "You just took an elevator."

Benton frowned. It had been twenty-six years since he had been in an elevator. "I guess I did." His mouth was just coming down on hers when Bugsy opened the door of her suite.

"I thought I heard you out here," he said, trying hard to pretend he had not interrupted anything. "I'm sorry to butt in, boss, but there's someone on the phone you should talk to." He cleared his throat. "Someone angry."

" 'Bye," Imogen said to Benton.

" 'Bye."

He kissed her on the lips. "See you at lunch."

"Um-hmm." He started walking down the corridor and she said, "You're going the wrong way. The stairs are in the other direction."

"I'm taking the elevator."

Imogen hugged herself as she walked into her room.

Benton went and stood in front of the elevator bank. He pushed the down button. The doors opened. He took a step in—

Nobody loves you, you little freak! a voice shouted in his head. *Nobody cares about you! You're a disgusting shit! PAY ATTENTION TO ME WHEN I TALK TO YOU!*

—and stopped.

He fumbled in his pocket for a piece of Juicy Fruit and turned, retracing his path to the stairs.

The voice on the other end of the phone was so loud Imogen had to hold it away from her ear. "Just what the hell are you doing out there, Imogen?"

She tilted the mouthpiece toward her. She could not stop smiling. She said, "Hi, Lex, how are you today?"

"Why haven't you been answering your phone for the last half hour?"

"I was on an airplane. Is there something in particular you wanted to talk to me about? I'm sort of busy."

"I know you've been busy. Have you checked your fax machine?"

"Not yet, I just—"

"Got home. I know. Go look at what I sent you. I'll hold on."

Imogen crossed to the fax machine and picked up the six sheets of paper. They were dark and each appeared to be part of a larger image. She organized them on the surface of the table and stepped backward.

It was a setup of the front cover of a tabloid. The photo showed a couple on the beach, each of them half-naked, embracing. The headline said "LOVERGIRL?"

It was her and Benton. It had to have been taken the night before, on the beach, when he was drying her with his sweatshirt. Beneath the headline the caption read: *The Inside Scoop on How the FBI Really Spends Its Time.* The publication date was the following week.

Imogen picked up the phone. She wasn't smiling anymore.

Lex said, "Well, what do you think? Are you proud of yourself?"

Oh golly, yes, she was tempted to say. I've always wanted to be a cover model. She said, "I think it's libel. Can you kill it before it hits the stands?"

"Yes. In exchange for dropping the charges you brought against that woman. Leslie Lite, the reporter."

"Do it."

"We are going to. And now I'll tell you what you are going to do. You are going to stay the hell away from Benton Arbor. You are not going to see him. You are not going to be in the same room with him. I don't even want him in Vegas. Do you understand?"

"Yes. You'll have to tell him."

"Elgin is on the phone with him right now. You're not going to see him before he leaves either, got that?"

Imogen nodded but said nothing.

"What did you think you were doing, Gigi?"

"I wasn't thinking," Imogen answered honestly. And she wasn't sorry either.

She listened through another ten minutes of Lex lecturing her. She hung up and called Benton. "Did you hear?" she asked when he answered on the first ring.

"Yes. I've got my walking papers. I'm leaving for Detroit in an hour. I'm not even allowed to come up and see you to say good-bye. They've got someone here baby-sitting me."

"I'm sorry, Benton."

"Me too. I was looking forward to having breakfast with you tomorrow."

Imogen smiled into the phone. "There's always next week," she heard herself say, and could not believe the words had come out of her mouth.

"That is what I like to hear. Look, I know you don't need me, but call if you just want to talk. Or if there is anything I can do."

"I will."

"Don't forget about me, okay?"

He sounded so much like a lonely child that she laughed. "I couldn't, even if I wanted to. And I don't want to."

Long pause.

"I love you, Imogen Page," he said and hung up, fast.

Imogen was still smiling when she put down the receiver. Then she turned to where Bugsy had repinned the collage to her wall. The smile vanished.

Not Loverboy's smile. His was big big big. He thought: *Roses are red, violets are blue, I've got Rosalind, and now, Imogen, I've got you too.*

Rosalind did not know how long she had been asleep, but she was sure it was too long. She had learned to recognize the different times of day from the amount of noise that filtered in from outside, and the faint sounds she heard now said it was daytime. He could be back at any moment. She had to rush.

She used her knee to open the heavy drawer of the drafting table, and picked out the manicure set with her teeth. She dropped it on the drafting table and bent over the zipper. It was tiny and recessed between the two sides of the leather case. Using her tongue, she was able to make it stick out so that her teeth could almost reach it. Almost.

Not good enough. She was losing precious minutes.

Her heart pounding, she turned around and propped her bound wrists on the edge of the table. Her fingers were numb and awkward from being without blood for so long. She closed her eyes and pictured the manicure set. There, right there, she could touch it, her right index finger could just make out its edge. *Good,* she told herself. *Keep going, Ros, you can do it.*

Her finger slid along the edge of the zipper until she found the pull. *Come on, thumb,* she urged her fingers, as if they weren't part of her. *Come on, dammit, come—*

Her index finger and thumb closed on the zipper pull. But

every time they moved, the manicure set moved too. She fought back the urge to cry. When did simple things become so hard?

She fumbled blindly with the zipper, anchoring the case against her back, pulling her arms as far down as they would go. From a great distance she heard the quiet hiss of the zipper coming undone. It was the best sound she had ever heard.

She pushed the manicure case open. Clumsy hands touched each piece in turn, as she tried to guess what would work best to cut through the duct tape he'd bound her wrists with. After four tries she managed to get her fingers into the holes of the nail scissors and turn them toward the tape.

They slipped off and fell onto the floor and as she bent to get them she heard the footsteps.

Dannie leaned over the table and handed her report around. Her cheeks were slightly flushed with excitement. "He did it in every city. The Florida case is less sure because they thought they had someone for it and the body was found in a swimming pool instead of a bathtub, but it sounds like our guy. They'd rather this didn't get out. Anyway, same MO, woman strangled after sex and left in a body of water. In every case where sheets were recovered, they had been sprayed with Poison perfume."

Tom, Harold, Bugsy, and Imogen all nodded. Imogen said, "Excellent work, Dannie. Did any of them have hickeys?"

"No. That's the other difference. And I haven't had time to figure out if they'd been on a date with their killer before they wound up dead. But I did notice another parallel. All of them except Marielle seem to have been killed at about the same point in Loverboy's cycle."

"Maybe that's connected to the hickey," Tom said. "Like he sort of lost control with her."

"Maybe," Imogen said. She scanned Dannie's report. "So they were all killed three days before the date on the collage. Three days before he killed his actual victim."

"Yes. Which would be—"

Bugsy glanced at the calendar pinned to the wall and said, "Tomorrow."

The table got quiet. Imogen slowly exhaled. She thought about the word-search page she'd found in the taxi.

Now someone must pay.

Was this what he meant?

"Payday," Imogen said to herself. She looked up abruptly and repeated it. "Payday. My God, that's it."

Dannie stopped evening the pages of the file she was putting away. Tom and Harold froze. Everyone knew what it meant when Imogen got that tone.

Bugsy said, "What?"

"That's the cycle. I could be wrong, but it tastes right. Every two weeks. *Payday.*"

"Why would payday make someone want to kill?" Dannie asked.

"Yeah," Tom put in. "I'm always happy on payday."

"I don't know," Imogen admitted. Tasted lime and burned leaves and heard her aunt's voice demanding, "Do you know how much we give up for you, ungrateful girl?"

Payday always made Aunt Caroline angry. It was always the worst time of the month. It was when she felt poorest, most taken advantage of. Most used by her ungrateful niece and nephew, her sinning sister's half-savage children.

Payday. Imogen spent most of them locked in her room without dinner.

"Maybe it is not about his pay cycle, but one of his parents'," Imogen suggested. The blank looks around the table told her the others did not understand what she meant. "It fits in with what I was thinking, about the collage. The name brands. Money, the power to buy things, held some sort of power in his home when he was growing up. He wanted things, yearned for things. Things mean something to him." The peanut taste in her mouth was stronger now. She was close.

She looked at the blank faces around her and it faded.

Close to what? What did any of that matter anyway? It brought them no closer to finding Rosalind.

She blew her bangs off her forehead. "I've been looking over the old case files, and I noticed another pattern. One that Dannie's discovery of the bodies fits into, as his way of blowing off steam. I think he has to have sex with the women as a sort of affirmation of his desirability and power, and he has to kill them so he does not kill his victims too early. Because although we don't really know how Loverboy spends the first half of the time he holds his victims hostage, I think we can have a pretty good idea of how he spends the last few days."

Imogen went to the whiteboard she'd had Bugsy bring in and wrote:

Three days before final day: Kills another woman.
Two days before final day: Begins torturing his victim.
One day before final day: Stops feeding them. More torture.
Final day: murder.

She faced her team. "I want to get him as soon as possible, obviously. But, given what he proposes to do to Rosalind Carnow, I think we all agree it's imperative we stop him before he gets here." Her finger rested on the heading *Two days before final day*. "That is the day after tomorrow. Which means we have today, tomorrow, and possibly the next morning to find him. I don't care what you have to do to run down leads, do it. Tom, stay on the Dumpsters. Dannie, you keep working on the dead women, but I want you to focus your attention on the local dry cleaners and laundries. I'm betting Loverboy won't have wanted to keep Rosalind's clothes lying around, possibly collecting clues, so he probably left them where he had them washed, which means he will have to be picking them up in the next day or two. Send around that description of the clothes Rosalind was taken in again. Metro should be able to help you with manpower on this. Harold, I want you to run the security tapes of supermarkets and convenience stores in a one-mile radius of the airport through Metro's face-recognition software. Loverboy must be buying food somewhere. If anyone matches my description of the cabdriver, or the craps dealer's, particularly if they are repeat visitors to the store in the last week, I want to hear about it." Her eyes went around the table. "If any of you find anything, no matter how small, call me or Bugsy right away. We've got to stop him this time."

Three nods, three chairs pushed away from the table. Silence as they filed out.

In her head, Imogen counted down. Three days, two days, one day, payday.

SOMEONE MUST PAY!

"Do you want me to turn off the air-conditioning, boss?" Bugsy asked. "You're shivering."

Imogen shook her head. "It won't help."

"Oh good, Ros, you're awake," he said, coming into the family room. Rosalind was panting and there was sweat running down her face but he didn't seem to notice. He did not even look around to make sure everything was in the right place.

She shifted in the recliner so the scissors weren't poking her in the back anymore.

"So I brought new tapes for us to watch." He held up two cassettes. Like all the others, these had stickers that said *BELLAGIO SECURITY DO NOT REMOVE* on them. "But I can't do it right now. I've got to go see a man about a car." He chuckled to himself.

Rosalind followed him with her eyes as he went to set the tapes and the grocery bag he was carrying on his desk. Please don't let him notice the hairpins are gone, she thought. Please don't let him notice—

The drawer wasn't closed all the way, and there was a piece of paper sticking out of it. How could she have been so careless? There was no way he wasn't going to notice that. Notice and know and—

But he just put the bag down on the desk and turned to face her.

"God, Ros, you look like you've been running a marathon. Why are you so sweaty?"

"I—I think I've got a cold," Rosalind stammered. "A fever."

He came and put his hand on her forehead. "I don't feel anything." He leaned down and stared in her eyes. "Are you sure you're not just making this up to get more attention?" His gaze moved to her lap. "Jeez, Ros, you've gotten yourself messy again." He picked a piece of fuzz from her nightgown. It must have stuck when she was crawling back into the recliner. *Now* he was going to know, now he was going to—

He stared at it intently. He held it out to her. "Make a wish, Ros," he said, and blew it onto the ground.

"I hope you wished for popcorn for lunch, because that's what you're having." He reached into the grocery bag and brought out a sack of cheese-flavored popcorn. "I didn't have time to get anything fancy."

"That's okay," she assured him.

"I knew it would be. I knew whatever I did would be okay with you. Because you like me SOOO much." He leaned his face right in front of hers. "Isn't that right, Rosalind?"

"That's right." She swallowed hard. She did not understand what he was doing.

He stood up. "I know." He reached into his coat pocket and pulled something out, then opened the bag of popcorn. "Sometimes, Ros, you make me feel so silly, do you know that?"

Rosalind looked at him warily. Slowly, she shook her head.

"Well, you do. Now open wide," he said. She did and he shoved a handful of popcorn into her mouth.

"Good, huh?" he asked. "Are you—"

His phone started to ring, interrupting him. He pulled it out of his pocket and looked at the caller ID. "Hey, Ros, it's a friend of yours." He held it out to her and the name *BITCH* flashed on the screen. "That's Julia. Want to talk to her?"

Rosalind chewed and swallowed as fast as she could. "Yes."

"Too bad! I don't think we'll take that call." He pushed a button and transferred it to his voice mail. "Now, where were we? Oh right. Time for another bite. Ready?"

"I'm not sure—"

He pushed popcorn into her mouth. This second helping was

bigger, and it took Rosalind a minute to realize what he had done. By then it was too late.

"Ha ha!" he said, rocking from one foot to the other. "I fooled you, didn't I, Ros? I snuck your medicine in with the popcorn. Ha ha ha!"

Rosalind tried to push the unchewed parts of the tranquilizer capsules under her tongue but she'd already swallowed at least one of them.

"Don't look at me that way, Ros," he scolded her. "It's for your own good. Pleasant dreams!"

He closed the door behind him.

CHAPTER 76

Bugsy picked up his phone on the third ring. "Yes." He listened for a moment, laughed, said, "Hold on."

He slid the phone from under his mouth. "It's Julia, boss. She wants to know if we've seen Wrightly Waring."

"No."

"No," Bugsy repeated into the mouthpiece.

Imogen was standing and looking at the maps with "family fun" sites marked on them from Loverboy's earlier kills. Over her shoulder she said, "Ask Julia if she knows if there is a racetrack near Yorba, California. And also where the Arbor Motors track is near Boston."

Bugsy relayed the questions, nodded, and hung up. "Julia says there's a defunct motor speedway in Anaheim that Arbor and a few other companies use as a test track, and that their facility in Boston is up the Lynnway near Route 1A."

Imogen marked both of those on the maps and studied them.

"Find anything?"

"No. Except that racing must be a very popular sport, because there seem to be racetracks near every large and small town in America." She turned around and took one of the last Tootsie Pops from the box. "You and Julia are certainly becoming good friends," she said.

Bugsy cracked up. "You sound like a mom from a 'fifties sitcom. Have you forgotten that I'm gay, or are you jealous?"

"No. But Cal might be if you don't watch out."

"I don't think I'm the one Cal needs to worry about."

"What do you mean? Do you think Julia is having an affair?"

"I'd say it's likely."

Imogen frowned. "That's so odd. She went on and on to me the other day about the joys of marriage. But you think she's sleeping with another man?"

Bugsy shook his head. "No. I think she's sleeping with Rachel."

"Rachel? J.D.'s assistant?"

"Exactly."

"Are you saying that Julia is bisexual?"

"Something like that. But she's not out—probably will never be out. She's terrified of what Benton would say, how he would react. The whole family. At least that's my take. She bends over backward to seem heterosexual and to make Cal happy. But I wouldn't be surprised if she and Rachel haven't been seeing each other clandestinely for some time."

Imogen thought back over the night when Rachel had given her a ride back to the Bellagio. Could she have been coming to see Julia?

"Do you think Cal knows?" she asked.

"No way. She's so terrified of anyone finding out that she acts the part of the perfect wife. Do anything for him, meet his needs before he's even thought of them himself. You know who does know, though, I think?"

Imogen nodded to herself. "J.D."

"Right. That's why she seems so scared around him. I think she's always afraid he's going to blurt it out."

"Poor Julia. It has got to be horrible for her to have such a big and important secret. That must be why she's so busy pretending not to have any."

"I hadn't thought of that. But I do think it's making her unhappy."

Imogen pictured her with Lancelot, the hairless dog she refused to touch, whom she called Little Ugly. "You can dress it up but underneath it's still ugly," Julia had said. At the time Imogen had wondered which of them she was talking about, but now she thought she knew.

"Do you think she'll live like that forever?"

"She doesn't think she has a choice. She's afraid her family will disown her."

Family. The crux of everything. The crux of the case. The word had always tasted cold and metallic to Imogen, something she was outside of. But now it had taken on a new undertone. Licorice.

Menace. Torment.

Family fun.

TICK-TOCK-TICK-TOCK!

Imogen glanced at the clock as she picked up the phone. It was just past midnight.

"Hello?"

"Knock, knock."

She laughed. "Who's there?"

"Pretty."

"Pretty who?"

"Pretty lonely here without you."

"How long did it take you to make that up, Benton?"

"Not so long. Some time. Did you like it?"

"What are you doing up so late?" she said instead of answering.

"Thinking about you. What are you doing?"

"Going crazy."

"Anything new today?"

"Nothing good. Nothing good enough."

He said, "It will come."

"I miss having you around."

There was a long pause. Imogen thought maybe she'd said something wrong. "Are you there?" she asked.

"Yes. I just—I didn't expect you to say that. It was nice."

"It's true."

"I miss being around you."

"How's Detroit?"

"Cold. And lonely. I don't want to talk about that. How's Rex?"

Imogen looked at him, back in his fancy tank. There was a little treasure chest in there with him now that she hadn't noticed before. "I think he's sleeping."

"What a novel idea. Why don't you try it?"

"I don't have time."

"You'll think better if you get some sleep."

"I'm too tense."

"Where are you?"

"In my bedroom. I'm working in bed."

"Alone?"

"Of course. Well, me and Rex."

"I mean, is Bugsy in the other room or something?"

"No."

"What are you wearing?"

"My pajamas."

"The ones with the flying toasters on them? The ones that are too big for you?"

"Yes."

"God, I wish I were there. Do you have any idea how sexy you look in those?"

"Benton." Imogen laughed. "That's absurd."

"No, really. When you answered the door wearing them the other day, you took my breath away."

It was the nicest compliment anyone had ever paid her. "Thank you."

"You are welcome. I wish I were there lying in bed next to you while you worked."

"I wish you were, too."

"Since I can't be, humor me by going to sleep. Just for a few hours."

"I'm not tired."

"Of course you aren't. If you turn out your light and unwrap one of the chocolates the hotel puts on your pillow, I'll tell you a bedtime story."

Benton's story had a very relaxing effect on Imogen. Ten minutes later, her body felt weightless and she could not keep her eyes open.

"Do you think you can sleep now?" Benton asked disingenuously.

"Sleep? I can hardly move. Benton, what did you do to me?"

He laughed, satisfied. "My work here is finished. I'll call you at breakfast time."

"I'll be waiting."

CHAPTER 78

"Sorry I couldn't get here until now," Dannie said, setting down her briefcase in "their room" at the Fun Motel. "Work is crazy."

Loverboy helped her out of her jacket, all polite. "Are there new developments in the case?" he asked. He was the Interested Boyfriend. He knew so many roles.

"Yes and no," she said. "Imogen thinks she knows why he kills every two weeks."

Loverboy was unbuttoning her blouse, pretending not to be listening too much. With each button, he kissed a little more skin. "Why does she think?"

Dannie's voice started to slur. "She says it has something to do with payday. That doesn't really make sense to me, but she's been right before."

Payday! Imogen was smart smart smart. Loverboy slid Dannie's blouse off and looked at her bra. It was bright pink with flowers on it. He could see her nipples through the mesh. It was a cheap brand, but he knew she'd bought it that day just for him, so it was special. She really liked him. Really really. He took her breasts in his hands and said, "Payday. Hmmm. Is that the only idea she can come up with?"

"No. I'm getting in touch with all the dry cleaners in the city to see if he left Rosalind's clothes with any of them."

"Why would he do that?" Loverboy asked. He hadn't expected them to think of the dry cleaners.

"To keep them clean. So there wouldn't be any clues."

His lips slid along the lacy polyester edge of the bra. "Sounds so iffy. And it sounds like a lot of work. Do you have to do that all by yourself?"

"Yes." It was more a sigh than a syllable.

He let his teeth nibble along the elastic band of the bra. "No wonder you have to work so late. Are you sure your Imogen is as good as she's supposed to be?"

"She is. There's something else too. We've also discovered that he kills a woman three days before he does his real murder. Like blowing off steam." His lips were on her nipples through the bra, but she stopped him now and pulled his face up so he was looking at her. "You understand I shouldn't be talking about this with you," she said.

"I shouldn't even be here," he pointed out to her. "But I can't help myself where you are concerned." He pulled her into his arms, Strong-Reliable-Man style, and let his MEMBER press against her thigh so she'd know he had other stuff on his mind. He'd already heard what he needed to know.

It worked. She reached for his waistband and said, "I don't want to talk about the case. This guy is a sick bastard."

He felt himself get even harder. He repeated, "Sick bastard." He pulled away and said in his sexy voice, "Do you know what I am? What I've been all day? All my life, practically?"

Dannie looked at him through her lashes. "No."

"A lonely bastard. Who was missing you."

He looked at his watch, saw it was half past midnight, and decided not to waste any more time with preliminaries. He ripped off her panties and slammed himself into her, backing her onto the bed. He felt incredibly alive. Incredibly powerful. Three days before the real victim. To let off steam. His hands caressed Dannie's shoulders, moved up her neck. He was a steam engine tonight!

Dannie was panting in ecstasy.

"Do you like me, Dannie?" he asked, using his sexy voice a little more.

"You know I do." Her nails were clinging to his ass. He started to make a checklist for later: *Nails*.

"A lot?" he asked.

"A whole lot." Her tongue skimmed his ear and she nipped at the lobe.

Teeth.

"Am I a good boy?"

Dannie laughed. "Yes. A very good boy." Her hand went between their legs. "And a big boy."

"Be careful, Dannie," he cautioned. "You're making me feel silly."

"Ooh, that sounds fun, big boy."

"Good boy," he corrected.

"Good boy."

"Say it again."

Dannie reached over her head and grabbed the headboard with both hands—

Headboard. Nightstand.

—pushing against it to take him deeper. "You're a very good— ooooh—boy."

Now he was so silly. Now the silliness took over.

"No, I'm not," he said. "I'm a bad boy." He jammed himself into her and his hands closed around her neck.

Dannie started to laugh again.

"Don't laugh at me, you lying bitch." His hands tightened.

What started out as a groan of pleasure became a primeval call for help. Her eyes got huge with surprise and her body convulsed around him frantically,

"You lied to me, you stupid faker bitch. You lied and said I was a good boy. You lied and said you liked me. And then you called me a sick bastard."

The sillies were so strong. He could feel them in his hands around her neck. He was letting off some steam now!

"Why are you trying to get away, Dannie?" His hands constricted more and more around her neck as he drove himself into her. "I thought you liked me." He tightened his hands, pounding into her. "I thought I was a good boy."

She was pulling and pushing against him now like a wild animal.

"You don't even know me. You only think you do. I'm not what you think I am at all."

Her struggling got more intense. She arched against him.

"You stupid bitch. You stupid lying bitch." He got his thumbs on her throat and pushed.

"Don't you even know who I am now? Don't you NOW? I AM NOT A GOOD BOY."

She arched up to him a final desperate time. As her throat rattled he came hard and fast, surging into her.

He lay on top of her, panting like a train, for five minutes.

It had been the best ever. He'd never felt anything like that before, never *let off so much steam*. He thought she came, too, just before she died. That was how good he was, letting her die in pleasure. He would have stayed inside her longer but he had a lot to do and her breath was starting to smell funny.

Besides, what if rigor mortis set in? That would be hard luck, wouldn't it, to get his dick stuck inside a dead lady? His engine caught in her tunnel?

Hard luck!

He laughed about that as he hauled her into the shower. He cleaned off her nails and teeth. He wiped the headboard and nightstand and vacuumed the sheets with his Dustbuster. He did a good job. He checked out the window and calculated he still had a few hours until dawn. Finally he put on the plastic shower cap from the bathroom and lay down in the bed. He should really try to get some shut-eye. From here on out, there wouldn't be time for sleeping. After this, it was work work work.

Chuga-chuga-chuga-chuga-CHOO CHOO! Full steam ahead!

Rosalind only has 3 days left!!!

Rosalind woke up abruptly, swimming against the current of unconsciousness. Something was digging into her thigh. What was—

The scissors. She remembered the scissors. From the manicure set.

Then she tasted cheesy popcorn in her mouth and remembered everything. Remembered his strange visit the night before. He had seemed distracted. Remembered how lucky she had been that he had not seen the open drawer.

She would not be so lucky again.

How many pills had he given her? She'd tried to count through the popcorn but couldn't. Two? Three?

He could be back at any moment.

She lurched to her feet and almost fell on her face as her knees buckled.

Be strong, Rosalind, she told herself. She leaned against the arm of the chair until a wave of queasiness passed. She turned to look at the seat. It was filthy, filled with crumbs and—

Don't think about that!

—scissors. She bent at the knees and leaned backward until her fingers touched the cushion, scrounging around through crumbs, where were they, where—

Her fingers found them. Slid into the tiny holes. This time she would make them work.

She sat on the edge of the chair, concentrating on keeping her breathing even, and pictured what her hands were doing behind her. Her fingers were even more numb than they had been before, and just making the blades open and close was an effort. The first try cut only air. The second and third pierced the tape and her palms, making her cry out in pain. Finally on the fourth try she felt the tiny blades catch at something and hold. She pushed them together and heard *snip* and almost started to cry.

Hold on, she told herself. *Hold on to yourself, Ros.*

Another snip. Her wrists were looser. She could move slightly more, another snip, slightly more, ano—

The scissors slipped from her hands and fell back onto the seat. They bounced to the floor.

NO!

Rosalind closed her eyes and blocked out the pain and, using every ounce of her strength, pulled her hands apart.

She tried not to look at them. She knew her nails were outlined with dark brown crusts from where he'd "accidentally" missed during her manicure, and she could not risk throwing up or passing out now. Fingers beginning to throb with the return of blood, she dug around the edges of the recliner's cushion to find where she had shoved the manicure kit. She found it, opened it. She could not keep her hands from shaking. *Come on,* she urged herself. *Concentrate.* Her fingertips skidded clumsily over the tiny manicure instruments. It was so hard to make them close around the thin edge of the nail file, *steady, steady*—

Got it.

Rosalind pushed the recliner into position underneath the rectangle and tried to stand on the arm. Her head swam for a moment and she steadied herself against the wall, tried again. Taking the nail file between her fingers she reached up toward the screws.

The pain in her shoulders was almost blinding. *Don't stop,* she ordered herself. *Think about something else, think about Jason, think about getting out of here—*

DO NOT STOP.

Her fingers trembled as she maneuvered the end of the nail file into the grooves of the Phillips-head screws. It skittered around, cutting scribbly lines in the paint around the screw, but she did not care. Eight screws. Concentrate on the screws, eight of them—

One out.

God, her arms ached.

Two out.

She collapsed for a few minutes after the third one because of the pain in her shoulders. After that it got easier. Five and six. Seven. Eight.

She dropped them on the seat of the recliner and pushed the panel away.

It did not move.

"Try harder," she said, talking to herself aloud now. "Try harder, Ros. You can do this."

She took a big breath and pushed as hard as she could. Something made a noise, but it refused to go up. She looked at the panel more closely. Maybe it didn't go up. Maybe it came—

She got her fingers around the edges and pulled and it opened down. Opened down with a ladder.

She had not permitted herself to wonder how she would get into the hole once she opened it, and now she didn't have to. It was a trapdoor to an attic with a ladder. She pulled the ladder down as far as it would go and climbed up it. She did not realize, or did not care, that she was sobbing.

The climb up the ten steps of the ladder seemed to take forever. Her arms, she could not keep her arms steady.

Hurry!

Finally she found herself in a cavernous space. Wherever she was being held had to be huge. There were a few moldering cardboard boxes with the words *FOOD SERVICE HOT CHOCOLATE MIX* on them pushed in a corner, but otherwise it was empty.

It should have been darker.

A window. There had to be a window. It took her a moment but she saw it, half-hidden behind a large cardboard drum. She ran toward it.

It was two filthy glass panes that went from the floor to the ceiling. She did not waste time trying to open them but wrapped a hand in the fabric of her nightgown and rammed it through the glass.

Fresh air, the noise of the city, gray light of early morning hit her at once, dazzling her. She looked out and saw the Las Vegas Strip in front of her. She could see the Eiffel Tower and maybe a corner of the Bellagio. Just blocks away. Heaven and hell separated by only blocks.

She looked down. She was up at the roof level, high above the ground. Below her was an asphalt parking lot. If she jumped she would definitely break her legs, and possibly die. *Not now,* she thought. *Not when I am so close.*

She looked out at the traffic passing by on the street, not much because it was so early. She looked at the cars in the lot and realized she recognized several of them.

She knew exactly where she was. She was safe. There was someone there to save her. She leaned out as far as she could. She opened her mouth to scream.

His face popped down from the roof in front of her. He said, "Hi, Ros! Going somewhere?" and shoved a rag in her mouth.

CHAPTER 80

He swung his body through the broken window from where he'd been hanging off the roof, purposely kicking her knees out from under her. She fell to the ground.

"Weren't expecting me, were you, Ros?" He chuckled to himself as he walked toward her. She was sprawled on the floor, struggling to get to her feet. "Thought I'd pay you a surprise visit. You sure look surprised, Ros. You should see the look on your face right now."

Rosalind gagged against the rag as he moved closer, rubbing his hands together. "It's neat up here, isn't it, Ros?" he asked, coming closer. "Really neat."

She was crawling backward on her knees.

"Yes, I knew you'd like it up here."

If she could get to the trapdoor, if she could get down the ladder, she would run into the hallway. She didn't care about nail guns now. She just wanted to be away from him. She was sobbing, struggling to breathe.

"So where did you think you were going, Ros? Going for a walk? A walk with Johnnie?" He reached into his back pocket and pulled out a pint bottle of Johnnie Walker red label.

"Here," he said, holding it out to her. "Don't you want it?"

"N-n-n—" she said through the rag.

He looked at the bottle. He looked at her. "You didn't want to go for a walk with Johnnie? Then what were you doing, Ros? You weren't running away from me, were you?"

Her back was against the other side of the attic now. There was nowhere for her to go. His face bent down to hers. He ripped the rag from her mouth. "Answer me, Ros."

"I—I—"

"Shut up!" He slapped her across the face with the wet fabric. He stood up and tossed the bottle to one side. "Don't lie. Don't try to fake me out. You were going to betray me, weren't you? After all the care I've taken of you, you were going to betray me." He defied her to deny it. "Why does this always happen to me? Every time! I do everything they ask just like I did everything you asked. I brought you your favorite food. I brought you hairpins. I made you pretty. And all you could think about was getting away from me. About hurting my feelings." He shook his head. "You said you liked me, Ros."

"I do." She was shivering uncontrollably.

"THEN WHY THE HELL WERE YOU RUNNING AWAY?" His leg bent back and he launched a hard kick at the Johnnie Walker bottle. It slammed against the wall behind Rosalind and shattered, splattering whiskey everywhere.

He stared at his feet. "Look what you made me do, Ros. You made me get my shoes dirty." He looked at her and smiled. "I'm afraid you'll have to clean them. The way you cleaned the mark off the back of the chair." He chuckled to himself. "You thought I didn't know. You thought I didn't know you were lying to me. YOU THOUGHT I WAS A STUPID LITTLE SHIT, DIDN'T YOU, ROS?"

"No-o-o." She could not keep her voice steady. This was worse than anything before.

"STOP LYING! Why are you trying to make me so silly? I get so silly when people lie to me. Why? Did you really think you could hide, Rosalind? Hide what you were thinking from me? Me, who knows you so well? ME, WHO'S SO GOOD AT HIDE-AND-SEEK?"

He reached down and dragged her up by the neck of her nightgown so she was standing in front of him.

"Why did you lie to me, Rosalind? Why did you try to run away?"

She tried to form words but he was holding her throat.

"WRONG ANSWER!" He eased up the pressure. His voice was level, sane. A parent to a bad child. "You shouldn't have done that. No, you really shouldn't have. I did not want to have to do this, but you made me. I trusted you and you betrayed me and now you have to be punished."

In one motion he hauled her to the trapdoor ladder and shoved her down. She landed on her knees at the bottom.

"Get into your chair, Rosalind," he said evenly as he climbed down.

She scampered into it.

"Good." He stood and looked around the room. "You really made a mess down here, Ros. We'll have to clean that up later. But first, it's story time!"

He went to his desk and opened the drawer. Rosalind was sure he was going to come back with the remains of the manicure set, but instead he brought out the large leather volume she had seen him looking at once. He tossed it into her lap.

The cover had the words FAMILY REMEMBRANCES embossed in gold on it. Rosalind's eyes filled with tears.

He saw it and nodded. "You remember when I bought that, don't you? When we were all in Italy together that time? You even helped me pick it out. Betcha didn't know I was saving a page in it for you!"

He started flipping through it and Rosalind saw pages and pages of newspaper clippings. "You can see how it's organized. Article from the day of disappearance on this side," he said, tapping a left-hand page with an article from the *North Florida Intelligencer* on it. "Then over here"—he touched the right-hand side—"the obituary. And maybe some pictures if I like them.

"There's other stuff, mostly about me, in here too," he explained as he riffled through the pages. He seemed to be looking for something.

Finally, near the back, he stopped. "Here it is. This is your section so far." On the left-hand page was an article from the day she disappeared from the *Las Vegas Review Journal*. "I always like to take the ones from the local papers. They're the best," he explained. The page opposite was empty. "This is where your obituary goes. I'm hoping they'll do a really big picture of you. And maybe one of me and Jason standing together at the funeral. Don't forget that I am one of his guardians."

The dull ache of horror Rosalind had been feeling galvanized into something far worse. Whatever happened, Jason could not fall into the hands of this madman.

"You *had* forgotten, hadn't you?" Loverboy said, hugging himself. "Oh boy, that's good. I'm so glad I remembered to remind you. You should really see your face, Ros. You look like shit."

"Why are you doing this?"

"*Sheesh.* Why does everyone always ask that? Why why why? Are you some kind of philosopher? What does it matter? I can and I am. Now look at this." He slipped an envelope out from the back of the album and sifted through it until he found what he was looking for. "This is the collage I made for you." He held it up at eye level and peered around at it, an artist admiring his work. "Do you see what I have in mind?"

Rosalind's eyes went to the six white chalk outlines of body parts. She had to force herself to keep breathing. "Are you—"

"I had a plan all set, but I thought it would be more fun to let you participate," he explained, interrupting her. "So here's what we're going to do. Since you like games so much, we're going to play one right now. It's called Loverboy Says. You'll notice I didn't bind your hands or feet. That's so you'll have the maximum range of motion for the game. It works just like Simon Says. If you move any part of your body without me telling you to, without me saying 'Loverboy Says,' I cut it off. Got it?" He turned to put the collage on the desk, and turned back with an enormous knife in his hands.

"Now smile," he commanded.

Rosalind struggled to pull the corners of her mouth up and he slapped her hard across the face and shouted, "I DID NOT SAY, 'LOVERBOY SAYS,' YOU IGNORANT SHIT!" He brought the knife to her lips. "I should cut these off, shouldn't I?"

Rosalind did not say anything, did not move. She was trembling inside, but worked to keep herself steady.

"ANSWER ME!" he yelled.

She did not move.

"LOVERBOY SAYS ANSWER ME!"

"Please don't cut my lips off," Rosalind pleaded.

The knife moved away. "I don't think I will. Not this time. That was a practice round. But you'd better be very careful from now on. From now on *anything* can happen."

CHAPTER 81

At 7:36 A.M. Imogen was pretty sure she knew Lover-boy's identity, but she could not get it confirmed for seven hours.

Unable to sleep at three A.M., she had started doing one of Martina Kidd's book of crossword puzzles. By six she had finished both of them and gone to take a shower.

That was where she remembered what Martina had asked her. At the end of their first visit with her. She'd sat down at the table, glanced at her crossword puzzle and said, "What is a six-letter word for 'plagiarize'?"

But that hadn't been a clue in any of the crossword puzzles. Imogen spent fifteen minutes making sure before she called the FBI research library.

"The definition of plagiarize is—"

Imogen interrupted the librarian. "I don't need the definition. I need the etymology."

"Plagiarize. From the Latin *plagiare*, meaning, 'to kidnap.' "

Kidnap. Martina had wanted her to get to the word *kidnap*. The connection seemed obvious—both to her last name, Kidd, and to a case where the killer kidnaps his victims and holds them for two weeks—but Martina was usually more subtle than that.

At 7:29 Benton called. "Breakfast time," he said, and as he spoke there was a knock on her door. "I took the liberty of ordering for you, ma'am, because I figured you would forget otherwise. You sound distracted."

"I am," Imogen said, shutting the door behind the room service waiter. "I'm chewing on something."

"I'll let you get to it. I'm sorry I'm not there to help."

"Me too. I feel like I'm in a race. I could use some of your expertise."

"Concentrate, keep your eyes on the track, and don't think about how much you have to go to the bathroom."

"Go to the bathroom?"

"It always happens in the middle of a race."

Imogen laughed. "Thanks for the tip."

"Anytime. Hey, is there any chance you could send that bridge problem I was working on to my computer fax? I haven't been able to solve it and it's nagging at me. It doesn't help that I don't seem to have anything else to do."

"I'll send it right now."

"Thanks. If you need any more driving lessons, just call."

Imogen was smiling as she poured her coffee and turned on the fax machine, and she smiled more when she lifted the lid on one of the two plates Benton had sent up and saw beneath it a pack of Juicy Fruit gum.

Don't forget about me, okay? Could anyone, ever?

It was 7:33.

As she fed the bridge newsletter into the fax machine, she looked up at the maps of family amusement sites tacked above it. *Concentrate, keep your eyes on the track.* Her eyes went to the blue and green circles that marked racetracks on each of the layouts. There were circles near the site of every killing. They were the only constant, the only type of family fun center that appeared everywhere. But they did not matter, she told herself, because the killer never kidnapped his victims from them.

She picked up the pack of Juicy Fruit and sniffed it, smelling Benton, as she let her mind wander.

Kidnap. She rolled the word around searching for a connection to something more substantial. Had the killer himself been kidnapped once? Taken from his family? Had someone in the case gone missing as a child? Could that be why he wanted to make a new family, destroy old ones?

Where had that idea come from, about families? It had come from—

"You can survive on Juicy Fruit gum for a week."

"The Greenways were not what I expected."

"I was trapped in an elevator once."

"Don't forget about me, okay?"

"It's a long story."

KIDNAPPED.

—Benton.

At 7:36 A.M. Imogen's mouth filled with the sick-sweet taste of Juicy Fruit. She dialed Bugsy's phone. "Is Sadie still here?"

"Good morning, boss."

"We don't have time for that." Her hands, her whole body, were shaking. "Is Sadie, Benton's grandmother, still here?"

"I think so."

"Get her up to my room as soon as possible. And get me a copy of the Arbor Motors race and test schedule and locations for the past two years."

At 8:26 A.M. Sadie settled into the cushions of Imogen's couch with a luxuriant yawn and said, "I am sorry, Ms. Page, but that is not for me to tell you."

"Who *can* tell me?" Imogen demanded.

"Ask his mother."

"Bugsy, go get Theresa Arbor."

At 9:15 A.M. Theresa sat nervously twisting the gold stud earring in her ear as she listened to Imogen's question. She thought for a moment, then shook her head. "I'm really not sure I should tell you about this."

"Why not?" Imogen asked, struggling to keep from shouting. *Deny it,* she wanted to beg. She felt like she was holding her breath with her entire body.

"Well, we tried to keep it from the FBI at the time, and now . . . after all these years . . . The rest of the family, Julia, her sister, they don't even know."

"After all these years, it won't matter," Imogen said. It was almost impossible for her to stay sitting on the chair facing the couch. "Please, Theresa. Please tell me about when Benton was kidnapped."

Theresa looked at Sadie, who did not seem to be paying attention, then at her lap. "Since you already seem to know about it, there's no harm, I guess."

You are wrong, Imogen's mind screamed. *There is more harm than you can possibly imagine.*

By the time Theresa looked up at her, Imogen had her face back under control. She spoke softly, as if someone might overhear. "It happened on his tenth birthday," she began. "As a surprise, Malcolm, his father, took him to work with him. He had promised to get Benji—that was his nickname—a pack of gum, but they forgot on the way up and Malcolm got caught on a phone call. But Benji—Benton—was so eager, such a big boy, that Malcolm let him go by himself. He bought a packet of Juicy Fruit. The woman who worked at the newsstand said he already had three pieces in his mouth by the time she gave him the change. He was such a funny boy." Theresa disappeared into the memory for a moment, then came back. "That woman was the last person to see Benton for a week.

"It was Malcolm's secretary who did it. Kidnapped him. Of course we did not know that at first. We never would have guessed—she seemed so faithful. She'd been with Malcolm forever. She was amazingly competent too. At everything. Even kidnapping. She kept Benton in an unused service elevator in the Arbor Motors building for five days. She gave him only a little food and water and told him it had to last until we paid her—or until the air ran out, whichever came first. She called him horrible names—disgusting S-word, freak—and told him that no one loved him, that we didn't care about him. She had told us that if we went to the police or the press she would kill Benton, so of course we did everything we could to keep the story quiet. But she used the newspapers, the fact that they did not say anything about him, to torture him. To convince my baby boy that we didn't love him."

She touched her eyes with a Kleenex. "At first the woman did not even set a ransom. She was crazy, you see. And when she did set a ransom, it was more than we could raise. We went to the family and asked them for help, and of course they came through with it, but—" She broke off and looked at Sadie.

Sadie said, "The story was leaked to the press. 'The sins of the fathers,' that was the headline. It was about how Malcolm was such an asshole that someone had taken his son to punish him. Which was not exactly true, because the motive was money. But Malcolm *was* an asshole. Anyway, he went berserk. Totally over the top. He accused all of us of having leaked the story, of trying to get rid of his dynasty, of—"

"We thought she was going to kill Benton," Theresa interjected. "Because of the story. He was scared." She looked at Imogen. "She probably would have killed Benton, too, but we managed to stop them from printing it in time. And the woman's husband, the dear, dear man, he just could not bear to have Malcolm in the back of his car weeping on his way back and forth to the office, so one morning he stopped the car by the side of the road and came forward and told us where to find my boy." She smiled radiantly. "Do you know, Benton lived on Juicy Fruit gum all that time. Gum. That's what he lived on!"

"I had some idea," Imogen said coolly. "You and Benton's father divorced after that, didn't you?"

"Yes," Theresa said, flapping a well-ringed hand. "You can imagine how it was. The constant bickering, the blame. It was too much for me."

"So you left the two of them."

Theresa sat forward. "Don't judge me, Ms. Page. I saved myself. Malcolm was entombing himself. He alienated the entire family and became strange. Erratic. Benton had to put his father on an allowance—the son putting the *father* on one. Can you imagine, a boy having to do that to his parent? Pay him an allowance every two weeks?"

Imogen tried not to let anything register on her face. "What about Benton? Did you worry about leaving him behind?"

"Oh no. I knew he would be fine. He was a divine little boy. He did not need me."

Imogen stared at the woman and wondered if she could really mean what she said.

"I was fairly useless as a mother anyway," Theresa went on. "I'm much better as a wife. You wouldn't understand. You're much more independent. But I was not made to be relied on. I was made to rely on others. That's just the way I am."

Sadie rolled her eyes. "You're full of it, Theresa. You were made to have a lot of money and you've used that Southern-belle excuse to cover up what amounts to prostitution."

Theresa turned on her. "What about you? You've used your money to buy a boy for you to play with."

"You'd like to reduce my relationship with Eros to that, wouldn't you? It would justify your own. But actually it's much more complicated—and more wicked. He says I remind him of his mother."

Theresa gave her a disapproving look so Sadie went on. "His mother died when he was very young and he's longed for her ever since. It's like a novel, isn't it?"

"Yes," Imogen agreed. Or a nightmare. She had not even considered Eros as a suspect. Eros. The god of love. Could he—

"But you did not want to talk about Eros. You were asking about Benton," Sadie put in. "So now you've met the family skeleton. But Benton got over it all beautifully—look at how he joined the Army Rangers hostage rescue squad, so he could help others who were in the position he'd been in. I have to say, really, I think it did more good than harm to the boy. He was pretty quiet before that, and afterward he became much more outgoing."

Outgoing. Imogen looked at the two women. Stood up. Smiled. "Thank you for telling me about that."

"I can't see that it has any bearing on the case," Theresa said.

Sadie winked at Imogen. "I think Ms. Page's interest in our Benton goes beyond the case, doesn't it?"

Imogen said, "I'm just trying to get all the pieces of the puzzle in place."

As they were leaving, Imogen said to Theresa, "What is the name of your perfume?"

"Poison," Theresa said. "It's my signature scent. Malcolm's favorite."

Of course it is, Imogen thought. She was calling Bugsy before the door had even shut. "I need the entire file every agency has on Benton Arbor and every press clipping ever printed. Everything. Now."

"What are you—"

"And also run 'Benji Arbor.' "

"Okay, but—"

"NOW."

She scooped Rex out of the fish tank and put him back in the fishbowl. He was looking as bad as she felt.

CHAPTER 82

It was after two when Imogen stood in front of the Loverboy profile—

Charming
Good-looking
Sense of humor
White male
Organized
Educated
Poor family in a rich neighborhood
Sick fuck
Between thirty and forty
Thrives on attention

—with a pen in her hand. She was not actually looking at the list. She was looking at the two blank categories below it:

Trigger?
Identity?

Her hand hovered over them. It fell to her side. She should write the answers. She knew them now.

Time to fill in the blanks.

She looked to her left, at the fax headed ARBOR MOTORS TEST SCHEDULE. *Is Imogen considering a purchase or merely curious?* Julia had written on the cover sheet. *Want to have a drink later, Bugs?* Imogen stared at her notes so she would not have to look at the sheets underneath. But she already knew what they said. There had been a race or a series of tests or both at a track near the site of each Loverboy murder in the weeks before it happened.

Finally, she moved her gaze to her right. She picked up the Xerox copy of the front cover of the *Inquisitor* that had come in one of the files, but her fingers refused to hold on to it. It slipped out and skidded to the floor.

She made her eyes follow it. She made herself look at it, hard, again. Look at the picture of Benton, dressed all in black, escorting Princess Artemis into a nightclub. Look at the date, two years earlier, a month before the first killing.

Look at the banner headline that screamed out across the top in all caps: "AMERICA'S LOVERBOY!"

Look at the face of the man she had thought she had so much in common with. The man she was so comfortable with. The man who made her feel so at home.

Look at the face of a serial killer.

She stood tapping the pen against the table, unable to make herself write, thinking, Thank God he is in Detroit.

That gave her time to find Rosalind before he got back.

Roses are red . . .

Loverboy came into the room, whistling a new tune. He carried two hangers covered with plastic dry-cleaning bags.

"Do you know what these are?" He held them in front of Rosalind.

She did not say anything. She did not move. Not even her eyes.

He stared at her, holding her gaze. She knew that if she blinked first he would cut off her eyelids. He had told her so earlier that morning. Her eyes started to water.

He bent toward her. His nose was touching hers. He screamed: "LOVERBOY SAYS, TELL HIM WHAT THESE ARE."

Every muscle in Rosalind's body was tensed. She said, "My clothes."

He turned away and moved to the desk, draping her clothes over it. "Good. Now, what do you say when someone picks up your clothes from the dry cleaners?"

His back was to her. Rosalind swallowed hard and fast, blinking almost obsessively, but kept her mouth closed.

"What do you say, Ros?" he asked again, this time with menace. He turned around slowly and moved toward her.

She pressed her lips closed.

"What do you say?" He was in her face again. His arms were on either side of the recliner and he was looming over her. "WHAT

DO YOU SAY, YOU DISGUSTING BITCH? PAY ATTENTION TO
ME WHEN I TALK TO YOU. *TELL ME WHAT YOU SAY!*"

Rosalind did not move. Tears streamed down her face.

He stood up, smiling. "Very good, Rosalind. Excellent. Now,
Loverboy says, tell me what you say."

"Thank you," Rosalind whispered. "You say thank you."

. . . violets are blue . . .

Imogen did not need or even want more proof, but she got it anyhow when she reached the bottom of the clippings file at 10:21 P.M. It started innocently with a small clipping, one inch by one inch, on yellowing newsprint, nineteen years old.

> *The Big Bess derailment took the maintenance staff of the seasonal carnival entirely by surprise. Chet Black, the head of the crew, gave this statement: "I can't even believe it. Me and Benji Arbor, we just looked Big Bess over yesterday. There's no way there was anything wrong with it."*
>
> *Only one young man, C.H., was willing to hazard a guess of what might have happened: "Looked to me like an act of God," he said, and from the paleness of his face, this reporter did not think he was joking.*
>
> *Bethany Samson remains in critical condition at Briggs Hospital.*

Three phone calls and forty-five minutes was all it took for Imogen to learn what she already knew.

The night nurse at the rehab center outside of Boston where paralyzed Bethany Samson had spent the past two decades of her life was not thrilled to get a call at 11:10 P.M., but the words *FBI investigation* perked her up.

"Hold on, I'll check," she said. Imogen listened to her shoes squeak away on the vinyl flooring. She listened to two other nurses have a conversation about the relative size of their sister-in-laws' engagement rings. She listened to the sound of her stomach rumbling.

The squishing returned, followed by the hiss of a body being lowered into an adjustable chair. "You were right, Bethany does have a stuffed animal, a big cat. You know, like Tom from the cartoon *Tom and Jerry*? One of those sort of hard ones that you'd win at a fair? She's had it a while too, at least six months.

"I checked the visitors' log while I was up," the nurse added, and Imogen was not sure whether she wanted to bless or curse her.

She held her breath.

"Not too many visitors. Her father's gone to live somewhere else." Imogen knew that. Part of what had taken her so long was getting him out of his golf game on Maui.

"In fact," the nurse went on, "there have only been three in the past year and a half."

Imogen pushed the point of her pen hard against the Bellagio notepad to keep it from skidding. "Were there any around the fifteenth of June of last year?"

"June thirteenth," the nurse confirmed.

Two days before Louisa Greenway disappeared. Imogen could taste it—she had just found the source of the thread on Louisa Greenway's sweater. Loverboy had seen Louisa at the Somerville fair, had won a toy, and had taken it to Bethany in the nursing home. Bethany, his first victim. Had he gone to celebrate with her? Or to rub it in?

Imogen forced herself to say, "What was the name of the visitor?"

She lived a century in the seconds it took the woman on the other end of the phone to make out the messy signature.

Finally the nurse said, "Benton Arbor."

"I'll be sending someone up to take a look at that," Imogen told her, surprised at how level her voice was. "In the meantime, is there a safe or something where you could lock the stuffed animal and the log up?"

"Lock up Beth's cat? And the visitors' log? Why on earth?"

"They are prime pieces of evidence in a murder investigation."

Imogen imagined that the nurses would not be discussing engagement rings for the rest of the night.

Her phone rang as soon as she hung up. It was Bugsy.

"Have you heard anything from Dannie?" she asked. "She should have checked in hours ago."

"No." His voice was tense. "I'm sure she's just running down leads and doesn't want to call empty-handed. Listen, boss." He paused.

"What is it, Bugsy?"

"We got a match on that partial print from the carabiner in the taxicab," he told her. He stopped.

"It is Benton's," she said, sparing him.

"Yes. J.D. is sure it's another one of those joke pieces of evidence—"

"It's not. Have a team in Detroit follow Benton. Our team, the best Detroit has got. I don't want anyone to know. I don't want to risk alerting Benton that we are on to him. We will also need a team on the ground here to arrest him as soon as his plane lands."

Imogen hung up without saying good-bye. Until now, until the print on the carabiner, everything had been circumstantial. She could make excuses, keep herself from believing.

Now she had no choice. She picked up her pen and went to the profile list. She filled in the blanks. She'd found the killer.

She forced herself to replay the investigation in her head. She remembered that very first day, the way he had antagonized her, then come and humbled himself and apologized. She now understood that had been calculated, a device to earn her trust. He was the one who had changed the security tapes. He had probably come to her room directly after having sex with Marielle Wycliffe the first time.

Two dates, he'd said, as if daring her to make a connection to a killer who didn't kill on the first date. *Loverboy is making a family,* he had suggested, teaching her all about himself. She had wondered how Loverboy and Martina were communicating and now she knew— she had BROUGHT him to the prison with her. And she herself had said that he and J.D.—her other prime suspect—were a lot alike. Handsome, organized, well-educated white males who thrived on attention.

"It was right in front of my face the whole time," she said to Rex.

Right there written in huge letters, and she hadn't seen it because she was too damn busy falling in love with him. Feeling connected with him. Feeling, for the first time, like she had found the best parts of herself. She had realized Loverboy was good at reading people. She just hadn't seen how good. He had known exactly what to do to get her to fall for him. And she'd gone along, thinking that her feelings for Benton were getting in the way of the case. She hadn't seen that they *were* the case.

She picked up the hotel phone and pushed the button for room service. "The best one you have. I don't care what it costs," she said. Listened. "Oh. Okay, then the second best."

When the waiter arrived she tipped him outrageously, told him she wouldn't need any glasses, and took her bottle of Dom Pérignon into the bathroom with her.

It was just after midnight.

She stood in front of the mirror and toasted herself. She made herself say the words out loud. "Congratulations, Imogen! You've found Loverboy with two days to spare! Well done."

Then she got into the shower and drank her champagne out of the bottle and cried.

No matter what she did she could not feel clean.

Rosalind is about to die . . .

"Does my humming bother you, Ros?" Loverboy asked over his shoulder. He was at his desk.

Rosalind didn't say anything.

"I'm getting tired of you not answering when I talk to you, Ros."

Rosalind ground her teeth to keep her mouth closed.

"It's making me feel silly," he warned.

She had learned what silly meant. It meant angry. It meant wanting to kill someone. She had learned a lot about him that evening, a lot she hadn't known, as they read his family album together. A lot she had not wanted to know.

"Loverboy says, tell me if my humming is bothering you, Ros."

"No," she answered. "It is nice. What song is it?"

"Did I tell you to say all that?" he demanded. "I didn't, did I?" His eyes lit up. "I could cut out your tongue! I could do that now and it wouldn't ruin the collage." He licked his lips. "I am going to cut out your tongue, Rosalind."

Rosalind fought to keep her breathing normal.

"Say bye-bye to your tongue, Ros." He came toward her, his big knife in his hand. "Loverboy says open your mouth, Rosalind."

Rosalind hesitated.

"LOVERBOY SAYS OPEN YOUR GODDAMNED MOUTH."

His eyes flashed and Rosalind felt the knife on her neck and she opened her mouth. She was crying.

"Hullese," she said, with her mouth open. "Hu-u-les don."

"DID I TELL YOU THAT YOU COULD TALK?"

She felt her tears falling on her hands. His face came close to hers and the knife moved across her chin, up to her lips—

"P.U., your breath stinks!" He jumped backward, taking the knife with him. "P.U.! I think I'll leave your tongue in there." He looked at her. "You look stupid like that, with your mouth open, Ros."

Rosalind did not move. She knew he was trying to get her to disobey him. To do something so he would have an excuse to hurt her.

"Shut your trap, Ros," he ordered her, stern.

Her mouth stayed open.

"Loverboy says to shut your trap, Ros."

She closed her mouth.

He turned, went back to the desk, and saw it was half past midnight. "Just two days to go, Ros," he told her. "Won't be long now."

He did not see her shudder. He was too busy getting everything ready. It was time for the ritual.

. . . and Imogen is too!!!

Imogen reached for the phone from the shower. "What?"

"I have bad news, Imogen," Bugsy said. "Benton is not in Detroit. He never went there. He gave our team the slip, sent his plane up—bottom line, we don't think he ever left Las Vegas."

Imogen dragged her clothes into the living room of her suite and dressed fast, her eyes not leaving the collage. *Come on, come on,* she urged herself. *Figure it out. Now. Figure it out. Goddamn you, Imogen, FIND ROSALIND NOW.*

Emergency! Emergency! the collage screamed at her.

Suddenly it made sense. She ripped the hangman's gallows with the twelve spaces Loverboy had faxed after the Marielle Wycliffe murder from the wall and began filling them in. Twelve spaces. She knew from the tape the address would be on the east side. She looked up at the list of items in the collage.

East side. E for *Emergency!*

There were eight other items with prominent names in the collage.

I for Intellivision.

N for Night Crawlers.

G for Great Houdini Magic Set.

O for Original Ouija board.

F for Ford County Library.

L for Liquid Paper.

A for Audrie Lumber.

M for Mead notebook.

I N G O F L A M. FLAMINGO. And with the *Emergency!* poster, E FLAMINGO. East Flamingo.

The bastard had simply been spelling it all along. Imogen had tried every kind of riddle but the answer had been so simple.

They still needed a number. If there really were only twelve spots and the E was part of the address, then the number would be only three digits. There was the 87 of the stereo, but that was only two.

Emergency!

The date on the license plate, the one Cal had pointed out to her. Yes! April 1980. 480. 480 East Flamingo.

She was out the door, punching numbers into her phone. Bugsy answered as she reached the lobby. "Bugsy, I need a backup team at 480 East Flamingo," she said, running through the casino. "I think I solved the collage. I'm going over there now to look around, but I won't go in until we have people in place."

"I'm afraid that might take a second, boss. I was just about to call you."

Imogen had reached the reception area. She stopped, panting. "What happened, Bugsy?"

"They—they found Dannie."

Imogen put her hand over her mouth. Her body filled with ice. SOMEONE MUST PAY. "No. Oh no. Oh—where?"

"At the Fun Motel. Opposite the Stratosphere at the end of the Strip."

"In the bathtub?"

"Shower. There is no bathtub."

"Oh God. Oh God, no, not Dannie." She was biting her lip, her hands smashing over her eyes.

"Her car was in the lot. It looks like she went there willingly. There was nothing you could do, boss."

SOMEONE MUST PAY.

Someone had.

"I could have caught him," Imogen said, hating herself. Hating herself to death. I could have not slept with him. I could—

"Bugsy, get me backup as fast as you can. I'll be somewhere around 480 East Flamingo."

"Don't get any vigilante-super-crime-fighter ideas. You know that cops who do that in movies always end up dead."

"This isn't a movie."

"All the more reason not to do it."

"I'll wait for backup."

The cabdriver, who Imogen ascertained was personally known to the valet parkers on duty, shook his head doubtfully when Imogen gave him the address. "You sure you want 480?" he asked as they made a right turn onto East Flamingo.

"I know it's a deserted lot or something."

"Actually, it's not," the cabbie said. He pulled over and pointed across six lanes of traffic. "It's that. The power grid."

Imogen stared at it. It didn't look right.

"If you're looking for deserted lots, there's the Bally's parking lot back there a ways," the cabdriver told her. "And there's the Ice Garden."

"The what?"

"Used to be a skating rink. Now that Benton Arbor guy uses it as his Vegas headquarters. You know, the race-car driver? Mostly it's empty, though. It's 804 East Flamingo. I know because it's got a big sign."

"Eight zero four," Imogen repeated, just to be sure she had it. "Like April 1980 but backward."

The cabdriver scowled. "I guess. I hadn't thought of it that way."

"Drive me over there. But drop me off a block away."

CHAPTER 87

The taxi driver hadn't lied. The address was written over the front of the Garden in huge letters that Imogen could see from where the taxi let her out. 804 E. Flamingo. Like an advertisement.

The cocky bastard. She was seething. She felt lethal. She was almost mad enough to go over and bang on the door, but she was not insane. There was a twenty-four-hour convenience store attached to a gas station next to the place. *Grumpy's,* the sign said. Perfect. She walked toward it as she phoned Bugsy the new address.

"Backup should be there in seven minutes, boss," he told her. "I'm going to keep you on the phone unless you promise not to go in there."

"I'm not going in," she promised. Thinking, I've already screwed up enough. "I won't jeopardize Rosalind's life now."

"Good."

It was only after she hung up that she heard the footsteps behind her.

She turned around. Benton stood right there holding a cup of coffee. Right there wearing his glasses, looking sheepish. "Imogen. I didn't—"

"Expect to see me?" she finished the sentence for him. "No, I bet not."

"I'm sorry I lied to you about being in Detroit."

Is that what you lied to me about? she wanted to scream. Was she really having this conversation?

She stared at him and he rushed on. "There was no way I could just leave town knowing that Rosalind's life hung in the balance," he said. "And maybe yours. I wanted to tell you, but with the feds—"

"Don't come any closer."

"Imogen?" Benton looked confused. He took another step.

"Stop right there!" she yelled. *Don't touch me, don't come near me, oh God, Benton, how could you, HOW COULD YOU?*

He took another step. Reached for her. "What is wrong?"

He is a killer. He has brutally tortured a woman for two weeks. He is not the man you thought he was. He is not the man you love.

Coming closer now. "Imogen? Why—"

She shot him.

Then she turned and ran.

She sprinted toward the Garden. If he was out there then she could get safely inside and save Rosalind. "Sorry, Bugsy," she whispered as she threw herself through the swinging glass door and locked it behind her. "I can't wait any longer."

CHAPTER 88

Loverboy took a deep breath and reseated himself on the desk chair to begin the ritual.

He flipped his family album open to the very first page and smoothed his hand over the single article pasted there. It was framed with gold corners to show it was special.

DEATHS:

Harwood, Edward. 58 years old, chauffeur. Of injuries sustained in car accident, which also killed his employer, Malcolm Arbor (see prev. page, main column).

Beloved father, survived by his only son, Cal Harwood, a sophomore at MIT. Memorial services private.

His eyes lingered, as they always did, on the words *beloved father, survived by only son.* That was the best part. He'd written it himself. He was so—

"Ros? Did you make a noise?" He turned around and fixed Rosalind with a mean stare.

But even as he looked at her and saw she wasn't moving, he heard the noise again. There was someone downstairs. There was someone—

"Hello?" the voice called. "Is there anyone here?"

Not someone. Imogen!

Loverboy's heart started to race. This was even better than he planned. Oh my goodness, was it good. He grabbed his jacket and the glasses he wore when he was being Cal. He leaned toward Rosalind's ear and said, "If you make a noise I'll make you eat Imogen's tongue before I cut yours out, got it?"

Rosalind nodded. Cal left the room and ambled quietly downstairs.

"Imogen?" he said, peering over the expanse of the Ice Garden toward her. He was coming down the stairs from the "offices," shading his eyes with one hand as if he couldn't make her out. As if he were just Mr. Hardworking Arbor Motors Employee.

She swung around toward him, aiming her gun at his stomach. When she saw who it was she let it fall to her side. "Oh my God, Cal, thank God you're here."

Someone started banging on the front door of the Garden and, turning around, Cal saw that it was Benton. He was bleeding out of his leg.

Imogen looked from him to Cal. She had her hand on his arm. "We've got to call the police, Cal. We've got to call them and you've got to help me search."

Cal felt her gun near his hand. He looked at her. "Imogen, are you okay?"

"No. Yes. It doesn't matter. Look, you were right, Cal. The registration on the fire truck on that *Emergency!* poster did mean something. It meant—"

"—804," Cal said. He cocked his head to one side. "Duh. I mean, why else would I have put it there?" He would have liked to take a few minutes and really enjoy her look of surprise, but he couldn't risk it. He reached out with the chloroform-soaked rag he had in his hand and covered Imogen's nose and mouth.

He carried her upstairs and laid her on the floor next to Rosalind's feet. Rosalind stared at her. "Ros, meet Imogen. I'm sure she'd say 'hi' if she could, but she's a little OUT OF IT right now.

Anyway, I hope you two like each other. You're going to spend the rest of your lives together."

He chuckled. Then he covered Rosalind's nose and mouth with chloroform until she passed out too.

He tied the two women together, slipped on his special outfit, and dumped their bodies into the laundry cart he'd stolen. As he worked he sang quietly to himself.

> London Bridge is falling down,
> Falling down
> Falling down
> Imogen and Rosalind falling down
> My fair ladies!

By the time the backup came Loverboy and his ladies were riding up up up in the world's fastest elevator and Benton was lying in front of the Garden door in a pool of his own blood.

CHAPTER 89

Loverboy rules!

Cal was sitting next to them, his back against the side of the observation platform, talking on his cell phone when Imogen regained consciousness. Her face was leaning against someone's back and her hands, taped together in front of her, were bound to someone else's. Rosalind, she guessed.

"Benton, is that you?" Cal was saying into the mouthpiece. He was wearing his glasses and workman's overalls with the name *Western Linen Supplies* stitched on the chest. Imogen strained to hear what he was saying. They were on top of the Stratosphere, on the outside observation deck more than a hundred stories above the Strip, and the wind carried Cal's voice away from her. "Are you paying attention?" she heard him ask. "Good. Ready? Get out your pencil and paper. If a man runs up stairs at an average pace of one floor every forty-five seconds, how long will it take him to climb a hundred and eight floors?"

There was a pause.

"Yep, that's right, eighty-one minutes. Assuming he doesn't have a gunshot wound in his leg. Now, I could wait that long. Or not. And guess what. I'm thinking NOT." He shifted so he was looking at Imogen. He winked and mouthed the words *Hi, there*. He turned his attention back to the phone. "Yeah, yeah, whatever, Benton. Look, you've got two and a half minutes before I push Imogen off the top. After that, Rosalind takes a tumble. By the way, the elevator only takes a minute and fifty-three seconds. Plenty of time—if you're not afraid of elevators. If you're not *chicken!* Toodles."

Cal hung up and got to his feet. He beamed at his two prisoners. "Well, look at you two. Pretty as a picture."

Imogen felt the woman she was tied to grab her hand. She held it and said to Cal, "I suppose in the next minute you are going to tell us why you've done all this?"

He shook his head. "No way. That always happens in the movies and the bad guy always dies. Why don't you tell me? That way you'll be the one to die."

"It was his mother," Rosalind said throatily. "She was the one who kidnapped Benton. When she was sent to prison—"

"That's enough from you," Cal hissed at her. "I want to hear Imogen."

Imogen felt the woman in front of her begin to tremble. My God, what had he done to her? Don't think about that now, she told herself. Get him talking. Delay him. She pictured the observation deck, round like a doughnut, and tried to think of ways off of it as she picked up where Rosalind had left off. "You missed your mother," she said. She turned her head and was staring right into his eyes and suddenly she could feel him. "You really missed her. Your father told you that she left because you weren't a good enough boy, right?"

Cal nodded. "He said she went away because she liked another boy better. Because I was a disgusting little shit."

"He lied to you because it was his own ineptitude he was covering up," Imogen said, commiserating. "They caught her because of him, didn't they? And he felt guilty. So he blamed you."

Cal began to rock back and forth. His expression changed and his voice was a whine when he said, "He gave her up. He gave my mommy up. I was her loverboy and he gave her up. She wanted the money so she and me could run away together, I know it, and the stupid shit ruined everything."

Imogen matched her tone to his. "You didn't know that, know

about any of it, until you were older, did you? You worked so hard to be perfect, when really it was your father who should have been working hard."

"That's right," Cal said, petulant. "Nothing I did was ever good enough. Pay attention, look at me, you're a freak, *buzz, buzz, buzz.*" Petulant became angry. "He was a pathetic bastard."

"And a drunk," Imogen said.

"Yeah, and a drunk. Every payday. Every payday he got drunk."

"He yelled at you, didn't he? He said mean things to you when he was drunk."

"He said I was a disgusting shit. He called me a pig."

"But he was the pig, wasn't he? Wallowing in his own filth. Especially the days after he got drunk. Those days he extra needed you, right?"

Cal stared at her. "How did you know?"

"I just do."

"Those were the days he would be so nice. He needed me to take care of him. Those days he said I was a good boy. His good boy. He said he was glad it was just the two of us. He said I was perfect and made him so proud." Cal shook his head in incomprehension. "And then on payday he got mad. On payday—" Cal's lip trembled and his eyes filled with tears.

"On payday he said things that erased all the ways he had been nice to you, right? So you never knew if you could trust him. Believe him? You were always waiting for him to betray you."

"Oh, he made me feel so silly when he did that," Cal said, talking to himself. He rubbed his arms with his palms. "He made me feel so full of sillies that I couldn't control. He slapped me so full of sillies that I think they never went away. I just wanted to—" He stopped.

"What, Cal?" Imogen asked in a gentle voice.

"I just wanted to hurt him so bad. I wanted to hurt him so bad. The lying bastard." His voice changed, became more shrill. "Some days he said he loved me and then the next day he'd say I was a freak. He said he hated me and I ruined his life. Took away everything. But he was the freak, you know? He was the one who was happy just to be Benton's father's chauffeur. And Benton's father kept him on just out of pity. Pity." He paused, his eyes focused like darts on Imogen. "But I showed them. I showed both of them good. I gave myself the best present a boy could have."

Imogen nodded. "You killed them. You did something to the car that your father was driving Benton's father in and you killed them. That was the same day you killed Susan Kellogg. After you had sex with her."

Cal smiled hugely. "Imogen, you are even smarter and prettier than I thought. Yeah, you're totally right. She was J.D.'s girlfriend, but she got around. She liked Benton, I could tell, so I knew she could like me. Benton was the boy my mommy wanted, after all. I had been her Loverboy but she wanted him more. So I wanted to be just like him. I've spent my life learning to be just like him."

"It must be hard sometimes, though."

"Wow, you really understand everything. I really tried to be like Benton, so everyone would like me. But sometimes I just knew they were lying to me and that made me feel so SILLY. So out of control."

"Is that what happened when you saw that newspaper that called Benton America's Loverboy?"

"Oh, that made me silly. Oh boy, I don't think I've ever been so silly. I was my mommy's loverboy. The *real* Loverboy. Not him. *Me.* That's when I saw that everything was his fault. My father, sure, but it was Benton who was at the root of it. He was the reason my mommy left. So I decided to punish him. Make it look like he did all the killings. Like HE was the freak. The faker. Why did he get to be the real Loverboy? But I wanted to enjoy myself too, you know?"

"Of course," Imogen agreed. Rosalind was squeezing her hand. "So you made yourself a family."

Cal smiled big again. "Oh man, it was a great family. Everyone nice and good-looking. And they all liked me so much. Until the end. Then they all got a little weird. They lied to me and tried to fake me out. That was when I had to punish them too. You could sort of feel it building and building. It was just like with my dad. They said they liked me. They said they needed me to take care of them, that I was a good boy, blah blah blah. But they were fakers. Every one of them. Every fucking one of them. They tried to run away from me because they didn't like me. They had been lying to me." He shook his head, trying to understand. His eyes, hard, metallic, swiveled to Imogen. "You are trying to fake me out too. You're trying to make me forget what we are doing up here."

She did not lie to him. "Maybe. But I also want to understand. Even if you are going to kill me, I want to understand."

The metallic edge was gone, replaced by something that looked like remorse. Cal sighed. "Oh, Imogen, you are way too good for him. You know, I was going to leave you alive, take you with me. You were going to be my *girlfriend*. Friends forever. But you turned out just like the others. In fact, you were worse than the others—you, who should have known better, you *still* chose him. I sent you presents and games. I thought about you all the time. I really felt like we were on the same wavelength, you know? And then you started paying all your attention to stupid Benton when you should have been paying attention to me."

His voice became nasty and he leaned over Imogen. "I'm the one who brought you here, not Benton. I'm the one who called you the first day to welcome you. *I'm* the one who made you come back to work in the first place. *ME*. I wanted to be *your* loverboy."

"What do you mean about making me come back to work?"

His lip curled. "Oh, no way. Haven't you understood yet? The R in my name? The center letter? No way!" He started to laugh. "That was for you! Or really, for your brother. My brother too." He smiled at her.

Imogen's mouth was suddenly completely dry. "What are you talking about, Cal?"

"Call me Loverboy. I'm talking about Sam. How I killed him. How I made him part of my F-A-M-I-L-Y!"

"He died of a blood infection."

"Oh yeah. I mean, he was sick, that's true, but he had another two or three weeks in him. Maybe even a month. Ask the doctors. Ask Dr. Stephen Gold, or better yet, ask his frisky receptionist. That's what I did. Anyway, he could have lived longer, but the problem was, I couldn't wait. I was on a schedule and you were part of it. I helped your brother in Rochester, Minnesota, so you'd come back to me."

Rochester. R. Imogen stared at him. "You killed my brother?"

"I needed you here with me."

An extraordinary sense of calm washed over Imogen. For only the second time in her life, she tasted nothing.

Cal cocked his head, looked at his watch, then at her. "I'm afraid now, Imogen, it's time for you to die too." He untied her hands from Rosalind's but kept her wrists and legs bound together.

Imogen held reassuringly on to Rosalind's fingers until the last possible moment. But when she let them go, she turned all her attention to Cal. To Loverboy. Freed from having to worry that she would be risking another woman's life if she acted, she threw herself on him.

"You bastard, you killed my brother," she said, bashing at him with her taped-together hands.

She caught him by surprise and he fell down under her onslaught. Imogen fell with him, striking him as hard as she could with the force of her combined fists. She no longer knew who she was or what she was doing. She had only one thought. "You killed my brother," she repeated over and over.

Cal was fighting back, fighting to push her away, but she was unstoppable. He had stolen Sam from her. He had stolen the only thing that mattered and she was going to make him pay.

"You bastard, you murdering bastard, you killed my brother, and you—"

Suddenly there were arms behind her, pulling her off, wrapping around her. "Shh, Imogen, it's all right," Benton's voice said in her ear.

In front of her, Cal lay curled in a ball on the ground, blood trickling from his lip. Four police officers had guns aimed at his head. "She hurt me, Mommy. She hurt me," he moaned, rocking back and forth. His eyes locked on Imogen. "Imogen, why did you hurt—"

His hand snaked out and caught one of the officer's pistols. Before the man realized it, Cal was on his feet, cheetahlike, aiming behind him.

" 'Bye, Imogen," he said, pulled the trigger, and took off.

Imogen staggered against the shot and fell to the ground, pulling Benton with her. She felt him crawl out from under her, lean over her, and saw him limp away. Footsteps pounded all around her and men ran in both directions around the circular observation deck to cut off Cal's escape.

She tried to crawl over to the dark form she thought was Rosalind but she couldn't do it. Everything was growing fuzzy, her range of vision shrinking. *Stay awake,* she told herself. *Pay attention. Pay—*

She heard more gunshots, this time from the other side of the building. There was a shout, a groan. The sound of horrible, manic laughter. Cal's voice screaming, "You'll never, ever get me, losers!"

Then silence. Silence that stretched forever. Stretched until the screeching of brakes and the dull thud of cars colliding and the horrified scream of a woman from 108 stories below pierced the air.

Imogen did not need to be told he had jumped. She did not need to be told it was over. She heard Rosalind say, hoarsely, "Benton, thank God you're here," and knew everything was back to normal.

Imogen lay back against the side of the building and lost consciousness.

CHAPTER 90

The hissing of the compressor was the first sound Imogen heard when she woke up. Sterile white walls, white gown, not hers.

The room was filled with balloons and flowers. It couldn't be her room, she thought, it's Sam's room, what was she doing back in Sam's room? Sam was dead, she was just dreaming about him.

Could she be dead too?

Ouch.

She tilted her chin down to see her arm and was looking at a tangle of tubes. She looked up and was staring into Cal's face.

She opened her mouth to scream and her eyes cleared and the face became Bugsy's.

"Hi, boss." He leaned over, smiling. "It's good to see you, too."

Imogen tried to speak. "How—" It came out like a croak.

"You're not supposed to talk yet. The bullet grazed your collarbone near your vocal cords. You can talk tomorrow," Bugsy told her. "Want to draw pictures?"

Imogen rolled her eyes. Looked around.

"Benton and Rosalind are down the hall. Julia had them put in a room together. Lex wouldn't let me put you in there too. He wants you under surveillance." Imogen followed his eyes to the door, where she saw two guards. One of them was chewing pink gum. As she watched he blew a huge bubble that popped on his face.

She rolled her eyes again.

"I know. Yes, they are both going to be fine," he said to the question in her eyes. "You managed to get there before he really started doing anything horrible. Besides getting her ears pierced, all of Rosalind's injuries are superficial, cuts and bruises. Mentally, she seems okay too. He really terrorized her, but she's a strong woman and she's determined to get past it. And knowing Cal was pulverized when he fell from the top of the Stratosphere certainly helps."

Imogen made a disgusted face.

"Pretty grim, I agree," Bugsy went on, to be talking, filling the silence. Trying to distract her. "Yep, about the only thing intact was the Western Linen Service uniform he was wearing so he could smuggle the laundry cart with you and Rosalind up in the service elevator. Make those from the same stuff they use for prison clothes. He got all that from a van at the motel where we found Dannie. The driver, Eddie, is still alive—just knocked him out, stripped off his uniform, and took the van, but for some reason didn't kill him. Anyway, they have had to get an anthropologist in from UNLV to piece together Cal's jaw for the final identification. They want to match it to the hickey on Marielle's neck and on that woman in Boston all those years ago. But they say it's going to take at least another week before they have enough pieces." Her attention drifted, so Bugsy changed the subject to one he knew she would care about. "They found out how he got to Sam."

Imogen looked up at him, clearly interested now.

"The bridge problem that Benton couldn't figure out? It was a code that Martina Kidd and Cal were using. They each posted bridge problems in the newsletter. That one was posted by Martina, who somehow found out the name of Sam's doctor. Benton deciphered it right before you shot him, but he didn't know what he'd found, since he'd never heard of Stephen Gold."

Imogen nodded and thought, Payback. That was the reason Loverboy had sent her to see Martina the first time, in exchange for the information about her brother.

Another puzzle solved. Too late.

She thought for a moment and mouthed the word *Julia*.

"She is doing better than you would expect. Right now I think she's keeping herself too busy to think by clucking over Benton and Rosalind, but I caught her in the hospital cafeteria yesterday and she seemed all right. She admitted, when she was questioned, that Cal wasn't with her the morning that Rosalind disappeared, but that she covered for him because he asked her to. He made it sound like it would just be simpler, that he didn't want to have to explain he'd been working at the Garden. She did not suspect him, her mild husband who thought only about cars and periodically couldn't get it up and sometimes came home smelling of another woman's perfume, so she didn't see anything wrong in going along with him. It also spared her having to admit publicly that she was with Rachel that morning. It seems like Cal knew exactly what his wife was doing, but rather than let on, he used it subtly, to control her. Like with her hairless dog—he wasn't allergic to dogs, he just did not want to risk leaving any telltale hairs around his crime scenes. But now Julia is completely out, at least to her family, and I think that is making her happy. She confided to me yesterday that when she told Sadie, her grandmother, Sadie said, 'Well, of course you're gay, dear. Everyone's known it for years.' "

Imogen tried to smile, but didn't manage very well. Something was tickling the back of her mind.

"Oh, and remember how Benton told you they moved the Arbor Motors operations from the Speedway because of sabotage?" Bugsy went on, hoping to lighten her expression. "It looks like Cal did the sabotage himself in order to get them to transfer everything to the Garden so he could keep Rosalind there. He planned it months ago. Harold had even run the security tapes from the convenience store you called me from, and they showed Cal buying frozen food and popcorn, which we now know was for Rosalind, but we never spotted it as an anomaly because he worked next door."

Imogen began to nod. Stopped and stared in front of her. Then struck her leg with her fist, shaking her head at herself in disgust. Julia had told her that she ran into Rosalind in the kitchen of the villa the morning Rosalind disappeared. Rosalind was throwing away champagne bottles and Julia was *pouring coffee for me and Cal.* But Cal did not drink coffee. He had told Imogen that himself when he came up to point out the clue in the *Emergency!* poster. How had she missed that? How could she not have seen—

Bugsy, misunderstanding her reaction, said, "Benton's fine too. It's a good thing you're not a very good shot or you two might not ever have children. You only grazed his kneecap. He can't walk, but the rest of him is in good working order. In case you were wondering."

Imogen swallowed hard. She and Benton. She had not even been able to aim at him properly, she remembered. Aiming low because she still had some glimmer of feeling for him even when she suspected he was a monster.

God, she was an idiot. With the memory of the shot, the final moments on top of the Stratosphere came back to her now. Benton cradling Rosalind. Rosalind clinging to him, sobbing on his shoulder.

There could be no Imogen and Benton, she understood. Even if he wanted it—*even if*—how could she take him from a woman who had suffered that? Rosalind deserved him.

Even if.

Every time he looked at her, Imogen knew, he would have to see the woman who could have spared Rosalind suffering if she'd been just a little bit smarter. Just a little better.

The answer had been in front of her the whole time and she hadn't seen it. *The whole time.* It had been so easy, just like with Sam at the hospice, and she'd failed. She hadn't understood.

"The place was mined," Bugsy told her, like a mind reader. "The room where he was keeping Rosalind at the Garden. If we had gotten there earlier, it would have gone up, taking a lot of lives with it."

Imogen shook her head for him to stop. She stared at the little blue flowers on the thin hospital blanket.

"It's true, boss."

She pinned Bugsy with her eyes. "Stop," she croaked at him. "No lies."

She spent the rest of the afternoon sitting up in the bed staring at the wall in front of her. Bugsy read her the cards that came with all her flowers. Irwin and Kathleen Bright, Lex and Elgin (the small ones), the director of the FBI, Clive Ross from Florida, the Boston Police Department, the Greenways with a drawing by Billy, Julia and Little Ugly, even J.D. Nothing from Benton.

The next day, she could speak.

The day after that, with a bandage on her throat, she was discharged. She walked to the door of the room Benton and Rosalind were sharing. Standing outside, she could hear their laughter. Rosalind's laughter. Her son, Jason, had flown in from Costa Rica and was sleeping on the floor of the room, Bugsy had told Imogen. Like one big family.

She stood and looked through the glass panel in the window. She watched for five minutes. None of them turned toward her. They really were a family. There was no place for her there.

She walked away.

Chicken! a voice in her head said, but this time she ignored it and kept walking.

CHAPTER 91

Irwin and Kathleen Bright's house
Kauai, Hawaii, two weeks later

Imogen sat with her arms around her knees on the sand and stared at the reflection of the half-moon on the ocean. It was her last night in Hawaii. Her plane ticket had her routed through Chicago, where she planned to spend a few days with Irwin and Kathleen Bright. After that, she had no idea what she was doing.

She knew what she wasn't doing, though. She was not going back to the FBI.

Irwin had managed to keep her phone number on the island a secret, but Elgin had used him as a conduit for his messages. For his bribes. Every day the ante went up. Her own office. Her own title. A promotion above Lex. She knew Elgin was actually serious when he offered her an expensive desk chair. And permission to bring her fish to work.

Like she'd ever subject Rex to that.

That morning Irwin had called with Elgin's biggest bait yet—a raise. But not even an extra five cents an hour (seven and a half during overtime, he made Irwin stress) was enough to make her take her old job back. There were better ways to earn a living than by dealing with death.

Her mind kept playing over the decision, but she knew it was not because she wasn't sure. It was because there were other decisions she should be rethinking. Harder decisions.

Behind her, in the house, the phone started ringing. It was nearly midnight, which meant that was Irwin calling to wish her sweet dreams. He and Kathleen had been acting like overprotective parents since she had finished the Loverboy case. While she chastised them and made fun of them, she had to admit she sort of liked it. Sort of liked having someone taking care of her.

She walked slowly to the house, but by the time she reached the porch the ringing had stopped. It was an incredibly still, peaceful night. In the far distance she heard the rumble of traffic, the whine of one moped, then another. Someone must be having a party. Closer by, the rustle of the leaves of a hibiscus plant.

A hand banging on her front door pierced the stillness.

Knock, knock.

She tensed, then relaxed as she remembered. Jackie, the Brights' caretaker, was supposed to stop by that night to get the keys from her before her early flight.

"Jackie? I'm around the back."

No answer. Again, *knock, knock.*

Imogen's instincts flamed to life. Her mouth filled with licorice.

"Who's there?" she called, the words of the joke out of her mouth before she realized it.

"Ben," a male voice answered.

Imogen could not move. It couldn't be. He—

"Ben who?" she asked silently pulling the back door closed.

Cal dropped from the ceiling right in front of her. "Ben waiting a long time to kill you, Imogen."

Imogen's fist came up and he caught it and twisted. Pain shot through her body like fire. "Miss me?" he asked, grabbing her other hand and holding them together by the wrists. He pulled her close to him. "Ah, Imogen, I can't tell you how happy it makes me to see you. Boy oh boy, do you make me feel *happy*."

Imogen watched his face. In the moonlight he looked even younger, even more like a deranged boy. "What are you doing here?"

"Gee, Imogen, I wonder. Either I came for a late, romantic dinner. Or I came to kill you." He grinned at her. "Or, possibly, both."

She kept staring at him. She felt both terrified and calm. "I'm afraid I don't have any food in the house."

He looked her up and down. "I'd say you're wrong."

STAY CALM, her head screamed. "You—you are supposed to be dead."

His grin broadened. "No, silly. YOU are supposed to be dead. And now you will be. See?" He held up a huge knife.

Calm calm calm calm. "But how did you—"

"Survive?" He chortled. "You did not really think I'd throw myself off that building, did you? Ugh, too icky. After all that? I could have escaped a hundred times if I'd wanted to."

It was true, Imogen realized. "Whose body was that?"

"Wrightly's, of course. Nobody missed him, not even Rosalind. He started to get all suspicious of me, wouldn't leave me alone. He claimed one day he thought I smelled like Rosalind's perfume. He was a weirdo. So I got rid of him. I dressed up like a window washer and hooked him to the side of the Stratosphere until I needed him, using Benton's rock-climbing gear. It looked really cool. Too bad you didn't see. The way I did it, it really seemed like it was me falling when all the time I was holding on to the steel ladder on the side. Oh, I also had to put his body in one of those Western Linen Service outfits, like the one I was wearing. You know, you can go anywhere in any hotel in the city if you're dressed like you're in maintenance of some kind. The customer's comfort is number one. Got to keep everything running smoothly. Yep, Vegas is a great town."

His eyes looked strange, hollow, and he kept licking his lips.

A late romantic dinner, he'd said.

Imogen swallowed hard. *CALM!* she repeated to herself. *Keep him talking.*

Why? What the hell will that do?

I DON'T KNOW JUST KEEP HIM TALKING.

"How did you find me here?" she asked.

"Professional secret. I bet you could figure it out if you put your mind to it. But you'd better hurry. Because I am here to put your mind to rest." The knife came up and the point pierced her forehead. He leaned into it, adding pressure. "For good."

Imogen ordered herself to stop trembling. "What are you going to do?"

"Well, since I didn't get to dismember Rosalind, I thought I might dismember you. I mean, if remembering means living in the past, then dismembering has to mean erasing the past, right? And I want to erase the past. I want a Fresh Start. Like the laundry detergent. And you're going to give it to me." The knife moved from her forehead, down to the tip of her nose. "I am thinking six main pieces. You know, head, two arms, two legs, torso, like in Hangman. But there are lots of smaller ones we have to get rid of before you die. Like, have you noticed that the hangman guy has no face?" He drew a circle with the knife around her lips, twice. "Or hands?"

His eyes followed the point of the knife as he moved it down her throat and along her arm, as if fascinated by the occasional dot of blood it summoned to the surface of the skin. "Blood looks so cool in moonlight, doesn't it?" he said. Imogen, assuming it was a rhetorical question, did not reply. "I think I'll have to kill you outside. That way I can really see it good."

The point of the knife came to rest on the inside of Imogen's right wrist. "This looks like a good starting place. We'll cut this one off and let the blood leave a trail outside. Like Hansel and Gretel!" His eyes swiveled to Imogen's fast. "Are you ready?"

NOW! her mind screamed.

"Yes," she said. She jerked her wrists up and the knife skidded away. Instinctively, Cal went for it, leaning sideways, and instinctively she kicked him in the shin. For an instant his grip on her wrists loosened and she pulled her hands from him, swinging with both fists. She aimed for his nose but connected with something harder—chin? shoulder? She heard the crack of a bone, did not stop, flew to the back door.

She was out on the porch, running down the beach. The closest neighbors were a quarter of a mile away, and they might not even be there, but that did not matter. All that mattered was getting away, running as hard and fast and far as she could.

Don't stop! her mind screamed.

It was dark and she nearly fell twice, tripping over rocks that hid in the shadowy indentations of the sand. Her heart was pounding and the wound on her neck began to throb. Over the sound of the blood pounding in her ears she heard his footfall.

He was quicker than she was.

Come on, Imogen.

He was bigger than she was.

Come on, come on, Imogen! You can do this—

He was coming up on her fast. She sprinted forward, pushing herself as hard as she could go. *Come on, come on—*

She tripped on a piece of driftwood and went flying facedown into the sand.

"Ha, ha!" he panted behind her.

COME ON!

She scrambled up, skidded, got her feet under her. His hand closed around her ankle.

She fell face-first into the sand again. His palm shoved the back of her head down into it, hard. She started to choke, spluttering sand.

"That wasn't nice, Imogen," he said, settling himself on the small of her back. He weighed at least twice what she did. Her arms and legs flailed but he sat there, unmoved. "You look like some freaky fish, Gigi," he said. "I can call you that, right? Gigi? That's what the people closest to you call you."

She gagged on the sand in her mouth.

"Good, I'm glad we agree on that. Well, here we are. I'd say it's time to get started." The knife came to rest against her neck. "If you don't stop flopping around, Gigi, you're going to get cut."

The metallic smell of the knife made Imogen gag again. She stopped moving.

"You know, it is really nice here. Under the stars like this with you. I forgot how nice it was to be with you." The knife traced a little heart shape on her cheek. "You're really great, Gigi. Know how much I like you? I like you so much that I read the play that your name is from. The Shakespeare one? *Cymbeline*." He slid the knife up and down against her neck, from her ear to her collarbone, as he spoke, and Imogen was sure he was watching the way the moonlight reflected in the blade. "Yep. I read *Shakespeare* for you. That's a lot of liking. Anyway, you know how in the play there is that servant who has orders to kill the princess Imogen? But he only pretends to, and he takes back some souvenir from her body but really leaves her alive?"

"That's not exactly how the play goes," Imogen said, spluttering sand.

"Close enough. Anyway, I'm thinking, what if we did it that way?"

Imogen's head turned as far as she could toward him. "I don't think I understand."

"I could just take something small from you, like, say, this"— the knifepoint bit into her pinkie, withdrew—"to send to Professor Kidd, sort of as a thank-you present for all her help. Pinkies have so many uses, particularly in an all-female prison ward. And then I could leave you alive. That way you could live happily ever after." He leaned down and whispered in her ear, "Hunting for me before I kill again."

"You are going to leave me alive?"

"It would be so exciting, wouldn't it? So dramatic? Me roaming the earth killing people. You roaming the earth after me. Who is the hunter and who is the prey? Ooh, it gives me chills. I just might do it. I think I could be persuaded to do it. If only—" His voice trailed off.

Imogen coughed out more sand. She asked, "If only what?"

"IF ONLY I WAS A FUCKING IDIOT!" Loverboy tipped his head back and laughed. "But I'm not. So I'm going to kill you. I just wanted to get your heart beating faster so there would be more blood. Now, which of the extra pieces do you want to eat first, Imogen? Your fingers or your ears? Because I really don't want to have to deal with a lot of cleanup, so you'll have to chip in and do your part." He shoved her face hard into the sand and said, "What? What? You have to speak up. Did you say your ear?"

The tiny *ping* registered somewhere deep in Imogen's mind, like something from a dream. *It couldn't be,* she told herself. She fought to keep breathing, unwilling to let herself believe as the point of the knife came to rest against her earlobe. This was it, she knew. It was over. She braced herself for the pain, for the feel of her own blood trickling down her cheek.

The world in front of her exploded with bright light. For three seconds she lay stunned on the ground seeing—

black and golden sand two clear sand crabs a piece of green sea glass the cross section of a driftwood twig a sand fly alighting a rainbow refracted

—nothing. Then as the lag of the flash-bang grenade faded, Cal's body dropped over her, *thud.* The point of his knife dug into her shoulder. She struggled to turn over, to wriggle away, but Cal's arms closed around her, hugging him to her.

"You are mine," he repeated over and over, his teeth gnashing her ear. "You are my girlfriend, Imogen. You are mine only—"

The sentence ended in another thud and a groan. His arms loosened and Imogen dragged herself from him. Without looking back, without asking what had happened, she started to run. *Don't stop,* she told herself, *keep going get away must get—*

"Imogen," a voice panted to her left. "Imogen, stop. Imogen, please stop. It's me. *IMOGEN!*"

She turned her head and through her tears she saw a black hood being pushed down. Saw a set of night-vision goggles being thrown aside. Saw a face, a pair of shoulders, a pair of arms. She hesitated for a moment, not daring to let herself believe it. Then she threw herself into them and said, "Benton, thank God you are here."

CHAPTER 92

Five hours later they sat on her terrace and watched the sun start to come up. The smell of Kentucky Fried Chicken still floated on the air. The SWAT operation had been a success. Cal, injured but alive, was on his way to Oahu by helicopter. Imogen was safe.

Elgin and Lex had been trying to sort out the implications of the report that had landed on their desks the previous morning, which said the body that had fallen from the Stratosphere was not the body that had given Marielle Wycliffe her hickey, when Kathleen Bright called. She had just realized that Lex should send the envelope he had for Imogen to her house, she explained, rather than to the address in Hawaii she'd given his assistant, because Imogen was leaving the next day.

Only Lex did not have an assistant anymore.

Benton had already been in Hawaii for four days looking for Imogen when he got J.D.'s call. By the time the SWAT team was assembled and flying out of Honolulu, Benton was on it.

But all of that was over. The last of the operational team had gone. The KFC buckets were stacked in a corner. Imogen and Benton were alone.

Now came the hard part. They faced each other across the tiny drinks table. They did not touch. They were both looking at their hands.

Imogen exhaled a big breath. She said, "Before this gets difficult, I want you to know that I understand. You don't have to feel bad. It is fine with me. We—we don't even have to talk about it."

Benton glanced from his hands to her face. "Oh. Good. I thought we should. But since we don't have to—" He shook his head, looking incredulous. "Imogen, I don't even know what you are talking about. What do you understand? What don't I have to feel bad about?" He put up a hand. "You know what? I don't even care about that. I just want to know why you left. Why you walked out of my goddamned life without saying good-bye."

His fist hit the table, startling Imogen.

"Are you angry?"

He stared at her, aghast. "I don't know what I am. Yes, I'm angry. But even more, I am hurt. I thought you—you wanted to be with me. Wanted to see if we could have something together. And instead, you just left."

"You had Rosalind. She needed you. And after what she suffered, she certainly deserved you."

"I am not a prize to be won at a carnival, Imogen."

"But I heard all of you together. I came to your room and I heard you laughing and saw all of you sitting together. Happy, like a family. You love her and she loves you and the three of you, with Jason, you are a family. A real family." She paused. Said, with feeling, "I was afraid to get in the middle of that. To ruin it."

"Is that really what you were afraid of?"

Imogen bit her lip.

Benton nodded. "You are right. We were happy to be together. Ecstatic. Are you kidding? After what Rosalind had gone through, after what she had *survived*? The only other choice was to dwell on it. To make her think about how horrible it had been. Yes, we were happy. Plus, we had a lot to talk about. And do you know what our favorite topic was? The one we returned to all the time?" He stopped speaking until she looked at him. "We talked about you, Imogen. About how great it would be when we could *all* be together. When you and Rosalind could get to know each other. She talked about how holding your hand during those last minutes on the Stratosphere gave her so much comfort. Julia told stories that made you sound like you leaped buildings and ate bad guys for breakfast. Every day we asked when we could see you and they said the next day and we waited. We even wrote a knock-knock joke for when we came to your room. And then one day we asked if we could see you. And they said you'd left."

He looked out at the ocean. "You just left. Without even meeting Rosalind. Without even saying good-bye."

The silence stretched until it became taut. Tiny waves lapped at the sand. Imogen's fingers brushed Benton's tentatively. Stayed there when he didn't pull away. Her voice was low, hard to understand. Confused. Shocked. She said, "You wrote a knock-knock joke? For me?"

He turned to her and saw that she was crying. Hard. "Yeah. A really, really bad one."

She started to cry harder. "Will you tell me?"

He reached out and cupped her cheek in his hand and said, "No."

"No?"

"I'm not in the mood for jokes. Right now I want to be serious." He extended his arms around the table toward her and she fell into them. He pulled her into his lap and held her against his chest. "Imogen, are you going to run away from me every time you get scared? Every time you have to take an emotional risk?"

"Probably," she said, sobbing.

He held her tighter. "Do you think you could wait until my knee heals completely before you run away again? You know, from where you shot me? Otherwise I won't stand a chance of catching up."

She laughed through her tears. "Probably."

"What happened to the Imogen Page who was not afraid of getting hurt? The one who propositioned me on the balcony of my beach house?"

Imogen shrugged, moved her eyes to her lap.

"The one who told me to call 1-800-Jerkoff?"

Imogen's eyes were still down, but Benton thought he caught a hint of a smile.

"The one who put me under arrest the first day we met?"

Imogen looked up. "You know, you're still under arrest. I never said you weren't under arrest anymore."

"Aha! You admit it."

"What?"

"That you are the same woman."

Imogen's eyes, bright from crying, searched his face. "You really want this, don't you?"

"Yes. And I will do whatever it takes to make it work."

She tucked her hair behind her ear and gave a nod. "Okay."

"Okay?"

"I owe you two dates. That's what we agreed on in Boston. Or now, one."

"What do you mean one?"

"Well, we sort of just had a date. So one more."

"That wasn't exactly what I had in mind when I said date. Psychopaths and SWAT teams and KFC."

"I don't know. I thought it was fun. Exciting."

Benton shook his head. "You would." Then said, "If you thought that was exciting, just wait until our next date."

"Okay, hot shot. When?"

"Are you doing anything right now?"

They were too occupied to grab the phone an hour later when Lex called to report that the helicopter carrying Cal Harwood to Honolulu had issued an SOS halfway through its flight and plunged precipitously into the shark-infested waters of Kauai Channel. The coast guard found no survivors.

"She knocked my socks off," says Arbor
By Storm Lark

Special to the Review-Journal

Serial wedding?
Even the staff of the Fontana Lounge at the Bellagio was kept in the dark about the names of the people throwing Saturday's blowout engagement party and their supersecret musical guest until the last minute. In fact, my spies tell me that when Tom Jones showed up for his sound check, one of the waitresses fainted and almost toppled the champagne fountain.

The lucky couple turned out to be Benton Arbor, multimillionaire head of Arbor Motors, and Imogen Page, the FBI agent who cracked the Loverboy case here this past winter. Arbor has homes in NYC, L.A., and Detroit, but the pair plan to make Las Vegas their base. Rumor has it that instead of a diamond engagement ring, Arbor proposed with a case of double-bond paper with the words Imogen Page Investigations *engraved on it. A hundred and fifty of their closest friends from around the globe—including one goldfish—joined them at the Bellagio bash, which showed no signs of stopping until well after dawn. No date has been made public for the wedding, but Tom Jones, who is a favorite of both Arbor and*

*Page, said privately that he has been asked to stay "on call" through-
out the summer.*

Ha, ha! Tom Jones and everything. What a riot. They were having fun now, but they would be missing him soon. Missing him and
thinking about him ALL the time. That he was sure of.

His next plan was going to blow them away totally. He was still
testing it, fine-tuning it, but even still it was better than anything
anyone else had ever done. It was going to make him superfamous.

He hit QUIT and pushed his chair away from the bank of moni-
tors in the Internet café. It was sultry in there, despite the fan, and he
couldn't wait to get outside. The pimple-faced boy at the cashier's
counter gave him a long look as he paid and a longer one as he leaned
over to pick up his package. He was getting used to having people
look at him that way. It had been strange at first, but it was really
growing on him.

Growing. Ha, ha!

He strolled to the post office. Everywhere he looked around
him, everyone was happy. He was too. He never felt silly anymore.
Now he just felt happy. Happy ALL the time.

He filled in the customs forms and slid them, with the box,
across to the man in the light blue shirt behind the counter. He sure
hoped Imogen liked this present. She'd never written to thank him
for the last one.

Of course, she didn't know where he was—

The post office man stroked his mustache as he read the forms
over. He shook his head. "You forget one," the man said, pointing a
bitten nail at one of the boxes on the form. "You forgot the condense."

He figured out what the man was saying. Contents. He slipped
the man a smile. "Silly me. Sorry." He took the form and wrote,
PIECE OF MIND. "How is that?"

"Just fine," the man told him. Gave him an appreciative once-
over. Added formally, "As are you, ma'am."

—or *what* he was.

"What is your name, handsome?" Cal, now short for Calista, asked with a flirtatious glance.

"Eduardo."

Calista rested a long red fingernail on the back of Eduardo's hand. "Someone should deal with that saucy tongue of yours, Eduardo."

"What about you, ma'am? Say, tonight?"

"Why, Eduardo, I can't tell you how *happy* that would make me," Calista said. Thought: Well, that's my Christmas shopping done.

The End
Not!

ABOUT THE AUTHOR

MICHELE JAFFE holds a Ph.D. in Comparative Literature from Harvard University. She is the author of *The Stargazer* and *The Water Nymph* as well as *Lady Killer, Secret Admirer,* and *Bad Girl.* She lives in Las Vegas. Please visit her website at www.michelejaffe.com.